Spinning Silver

Spinning Silver

Naomi Novik

DEL REY

NEW YORK

Copyright © 2018 by Temeraire LLC

Published in the United States by Del Rey, an imprint of Random House, a division of Penguin Random House LLC, New York.

DEL REY and the HOUSE colophon are registered trademarks of Penguin Random House LLC.

LIBRARY OF CONGRESS CATALOGING-IN-PUBLICATION DATA
Names: Novik, Naomi, author.
Title: Spinning silver / Naomi Novik.
Description: New York : Del Rey, [2018]
Identifiers: LCCN 2018005791 | ISBN 9780399180989 (hardback) |
ISBN 9781984817556 (international edition) | ISBN 9780399181009 (ebook)
Subjects: | BISAC: FICTION / Fantasy / Epic. | FICTION / Fairy Tales,
Folk Tales, Legends & Mythology. | FICTION / Action & Adventure. |
GSAFD: Fantasy fiction.
Classification: LCC PS3614.O93 S65 2018 | DDC 813/.6—dc23
LC record available at https://lccn.loc.gov/2018005791

Illustrations by Tara O'Shea

Printed in the United States of America on acid-free paper

randomhousebooks.com

2 4 6 8 9 7 5 3

Book design by Jo Anne Metsch

Spinning Silver

Chapter 1

The real story isn't half as pretty as the one you've heard. The real story is, the miller's daughter with her long golden hair wants to catch a lord, a prince, a rich man's son, so she goes to the moneylender and borrows for a ring and a necklace and decks herself out for the festival. And she's beautiful enough, so the lord, the prince, the rich man's son notices her, and dances with her, and tumbles her in a quiet hayloft when the dancing is over, and afterwards he goes home and marries the rich woman his family has picked out for him. Then the miller's despoiled daughter tells everyone that the moneylender's in league with the devil, and the village runs him out or maybe even stones him, so at least she gets to keep the jewels for a dowry, and the blacksmith marries her before that firstborn child comes along a little early.

Because that's what the story's really about: getting out of paying your debts. That's not how they tell it, but I knew. My father was a moneylender, you see.

He wasn't very good at it. If someone didn't pay him back on time, he never so much as mentioned it to them. Only if our cupboards were really bare, or our shoes were falling off our feet, and my mother spoke quietly with him after I was in bed, then he'd go, unhappy, and knock on a few doors, and make it sound like an apology when he asked for some of what they owed. And if there was money in the house and someone asked to borrow, he hated to say no, even if we didn't really have enough ourselves. So all his money, most of which had been my mother's money, her dowry, stayed in other people's houses. And everyone else liked it that way, even though they knew they ought to be ashamed of themselves, so they told the story often, even or especially when I could hear it.

My mother's father was a moneylender, too, but he was a very good one. He lived in Vysnia, forty miles away by the pitted old trading road that dragged from village to village like a string full of small dirty knots. Mama often took me on visits, when she could afford a few pennies to pay someone to let us ride along at the back of a peddler's cart or a sledge, five or six changes along the way. Sometimes we caught glimpses of the other road through the trees, the one that belonged to the Staryk, gleaming like the top of the river in winter when the snow had blown clear. "Don't look, Miryem," my mother would tell me, but I always kept watching it out of the corner of my eye, hoping to keep it near, because it meant a quicker journey: whoever was driving the cart would slap the horses and hurry them up until it vanished again.

One time, we heard the hooves behind us as they came off their road, a sound like ice cracking, and the driver beat the horses quick to get the cart behind a tree, and we all huddled there in the well of the wagon among the sacks, my mother's arm wrapped around my head, holding it down so I couldn't be tempted to take a look. They rode past us and did not stop. It was a poor peddler's cart, covered in dull tin pots, and Staryk knights only ever came riding for gold. The hooves went jangling past, and a knife-wind blew over us, so when I sat up the end of my thin braid was frosted white, and all of my mother's sleeve where it wrapped around me, and our backs. But the frost faded, and as soon as it was gone, the peddler said to my mother, "Well, that's enough of a rest, isn't it," as if he didn't remember why we had stopped.

"Yes," my mother said, nodding, as if she didn't remember either, and he got back up onto the driver's seat and clucked to the horses and set us going again. I was young enough to remember it afterwards a little, and not old enough to care about the Staryk as much as about the ordinary cold biting through my clothes, and my pinched stomach. I didn't want to say anything that might make the cart stop again, impatient to get to the city and my grandfather's house.

My grandmother would always have a new dress for me, plain and dull brown but warm and well-made, and each winter a pair of new leather shoes that didn't pinch my feet and weren't patched and cracked around the edges. She would feed me to bursting three times every day, and the last night before we left she would always make cheesecake, her cheesecake, which was baked golden on the outside and thick and white and crumbly inside and tasted just a little bit of apples, and she would make decorations with sweet golden raisins on the top. After I had slowly and lingeringly eaten every last bite of a slice wider than the palm of my hand, they would put me to bed upstairs, in the big cozy bedroom where my mother and her sisters had slept as girls, in the same narrow wooden bed carved with doves. My mother would sit next to her mother by the fireplace, and put her head on her shoulder. They wouldn't speak, but when I was a little older and didn't fall asleep right away, I would see in the firelight glow that both of them had a little wet track of tears down their faces.

We could have stayed. There was room in my grandfather's house, and welcome for us. But we always went home, because we loved my father. He was terrible with money, but he was endlessly warm and gentle, and he tried to make up for his failings: he spent nearly all of every day out in the cold woods hunting for food and firewood, and when he was indoors there was nothing he wouldn't do to help my mother. No talk of woman's work in my house, and when we did go hungry, he went hungriest, and snuck food from his plate to ours. When he sat by the fire in the evenings, his hands were always working, whittling some new little toy for me or something for my mother, a decoration on a chair or a wooden spoon.

But winter was always long and bitter, and every year I was old enough to remember was worse than the one before. Our town was unwalled and half nameless; some people said it was called Pakel, for being near the road, and those who didn't like that, because it reminded them of being near the Staryk road, would shout them down and say it was called Pavys, for being near the river, but no one bothered to put it on a map, so no decision was ever made. When we spoke, we all only called it *town*. It was welcome to travelers, a third of the way between Vysnia and Minask, and a small river crossed the road running from east to west. Many farmers brought their goods by boat, so our market day was busy. But that was the limit of our importance. No lord concerned himself very much with us, and the tsar in Koron not at all. I could not have told you whom the tax collector worked for until on one visit to my grandfather's house I learned accidentally that the Duke of Vysnia was angry because the receipts from our town had been creeping steadily down year to year. The cold kept stealing out of the woods earlier and earlier, eating at our crops.

And the year I turned sixteen, the Staryk came, too, during what should have been the last week of autumn, before the late barley was all the way in. They had always come raiding for gold, once in a while; people told stories of half-remembered glimpses, and the dead they left behind. But over the last seven years, as the winters worsened, they had grown more rapacious. There were still a few leaves clinging to the trees when they rode off their road and onto ours, and they went only ten miles past our village to the rich monastery down the road, and there they killed a dozen of the monks and stole the golden candlesticks, and the golden cup, and all the icons painted in gilt, and carried away that golden treasure to whatever kingdom lay at the end of their own road.

The ground froze solid that night with their passing, and every day after that a sharp steady wind blew out of the forest carrying whirls of stinging snow. Our own little house stood apart and at the very end of town, without other walls nearby to share in breaking the wind, and we grew ever more thin and hungry and shivering. My father kept making his excuses, avoiding the work he couldn't bear to do. But even when my mother finally pressed him and he tried, he only came back with a scant handful of coins, and said in apology for them, "It's a bad winter. A hard winter for everyone," when I didn't believe they'd even bothered to make him that much of an excuse. I walked through town the next day to take our loaf to the baker, and I heard women who owed us money talking of the feasts they planned to cook, the treats they would buy in the market. It was coming on midwinter. They all wanted to have something good on the table; something special for the festival, their festival.

So they had sent my father away empty-handed, and their lights shone out on the snow and the smell of roasting meat slipped out of the cracks while I walked slowly back to the baker, to give him a worn penny in return for a coarse half-burned loaf that hadn't been the loaf I'd made at all. He'd given a good loaf to one of his other customers, and kept a ruined one for us. At home my mother was making thin cabbage soup and scrounging together used cooking oil to light the lamp for the third night of our own celebration, coughing as she worked: another deep chill had rolled in from the woods, and it crept through every crack and eave of our run-down little house. We only had the flames lit for a few minutes before a gust of it came in and blew them out, and my father said, "Well, perhaps that means it's time for bed," instead of relighting them, because we were almost out of oil.

By the eighth day, my mother was too tired from coughing to get out of bed at all. "She'll be all right soon," my father said, avoiding my eyes. "This cold will break soon. It's been so long already." He was whittling candles out of wood, little narrow sticks to burn, because we'd used the last drops of oil the night before. There wasn't going to be any miracle of light in our house.

He went out to scrounge under the snow for some more firewood. Our box was getting low, too. "Miryem," my mother said, hoarsely, after he left. I took her a cup of weak tea with a scraping of honey, all I had to comfort her. She sipped a little and lay back on the pillows and said, "When the winter breaks, I want you to go to my father's house. He'll take you to my father's house."

The last time we had visited my grandfather, one night my mother's sisters had come to dinner with their husbands and their children. They all wore dresses made of thick wool, and they left fur cloaks in the entryway, and had gold rings on their hands, and gold bracelets. They laughed and sang and the whole room was warm, though it had been deep in winter, and we ate fresh bread and roast chicken and hot golden soup full of flavor and salt, steam rising into my face. When my mother spoke, I inhaled all the warmth of that memory with her words, and longed for it with my cold hands curled into painful knots. I thought of going there to stay, a beggar girl, leaving my father alone and my mother's gold forever in our neighbors' houses.

I pressed my lips together hard, and then I kissed her forehead and told her to rest, and after she fell fitfully asleep, I went to the box next to the fireplace where my father kept his big ledger-book. I took it out and I took his worn pen out of its holder, and I mixed ink out of the ashes in the fireplace and I made a list. A moneylender's daughter, even a bad moneylender's daughter, learns her numbers. I wrote and figured and wrote and figured, interest and time broken up by all the little haphazard scattered payments. My father had every one carefully written down, as scrupulous with all of them as no one else ever was with him. And when I had my list finished, I took all the knitting out of my bag, put my shawl on, and went out into the cold morning.

I went to every house that owed us, and I banged on their doors. It was early, very early, still dark, because my mother's coughing had woken us in the night. Everyone was still at home. So the men opened the doors and stared at me in surprise, and I looked them in their faces and said, cold and hard, "I've come to settle your account."

They tried to put me off, of course; some of them laughed at me. Oleg, the carter with his big hands, closed them into fists and put them on his hips and stared at me while his small squirrelish wife kept her head down over the fire, darting eyes towards me. Kajus, who had borrowed two gold pieces the year before I was born, and did a good custom in the krupnik he brewed in the big copper kettles he'd bought with the money, smiled at me and asked me to come inside and warm myself up, have a hot drink. I refused. I didn't want to be warmed. I stood on their doorsteps, and I brought out my list, and I told them how much they had borrowed, and what little they had paid, and how much interest they owed besides.

They spluttered and argued and some of them shouted. No one had ever shouted at me in my life: my mother with her quiet voice, my gentle father. But I found something bitter inside myself, something of that winter blown into my heart: the sound of my mother coughing, and the memory of the story the way they'd told it in the village square so many times, about a girl who made herself a queen with someone else's gold, and never paid her debts. I stayed in their doorways, and I didn't move. My numbers were true, and they and I knew it, and when they'd shouted themselves out, I said, "Do you have the money?"

They thought it was an opening. They said no, of course not; they didn't have such a sum.

"Then you'll pay me a little now, and again every week, until your debt is cleared," I said, "and pay interest on what you haven't paid, if you don't want me to send to my grandfather to bring the law into it."

None of them traveled very much. They knew my mother's father was rich, and lived in a great house in Vysnia, and had loaned money to knights and even, rumor had it, to a lord. So they gave me a little, grudgingly; only a few pennies in some houses, but every one of them gave me something. I let them give me goods, too: twelve yards of warm woolen cloth in deep red, a jar of oil, two dozen good tall candles of white beeswax, a new kitchen knife from the blacksmith. I gave them all a fair value— the price they would have charged someone else, not me, buying in the market—and I wrote down the numbers in front of them, and told them I would see them next week.

On my way home, I stopped in at Lyudmila's house. She didn't borrow money; she could have lent it herself, but she couldn't have charged interest, and anyway no one in our town would have been foolish enough to borrow from anyone but my father, who would let them pay as they liked or didn't. She opened the door with her practiced smile on: she took in travelers overnight. It came off when she saw me. "Well?" she said sharply. She thought I had come to beg.

"My mother is sick, Panova," I said, politely, so she'd keep thinking it just a little longer, and then be relieved when I went on to say, "I've come to buy some food. How much for soup?"

I asked her the price of eggs after, and bread, as though I were trying to fit them to a narrow purse, and because she didn't know otherwise, she just brusquely told me the prices instead of inflating them twice over. Then she was annoyed when I finally counted out six pennies for a pot of hot soup with half a chicken in it, and three fresh eggs, and a soft loaf, and a bowl of honeycomb covered with a napkin. But she gave them to me grudgingly, and I carried them down the long lane to our house.

My father had come back home before me; he was feeding the fire, and he looked up worried when I shouldered my way in. He stared at my arms full of food and red wool. I put my load all down and I put the rest of the pennies and the one silver kopek into the jar next to our hearth, where there were only a couple of pennies left otherwise, and I gave him the list with the payments written on it, and then I turned to making my mother comfortable.

After that, I was the moneylender in our town. And I was a good moneylender, and a lot of people owed us money, so very soon the straw of our floor was smooth boards of golden wood, and the cracks in our fireplace were chinked with good clay and our roof was thatched fresh, and my mother had a fur cloak to sleep under or to wear, to keep her chest warm. She didn't like it at all, and neither did my father, who went outside and wept quietly to himself the day I brought the cloak home. Odeta, the baker's wife, had offered it to me as payment in full of her family's debt. It was beautiful, dark and light browns; she'd brought it with her when she married, made of ermines her father had hunted in the boyar's woods.

That part of the old story turned out to be true: you have to be cruel to be a good moneylender. But I was ready to be as merciless with our neighbors as they'd been with my father. I didn't take firstborn children exactly, but one week late in the spring, when the roads were finally clear again, I walked out to one of the peasant farmers in the far fields, and he had nothing to pay me with, not even a spare loaf of bread. Gorek had borrowed six silver kopeks, a sum he'd never repay if he made a crop every year of the rest of his life; I didn't believe he'd ever had more than five pennies in his hand at once. He tried to curse me out of the house at first, casually, as many of them did, but when I held my ground and told him the law would come for him, real desperation came into his voice. "I have four mouths to feed!" he said. "You can't suck blood from a stone."

I should have felt sorry for him, I suppose. My father would have, and my mother, but wrapped in my coldness, I only felt the danger of the moment. If I forgave him, took his excuses, next week everyone would have an excuse; I saw everything unraveling again from there.

Then his tall daughter came staggering in, a kerchief over her long yellow braids and a heavy yoke across her shoulders, carrying two buckets of water, twice as much as I could manage when I went for water to the well myself. I said, "Then your daughter will come work in my house to pay off the debt, for half a penny every day," and I walked home pleased as a cat, and even danced a few steps to myself in the road, alone under the trees.

Her name was Wanda. She came silently to the house at dawn the next morning, worked like an ox until dinner, and left silently after; she kept her head down the entire time. She was very strong, and she took almost all the burden of the housework even in just that half day. She carried water and chopped wood, and tended the small flock of hens we now had scratching in our yard, and scrubbed the floors and our hearth and all our pots, and I was well satisfied with my solution.

After she left, for the first time in my life my mother spoke to my father in anger, in blame, as she hadn't even when she was most cold and sick. "And you don't care for what it does to her?" I heard her crying out to him, her voice still hoarse, as I knocked the mud from my boot heels at the gate; without the morning work to do, I had borrowed a donkey and gone all the way to the farthest villages to collect money from people who'd probably thought they'd never see anyone ever come for it again. The winter rye was in, and I had two full sacks of grain, another two of wool, and a big bag of my mother's favorite hazelnuts that had been kept fresh all winter out in the cold, along with an old but good nutcracker made of iron, so we wouldn't have to shell them with the hammer anymore.

"What shall I say to her?" he cried back. "What shall I say? No, you shall starve; no, you shall go cold and you will wear rags?"

"If you had the coldness to do it yourself, you could be cold enough to let her do it," my mother said. "Our daughter, Josef!"

That night, my father tried to say something to me quietly, stumbling over the words: I'd done enough, it wasn't my work, tomorrow I'd stay home. I didn't look up from shelling the hazelnuts, and I didn't answer him, holding the cold knotted under my ribs. I thought of my mother's hoarse voice, and not the words she'd said. After a little while he trailed off. The coldness in me met him and drove him back, just as it had when he'd met it in the village, asking for what he was owed.

Chapter 2

Da would often say he was going to the moneylender. He would get money for a new plow, or to buy some pigs, or a milch cow. I did not really know what money was. Our cottage was far from town and we paid tax in sacks of grain. Da made it sound like magic, but Mama made it sound dangerous. "Don't go, Gorek," she would say. "There's always trouble where there's money owed, sooner or later." Then Da would shout at her to mind her own business and slap her, but he wouldn't go.

He went when I was eleven. Another baby had come and gone in the night and Mama was sick. We hadn't needed another baby. We already had Sergey and Stepon and the four dead ones in the ground by the white tree. Da always buried the babies there even though the ground was hard to dig, because he didn't want to spare planting ground. He could not plant anything too close to the white tree anyway. It would eat up anything around it. The rye seedlings would sprout and then one cold morning they would all be withered and the white tree would have some more white leaves on it. And he could not cut it down. It was all white, so it belonged to the Staryk. If he cut it down, they would come and kill him. So all we could plant there was the dead babies.

After Da came back in angry and sweating from burying the new dead baby, he said loudly, "Your mother needs medicine. I am going to the moneylender." We looked at each other, me and Sergey and Stepon. They were only little, too scared to say anything, and Mama was too sick to say anything. I didn't say anything either. Mama was still lying in the bed and there was blood and she was hot and red. She did not say anything when I talked to her. She only coughed. I wanted Da to bring back magic and make her get out of bed and be well again.

So he went. He drank up two kopeks in town and lost two gambling before he came home with the doctor. The doctor took the last two kopeks and gave me some powder to mix with hot water and give to Mama. It didn't stop the fever. Three days later I was trying to give her some water to drink. She was coughing again. "Mama, I have some water," I said. She did not open her eyes. She put her big hand on my head, strange and loose and heavy, and then she died. I sat with her the rest of the day until Da came home from the fields. He looked down at her silently, and then he told me, "Change the straw." He took her body over his shoulder like potatoes and carried her out to the white tree and buried her next to the dead babies.

The moneylender came a few months after that and asked for the money back. I let him in when he came. I knew he was a servant of the devil but I wasn't afraid of him. He was very narrow, hands and body and face. Mama had an icon nailed to the wall that was carved out of a skinny branch. He looked like that. His voice was quiet. I gave him a cup of tea and a piece of bread because I remembered Mama always gave people something to eat if they came to the house.

When Da came home he shouted the moneylender out of the house. Then he beat me five big wallops with his belt for letting him in at all, much less giving him food. "What business has he got coming here? You can't get blood from a stone," he said, putting his belt back on. I kept my face in my mother's apron until I stopped crying.

He said the same thing when the tax collector came to our house, but he only said it under his breath. The tax collector always came the day we brought in the last of the grain harvest, winter and spring. I didn't know how he always knew, but he knew. After he left, the tax was paid. Whatever he did not take, that was for us to live on. There was never very much. In winter, Mama used to say to Da, "We will eat that in November, and that in December," and point to this and that until everything was divided up until spring. But Mama was not there anymore. So Da took one of the kid goats away to town. That night he came back very late and drunk. We were sleeping in the house next to the oven and he tripped over Stepon when he came in. Stepon cried and then Da got angry and took off his belt and hit us all until we ran out of the house. The mama goat stopped giving milk, and we ran out of food at the end of winter. We had to dig under the snow for old acorns until spring.

But the next winter when the tax collector came, Da took a sack of grain to town anyway. We all went to sleep in the shed with the goats. Sergey and Stepon were all right, but Da beat me the next day anyway when he was sober, because his dinner was not ready when he came home. So the next year I waited in the house until I saw Da coming down the road. Da had a lantern with him that was swaying in big circles because he was so drunk. I put the hot food in a bowl on the table and ran out. It was already dark but I did not take a candle because I did not want Da to see me leaving.

I meant to go to the shed, but I kept looking behind me to see if Da was coming after me. His lantern was swinging inside the house, making eyes of the windows, looking for me. But then it stopped moving, so he had put it onto the table. Then I thought I was safe. I started to look where I was walking, but I could not see in the dark, because I had been looking at the bright windows, and I was not on the path to the shed. I was in the deep snow. There was no sound of the goats or even the pigs. It was a dark night.

I thought I would come to the fence or the road sooner or later. I kept walking with my hands held out to catch the fence but I didn't come to it. It was dark and first I was afraid, and then I was only cold, and then I was also getting sleepy. My toes were numb. Snow was getting into the cracks between the woven bark of my shoes.

Then ahead of me there was a light. I went towards it. I was near the white tree. Its branches were narrow and all the white leaves were still on it even though it was winter. The wind blew them and they made a noise like someone whispering too quiet to hear. On the other side of the tree there was a broad road, very smooth like ice and shining. I knew it was the Staryk road. But it was so beautiful, and I still felt very strange and cold and sleepy. I did not remember to be afraid. I went to walk onto it.

The graves were in a row under the tree. There was one flat stone at the top of each one. Mama had gotten them out of the river for the others. I had gotten one for her, and the last baby. Theirs were smaller than the others because I could not carry as big a stone as Mama yet. When I stepped over the row of stones to go to the road, a branch of the tree hit me on my shoulders. I fell down hard. All my breath was knocked out. The wind blew the white leaves and I heard them say, *Run home, Wanda!* Then I was not sleepy anymore, and I was so afraid I got up and I ran all the way back to the house. I could see it a long way off because the lantern was still in the windows. Da was already snoring on his bed.

A year later old Jakob our neighbor came to the house and asked
Da for me. He wanted Da to give him a goat, too, so Da threw
him out of the house, saying, "A virgin, healthy, a strong back,
and he wants a goat from me!"

I worked very hard after that. I took as much of Da's work as
I could. I didn't want to make a row of dead babies and die. But I
got tall and my hair was yellow and long and my breasts grew.
Two more men asked for me over the next two years. The last one
I didn't know at all. He came from the other side of town, six
miles away. He even offered a bride price of one pig. But my hard
work had made Da greedy by then, and he said three pigs. The
man spat on the floor and walked out of the house.

But the harvests were going very bad. The snow melted later
every year in spring and came sooner in the fall. After the tax collector took his share, there was not much left for drinking. I had
learned to hide food in places so we did not run out so badly
in winter as the first year, but Sergey and Stepon and me were
all getting bigger. The year I was sixteen, after the spring harvest,
Da came back from town only half drunk and sour. He didn't
beat me, but he looked at me like I was one of the pigs, weighing
me in his head. "You'll come to market with me next week," he
told me.

The next day I went out to the white tree. I had stayed away
from it ever since that night I saw the Staryk road, but that day I
waited until the sun was up high. Then I said I was going for
water, but I went to the tree instead. I knelt down under the
branches and said, "Help me, Mama."

Two days later, the moneylender's daughter came to the house.
She was like her father, a skinny branch with dark brown hair and
thin cheeks. She was not as high as Da's shoulder, but she stood in
front of the door and threw a long shadow into the house and said
she would have the law on him if he did not pay her back the

money. He shouted at her, but she was not afraid. When he was done telling her there wasn't blood to be had from a stone, and showing her the empty cupboard, she said, "Your daughter will come and work for me, then, in payment of your debt."

When she was gone, I went back to the white tree and said, "Thank you, Mama," and between the roots I buried an apple, a whole apple, though I was so hungry I could have eaten it with all the seeds. Above my head, the tree put out a very small white flower.

I went to the moneylender's house the next morning. I was afraid to go to town alone, but it was better than going to the market with Da. I didn't really have to go into town anyway: their house was the first out of the forest. It was big, with two rooms and a floor of smooth fresh-smelling wood boards. The money-lender's wife was in bed in the back room. She was sick and coughing. It made my shoulders tight and hard to hear it.

The moneylender's daughter was named Miryem. That morning she put on a pot of soup, steam filling the cottage with a smell that made my empty stomach tighten like a knot. Then she took the dough rising in the corner with her and went out. She came back in the late afternoon with a hard face and dusty shoes and a loaf of dark brown bread fresh from the baker's ovens, a pail of milk and a dish of butter, and a sack over her shoulders full of apples. She put out plates on the table, and laid one for me, which I didn't expect. The moneylender said a magic spell over the bread when we sat down, but I ate it anyway. It tasted good.

I tried to do as much as I could, so they would want me to come back. Before I left the house, the moneylender's wife said to me in her cough-hoarsened voice, "Will you tell me your name?" After a moment I told her. She said, "Thank you, Wanda. You have been a great help." After I left the house, I heard her saying

I had done so much work, surely the debt would be paid soon. I stopped to listen outside the window.

Miryem said, "He borrowed six kopeks! At half a penny a day she'll be four years paying it off. Don't try to tell me that's not a fair wage when she gets her dinner with us."

Four years! My heart was glad as birds.

Chapter 3

Flurries of snow and my mother's cough both kept coming back long into the spring, but at last the days warmed, and the cough finally went away at the same time, drowned in soup and honey and rest. As soon as she could sing again, she said to me, "Miryem, next week, we'll go see my father."

I knew it was desperation, trying to break me loose from my work. I didn't want to leave, but I did want to see my grandmother, and show her that her daughter wasn't sleeping cold and frozen, that her granddaughter didn't go like a beggar anymore; I wanted to visit without seeing her weep, for once. I went on my rounds one last time, and told everyone as I did that I was going to the city, and I would have to add on extra interest for the weeks I was gone unless they left their payments at our house while I was away. I told Wanda she still had to come every day, and get my father's dinner, and feed the chickens and clean the house and yard. She nodded silently and didn't argue.

And then we drove to my grandfather's house, but this time I hired Oleg to take us all the way with his good horses and his comfortable wagon, heaped with straw and blankets and jingling bells on the harness, with the fur cloak spread over all against the wind. My grandmother came out surprised to meet us when we drew up to the house, and my mother went into her arms, silent and hiding her face. "Well, come in and warm up," my grandmother said, looking at the sledge and our good new dresses of red wool, trimmed with rabbit fur, and a golden button at the neck on mine that had come out of the weaver's chest.

She sent me to take my grandfather fresh hot water in his study, so she could talk to my mother alone. My grandfather had rarely done more than grunt at me and look me up and down disapprovingly in the dresses my grandmother had bought. I don't know how I knew what he thought of my father, because I don't remember him ever having said a word about it, but I did know.

He looked me over this time, out from under his bristling eyebrows, and frowned. "Fur, now? And gold?"

I should say that I was properly brought up, and I knew better than to talk back to my own grandfather, but I was already angry that my mother was upset, and that my grandmother wasn't pleased, and now to have him pick at me, him of all people. "Why shouldn't I have it, instead of someone who bought it with my father's money?" I said.

My grandfather was as surprised as you would expect to be spoken to like this by his granddaughter, but then he heard what I had said and frowned at me again. "Your father bought it for you, then?"

Loyalty and love stopped my mouth there, and I dropped my eyes and silently finished pouring the hot water into the samovar and changing out the tea. My grandfather didn't stop me going away, but by the next morning he knew the whole story somehow, that I'd taken over my father's work, and suddenly he was pleased with me, as he never had been before, and as no one else was.

His other two daughters had married better than my mother, to rich city men with good trades, but none of them had given him a grandson who wanted to take up his business. In the city, there were enough of my people that we could be something other than a banker, or a farmer who grew his own food. City people were more willing to buy our goods, and there was a thriving market in our quarter behind our wall.

"It's not seemly for a girl," my grandmother tried, but my grandfather snorted.

"Gold doesn't know the hand that holds it," he said, and frowned at me, but in a pleased way. "You'll need servants," he told me. "One to start with, a good strong simple man or woman who won't mind working for a Jew: can you find one?"

"Yes," I said, thinking of Wanda: she was already used to coming, and in our town there wasn't much other chance for a poor farmer's daughter to earn a wage.

"Good. Don't go yourself to get the money anymore," he said. "Send the servant, and if the customers want to argue, they have to come to your house. Get a desk, so you can sit behind it while they stand."

I nodded, and when we went home, he gave me a purse full of pennies, five kopeks' worth, to lend out to towns near ours that hadn't any moneylender of their own. When we came home, I asked my father if Wanda had come while I was gone. He looked at me sadly, his eyes deep-set and sorrowful even though we hadn't gone hungry for months now, and he said quietly, "Yes. I told her she need not, but she came every day."

Satisfied, I spoke to her that day after she finished her work. Her father was a big man, and she too was tall and broad-shouldered, big square hands made red with work, the nails close-trimmed, her face dirty and her long yellow hair hidden away under a kerchief, dull and silent and oxlike. "I want more time to spend on keeping the accounts," I said. "I need someone to go round and collect money for me. If you will take the work, I will pay you a penny a day, instead of half."

She stood there a long moment, as though she was not sure she understood me. "My father's debt would be cleared sooner," she said finally, as if making sure.

"When it is clear, I will keep paying you," I said, half recklessly. But if Wanda did my collecting, I could do a circuit round the neighboring villages and make new loans. I wanted to loan out that little lake of silver my grandfather had given me, and set a river-flow of pennies coming back.

Wanda was silent again, then said, "You will give me coin?"

"Yes," I said. "Well?"

She nodded, and I nodded back. I didn't offer to shake hands; no one would shake hands with a Jew, and anyway I knew it would have been a lie if they had. If Wanda didn't keep to the bargain, I would stop paying her; that was a better guarantee than any other I could have.

Da had been angry and sullen ever since I went to work in the moneylender's house. He couldn't sell me to anyone, and I wasn't home to work, and still we didn't have much to eat. He shouted more and swung his hand harder. Stepon and Sergey spent most of their time with the goats. I ducked as much as I could and took the rest in silence. I closed my mouth with counting. If four years would have cleared my father's debt, at half a penny, then two years would do it now. So two years was six kopeks. And I could work for two years more before my father would think the debt was paid. I would have six kopeks. Six silver kopeks of my own.

I had only ever caught a glimpse of so much money, my father letting two coins slip gleaming into the doctor's open hand. Maybe if he hadn't drunk and gambled up the other four, it would have been enough.

I didn't mind going to strangers' houses and knocking and asking them for money. It wasn't me asking, it was Miryem, and it was her money, and she was going to give some of it to me. Standing on their stoops I could see inside, handsome furniture, warm fires. No one in their houses coughed. "I am here from the moneylender," I said, and told them how much they owed, and I did not say anything when they tried to tell me the number was wrong. At a few houses, someone said they couldn't pay, and I told them they needed to go speak to her at her house if they did not want her to send it to the law. Then they gave me something after all, so they had been lying. I minded even less, then.

I carried a big sturdy basket and I put inside it everything they gave me. Miryem was worried I would forget who gave what, but I didn't forget. I remembered every coin and all the different goods. She wrote it all down in her big black book, the thick goose-feather pen scratching surely in her hand without a pause. On market day, she would sort out any goods she did not want to keep, and I would follow her with the basket into town. She sold and traded until the basket was empty and the purse she carried full, turning cloth and fruit and buttons into coins. Sometimes she took another step first: if a farmer had given her ten skeins of wool, she would take them to a weaver in her debt and have her work off a payment in making it into a cloak; then she would sell the cloak in the market.

And at the end of the day she would pour out a lake of pennies on the floor and roll them in paper to turn them into silver; one roll of pennies the length of my ring finger was the same as a kopek. I knew because when she took that roll into the market the next time, very early in the morning, she would find a merchant who had traveled in from out of the town, still putting up his stand, and she would give him that roll and he would open it and count the pennies and then he would give her one silver kopek back. The silver coins she did not spend or change in the market.

She brought them home and rolled them in paper also, and a roll as long as my little finger, that was the same as a coin of gold. She put them away into the leather purse her grandfather had given her. I never saw that purse except on market days, and on market days it was out on the table when I came, and it stayed there until after I had gone for the day. She did not hide it or take it out where I could see, and her father and her mother never touched it.

I didn't understand how she guessed how much each thing would be worth to someone else, when she didn't care to keep them herself. But little by little I learned to read the numbers she wrote down in her book when she valued the payments, and when I overheard the prices she got in the market, the two were nearly the same, every time. I wanted to understand how she did it. But I didn't ask. I knew she only thought of me as a horse or an ox, something dull and silent and strong. I felt so, around her and her family. They talked all the day it seemed to me: talked or sang or even argued. But there was never shouting or raised hands. They were always touching one another. Her mother would put a hand on Miryem's cheek or her father would kiss her on the head, whenever she passed nearby. Sometimes when I left their house at the end of the day, once I was down the road and into the fields and out of sight, I would put my hand on the back of my head, my hand that had grown big and heavy and strong, and I tried to remember the feeling of my own mother's hand.

In my house there was only a silence like solid earth. We had gone a little hungry all the winter, even me with my extra dinner. I had a walk of six miles to go with it. Now spring was here, but we were all still hungry. When I walked home I picked up mushrooms and if I was lucky a wild turnip and whatever greens I saw. There were not many. Most of them we could not eat. Those went to the goats. Then in our garden I dug some of the new potatoes, which were too young to be worth eating but we ate them anyway. I would cut off the smallest piece with an eye and bury it again. I went inside and stirred up the coals under the pot that I had put on in the morning with our cabbage. I put the small lumps of potatoes in with whatever else I had found. We ate sitting around the table with our heads bent, never speaking.

Nothing grew well. The ground stayed packed hard and cold into April, and the rye grew sluggishly. When at last Da was able to start planting beans, a week later snow fell again and killed half the plants. That morning when I woke I thought it was still night. But it was stone-grey outside, and snow was coming down so we could not see the neighbor's fence. Da started cursing and cuffed us out of bed. We all hurried outside to bring in the goats, the five baby goats. One of them was already dead. The rest we brought into the house with their mothers. They brayed and chewed our blankets and nearly got into the fire, but they stayed alive. After the snow stopped, we butchered the dead one and salted what little meat there was. I made soup of the bones and we ate the liver and lungs. For one day we weren't hungry.

Sergey could have eaten three times his share. He was starting to get big himself. I thought he was hunting sometimes, even though he knew he would be hanged for poaching, or worse if he was taking them from the forest. The only animals we could take from the forest were the marked ones, the ones with some spot of black or brown. But there were almost none like that left, and the white animals, all white, belonged to the Staryk. I did not know what they would do to someone who hunted their animals, because nobody did it, but I knew they would do something. You could not take anything from the Staryk that was theirs. They came and stole from people, but they did not like it when anyone stole from them.

But sometimes Sergey came in and ate without looking up, without stopping, his full share, the same way I ate mine. As if he knew he had eaten more than the others at the table. So I thought he was hunting where no one else saw. I did not tell him not to do it: he knew. Anyway it was not the same in my house as the money-lender's house. I did not think the word *love*. Love was buried with my mother. Sergey and Stepon were only more of the babies who made my mother sick. They had not died, but so they had made even more work for her and now me. They ate some of the food, and I had to spin the goats' wool and knit and wash their clothes. So I did not worry very much about what if the Staryk did something to Sergey. I did think maybe I should tell him to bring me the bones to make soup, but then I thought, if we all ate, we would all be in trouble, and not worth it just for some cracked bones he had already sucked clean.

But Stepon did love Sergey. I had made Sergey take care of him, when my mother died. I was eleven and I could spin, and Sergey was only seven years old, so Da let me. By the time Sergey was big enough to go to the fields, he had gotten used to putting up with Stepon and didn't push him back on me. Stepon would follow him and keep out of the way and bring them water. He helped with the goats, and together they could sleep warm out of the house if my father was angry, even in winter. Sergey would cuff him sometimes but not very hard.

So Stepon came to me the day Sergey got sick. It was not yet noon. I was working in the moneylender's garden, cutting off the heads of their cabbages. They were not really ready yet, but that night it had frozen a little, even though it was still early in autumn, and Miryem had said better to bring them in for what good they would be. I kept an eye on the door. Soon it would open and the moneylender's wife would call me inside for dinner. That morning there had been a crust of stale bread in among the grain to go to the hens, and I had taken it myself and gnawed it up bit by bit, making it soft in my mouth with swallows of water out of the rain barrel, cold from under a crust of ice, but my belly was still pinched tight. I was looking at the door again when Stepon cried,

"Wanda!" He was leaning on the fence breathing in big gulps. "Wanda!"

When he shouted my name I jerked as though Da had come down on my back with a switch. "What is it?" I was angry with Stepon for coming. I didn't want him there.

"Wanda, come," he said, beckoning me. He never talked much. Sergey understood him without talking, most of the time, and when my father filled our house with his voice, he got out of it if he could. "Wanda, come."

"Is something wrong at home?" The moneylender's wife was standing in the doorway, with a shawl around her for the cold. "Go on, Wanda. I will tell Miryem I sent you home."

I didn't want to go. I guessed something had happened to Sergey, because that was why Stepon would come. I didn't want to give up my dinner to go help Sergey, who had never helped me. But I couldn't say so to the moneylender's wife. I got up and went silently out of the gate, and after we were down the road and into the trees I shook Stepon and said, angry, "Don't ever come for me again." He was only ten, still small enough for me to shake.

But he only grabbed my hand and pulled me on. I went with him. There was nothing else for me to do but go home and tell Da that Sergey had gotten himself into trouble, and that I wouldn't do. Sergey was not someone I loved, but he would not tell Da on me, and I would not tell on him. Stepon kept trying to run. I began to catch the haste from him, so I would run a little way without thinking, and then I would stop running, and he would stop to catch his breath, and then he would start us going again. We went the six miles in only an hour. A little way before we reached our house, he started to lead me off the road, into the forest. Then I began to be wary. "What has happened to him?" I demanded.

"He won't get up," Stepon said.

Sergey was at the creek where sometimes we had to go for water in the summer, if the stream closer went dry. He was lying on his side on the bank. He did not look asleep. His eyes were open, and when I put my finger on his lips I could feel that he was breathing, but there was nothing stirring in him. His arms were heavy and limp when I tried to lift one. I looked around. Half in the water next to him there was a white rabbit dead, with a string of rough twisted goat-hair around its leg. It did not have any markings. There was frost all over the paths and ice creeping out of the edges of the creek. So then I knew the Staryk had caught him hunting and taken his soul away.

I put his arm down again. Stepon looked at me as if he thought I would do something. But there was nothing to do. The priest wouldn't come to help us here so far from town, and anyway Sergey had been stealing when he knew better. I did not think God would save you from the Staryk when it was your own fault.

I didn't say anything. Stepon didn't say anything, but he kept staring at me, as if he knew I could do something, until I began to feel in my own stomach that I could, too, even though I didn't want to. I closed my teeth together and tried not to think of anything to try, and then I tried to slap Sergey awake, and then to throw cold water in his face, even though I knew that was no good. And it was no good. He didn't stir. The water ran down over his face and some drops even slid into his eyes and then ran over them and came out again like tears, but he wasn't crying, he was only lying there empty as a dead log rotted from inside.

Stepon didn't look at Sergey. He watched me the whole time almost without blinking. I wanted to slap him, or chase him away with my stick. What good had either of them ever done me that I owed them anything? I stopped trying and stood with my hands made into fists, and then I said, the words tasting like old rotten acorns in my mouth, "Pick up his legs."

Sergey was not so big yet that we couldn't carry him together. I pushed him onto his back and I took him under the arms, and Stepon put Sergey's ankles onto his thin shoulders, and together we carried him slowly out of the forest all the way to the edge of our fields, all the way to the white tree. I was angrier when we got there than when we began. I fell down three times in the forest, walking backwards with his weight dragging at my hands, falling over roots and slipping in half-frozen mud. I bruised myself on a stone, and covered myself in dirt and crushed poison berries I would have to wash out of my clothes. But that was not what made me angry. They had taken her from me, all of them: Sergey and Stepon and the rest of those dead boys in the dirt. They had taken my mother. I had never wanted to share her with them. What right did they have to her?

But I didn't say anything out loud. I let Sergey's shoulders drop to the ground by the white tree in a heap, beside our mother's grave, and I stood there by the tree and I said, "Mama, Sergey is sick."

The air was still and cold. Beyond us the rye was just barely up in a long half-green field going away, the plants much smaller than they should have been, and I could see the smoke from our house going up in a straight grey line. Our father was not in sight. There was no wind blowing, but the white tree sighed and its branches shivered, and a little piece of its bark sprang off at one end. I took hold of it and peeled it off the trunk, one long strip.

We picked Sergey up and carried him the rest of the way to our creek, and I sent Stepon to the house to bring me back a hot coal and a cup. I pulled dry dead grass and twigs and raked it into a pile, and when Stepon came I lit it into a small fire, and boiled a tea from the bark. The water turned cloudy ash, and a smell like earth came from the cup, and then we held up Sergey's head and made him swallow some of it. He shuddered all over like a beast shaking off flies in summer. I gave him another swallow, and a third, and then he turned over and began to vomit, again and again, a heap of steaming raw red flesh coming out of him onto the dirt, stinking and awful. I scrambled away not to be sick, too.

When at last he stopped he crawled away from the pile himself, crying a little.

I gave him some water to drink, and Stepon buried the heap of raw meat that had come out of him. Sergey wept a little longer, gasping. He looked gaunt and scraped-thin, as if he had been starving, but at least he was there again. He had to lean on me when we stood up. We went along the creek to the rock where the goats drank, and they were there, grazing and mumbling at the leaves along the bank. The oldest goat wandered over to us, ears wagging forward, and Sergey put his arms around her neck and pressed his face against her side while I milked a cup and gave it to him to drink.

He swallowed every drop and licked the cup clean, and then he looked at me, wary. Our father paid attention if one of the goats did not give as much milk as she should, and we would all be beaten for it, if he did not know who had taken it. But I took the cup from Sergey's hand and milked another for him, and gave it to him again. I don't know why I did it. But I did, and then in the morning when my father came in from the milking pails and began to shout, I stood up and said to him loudly, "Sergey needs more food!"

My father stared at me, and so did Sergey and Stepon. I would have stared, too, if I were outside myself. After a moment he slapped me and told me to keep my mouth to myself, but then he went back out, and that was the end of it. Sergey and Stepon and I all stood inside the house, half waiting, but he didn't come back. There was no beating. Sergey looked at me and I looked back at him, and we didn't say anything. After a minute more, I took my kerchief and my sack and left for work. My clothes were still dirty and hard with mud. I wouldn't have time to wash them until washing-day.

When I came home at midday, Sergey had brought out the washing-tub and Stepon had filled it from the creek. They had even boiled some water to make it hot, so the clothes would wash easily. I looked at it, and then out of my pocket I showed them the three eggs I had gotten from the moneylender's wife. She had asked me what had happened. When I told her my brother had been sick with something he ate, she said that the best for a bad stomach was fresh raw eggs and gave me three. I ate one, Sergey one and a half, and Stepon the last half. Then they cut our own small cabbages for me while I washed my clothes, and when I was done, I made dinner.

Chapter 4

All that cold year, I sowed my silver. The spring had come late again, and the summer was short, and even the vegetable gardens grew slowly. The snow kept falling well into April. People came to me from far off, dozens of villages around, and borrowed money to carry them through. When we went back to Vysnia the next spring, I brought my grandfather's purse back with me full of kopeks rolled and ready to be changed into gold zlotek and put into the bank, safe from Staryk raiders behind the thick walls of the vault and the thicker city walls outside. My grandfather said nothing, only held the purse a little while, balanced on his palm, weighing it, but I saw he was proud of me.

My grandparents hadn't usually had guests over when we were visiting, except my mother's sisters. I hadn't noticed before, but I noticed now, because suddenly the house was full of people coming to drink tea, to stay to dinner, lights and bustling dresses and laughing voices. I met more city people in those two weeks than I had in all the visits before. I had always vaguely thought of my grandfather as an important man, but now I saw it ten times over:

people addressed him formally as Panov Moshel, even the rabbi, and at the table he and several other men discussed seriously the politics of the quarter, and often settled arguments there, among themselves, as though they had a right to do it.

I didn't understand why the guests hadn't come before. All of them were kind, and pleased to see me. "Can this be little Miryem?" Panova Idin said, smiling at me and touching my cheeks: she was the wife of one of my grandfather's friends. I didn't remember ever meeting her before, it had been so long. "So grown-up already! Surely we will be dancing at your wedding soon." My grandmother, hearing her, kept her mouth pursed; my mother looked still unhappier. She kept to a corner of the sitting room when the guests came, bent over a shirt of plain linen she was sewing for my father, and said only enough to all the visitors to be not-quite-polite: my mother, who was kind to people in our village who had taken food out of her mouth, and who would not have her in their houses.

"I don't believe in selling a sow's ear for a silk purse," my grandfather told me bluntly, when I finally asked him about the guests. "Your father couldn't dower you as the guests who come to this house would expect of my granddaughter, and I swore to your mother when she married him that I would never put more money in his pocket, to fall back out again."

I understood then why he hadn't invited his rich guests, and why he hadn't wanted my grandmother buying dresses for me, as he'd thought, with fur and gold buttons on them. He wouldn't try to make a princess out of a miller's daughter with borrowed finery, and snare her a husband fool enough to be tricked by it, or one who'd slip out of the bargain when he learned the truth.

It didn't make me angry. I liked him better for that cold hard honesty, and it made me proud that now he did invite guests, and even boasted of me to them, how I'd taken away a purse of silver and brought back one of gold. I liked to feel their eyes on me, weighing me like a purse, and being able to hold my head up when they did it, feeling my own worth.

I found myself getting angry at my mother instead. Her sisters came to dinner again, the last night before we left, twelve of us around the table and many little ones yelling and noisy in the courtyard. My cousin Basia sat next to me: a year older, beautiful with plump arms and sleek shining brown hair and a necklace and earrings of pearls, self-possessed and graceful. She had visited the matchmaker a month ago, and she looked down with a smile in her eyes and the corners of her mouth when her mother spoke about one young man they were considering: Isaac, a jeweler like her father and skillful, although my grandfather shook his head a bit skeptically and asked many questions about his business. Her hands were smooth and soft. She had never had to do hard work, and her clothing was finely stitched, embroidered beautifully with flowers and birds singing.

I didn't envy her, not now when I could buy myself an embroidered apron, if I wanted to spend my money so. I was glad to have my work. But I felt my mother drawn tight near me, as if she would have put out a hand to bar me from seeing Basia's life and wanting anything of it. The next day we flew home in the sleigh over the frozen crust of snow, cutting through the dark forest. It was a bitter cold for spring, but I had my own fur cloak, and three petticoats underneath my dress, and there were three blankets tucked around us, snug and comfortable. But my mother's face was full of misery. We didn't speak. "Would you rather we were still poor and hungry?" I burst out to her finally, the silence between us heavy in the midst of the dark woods, and she put her arms around me and kissed me and said, "My darling, my darling, I'm sorry," weeping a little.

"Sorry?" I said. "To be warm instead of cold? To be rich and

comfortable? To have a daughter who can turn silver into gold?"
I pushed away from her.

"To see you harden yourself to ice, to make it so," she said. I
didn't answer her, only huddled into my robes. Oleg was speaking
urgently to his horses: a silver gleam had appeared between the
trees in the distance, the Staryk road peeking out. The horses trotted on more swiftly, but the Staryk road kept pace with us all the
way home, shining between the trees. I could feel it on my side, a
shimmer of colder wind trying to press against me and pierce
through to my skin, but I didn't care. I was colder inside than out.

Wanda was late coming to the house the next morning, and when
she came in, she was out of breath and her face ruddy with sweating and her stockings and skirt covered in a crust of clumped
snow, as though she had come through the fields forcing a new
way, instead of walking on the village road. "The Staryk are in
the woods," she said without looking up. When we stepped into
the yard in front of our house, we saw the Staryk road still there,
glimmering faintly between the trees, not a quarter of a mile distant.

I had never heard of the road coming so near to town. We did
not have a wall, but we were not rich enough to tempt them. Our
taxes were paid in grain and wool, and the rich men changed
their silver for gold behind city walls and left it in banks, just like
me. Maybe a woman had a necklace of gold or a ring—I thought
belatedly of the button on my own collar—but they could not
have harvested even one small chest of golden jewelry if they had
smashed into every house along the main lane.

A bitter cold was radiating out of the wood; if you knelt down and put out your bare hand, you could feel the chill creeping along the ground as though breathed out faintly by some distant giant, and the air had a thick strong smell of broken pine branches. The forest was deep in snow, but it felt too cold for nature even so. I looked back at the town and saw other people standing in their yards in the houses nearest ours, looking at the road just as we were. Panova Gavelyte scowled at me when our eyes met, before she went back into her house, as though it was our fault.

But nothing else happened, and the morning work had to be done, so little by little we all went inside, and when we couldn't see the road, we stopped thinking about it. I sat down with my books to look over everything that Wanda had brought into the house the two weeks we had been gone. She took the basket full of stale bread and grain for the chickens and went out to feed them and gather the eggs. My mother had finally given up trying to do any of the outdoor work, and I was glad: she was sitting at the table paring potatoes for our dinner, warm by the fire, and there was a little color in her cheeks, a little roundness that had been eaten away last winter. I refused to care at the way she looked over at me with my books.

The numbers were all tidy and clean, and all the right amounts had come in. My grandfather had asked me about my servant, and whether she was good; he hadn't thought I was foolish to have promised to pay Wanda in money. "A servant is easy to make dishonest when they bring you coin and never touch any themselves," he said. "Let her feel that her fortune rises with yours."

I was a little wary of my own fortune rising, even with fourteen gold coins in the heavy vault in my grandfather's bank. I knew that money was not really from my own lending work; it was my mother's dowry, coming back to us at last. My father had lent it out so quickly after they were married, it was all gone into other pockets almost before I was born, and so little had ever been paid back that every one of our neighbors for miles around was still in our debt. They had fixed their houses and their barns, they had bought cattle and they had bought seed grain, they had married their daughters and started their sons in the world, and meanwhile my mother had gone hungry and my father had been chased out of their yards. I meant to get back every coin and all the interest besides.

But I had already gathered the easy money. Some of it would never come back. Some who had borrowed from my father had died, or gone away so far I did not have their direction. I was already having to take more than half my payments in goods or work or something else, and turning those into coin wasn't easy. Our house was snug now, and we had a flock of chickens as big as we could manage. People had offered me a sheep or a goat, too, but we didn't know anything about keeping them. I could sell them on again, but that was difficult, and I knew better than to try and give any of my debtors one penny less in credit than the full amount I got for their goods in the market. They would call it cheating, even though it was my time spent on the work of selling it.

I was lending new money only to those who had some reasonable hope of having it to repay, and in small and cautious amounts, but that only brought in an equally cautious stream of payments, and I didn't know how many would yet default before their full debt was paid. But even so, looking at my accounts with all the tidy amounts brought in, I decided I would start to pay Wanda now: each day she would clear half a penny of her father's debt, and take half a penny home, and have real coin to keep, so she and her father would feel that she was earning money; it wouldn't just be a number written in my books.

I had just settled with myself that I would tell her this afternoon, before she went home, when the door banged open and she rushed back in with the basket clutched against her chest, still full of grain. She said, "They've been outside the house!"

I didn't know who she meant at first, but I stood up in alarm anyway; her face was white and afraid, and she wasn't given to startling. My father said, "Show me," and took the iron poker from the fireplace.

"Is it burglars?" my mother said in a low voice: my own first thought, too, as soon as I had one. I was glad I had taken my money away and put it in the bank. But then we followed my father outside, around the back of the house where the chickens were still squawking loudly in disappointment, waiting for their food, and Wanda showed us the marks. It wasn't burglars at all.

The hoofprints were barely a shallow impression in the top dusting of fresh snow. They hadn't broken through the ice crust beneath, but they were very large, the size of horse hooves, except cloven like deer, and with spiky indentations at the front ends. They came right to the wall of the house, and then someone had climbed down and looked through our window: someone wearing strange boots with a long pointed toe.

I didn't quite believe in it, at first. It was certainly something strange, but I thought someone was playing a trick on us, like the village boys who had thrown rocks at me sometimes when I was little. Someone had come creeping over to leave the marks to scare us, or maybe something even more malicious: to make an excuse for a robbery they planned. But before I opened my mouth to say so, I realized no one could have made the marks without breaking the snow themselves, unless they had leaned down somehow with a stick from the roof. But the roof was unmarred, and the cloven hoofprints made a long trail across our yard and all the way back into the forest, where under the trees they vanished. And when I looked in that direction, I saw the silver road gleaming between the trees still there.

I didn't say anything, and neither my mother or my father said anything either, all of us looking into the woods at the road, and only Wanda said, flatly, "It's the Staryk. The Staryk came here."

But the Staryk didn't belong in the yard with our chickens, peering in through the window into our big room. I bent down to look through myself: there was nothing to see over my narrow bed but the fireplace with its small cooking pot, the cupboard my father had made as a present for my mother, the sacks of grain in our pantry. My home looked so ordinary and so plain it only made the idea more ridiculous, and I straightened up and stared at the prints again, half expecting them to go away and stop making the world untidy and absurd.

And then my father took the poker and stirred it right into the prints, and trudged along the line of them dragging it through, all the way to the forest's edge, and then he came back walking over them. He came up to us and said, "Let's not hear any more talk like that. Who knows who made it, probably just some children making a stupid joke. Go back to your chores, Wanda."

I stared at him. I had never heard my father sound so hard. I didn't know he could speak so. Wanda hesitated. She looked where the prints had been, but then she slowly stepped over the trampled snow and began to feed the chickens. My mother was standing silently by with her shawl wrapped tight, her lips pressed tight, her hands clenched tight. She said, "Come back in the house, Miryem, I need your help with the potatoes." I followed my mother back to the house, and as we did, she glanced down the road towards the town. But everyone else had all gone to their chores and into their houses; no one was still outside watching.

When we were inside, my father went to the window over my bed with a narrow stick out of the woodpile and measured its length and width with cuts of his knife, and then he took his coat and his small axe and his hat and went out again, carrying the stick. I watched him go, and then I looked at my mother, who was peering out the back at Wanda already busy sweeping the yard.

"Miryem," my mother said, "I think it would be good for your father to have a young man's help. We will ask Wanda's brother to come stay with us at night, and pay him."

"Pay someone just to sleep in the house? What good would he even do, if one of the Staryk did come?" I laughed even as I said it out loud: the idea of it was so ridiculous. I couldn't quite remember why I had ever thought it *was* anything but a joke. I had a feeling as though I'd just been having a dream, and it was already fading.

But my mother said sharply, "Don't speak of such things. I don't want you to say anything like that again. And don't talk of the Staryk to anyone, anywhere in town." I understood that even less. Everyone would be talking of the Staryk, with the road there in the woods, and tomorrow was market day. "Then you won't go," she said, after I said so, and when I protested I had goods from Vysnia to take and sell, she took me by the shoulders and said, "Miryem. We will pay Wanda's brother to stay at night, so she won't say to anyone that the Staryk are visiting our house. And you will not say to anyone that they have come near."

I stopped arguing. My mother said softly, "Two years ago, outside Minask, a band of Staryk went through the countryside to three towns, towns not much bigger than this. They burned the churches and the houses of rich men, and took all the little gold they could find. But they rode past Yazuda village, where the Jews lived, and they did not burn their houses. So the people said the Jews had made a pact with the Staryk. And now there are no Jews in Yazuda. Do you understand, Miryem? You will not speak of the Staryk coming to our house."

That wasn't elves or magic or absurdity. That was something I understood very well. "I'll go to market tomorrow," I said, after a moment, and when my mother would have spoken, I went on, "It would be strange if I didn't. I'll go, and sell the two new dresses I bought, and talk of the new fashions in Vysnia."

My mother nodded after a moment, and stroked my head with her hand, and cupped my cheeks. Then we sat down together at the table and began to peel the rest of the potatoes. Outside I heard Wanda working on chopping wood, the steady *thwack-whack* of the axe going in even rhythm. My father came back after only a short while with an armful of green boughs, and he spent the rest of the morning by the fire whittling them and fitting them together into small grates that he nailed across our window frames.

"We have been thinking we might hire Wanda's brother to come stay for the nights," my mother said without looking up from her knitting, while he worked.

"It would be good to have a young man around," my father agreed. "I worry whenever we have money in the house. Anyway, I could use the help. I am not as young as I was."

"Maybe we could keep some goats after all," I said. "He could look after them for us."

That morning after she came back, Miryem said to me, "Wanda, we would like to have a young man staying here at night to help look after the house, and to take care of some goats we are going to get. Would your brother be able to come and help us?"

I didn't answer her right away. I wanted to say no. I had kept her books, all those two weeks while she was away. Me, alone. Every day I went on my rounds, every day to a different set of houses, and then I came back to the house and set dinner to cook for me and her father the moneylender, and I sat down at the table and with my hands trembling a little I carefully opened the book. The leather was so soft beneath my hands, and inside, every thin fine page was covered with letters and numbers. I turned them one after another to find the houses I had visited that day. She had a different number on the page for each house, and next to it the name of the person who lived there. I dipped my pen, and wiped the nib, and dipped it again, and I wrote very slowly and shaped every number as well as I could. And then I closed the book up again, and cleaned the pen, and put it and the ink away on the shelf. I did all that by myself.

All that summer, when the days were long and I could linger a little, Miryem had taught me how to write the numbers with a pen. She would take me outside after dinner and shape them in the dirt with a stick, over and over. But she didn't only teach me how to put them down. She taught me how to *make* them, one new number growing out of two, and how to take one number away from another also. Not just little numbers that I could make on my hands or by counting stones, but big numbers. She taught me how to make a hundred pennies into a kopek and twenty silver kopeks into a golden zlotek, and how to break a piece of silver back into pennies again.

I was afraid at first when she began. It was five days before I picked up the stick and traced the lines she had drawn. She spoke as if it was ordinary, but I knew she was teaching me magic. I was still afraid afterwards, but I couldn't help myself. I learned to draw the magic shapes in the dirt, and then with an old worn-out pen and ash mixed with water on a smooth flat rock, and finally with her own pen and ink on an old piece of paper, marked up to grey from all the writing that had been done and bleached away. And by the end of the winter, when she went away visiting, I could keep the books for her. I was even starting to be able to read the letters. I knew the names out loud and on each page, I would say them softly to myself and touch the letters with my finger and I could see which letters made each sound. Sometimes when I was wrong Miryem would stop me and tell me the right one. That was how much magic she had given me, and I didn't want to share.

A year ago, I *would* have said no to her, to keep it to myself. But that was before I had saved Sergey from the Staryk. Now, when I came home late, he had put the dinner on for me. He and Stepon had gathered me goat-hair from the bushes and the hay, all winter long, enough so I could make a shawl to wear when I walked to town. He was my brother.

Then I almost said no anyway for fear. What if he let the secret out? It was so big that I could hardly keep it inside me anyway. Every night I went to sleep thinking of six silver kopeks tight in my fist, shining and cold. I made them out of adding pennies, one by one, as long as I could before sleep took me.

But after a moment, I said slowly, "Would his work help pay the debt sooner?"

"Yes," Miryem said. "Every day you and he will earn two pennies. Half will go to the debt until it is paid, and I will give you half in coin. And here is the first, for today."

She took out a round clean penny and put it shining in my hand, like a reward for thinking yes instead of no. I stared down at it, and then I closed my hand around it in a fist. "I will talk to Sergey," I said.

But when I told him, in a whisper, in the woods, far from where Da might be to overhear, he asked, "They only want me to stay in the house? They will give me *money*, just to stay in the house, and feed their goats? Why?"

I said, "They're afraid of burglars," but as soon as the words came, I remembered that it wasn't true. But I couldn't remember what the truth was.

I had to stand up and pretend to be holding the basket for the chickens, and walk around, before the memory of that morning would even come back into my head. I had gone outside and quietly eaten some of the stale bread, standing at the corner of the house where they wouldn't see me, and neither would the chickens, and then I had gone around the corner and I had seen the footprints—

"The Staryk," I said. The word was cold in my mouth. "The Staryk were there."

If Miryem hadn't given me the penny, I don't know what we would have done. I knew my father's debt didn't matter anymore. No law would make me go to a house where the Staryk were coming and looking in the windows. But Sergey looked at the penny in my hand, and I looked at it, and he said, "A penny each, every day?"

"Half of it goes to the debt, for now," I said. "One penny each day."

"You will keep this one," he said after a moment, "and I will keep the next."

I didn't say, *Let us go to the white tree and ask for advice.* I was like Da then. I didn't want to hear Mama's voice saying, *Don't go, it'll be trouble.* I knew there would be trouble. But I also knew what would happen if I stopped working. If I told Da, he would say I didn't have to go back another minute to a house of devils, and then he would sell me in the market for two goats, to someone who wanted a wife with a strong back and no numbers in her head. I would not even be worth as much as six kopeks.

So instead I told my father that the moneylender wanted someone to help tend goats, and it would pay his debt quicker if he let Sergey go to them at night. He scowled and said to Sergey, "Be back an hour after sunrise. When will the debt be paid?"

Sergey looked at me. I opened my mouth and said, "In three years."

I expected him to hit me, to shout I was a fool who couldn't do my sums. But Da only growled, "Bloodsuckers and leeches," and then he added to Sergey, "You will tell them they must give you breakfast there! We will have no more taking milk from the goats."

So we had three years now. First there would be a penny every other day, and then a penny every day. Sergey and I clutched hands together behind the house. He said in a whisper, "What will we buy with it?"

I didn't know how to answer him. I hadn't thought of buying anything with the money. I only thought of having it, real in my hands. Then Sergey said, "If we spend any of it, he'll find out. He'll make us give it to him."

First I thought, at least Da would not want to take me to the market. If I brought home a penny every day, he would be glad to let me keep working for the moneylender. But then I thought of him taking my pennies, of having to put each shining one into his hand. I thought of him going to town and drinking them up, gambling, never working anymore. He would be happy every day. "I won't," I said. My stomach burned. "I won't let him have any of it."

But we didn't know what to do. Then I said, "We'll hide it. We'll hide it all. If we work for three years, and don't spend it, we will have ten kopeks, each. Together that will be one zlotek. A coin of gold. And we'll take Stepon and go away."

Where could we go? I didn't know. But I was sure that when we had so much money, we could go anywhere. We could do anything. And Sergey nodded; he thought so too. "Where can we hide it?" he asked.

So we went to the white tree, after all, and beneath the stone on my mother's grave we dug a hollow and we put the penny into it, and covered it again with the stone. "Mama," I said, "please keep it safe for us." Then we hurried away and didn't wait to see if anything would happen. Sergey didn't want to hear Mama tell us not to do it, either.

That night after dinner he went to town, with a cap I tied together from rags around his head to keep his ears warm. I stood in the front yard watching him go. The Staryk road was still lingering near in the forest, shining. It wasn't like a lamp, but like stars on a cloudy night. If you tried to look right at it, you couldn't see it. If you looked away, it was there gleaming in the corner of your eye. Sergey had been staying away from it as much as he could. He didn't like to go to the forest anymore. He stayed all the way on the shoulder of the village road, along the opposite edge across from the trees, even though he had to stamp through the snow there, and the road was packed hard by now. But soon he was gone into the dark.

In the morning, I could see his tracks still in the snow as I walked to town myself. I half wished he had walked in the road so I wouldn't see them, because I was afraid that they would just stop somewhere along the way. But they didn't. I followed them all the way to Miryem's house, and Sergey was there at the table eating a bowl of nut-smelling hot kasha. It made my stomach hungry, too. We didn't eat breakfast at our house anymore. There wasn't enough food.

"Everything was quiet all night," he said to me, and I took the basket and went out to the hens. There was a whole heel of bread in the basket, the middle of it still soft. I ate it and then I went to the hens, but they didn't come out to meet me.

Slowly, I went closer. There were tracks all around the coop. The hoof like a deer, but big, with claws. The little window at the top, that I had closed yesterday when I left, was opened wide as if something had put its nose in. I bent down and put my hand inside the coop. The hens were there, sitting all together, crouched with their feathers all fluffed big. There were only three small eggs, and when I brought them out, one of them had a grey shell, pale whitish grey like ash in a fireplace.

I threw the grey one away into the forest as hard as I could and thought of brushing away the tracks and pretending I had not seen them. What if the moneylender told Sergey not to come again, because he had not kept away the Staryk? Maybe they would send me away, too. And if I brushed the snow clean, I would forget the tracks myself, just like I had yesterday. It would almost be as though they hadn't been there at all. I went and got the broom that I used to sweep the yard. But it was leaning against the side of the house, and when I went to take it, I saw the boot marks. There were many of them. The Staryk had come to the back of the house, the same one with the pointed boots, and he had walked back and forth along the wall three times, right there where they slept.

Chapter 5

Wanda's brother wasn't much more than a boy: tall and broad and raw, a half-starved horse with his big bones poking out at elbows and wrists. When he arrived for the first time that evening, he said without looking up that his father would let him come if we gave him supper and breakfast, and when he sat down at the table, I could see Gorek was no fool to set those terms: he ate like a wolf. We might as well have doubled his wages, with the price of food going as it was. But I didn't say anything, even when my mother gave him another piece of bread and butter. My parents had moved my bed into their room, and they gave Sergey a pair of blankets to sleep on in its place.

I woke up in the dark middle hours. My father was going into the living room, and the door was creaking open, letting in a gust of biting air. I heard Sergey stamping snow off his boots, and he said to my father briefly, "Everything is quiet."

"Go back to sleep, Miryem," my mother said softly. "Sergey was only looking around outside."

I opened my eyes twice more at night to the sound of him going out and the sharp lick of the cold air, but I closed them again right away afterwards. Nothing happened. We rose in the morning and began cooking the kasha for breakfast. Sergey was outside hammering posts into the ground, to make a pen that would keep goats in. The Staryk road was still there in the trees, but when I peered at it from the window I thought maybe it was a little farther away. It was a grey cold day, and the sun did not come out, but the road glittered anyway. Some of the village boys were outside the village past our house, daring each other to try and throw a rock onto the Staryk road, or to touch it; I could hear their gleeful high voices taunting each other.

Wanda came while her brother was still at the table eating, and went out with the basket for the hens. She came back with the basket almost empty, only two eggs, though we had nine laying hens now. She set it on the table and we all looked at them. The eggs were small, the shells very white, and then she said abruptly, "There are more tracks behind the house."

We went and looked at them. I recognized them when I saw them, although I had already forgotten what they looked like: until Wanda said anything, I had half forgotten they had ever been there at all. The long-toed boots had prowled round the back wall of the bedroom, back and forth three times, and the cloven-hooved animal had been standing beside the coop, leaving marks all over the snow around it like a fox sniffing round to find a hole to get in. The hens were all huddled together inside in a single feathery heap.

"I looked, I swear!" Sergey said, but my father said, "Never mind, Sergey." Wanda brushed the yard, and we threw the two eggs into the midden. My mother's arm was tight around my shoulders as we went back into the house.

Sergey went back to his father's farm, and Wanda did the cleaning and went for water. I didn't forget about the footprints again, even though I wanted to, but when Wanda came in, I stood up and said, "Come, we're going to market," and went for my shawl, as if there hadn't been anything strange or out of the ordinary about the day. When we went out, I kept my back turned to the woods. The wind at my heels was cold, curling fingers up under the long hem of my dress. I didn't turn to look and see if the silver glimmer of the Staryk road was still there.

Wanda carried the basket with all the small trinkets I had bought in Vysnia to sell, and also the two dresses I had bought myself in a defiant extravagance, because my mother wouldn't let me buy one for her. They were warm dresses and also beautiful, woolen with large flowers glowing out along the hem, deep green and blue colors on red cloth. I went straight to the dressmaker Marya's stall and pulled out the hems to show her and said, "Look at the new pattern they have in Vysnia this year."

A group of women gathered round me to look at them at once, a wall of safety against any other gossip that might be going on. A new pattern was more important to them than the Staryk road, which no one wanted to think about too much anyway. In the market square you couldn't see it. Of course Marya asked me what I wanted for the dresses. I didn't answer her at once. There were six women standing round me, their eyes on my face like crows ready to peck. For a single sharp moment I thought of letting the dresses go cheap, to leave a friendly feeling behind me, a feeling that might argue for me if someone began to speak of the Staryk road and how near it was to our house. Suddenly I understood my father better.

I took a breath and said, "I don't know if I can sell them right away. You can see how much work went into them, and from the finest hand in Vysnia. They were made for wedding clothes, and I paid high to get them and bring them all this way. I can't sell them for less than a zlotek, each."

I spent the whole day at market standing in one place, while women came and looked at the dresses worth a zlotek, murmuring to each other about the embroidery, the cut, the bright colors. They examined the seams and nodded in agreement when I solemnly pointed out how careful and perfect the small stitches were, and how you could tell they had used very fine thread. I sold them all the other goods in between, the other things I had brought from Vysnia. All of them went for more than I had hoped, as if they also had acquired a luxurious glow. And at the end of the day, the tax collector came by, who liked to stop in at the market now and again even though he had a servant who did his shopping for him, and he paid me two zlotek and took the dresses for his daughter's wedding chest.

I came back to the house with my heart pounding, a kind of ferocious triumph in my throat, half afraid: I didn't know what to do with myself. I had only paid a kopek for each dress. My mother and father didn't say anything when I put the two zlotek on the table, with all the pennies and the three kopeks I had also earned, selling. My father sighed a little, almost without noise. "Well, my daughter really can turn silver to gold," he said, almost helplessly, and he put his hand on my head and stroked it, as if he was sorry instead of proud.

Hot angry tears came prickling into my eyes, but I set my teeth and put the gold away into my purse, and then I gave my mother the jar of preserved cherries I had bought for us as a treat. After dinner, she made strong tea and put out the cherries in a glass dish with a tiny silver spoon, the last part of the tea service she had brought with her when she was married. The rest of it had gone in the market over the years, when we had been hungry. We put the sweet cherries into the tea and drank up the hot sweet liquid and then ate each soft warmed-through cherry and let the pits out onto our spoons from our lips very delicately.

Wanda cleared the table and put her kerchief on her head, making ready to go, and then she stopped and looked up as the whole room grew dark. Outside the windows snow was coming down suddenly, and when we opened the door, it was falling so strong already that we couldn't see the next house over in the village. In the other direction, the Staryk road was still visible, gleaming somehow brighter through the snow, and for a moment I almost thought I saw something moving in the trees upon it.

My mother said, "You can't go in this weather. You'll stay until it stops." Wanda stepped back and pushed the door shut against the wind with an effort.

The snow didn't stop, though, all the rest of the afternoon. It didn't even slacken. As the night came on, Wanda and my father went out and knocked snow off the top of the chicken coop and from around the sides, so the hens wouldn't smother. We huddled back inside the house like chickens in a coop ourselves. The smell of the stew had vanished, even though the rest of it was still in the back of the fire, keeping warm, and my mother had put potatoes into the ashes to roast for our supper. The air was full of a bitter cold that left a sharp biting feeling in my nostrils with nothing warm or alive in it, not even any smell of earth or rotting leaves. I tried to see to go over my books, and then to sew, and had to give all of it up. It was too dark, and the candlelight didn't seem to be able to spread far over the table.

"Come, we shouldn't sit here so dull," my father said finally, as we all sat in silent lumps under fur coats and shawls and blankets. "Let's sing together."

Wanda listened to us sing and asked abruptly, when we had a pause for breath, "Is that magic?"

My father stopped singing; my mother said firmly, "No, Wanda, of course not. It is a hymn to God."

"Oh," she said, and nothing more, and after that none of us sang anymore for a while, and then she said, "So it would keep them off, wouldn't it?"

After a moment, my father said quietly, "I don't know, Wanda. God does not save us from suffering on this Earth. The Staryk afflict the righteous as well as the sinful, just as do illness and sorrow."

He told us the story of the book of Job, then, from memory. It wasn't comforting, of course, unless you liked the end, which I didn't, but my father never reached it that day; he was just where Job was lamenting the injustice of God, his whole family gone, when the blow came on the door, a heavy thump like a hard stick knocking on the door. We all jumped, and my father stopped talking. We all sat in silence staring at the door. Finally, my father said abruptly, "Why, Sergey shouldn't have tried to come in this."

He got up and went to the door. I wanted to shout a protest, to tell him to keep back; I saw Wanda draw deep into the knot of her blankets with a wide, wary face. She didn't think it was her brother, either. Even my father didn't really think it; he took the poker with him as he went to the door, and then he reached over with his left hand and pulled it open with a swift jerk, the poker raised high.

But there was no one at the door. Not even the wind came in. The snow had stopped as quickly as it had come, and outside it was only the ordinary dark of night, a last few floating flakes catching the firelight as they finished drifting down past our doorway. I stared and turned to look out the barred window, towards the forest: the Staryk road was gone.

"What is it, Josef?" my mother said.

My father was still in the doorway, looking down. I pushed aside my blankets and got up and went to his side. It wasn't even very cold out anymore; my shawl was enough. But the path from our house had been filled in again as high as my knees, and even under the eaves, snow covered our old stone stoop thickly. A line of the cloven hoofprints came around the house from the back, and a pair of long pointed boot prints was pressed into the fresh snow before our house. In the very center of the stoop, resting lightly on the surface, was a small bag of white leather drawn shut.

My father looked round. We could see our neighbors now: all the houses had become squat white mushrooms with the tops of yellow-lit windows peering out over the snow covering their sills. There was not a soul anywhere in the road, but even as we watched, I saw movement in a window, a child's hand rubbing a clear circle in the frozen glass. Swiftly my father bent down and took the leather bag. He brought it inside, and I closed the door behind him.

He put the bag down on the table. We all gathered around and stared at it as though it were a live coal that might at any moment set the whole house ablaze. It was made of leather, white leather, but not dyed by any ordinary method I'd ever heard of: it looked as though it had always been white, all the way through. There wasn't a seam or stitch to be seen on its sides. Finally, when no one else moved to touch it, I tugged open the top, drawn by a white silken cord, and emptied out the coins within. Six small silver coins, thin and flat and perfectly round, slid onto the table in a little heap with a chiming like bells. Our house was full of warm firelight, but they shone coldly, as if they stood under the moon.

"It's very kind of them to make us such a present," my father said, dry. Of course, the Staryk would never do such a thing. Sometimes you heard stories of fairies who came with gifts. My own grandmother told a story sometimes that her grandmother had told her, that when *her* grandmother had been a little girl in Elkurt in the west, she had one day found a fox bleeding on the ledge of the window of her attic bedroom, torn as if by a dog. She brought it inside and tended its wound and gave it some water. It lapped it up and then said to her in a human voice, "You have saved me, and one day I will repay the favor," and then leapt out the window again. And when she was a grown woman, with children of her own, one day she opened her kitchen door to scratching and the fox was there, and it told her, "Take all your family and any money you have in the house and go hide in the cellar."

And she did as the fox said, and even as they hid, they heard outside a roaring of angry voices. Men came into their house, knocking over furniture and breaking things above their heads, and there was a smell of smoke thick in the air. But somehow the men did not find the cellar door, and the smoke and fire did not come down.

They crept out again that night at last and found their house and the synagogue and all their neighbors' houses on every side burned down. They took their few remaining possessions and ran to the edge of the quarter and hired a man with a cart to drive them east, and so came to Vysnia where the duke then had opened the doors to the Jews, if they came with money.

But that was a story from another country. You did not hear stories like that about the Staryk. Here, you heard that once a strange white beast had come to a peasant's barn with a wounded Staryk knight drooping on its back, and in fear the peasants had taken him into their house and tended his wounds. And when he woke, he took up his sword and killed them, and then dragged himself out to his steed and rode back into the woods still dripping blood, and the only way anyone knew what happened was the mother had sent her two young children to hide in the hayloft of the barn and told them not to stir out of it until the Staryk was gone again.

So we knew that the Staryk had not given us a purse of silver to be kind. I couldn't think why they *had* left it, yet there it was on our table, shining like a message we couldn't understand. And then my mother drew a sharp breath and looked at me and said, low, "They want you to turn it into gold."

My father sat down at the table and covered his face, but I knew it was my own fault, talking in the deep woods, in a sleigh driving over the snow, about turning silver to gold. The Staryk always wanted gold.

"We'll take the money from the vault," my mother said. "At least we have it."

What I said was, "I'll go back to the city tomorrow." But I

went outside and stood in the yard of our house on the fresh-
fallen snow with my hands squeezed into fists. The crust was already frozen hard and solid: it would make for good traveling, fast
traveling. There were six silver coins in the bag, and I had put
fourteen gold coins away, just this last visit. I could hire Oleg's
sleigh and drive back to Vysnia and take six gold coins out of my
grandfather's bank vault and give them to the Staryk, six gold
coins I had worked for, and use them to buy my safety.

Wanda came out in her shawl, to go and feed the new goat we
had brought home from market. Sergey hadn't come, of course,
in the storm, and it was late for her to walk home now. She looked
at me and silently went into the barn, and when she came back
out, she asked me abruptly, "Will you give them your gold?"

"No," I said, speaking as much to the Staryk in the forest as to
her. "No, I won't give them a thing. They want silver turned to
gold, so that's what I'll do."

Chapter 6

The next morning, Miryem took the Staryk's purse and went to Oleg's house and asked him to take her back to Vysnia. She did not ask me to keep the books. She did not even remind me to go get the payments. Her mother saw her off at the gate and stood there a long time, holding her shawl around her shoulders, even after the sleigh was gone.

But I did not need to be reminded. I took the basket and went on my rounds. It was the sixth day of the month, so I was collecting in town today. Nobody liked to see me coming, but Kajus always smiled at me anyway, like we were friendly, even though we were not. When I had first begun to work for Miryem, he would always pay in jugs of krupnik. Miryem did not like that, because he sold the same krupnik in the market every week, hot from a kettle in winter, and everyone would buy it from him and not her. She had found a guesthouse down the road where they would buy it, when she had ten jugs to sell, but that was more trouble than she liked, and she had to pay to send it to them.

But then he had given me a bad bottle, which looked all right from the outside, but Miryem sniffed the top near the seal, and then she opened it, and a smell like rotten leaves came out. She looked at it with an angry mouth, but then she told me to put the bottle apart from the rest, in a corner of the house, and say nothing to him. He gave me two more bad bottles in a row, the next two months. After the third one, she gave me all three corks and sent me back with them to tell him three times was too many to go bad, and she would not take any more krupnik from him in payment. So now he had to pay in pennies. That time, he did not smile at me.

But today he smiled. "Come in and keep warm!" he said, although it was not so very cold anymore today. "You will have to wait a little while. My oldest boy has gone to take Panova Lyudmila my new batch. He will bring back the money." He even gave me a glass of krupnik to drink. Usually he had the money waiting, so he would not need to invite me in at all. "So Miryem is going back to Vysnia for more dresses? She is doing a good business! And she is lucky to have you here at home to mind the store for her."

"Thank you," I said politely, putting down the glass. "It is good krupnik." I wondered if he meant to try and bribe me to take less. Some other people had tried. I did not understand why they thought I would do it. If I took less back to Miryem, and lied and told her they had no more, she would put down the smaller number in her book, and they would keep owing whatever they hadn't paid. It would only save them money if they meant to say that I had stolen the money when the time came to claim their debt was paid, and why shouldn't they cheat me, if I had helped them cheat.

"Yes, she knows what she is about," Kajus continued. "Trust her to find a hardworking girl to help her. You aren't just a pretty face! Ah, here is Lukas."

His son came back into the house, with a box of empty jugs. He was a little older than Sergey, not as tall as him or me, but his face was round, and there was meat on his bones. He did not go hungry. He looked at me, up and down, and his father said, "Lukas, give her seven pennies for the moneylender." Lukas counted out the seven pennies into my hand. It was more than they needed to pay. "I have been doing a good business, too," Kajus said to me, with a friendly wink. "All this cold weather! A man needs something to put heat in his belly. It must be especially bad, out on your farm," he added. "I haven't seen your father in town in a while."

"Yes," I said, wary. My father didn't come because we didn't have anything to spare for liquor.

"Here," Kajus said, handing me a sealed jug, a small one, the kind he sold in the market for a few bits if you brought him back the jug. I only stared at it without taking it. I didn't know what it was for; he had already paid me. But Kajus pressed it on me again. "A gift for your father," he said. "You'll bring back the jug when you have a chance."

"Thank you, Panov Simonis," I said, because I had to. I did not want to take my father a jug of krupnik, so he could get drunk at home and beat us, but I didn't see any way out of it. The next time Da did come to town, Kajus would expect to be thanked, and if it came out I hadn't given it to him, I would really get a beating then. So I put the jug in my basket.

No one else in the other houses invited me in for krupnik. Marya the dressmaker was the only one who said anything to me, besides handing me the money. "So Miryem is going to get more dresses from Vysnia, is she?" she said abruptly. She had only given me a single penny. "It seems a long way to go, and for very dear goods. Who knows if she will be able to sell anything more."

"I don't know if she will bring more dresses, Panova," I said.

"Well, she will suit herself and no one else, that's certain," Marya said, and shut the door hard in my face.

I went back to the house and unpacked the payments. One of the borrowers had given me an old chicken that had stopped laying, ready for the pot. "Will you want it today, Panova Mandel-stam?" I asked Miryem's mother. "I can wring its neck and pluck it if you want."

She was sewing, and when I asked her, she looked up and turned her head around the room as if she was looking for something she had lost. "Where is Miryem?" she asked me, as if she had forgotten, and then she shook her head and said, "Oh, I am being silly. She went back to Vysnia for more dresses."

"Yes, she went to Vysnia for dresses," I said slowly. Something about it sounded wrong to me. But of course, that was why she had gone back. Everyone else thought so.

"Well, there is enough food in the house. We will save the chicken," Panova Mandelstam said. "Put it with the others for now, and then come back inside. It is time for dinner."

I took the old hen to the coop and put her inside. Then I stood looking at the snow behind the house, deep-drifted and unmarked now, with the broom leaning half buried against the wall: the broom I had used to sweep away the footprints of the Staryk, who had come to the house last night, and left a purse of silver for Miryem to turn into gold. I shivered all over and went back in so I could forget again.

After dinner, I had to go. My father would already be angry that I had not been home to get his dinner yesterday, because of the storm. But I swept the floor and went to look in at the chickens and wrote down everything in the book before I left. I had slept the night on the pallet they had made for Sergey, warm and cozy in the big room with the oven and the smells of dough and stew and honey and kasha. My house did not smell like that. Miryem's mother gave me a cup of fresh rich cow's milk with my dinner, out of a big pail that Panova Gizis had paid with, and two pennies for two days, even though Sergey hadn't come last night in the storm, and a bundle for my basket with some bread and butter and eggs in it. "Sergey didn't get supper or breakfast," she said. I put on my shawl and went, with her kindness heavy on my arm.

I went around through the forest and hid the bundle in among the roots of the white tree, and again I buried the pennies. I put one each in my pile and Sergey's pile. Then I went on to the house. Stepon was there trying to stir a pot of porridge that had gone solid. There was a strong red mark on his face, and he was wincing when he moved. He looked up at me, unhappy. So our father had told him to get dinner last night and then hit him because he did not know how to do it. "Sit and rest," I told him. "There's something for later."

I thinned the porridge with some water and cooked some cabbage. My father came in angry, shouting even while he took off his boots that I had no business staying in town because of a little snowfall, over so quickly, and the moneylender would take an extra day's payment off the debt for keeping me. "I will tell them so," I said, putting the cabbage on the table quickly, before he was even all the way inside the house. "Panov Simonis gave me a present for you, Da." I put the bottle of krupnik on the table. I thought I might as well use it to avoid a beating now, since he was going to be drunk later anyway.

"What is Kajus giving me presents for?" Da said, and he sniffed the jug suspiciously when he opened it. But soon he was drinking it in big swallows, the whole thing, while he ate half the cabbage and the porridge. The rest of us ate our share quickly, without looking up.

"I will go get wood now, since I wasn't home," I said. Da didn't tell me not to go. Sergey and Stepon slipped out with me, and I took them to the white tree. The bundle was still there where I had left it, and it hadn't frozen. We shared the food, and afterwards they helped me gather wood. After that, Sergey went down the road to town. Stepon huddled together with me outside against the woodpile, helping me keep warm while we listened through the cracks to Da singing loudly.

Once he paused and shouted for me. "Stupid girl, went too far," he said, grumbling, when I didn't answer. "Now the fire is dying." It was a long time before he went to bed and began to snore. Stepon and I were very cold by then. We crept into the house as quiet as we could and banked the fire, so it would not be dead before morning, and I put on the kasha to cook for breakfast. I showed Stepon how to do it so he would know next time. Then we crawled into bed and went to sleep. In the morning, my father beat me six hard wallops with his belt for having gone too far, even though the fire was all right and breakfast was ready. I think he was mostly hitting me because I hadn't been there to hit last night. But he had a bad headache and he was hungry, so when Stepon put a big bowl of steaming kasha on the table, he stopped hitting me and sat down to eat. I wiped my face and swallowed and sat down next to him.

It was late when I reached Vysnia in Oleg's sleigh. I slept that night in my grandfather's house, and early the next morning I went down to the market in our quarter and asked around until I found the stall of Isaac the jeweler, the one my cousin Basia meant to marry. He was a young man with spectacles and stubby but careful fingers, handsome, with good teeth and nice brown eyes and his beard trimmed short to stay out of his work. He was bent over an anvil in miniature, hammering out a disk of silver with his tiny tools, enormously precise. I stood watching him work for maybe ten minutes before he sighed and said, "Yes?" with a faint hint of resignation, as though he'd hoped I would go away instead of troubling him to do any business. I brought out my white pouch and spilled the six silver coins onto the black cloth he worked upon.

"That's not enough to buy anything here," he said, matter-of-fact, with barely a glance; he started to go back to his work, but then he frowned a little and turned around again. He picked one coin up and peered at it closely, and turned it over in his fingers, and rubbed it between them, and then he put it down and stared at me. "Where did you get these?"

"They came from the Staryk, if you want to believe me," I said. "Can you make them into something? A bracelet or a ring?"

"I'll buy them from you," he offered.

"No, thank you," I said.

"To make them into a ring would cost you two zlotek," he said. "Or I'll buy them from you for five."

My heart leapt: if he would buy them from me for five, that meant he thought he could sell whatever he made for more. But I didn't try to bargain up his price. "I have to give the Staryk back six gold coins, in exchange," I said instead. "So I can pay you one zlotek to make a ring for me, or if you like, you can sell whatever you make, and we'll divide whatever profit there is left after the Staryk is paid off," which was what I really wanted; I was sure Isaac could sell a piece of jewelry better than I could. "I'm Basia's cousin, Miryem," I added, at the end, saving it for the last.

"Oh," he said, and looked down at the six coins again and stirred them with his fingers; then finally he agreed. I sat down on a stool behind his counter, and he set about the work. He melted the coins in a small hot oven that the jewelers shared, in the middle of their stalls, and then he poured the liquid silver into a mold, a thick one made of iron. When it had half cooled, he took it out with his leathered fingertips and engraved a pattern into the surface, fanciful, full of leaves and branches.

It didn't take him long: the silver melted easily and cooled eas-

ily and took the tiny tip of his engraving knife easily. When he was
done, he tipped the ring onto black velvet, and we just looked at it
together in silence for a while. The pattern seemed oddly to move
and shift: it drew the eye and held it, and shone cold even in the
midday sun. Then Isaac said, "The duke will buy it," and sent his
apprentice running into the city. A tall, imperious servant in velvet
clothes and gold braid came back with the boy, making clear in
every line of his expression how annoyed he was by the interrup-
tion of his own important work, whatever that might have been,
but even he stopped being annoyed when he saw the ring and
held it on his palm.

He bought the ring for ten zlotek on the spot, and carried it
away in a closed box that he held carefully with both hands. Isaac
had ten golden zlotek in his hand, and even so all he and I did was
sit there and watch the duke's servant until he was all the way out
of sight, as if even inside the box the ring was pulling our eyes
after it. The man grew more and more distant along the busy
market lane, and still I had no trouble finding him in the crowd.
But at last he walked through the gates of the quarter and was
gone, and we were set free to look down at our reward, the ten
gold coins we had made out of Staryk silver.

I put six of them back into the little white pouch. Isaac kept
two—it would help pay a good bride price—and then I took the
last two back to my grandfather's house and proudly gave them to
him, to go into the vault with the rest of my gold. He smiled a
hard little smile at me, full of satisfaction, and tapped my forehead with his forefinger. "There's my clever girl," he said, and I
smiled back, just as hard, just as satisfied.

"You don't mean to leave so late!" my grandmother said a little reproachfully when I meant to put on my wraps after dinner:
it was Friday.

"I'll get there before sundown, if we go fast," I said. "And Oleg
will be driving, not me." I had gotten him to wait for me a night,

in exchange for forgiving him his next payment; it was cheaper than paying a carter from Vysnia to take me home. He had slept in my grandfather's stable with his horse, but he wouldn't want to stay longer, not without more payment, and we couldn't have left until after sundown tomorrow. Anyway, the Staryk didn't keep Shabbat, and I wasn't sure how I was meant to get them back their changed money. I thought perhaps I would have to leave it on the doorstep of my house, for them to come and take away.

"She will get there in time," my grandfather said with finality, making it all right. So I climbed back into Oleg's sleigh.

We made good time over the hard frozen snow, the horse trotting quickly with only my weight in back. It grew dark under the trees, but the sun had not quite gone down yet, and we were close to home. I hoped we would make it, but then the horse slowed, and then dropped to a walk, and then halted entirely. She stood there unmoving with her ears pricked up anxiously, warm breath gusting out of her nostrils. I thought perhaps she needed a little rest, but Oleg hadn't said anything to her, and he didn't move to make her start jogging again.

"Why are we stopping?" I asked finally. Oleg didn't answer me: he slumped in his seat as though he slept. A chill wind rose, murmuring against my back, creeping over the edges of the sledge and wriggling its way through the covers to get to my skin. Blue shadows stretched out over the snow, cast by a pale thin light shining somewhere behind me, and as my breath rose in quick clouds around my face, the snow crunched: some large creature, picking its way towards the sleigh. I swallowed and drew my cloak around me, and then I summoned up all the winter-cold courage I'd ever found and turned.

The Staryk didn't look so terribly strange at first; that was what made him truly terrible. But as I kept looking slowly his face became something inhuman, shaped out of ice and glass, and his eyes like silver knives. He was beardless like a boy, but his face was a grown man's, and he was tall, too tall when he drew near and loomed over me like the marble statue in the square of Vysnia, carved larger than life. He wore his white hair in long braids. His clothes, just like his purse, were all in that same unnatural white leather, and he was riding a stag, larger than a draft horse, with antlers branched twelve times and hung with clear glass drops, and when it put out its red tongue to lick its muzzle, its teeth were sharp as a wolf's.

I wanted to quail, to cower. Instead I held my fur cloak tight at the throat with one hand against the chill that rolled off him, and with my other I held out the purse to him as he came close to the sleigh.

He paused, surveying me out of one silver-blue eye with his head turned sideways, like a bird looking me over. He put out his gloved hand and took the bag, and he opened it and poured the six gold coins out into the cup of his hand, the faint jingle loud in the silence around us. The coins looked different in his hand, warm and sun-bright, shining against the unnatural cold white of his glove. He looked down at them and seemed surprised and also vaguely disappointed, as though he was sorry I'd managed it. He poured them back into the bag and pulled the drawstring tight around the golden light, like closing away a sunbeam, and the bag vanished beneath his long cloak.

The Staryk road was a wide shining lane behind him, just through the trees. He turned his steed towards it without saying a word, taking those six gold coins I had gotten with my work and fear as though they were only his due, and anger rose up in me. "I'll need longer next time, if you want more of them changed," I called after him, throwing my words against the hard icy silence like a shell around us.

He turned his head round and stared at me, as though surprised I'd dared to speak to him, and then the sharp-antlered deer took a step onto the road, and he wasn't there anymore; Oleg shook himself all over and chirruped to the horse, and we were trotting again. I fell back into the blankets shivering as though the air had grown suddenly much colder; the tips of my fingers where I'd held out the purse were numbed. I pulled off my glove and tucked them underneath my arm to warm them up, wincing as they touched my skin. A feathery snowfall began to come down around us as we drove the rest of the way.

I noticed the silver ring on my father's hand that night as his finger beat out his irritation against the side of his goblet, in steady clinks. He commanded me to a formal dinner at his table one night a week; to improve my manner in polite company, he said. My manners did not need improving—Magreta had seen to that—but whatever my father's real reason, it was certainly not for his own pleasure. He was dissatisfied every time he saw me, as though he'd hoped I might have become more beautiful, more witty, more charming. Alas, no. But I was his only child old enough to bother with yet, as my half brothers were still in the nursery, and my father disliked for anything he owned to be idle.

So I came down to dinner and performed my correct company manners, so Magreta would not come in for punishment, and when he had a knight or boyar or occasionally a visiting baron at his table, I kept my eyes modestly downcast and listened to them talk of armies or tax rolls or borders and politics, glimpses into a wider world as far removed from my narrow upstairs rooms as paradise. I would have liked to think I had a chance of moving in that world someday; my stepmother did, smiling with her open hands to greet our guests, making sure that her table and her hospitality suited each one's pride and deserts, cutting a fine and jeweled figure at my father's side when we went visiting ourselves, or

7 0

hosted nobles of greater rank. She gleaned the truth about the state of their holdings from wives and sisters and daughters, and in the evenings my father would listen to her advice and counsel; she had a voice in her husband's ears. I would have liked to hope for one myself.

But my father's irritation told me otherwise. I had been a disappointment to him from the beginning, my mother having taken an excessive number of years to produce me, and shortly afterwards miscarrying the overdue son and dying with him. It had required some few years to settle on the best replacement, and though Galina had done her best, even so he still had nothing to work with yet but me and two little boys in the nursery, just when all the men of his cohort, the ones who had helped the old tsar to his throne, had daughters ready to marry, and sons wanting more beauty and grace in a wife than I could offer, or at least more money than my father would offer to compensate for their lack.

When I was younger, and there was still some chance of my growing into real usefulness, he would sometimes ask me sharp questions about books I had read, or demand that I recite him all the names of every noble in Lithvas from the tsar down to the counts in order of their precedence, but lately he had stopped bothering. My last governess now had begun to teach my older brother his letters, and if I had a book to read, it was because I had managed to slip it off the downstairs shelves myself in a rare chance. And when there was no one else at his table to distract him from my silence and my pallid, narrow face, my father frowned at me and tapped his fingers against his cup.

That night there was no guest at the table. The tsar was coming for a visit soon, and no one else had been invited for months leading up to it, to save for the unavoidable expense. My father meant to spend as little as he could, but even so the waste of it made him more dissatisfied with me than usual. Perhaps it brought home more forcibly to his mind that he would get little return on me, although even if I had been beautiful, surely he would never have been one of the lords who spent themselves into debt hosting the tsar, dangling their daughters like bait and making fools of themselves in hope.

The tsar was not going to marry any of them, however beautiful they were; he would marry Princess Vassilia. She was not beautiful any more than I was, but her father was Prince Ulrich, who ruled over three cities, not one, and had ten thousand soldiers and the great salt mine under his hand, so she did not need to be beautiful to become tsarina. The tsar should have married her already, but he evidently preferred to keep his other nobles hoping for a little longer; a dangerous game to play with Ulrich's pride, but one that gave the tsar an excuse to travel a great deal and spread the expenditure of his lavish court around, instead of offering hospitality himself.

And my father had a marriageable daughter, in theory, and therefore could be imposed upon. So now I was become an expense beyond my value, especially as my father plainly did not even hope for some secondary benefit—that some useful member of the tsar's court would think of me for a son or cousin somewhere. I was glad to be beneath the notice of the tsar, who was young and handsome and cruel, but I would have liked to be pretty enough or charming enough that at least someone might want to marry me, instead of only taking me as a codicil to whatever begrudging dowry they could wring out of my father. Or even to be sure that anyone *would* marry me: my only escape from a life spent between narrow walls. My father's irritation spoke wordlessly of a dismal fate for me.

But as his ring tapped a faint high chiming against the side of his cup, I watched the cool silver of it catching the light, and I forgot that it was driven by impatience. I thought only of snowflakes falling past a lit window, the silence of the start of winter, standing outside in the garden on a day when the leaves were coated in shining clear ice. I even forgot to listen to what he was saying to me, until he said sharply, "Irina, are you attending?"

I had only the refuge of honesty. "Forgive me, Father," I said. "I have been looking at your ring. Is it magic?"

That had been another of my mother's disappointments: her magic, of which she'd had none. Her great-grandmother had been raped by a Staryk knight during a midwinter night's raiding that killed her husband, and the boy she bore afterwards had silver hair and silver eyes and could walk through blizzards and make things cold with a touch. His children had silver hair, too, although not much of his power, and my father had married my mother on the strength of the legend and her pale eyes and a lock of silver hair that waved back from her forehead.

But her looks were all the magic she had, and I had not even so much as that, only plain brown hair, and my father's brown eyes, and I shivered like anyone else in the cold. Yet when I looked at my father's ring, I felt snow falling. My father paused, and looked down at it on his own hand. It was a little small for him. He was wearing it above the knuckle of his index finger, on his right hand, and his thumb rubbed the surface. He had been touching it all through the meal, absently. After a moment he said, "Unusual craftsmanship, that is all," with the final tone that meant we were not to discuss the matter further. So he had not known that it was magic, did not know any power it had, and did not care for anyone else to know more than he did.

I said nothing more and lowered my eyes and paid careful attention the rest of the meal as he told me flatly what was expected of me during the tsar's visit—which was nothing. He did not want the expense of buying me several new gowns. So I was to be a little sick and stay upstairs and out of the way, and Galina would have three new gowns instead. He said nothing else about the ring, and also did not mention my earlier distraction.

I was glad to stay out of the tsar's way, but three new gowns would have been more useful for me than for Galina, if my father had meant to begin offering me around anytime soon. That night I put my candle on the windowsill and watched the snowflakes falling through the candlelight while Magreta brushed my hair; carefully clearing the tangles from the bottom up with the silver comb and brush that she always kept on her in the purse tied at her waist; then there would be seventeen strokes from the roots for good measure, one for every year it had been growing. She tended my hair like a garden, and it rewarded her attention; by now it was longer than I was tall, and I could sit by the window while she brushed the ends from her chair near the fire. "Magra," I asked, "did my father love my mother?"

She was so surprised she stopped brushing. I knew she had served my mother before I was born, but I had never asked about her before. It had never occurred to me to ask. I had been so young when she died that I only thought of her as of an ancestor a long time gone. My father had told me about her in precise and accurate terms, enough that I understood she had been a failure. He had not made me want to know more.

Magreta said, "Why yes, dushenka, of course he did," and while she would have said so even if it wasn't true, she hadn't hesitated first, which meant she at least believed her own words. "He married her with no dowry, didn't he?" she added, though, and then it was my turn to look around and be surprised. He had never told me *that*. It was almost unimaginable.

"He doesn't speak of her as though he'd loved her," I said, incautious in my own turn.

Magreta did hesitate then before she said, "Well, there is your stepmama to think of."

I did not really need Magreta to tell me that love had caught my father like an unwilling fish, and that having slipped the hook, he had been glad to forget he had ever been on it in the first place. Certainly my stepmother had only come with a fat dowry of gold coins, a heavy chest bigger than I was, which now rested deep in the treasury under the house. My father had not been caught a second time. And likely he had been all the more disappointed in my mother, if she'd had enough magic to enchant him into stupidity but not for anything more.

I dreamed of the ring that night, only it was worn by a woman with a silver lock falling from her forehead—a lock that matched the ring on her hand. Her face wouldn't come clear in the dream, but she turned away from me and walked through a forest of white and silver trees. I woke thinking not of my mother, but of the ring; I wanted a chance to touch it, to hold it.

Magreta normally kept me well out of my father's way, but every day she took me down to a corner of the gardens for walking exercise, even in cold weather. That morning I took the turning into the older part of the gardens, away from the house; there was a neglected chapel still there, half buried beneath leafless vines, the grey wood rotting a little, carved points like thorns poking out through the dusting snow on the roof. Magreta stayed below and twittered worry at me, but I climbed the creaking steps up into the empty belfry so I could look out the round window over the garden wall and see into the great courtyard where my father daily drilled his men.

That was a duty he never neglected. He was no longer a young man, but he had been born a boyar and not a duke, and many years ago he had killed three knights in a single day's battle and broken the walls of Vysnia for the tsar's father, for the right to make the city his own. He still oversaw the training of his own knights, and took sturdy boys from farmers and made them men-at-arms in the city. Even two archdukes and a prince had deigned to send him their sons to foster, because they knew he would send them back well trained.

I thought perhaps he would have taken the ring off for drill; if so, it might be in his study somewhere, on his desk. I was already making plans. Magreta wouldn't let me go in there, but I could coax her to step into the library next door to it, and lose her between bookshelves; I might go in and put my hand on it for just a moment.

But when I looked into the courtyard, where the soldiers were going through their paces under his taskmaster voice, my father was bare-handed, though ordinarily he wore heavy gloves or sometimes metal gauntlets. His hands were clasped loosely behind his back, the left holding the right wrist. The silver band was shining as if in sunlight, though the sky was dark grey and snow was drifting, as far from my reach as another world.

The Staryk lord kept coming back into my head even after I was back home again. I didn't remember him all the time; only in the moments when I was alone somewhere and in the middle of some other task. When I went outside behind the house to tend the chickens, I remembered his footprints there, and was glad to see the snow unmarked. In the shed, feeding the goats in the dim early-morning light, I looked into a corner where a rake stood in shadows and remembered him coming out of the dark trees with his white braids and his cruel smile. When I went out to get a little snow for water, to make tea, my hands grew cold and I thought, *What if he comes back.* It made me angry, because being angry was better than being afraid, but then I came in with the pail of snow and found myself standing before the fire angry for no reason, and my mother looking at me, puzzled.

She hadn't asked me anything about the Staryk, only how my grandmother and my grandfather were, and if I'd had a good journey, as if she too had forgotten why I'd gone to Vysnia in the first place. I didn't have any of the fairy silver left to fix it in my own head, not even the little white purse. I remembered going to the marketplace, and I remembered Isaac working, but I couldn't see the ring he'd made in my mind's eye.

But I remembered enough that every morning I went again to look behind the house, and on Monday, Wanda came out to feed the chickens while I was still there. She joined me and looked down at the smooth unbroken surface, and unexpectedly she said, "You paid him, then? He's gone?"

For a moment I almost said, *Whom do you mean*, and then I remembered again, and my hands clenched. "I paid him," I said, and Wanda nodded after a moment, one single jerk of her head, as though she understood that I was saying that was all I knew: he might come back, or he might not.

I had brought some aprons with me from Vysnia in the new embroidered pattern—aprons instead of dresses, so I could sell them for less than a zlotek without making it seem as though the dresses had been a cheat. All of them went quickly that market day, and the handkerchiefs I'd also bought. A woman from a farm out in the country even asked me if I was going back to Vysnia soon, and if I thought I could get a good price for her yarn there. No one had ever done business with me before, if they could help it, except to buy from me cheap and sell to me dear; usually she would have asked one of the carters instead, Oleg or Petrov, to take it to town if she couldn't sell it herself at market. But these last few years all the sheep and goats were growing their coats so thick, in the long cold winters, that the price of wool was falling low, and they couldn't have gotten her much.

Hers was better than the usual, soft and thick; I could tell she had combed it and washed it and spun it carefully. I rubbed a strand between my fingers and remembered that my grandfather had said he would be sending some goods south, down the river, when spring came: he had hired a barge. He meant to pack his goods with straw, but maybe he could pack them with wool instead, and we could sell it for more in the south, where it had not been so cold.

"Give me a sample and I'll take it the next time I go, and I'll tell you what I can get" was all that I told her. "How much of it do you have to sell?" She only had three bags, but I saw others listening as we spoke. There were many at the market who sold wool for a little income, or even their livelihood, and were being squeezed by the falling prices; I was sure if I came back to the market and told her where others could overhear that I could offer her a good price, many more would come quietly to see me.

By the time I went home from the market that day, it was settled in my head that I had gone to Vysnia for more goods to sell, to make more business for myself. There were three brand-new goats on a string behind me, bought cheap because of the falling price of wool, and even more plans in my head: I would ask my grandfather to take my profits from the wool and buy me some dresses from the south, in just a little bit of a foreign style, to sell in Vysnia and in the market here, too.

That night there was a brown roast chicken on the table and carrots glazed with fat, and for once my mother dished out the good food without looking as though every bite would poison her. We ate, and afterwards Wanda went home and we settled in together around the fire. My father was reading to himself, his lips moving silently, from the new Bible I had bought him in Vysnia; my mother was crocheting lace from some fine silk thread, a piece that could someday go into a wedding dress, maybe. The golden light shone in their faces, kind and worn, and for a moment I felt the whole world suspended in happiness, in peace, as though I had reached a place I had never been able even to imagine before.

The knocking came on the door, heavy and vigorous. "I'll get it," I said, putting my sewing aside. But when I stood, my parents hadn't even glanced up. I held there frozen in place a moment, but they still didn't look; my mother was humming softly, her hook swinging in and out of the thread. Slowly I went to the door and opened it, and the Staryk was on the stoop with all of winter behind him, a whirling cloud of snow that wasn't falling past the windows.

He held another purse out to me, clinking like chains, and spoke with a high thin voice like wind whistling through the eaves. "Three days you may have, this time, before I come to have my own back again," he said.

I stared at the purse. It was large and heavy with coin, more silver there than I had in gold even if I emptied my vault; far more. Snow was drifting in to melt cold against my cheeks, flecking my shawl. I thought of accepting it in silence, of keeping my head bowed and afraid. I *was* afraid. He wore spurs on his heels and jewels on his fingers like enormous chips of ice, and the voices of all the souls lost in blizzards howled behind him. Of course I was afraid.

But I had learned to fear other things more: being despised, whittled down one small piece of myself at a time, smirked at and taken advantage of. I put my chin up and said, as cold as I could be in answer, "And what will you give me in return?"

His eyes widened and all the color went out of them. The storm shrieked behind him, and a lance of cold air full of snow and ice blew into my bare face, a stinging prickle of pins-and-needles on my cheeks. I expected him to strike me, and he looked as though he wanted to; but instead he said to me, "Thrice, mortal maiden," in a rhythm almost like a song, "Thrice you shall turn silver to gold for me, or be changed to ice yourself."

I felt half ice already, my hands so cold that I imagined I could feel my finger bones aching under the numb flesh. At least I was too cold even to shiver. "And then?" I said, and my voice didn't shake.

He laughed at me, high and savage, and said, "And then, if

you manage it, I will make you my queen," mockingly, and threw the purse down at my feet, jingling loud. When I looked back up from it, he was gone, and my mother behind me said, slow and struggling, as if it was an effort to speak, "Miryem, why are you keeping the door open? The cold's coming in."

Chapter 7

The purse that the Staryk had left was ten times as heavy as before, full of shining coins. I counted them out into smooth-sided towers, trying to put my mind into order along with them. "We'll leave," my mother said, watching me build them. I hadn't told her what the Staryk had promised, or threatened, but she didn't like it anyway: a fairy lord coming to demand I give him gold. "We'll go to my father, or somewhere else away," but I felt sure that wasn't any good. How far would we have to go to run from winter? Even if there were some country a thousand miles away beyond his reach, it would mean bribes to cross each border, and a new home wherever we found ourselves in the end, and who knew how they'd treat us when we got there. We'd heard enough stories of what happened to our people in other countries, under kings and bishops who wanted *their* debts forgiven, and to fill their purses with confiscated wealth. One of my great-uncles had come from a summer country, from a house with orange trees inside a walled garden; someone else now picked those oranges, that his family had carefully planted and tended, and they were lucky to have made it here.

And even in a summer country, I didn't think I could escape

forever. One day the wind would blow and the temperature would drop, and in the middle of the night a frost would creep over my threshold. He would come to keep his promise, a final revenge after I'd spent my life running around the world breathless and afraid, and he'd leave me frozen on a desert stoop.

So I put the six towers of coins, ten in each, back into the purse. Sergey had come by then; I sent him to Oleg, to ask him to come round with his sledge and drive me to Vysnia that very night. "Tell him I'll clear a kopek from his debt, if he'll take me and bring me back on Saturday night," I said grimly: that was twice what the cost of the drive should have been, but I needed to go at once. The Staryk might have given me three days, but I had only until sundown on Friday to get the work done; I didn't think he would take Shabbat as an excuse.

I was in the market at first light the next day, and the instant Isaac saw me in front of his stall, he demanded eagerly, "Do you have any more of the silver?" Then he flushed and said, "That is, welcome back," remembering he had manners.

"Yes, I have more," I said, and spilled the heavy purse out in a shining swath on his black velvet cloth; he hadn't even put out his goods for the day yet. "I need to give back sixty gold this time," I told him.

He was already turning the coins over with his hands, his face alight with hunger. "I couldn't *remember*," he said, half to himself, and then he heard what I'd said and gawked at me. "I need a little profit for the work that this will take!"

"There's enough to make ten rings, at ten gold each," I said.

"I couldn't sell them all."

"Yes, you could," I said. That, I was sure of: now that the duke had a ring of fairy silver, every wealthy man and woman in the city needed a ring just like it, right away.

He frowned over the coins, stirring them with his fingers, and sighed. "I'll make a necklace, and see what we can get."

"You really don't think you can sell ten rings?" I said, surprised, wondering if I were wrong after all.

"I want to make a necklace," he said, which didn't seem very sensible to me, but perhaps he thought it would show his work off and make a name for him. I didn't really mind as long as I could pay off my Staryk once more, and buy myself some time.

"And it has to be done before Shabbos," I added.

He groaned. "Why must you ask for impossibilities!"

"Do *those* look possible, to you?" I said, pointing at the coins, and he couldn't really argue with that.

I had to sit with him while he worked, and manage the people who came to the stall wanting other things from him; he didn't want to talk to anyone and be interrupted. Most of the ones who came were busy and irritated servants, some of them expecting goods to be finished; they snapped and glared, wanting me to cower, but I met their bluster and said coolly, "Surely you can see what Master Isaac is working on. I'm sure your mistress or your master wouldn't wish you to interrupt a patron I cannot name, but who would purchase such a piece," and I waved to send their eyes over to the worktable, where the full sunlight shone on the silver beneath his hands. Its cold gleam silenced them; they stood staring a little while and then went away, without trying to argue again.

Isaac kept working without a pause until the sun's rays finally vanished, and began again the next morning at dawn. I noticed that he tried to save a few of the coins aside, while he worked, as though he wanted to keep them to remember. I thought of asking him for one to keep myself; but there was no use. At noon he sighed and took the last of the ones he'd saved and melted it down, and strung a last bit of silver lace upon the design. "It's done," he said, afterwards, and picked it up in his hands: the silver hung over his broad palms like icicles, and we stood looking at it silently together for a while.

"Will you send word to the duke?" I asked.

He shook his head, and took out a box from under his table: square and made of carved wood lined with black velvet, and he laid the necklace carefully inside. "No," he said. "For this, I will go to him. Do you want to come?"

We went together to the gates of our quarter, and walked into the streets of the city. I had never gone through this part of town on foot before. The houses nearest the walls were mean and low, run-down; but Isaac led me to the wider streets, past an enormous church of grey stone with windows like jewelry themselves, and finally to the enormous mansions of the nobles. I couldn't help staring at the iron fences wrought into lions and writhing dragons, and the walls covered with vining fruits and flowers sculpted out of stone. I wanted to be proud, to remember I was my grandfather's daughter, with gold in the bank, but I was glad not to be alone when we went up the wide stone steps swept clear of snow.

Isaac spoke to one of the servants. We were taken to a small room to wait. No one offered us anything to drink, or a place to sit, and a manservant stood looking at us with disapproval. I was almost grateful, though: the irritation made me feel less small and less tempted to gawk. Finally the servant who had come to the market last time came in and demanded to know our business. Isaac brought out the box and showed him the necklace; he stared down at it, and then said shortly, "Very well," and went away again. Half an hour later he reappeared, and ordered us to follow him. We were led up the back stairs and then emerged into a hall more sumptuous than anything I had ever seen, the walls hung with tapestries in bright colors and the floor laid with a beautifully patterned rug.

It silenced our feet and led us into a sitting room even more luxurious, where a man in rich clothes and a golden chain sat in an enormous chair covered in velvet at a writing table. I saw the ring of fairy silver on the first finger of his hand. He didn't look down at it, but I noticed he thumbed it around now and again, as though he wanted to make sure it hadn't vanished from his hand. "All right, let's see it," he said, putting down his pen.

"Your Grace." Isaac bowed and showed him the necklace.

The duke stared into the box. His face didn't change, but he stirred the necklace gently on its bed with one finger, just barely moving the delicate looped lacelike strands of it. He finally drew a breath and let it out again through his nose. "And how much do you ask for it?"

"Your Grace, I cannot sell it for less than a hundred and fifty."

"Absurd," the duke growled. I had a struggle to keep from biting my lip, myself: it was outrageous.

"Otherwise I must melt it down and make it into rings," Isaac said, spreading his hands apologetically. That was rather clever bargaining: of course the duke would rather no one else had a ring like his.

"Where are you getting this silver from?" the duke demanded. "It's not ordinary stuff." Isaac hesitated, and then looked at me. The duke followed his eyes. "Well?"

I curtseyed, as deeply as I could manage and still get myself back up. "I was given it by—one of the Staryk, my lord. He wants it changed for gold."

I feared whether he would believe me. His eyes rested on me like weights, but he didn't say *nonsense,* or call me a liar. He looked at the necklace again and grunted. "And you would like to do it through my purse, I see. How much more of this silver will there be?"

I had been worrying about that, whether the Staryk would bring even more silver next time, and what I would do with it if he did: the first time six, the second time sixty; how would I get six hundred pieces of gold? I swallowed. "Maybe—maybe much more."

"Hm," the duke said, and studied the necklace again. Then he put his hand to one side and took up a bell and rang it; the servant reappeared in the doorway. "Go tell Irina I want her," he said, and the man bowed. We waited a handful of minutes, not very long, and then a girl came to the door. She was near my age, slim and demure in a plain grey woolen gown, modestly high-necked, with a fine grey silken veil trailing back over her head. Her chaperone came after her, an older woman scowling at me and especially at Isaac.

Irina curtseyed, without raising her downcast eyes. The duke stood up and took the necklace over to her, and put it around her neck. Then he stepped back, three paces, and stopped there to look at her. She wasn't especially pretty, I would have said, only ordinary, except her hair was long and thick and lustrous; but it didn't really matter with the necklace on her. It was hard even to glance away from her, with winter clasped around her throat and the silver gleam catching in her veil and in her dark eyes as she looked at herself in the mirror on the wall there.

"Ah, Irinushka," the chaperone murmured, approvingly.

The duke nodded. He didn't look away from her as he said, "Well, jeweler, you are in luck. You may have a hundred gold coins for your necklace, and the next thing you make will be a crown fit for a queen, to be my daughter's dowry: and you will have ten times a hundred gold for it when I see it on her brow."

"His Grace wants you, milady," the maid said, and even gave me a curtsey, more than the senior servants usually did; *milady* to them was my stepmother. She herself was a message, in her neat grey dress: she was one of the upper maids who was allowed to polish furniture, not one of the lowly peasant scullery-girls who scrubbed the floors and tended the fires; those were the ones who made up my room. There was nothing very valuable in it for them to damage.

"Quickly, quickly," Magreta said, dropping her own sewing, and she bustled me up and touched the braid wound around my head that she had put in two days ago; I could feel her wishing she had time to do it over again, but then she shook her head and just made me take off my apron, and brushed my shoes and the bottoms of my skirts. I stood still and let her do it while I considered my vanishing-few options.

Of course there was only one reason my father would summon me during the day to his study, a thing he had never done, when he would see me at dinner that night anyway: someone wanted to marry me after all, and the matter was well advanced. Either there was a dowry already promised, or at least a serious negotiation under way; I was sure of it, even though there hadn't been so much as a whisper of such a thing when I'd dined with him last.

The haste of it made excellent sense: if he couldn't avoid the expense of the tsar's visit, at least he would save the separate expense of my wedding, and more besides; it would serve his consequence and his purse both to make the tsar and his court guests at his daughter's wedding. They would have to toast me and my husband, and they would have to give gifts whose value would undoubtedly be factored into the dowry under discussion.

But I couldn't imagine there would be anything for me to like in the marriage. Of course I would have liked to be mistress of my own home, secure from all those dismal alternatives I saw ahead of me, but not in this hurried haste and so clearly for the sake of my father's convenience. A man who'd marry me like this wasn't marrying me at all; he was making a bargain for a girl-shaped lump of clay he meant to use at *his* convenience, and he wouldn't need to value me highly when my father made it so clear that *he* didn't. My best hope would be someone of low rank, a rich ambitious boyar who owed my father fealty, and who was willing to take the duke's daughter at a bargain price to make himself a high man within the duchy; then I would at least have been worth that much to him. But I couldn't think of any candidates. After seven years of bad winters, my father's boyars were spending more time thinking of their lean purses than of their standing in the court. None of them were likely to want an expensive wife.

Anyway, such a man would be very little use. More likely, my father had found a nobleman who couldn't get a young wife of equal rank otherwise: someone distasteful enough that at least some fathers would hesitate before handing over their daughters. A cruel man perhaps, who would be all the more eager for a girl with a parent who would not object very much to whatever might happen to her.

I went downstairs even so, of course; I had no choice. Magreta was nearly quivering as we went down the stairs. She understood as well as I did what was in the offing, but she did not like to think of troubles before they appeared, so she was dreaming of a good and happy marriage for me, and being the old retired nurse of the mistress of the house instead of mured up in the attic rooms with a neglected daughter. I let her be excited while I wondered if I was about to meet the man himself, and if so, how I could tell whether it was worth infuriating my father by trying to make myself look like a bad bargain. It was an unpleasant scrap of hope to cling to.

But when the door opened, there was no betrothal waiting for me, no one who could even have been the agent of a potential husband; only two Jews, a man and a woman, thin and brown and dark-eyed, and the man was holding a box full of winter. I forgot to think of anything else, to think at all: the necklace blazed cold silver at me out of black velvet, and I was at the window in the garden again with the breath of winter on my cheeks and frost creeping over a windowsill beneath my fingers, yearning at something out of reach.

I almost went towards it with my hands stretched out; I clutched them into my grey wool skirts and curtseyed with an effort, forcing my eyes low for a moment, but when I stood again, I looked again. I still wasn't thinking; even as my father went and took the necklace from the box I wasn't thinking, and when he brought it over to me, I looked up at him only in blank surprise: it was all wrong. He couldn't mean to give such a thing to me. But he gestured with impatience, and after a moment I slowly turned my back, and bent my head to let him put it around my neck.

The room was warm, warmer by far than my narrow rooms upstairs, with a healthy fire crackling. But the metal felt cold against my skin, cold and wonderful, refreshing as putting wet hands on your cheeks on a hot day. I lifted my head and turned, and my father was looking at me. All of them were looking at me, staring. "Ah, Irinushka," Magreta murmured tenderly. I put my fingers up to brush over the fine links. Even lying on my skin, it still felt cool to the touch, and when I looked at myself in the mirror, in the glass I was not standing in my father's study. I was in a grove of dark winter trees, under a pale grey sky, and I could almost feel the snow falling onto my skin.

I stayed there for a long timeless moment, breathing in deep sweet cold air that filled my lungs, full of freshly cut pine branches and heavy snow and deep woods wide around me. And then distantly I heard my father promise the Jews that he would give them a thousand pieces in gold, if they would make a crown to be my dowry, so I had been right: he did have a betrothal in mind, and the arrangements were most urgent indeed.

He did not let me keep the necklace, of course. After the Jews left, he beckoned me over, and though he paused a moment, staring at me again, he reached back around my neck and took the necklace off and laid it back into the box. He looked at me afterwards hard, as if he had to remind himself what I really was without it, and then he shook his head and said to me crisply, "The tsar will be here the week after next. Practice your dancing. You will dine with me every night until then. See to her clothes," he added to Magreta. "She must have three new dresses."

I curtseyed and went back upstairs with Magreta hovering, like a cloud of anxious birds that go bursting out and fly madly before they settle back into the tree. "I must get some of the maids to help me," she said, swooping to snatch up her knitting, to have something to close her hands around. "So much to be done! Nothing is ready. Your chest is not half full! And three dresses to be made!"

"Yes," I said. "You should speak to the housekeeper at once," and Magreta said, "Yes, yes," and flew out of the room again and left me alone at last, to sit down by the fire with my own sewing, a white nightgown being elaborated with embroidery for a wedding-bed.

I had met the tsar once before, seven years ago, when his father and brother had just died; my father had come to Koron for the coronation, to do homage to the new tsar or more accurately to the new regent, Archduke Dmitir. I saw Mirnatius first in the church, while the priest was droning through the ceremony, but I didn't pay him very much attention then; I was so bored that I was nodding on the seat beside Galina in my hot and stiff clothing, until I jerked awake and jumped to my feet when they finally crowned him, with a feeling like being jabbed hard with a needle, a moment even before everyone else was rising so we could acclaim him.

No one else paid very much attention to him afterwards. The great lords dined and talked together at the tsar's table, paying court to Dmitir, and Mirnatius came out alone into the gardens behind the palace, where I was also playing, of no importance myself. He had a small bow and arrow, and shot squirrels, and when he hit them, he came and looked at their little dead bodies with pleasure. Not in the ordinary way of a boy proud of being a good hunter: he would take hold of the arrows and jiggle them, to make the bodies twitch and jerk if he could, staring down with a wide blank fascination in his eyes.

He caught me staring at him indignantly. I was too young to have learned to be cautious. "Why are you staring so?" he said. "It's only a little life still left in them. It's not witchcraft."

He might well have known the difference: his mother had been a witch, who seduced the tsar after his first tsarina died. Nobody approved of the marriage, of course, and after only a few years she was put to death by flame when she was caught trying to have the first tsarina's son killed, to make her own son the heir. But now the tsar and the eldest prince had died of fever, and so the witch's son had become tsar anyway, which, as Magreta used to say, was a lesson to everyone that being a witch was not the same thing as being wise.

I too was not wise at the time, although I had the excuse of being a young girl. Even though he was the tsar, I said, "You've already killed them. Why can't you leave them alone?" Which was not very coherent, but I knew what I meant: I didn't like him mauling the little bodies around, making them flinch for his pleasure.

His beautiful green eyes narrowed pig-small and angry, and he raised the bow and aimed an arrow at me. I was old enough to understand that was death looking at me. I wanted to run, but instead I simply froze, my whole body stopped in place and my heart with it, and then he laughed and lowered the bow and said mockingly, "All hail the defender of dead squirrels!" and made me a great formal bow like at a wedding before he strolled away. All the rest of that week, whenever I played in the garden, I was sure to come across a dead squirrel—always tucked away somewhere out of the gardeners' sight, and yet my ball would roll to it, or if I ran to hide and seek with Magreta, I would crouch into a bush only to find one cut open, lying there in wait for me.

I thought of telling on him: I was sure everyone would have believed me, because Mirnatius was so beautiful, and because of his mother. People even whispered about him already. But I told Magreta first, and when she got the whole story out of me, she told me that trouble came to those who made it, as the squirrels should have shown me, and I wasn't to stir up any more. And then she kept me indoors in our room, spinning yarn all the rest of our visit, except for hasty meals.

We'd never spoken of it since, but I knew Magreta hadn't forgotten any more than I had. We had gone back to Koron, four years ago, for Archduke Dmitir's lavish funeral. Mirnatius had commanded the attendance of most of the nobility, presumably to make clear that he no longer had nor required a regent, and he'd made them all swear fealty over again to him personally. We'd been there for two weeks. Magreta kept me very close throughout, and never let me leave my rooms without my veil over my face, even though I wasn't a woman yet, and she brought me all my meals from the kitchens with her own hands. Mirnatius had stood as chief mourner: he'd been sixteen then, tall and full-grown and even more beautiful, with his black hair and light eyes that looked like jewels shining out of his Tatar-dark skin, and his mouth full of even white teeth, and with the crown and his golden robes he might have been a statue, or a saint. I watched him through the faint haze of my fine veil, until his head turned in my direction, and then I quickly dropped my eyes and made sure I was small and insignificant in the third row of princesses and dukes' daughters.

But in two weeks' time, he would come to my father's house, and there would be no camouflage. My father would not give him three good dinners and take him boar hunting in the dark woods and minimize his expense. Instead he would make an extravagant feasting that would last all three days, with jugglers and magicians and dancers to keep the tsar and his court entertained indoors, and he would give me three new dresses after all, and make an offering of me. It seemed my father did mean to try and catch the tsar for his daughter, with a ring and a necklace and a crown of magic silver to bait his trap.

I looked at my face in the window's reflection and wondered what my father's hard eyes had seen, with that necklace around my throat, to make him think it a chance worth taking. I didn't know. I couldn't see my own face when I wore it. But I didn't have the comfort of thinking him a fool.

I was still standing by the window, my hands resting on the cold stone and my sewing abandoned, when Magreta came back to the room still twittering, to press a cup of hot sweet tea into my hands. She had even brought up a thick slice of my favorite poppy-seed cake, which she must have coaxed out of the cook; I did not get such treats every day. A maid was trailing her with a few extra logs for the fire. I let her draw me back to the hearth, grateful for what she was trying to do, and I didn't tell her that it was all wrong. What I really wanted was the silver necklace, cold around my neck, even though it was bringing my doom; I wanted to put it on and find a long mirror and slip away into a wide dark winter wood.

It was Saturday night after sundown when I climbed back into Oleg's sledge. I had put twenty gold pieces more into my grandfather's vault, and I carried the Staryk's swollen white purse with me, the leather straining with the weight of the gold. My shoulders tightened as we plunged into the forest, and I wondered with every moment when and if the Staryk would come upon me once more, until somewhere deep in the woods, the sledge began to slow and came to a stop under the dark boughs. I went rabbit-still, looking around for any signs of him, but I didn't see anything; the horse stamped and snorted her warm breath, and Oleg didn't slump over, but hung his reins on the footboard.

"Did you hear something?" I said, my voice hushed, and then he climbed down and took out a knife from under his coat as he came towards me, and I realized I'd forgotten to worry about anything else but magic. I shoved the heaped blankets and straw towards him as a too-fragile barricade as I scrambled out the other side of the sledge. "Don't," I blurted. "Oleg, don't," my heavy skirts dragging in the snow as he came around for me. "Oleg, please," but his face was clenched down, cold deeper than any winter. "It's not my gold!" I cried in desperation, holding the purse out between us. "It's not mine, I have to pay it back—"

He didn't stop. "None of it's yours," he snarled. "None of it's yours, little grubbing vulture, taking money out of the hands of honest working men," every word out of his mouth familiar as a knife: it was the story again, only a little different; a story Oleg had found to persuade himself he wasn't doing wrong, that he had a right to what he'd take or cheat, and I knew he wouldn't listen to me. He would leave my body for the wolves, and go home with the gold hidden under his coat, and say I had been lost in the woods.

I dropped the purse and gripped two big handfuls of my skirts and struggled back, floundering through the deep snow, higher than my thighs. He lunged, and I flung myself away, falling backwards. The crust atop the snow gave beneath my weight, and branches out of the underbrush clawed my cheek. I couldn't get up. He was standing over me, his knife in one hand and the other reaching down to grab me, and then he halted; his arms sank down to his sides.

He wasn't showing me mercy. A deeper cold was coming into his face, stealing blue over his lips, and white frost was climbing over his thick brown beard. I struggled back to my feet, shivering. The Staryk was standing behind him, a hand laid upon the back of his neck like a master taking hold of a dog.

After a moment he dropped his hand. Oleg stood blank between us, bloodless as frostbite. He turned and slowly went back to the sledge and climbed into the driver's seat. The Staryk didn't watch him go, as if he cared nothing for what he had done; he only looked at me with his eyes as gleaming as Oleg's blade. I was shaking and queasy. There were tears freezing on my eyelashes, making them stick together. I blinked my eyes open and held my hands tight until they stopped trembling, and then I bent down and picked up the purse out of the deep snow, and held it out.

The Staryk came closer and took it from me. He didn't pour the purse out: it was too full for that. Instead he dipped his hand inside and lifted out a handful of gold to tumble ringing back into the bag through his fingers, until there was only one last coin held between his white-gloved fingers, shining like sunlight. He frowned at it, and me.

"It's there, all sixty," I said. My heart had slowed, because I suppose it was that or burst.

"As it must be," he said. "For fail me, and to ice you shall go, though my hand and crown you shall win if you succeed." He said it as if he meant it, and also angrily, although he had set the terms himself: I felt he would almost have preferred to freeze me than get his gold. "Now go home, mortal maiden, until I call on you again."

I looked over helplessly at the sledge: Oleg was sitting in the driver's seat, staring with his frozen face out into the winter, and the last thing I wanted was to get in with him. But I couldn't walk home from here, or even to some village where I could hire another driver. Oleg had turned off the road to bring us here: I had no idea where we were. I turned to argue, but the Staryk was already gone. I stood alone under pine boughs heavy with snow, with only silence and footprints around me, and the deep crushed hollow where I had fallen, the shape of a girl outlined in the drift, like a child playing might have made.

It began to snow even while I stood there, a thick steady snow that forced my hand. I picked my way gingerly to the sledge and climbed back inside. Oleg shook the reins silently, and the mare started trotting again. He turned her head towards the trees, away from the road, and drove deeper into the forest. I tried to decide whether I was more afraid to call out to him and be answered, or to get no reply, and if I should try to jump from the sledge. And then suddenly we came through a narrow gap between trees onto a different road: a road whose surface was pale and smooth as a sheet of ice, gleaming white. The rails of the sledge rattled once, coming onto the road, and then fell perfectly silent. The horse's heavy-shod hooves went quickly on the ice, the sledge skating along behind her. Around us, trees stretched tall and birch-white, full of rustling leaves; trees that didn't grow in our forest, and should have been bare with winter. I saw white birds and white squirrels darting between the branches, and the sleigh bells made a strange kind of music, high and bright and cold.

I didn't look behind me, to see where the road came from. I huddled back into the blankets and squeezed my eyes shut and kept them so, until suddenly there was a crunching of snow beneath us again, and the sledge was already standing outside the gate of my own yard. I all but leapt out, and darted through the gate and all the way to my door before I glanced around. But I needn't have run. Oleg drove away without ever looking back at me.

Chapter 8

"Wanda," Miryem said to me, the morning after she came back, "will you take this to Oleg's house? I forgave him a kopek for waiting for me, in Vysnia." She gave me a written receipt, but she didn't meet my eyes as she asked. There were red scratches across the back of her jaw and cheek, as though a branch had caught her there, or something with claws.

I said, "Yes, I will go." I put on my shawl and took the note, but when I came to Oleg's house, down the lane and around a corner, I stopped across the street and stood watching. Two men were carrying away his body to the church. I saw his face for a moment. His eyes were open and staring, and his mouth was blue. His wife was sitting huddled near the stables. The neighbors were converging on the house with covered dishes. One of them stopped in front of me. I had met Varda: she had still owed a small sum when I had started collecting, and she had paid the balance off with three young, laying chickens. She said to me sharply, "Well? What do you want in this house? The flesh of the dead?"

Kajus was coming to the house too with his wife and son, carrying a big steaming jug of krupnik. "Come now, Panova Kubilius, it is Sunday. Surely Wanda is not collecting," he said.

"He earned a kopek off his debt for driving Miryem to Vysnia," I answered. "I came to bring the receipt."

"There, you see," Kajus said to Varda, who scowled back at him and me both.

"A kopek!" she said. "One less for his poor wife to take out of her children's mouths to fatten the Jew's purse. Give it to me! I will take it to her, not you."

"All right, Panova," I said, and gave her the paper. Then I went back to Miryem and told her that Oleg was dead, outside his own stables, found lying frozen and staring blindly upwards, his horse and sledge put away.

She heard me out silently, and said nothing. I stood with her a few moments, and then because I could think of nothing else to do, I said, "I will go and feed the goats," and she nodded.

The next day I was collecting out of town, down the east road. Everyone had heard by then. They asked me if it was true and were sorry when I said it was. Oleg had been a big cheerful man who would buy beer and vodka for friends in the roundhouse during winter, and he would bring a widow a load of firewood when he was driving one for himself. Even my father, when I came home and told him, exclaimed in regret. When they buried him on Tuesday, his widow was the only one of the mourners who came back from the churchyard with dry eyes.

Everyone spoke of it, but not as a thing that the Staryk had done. His heart had burst, they said, shaking their heads. It was sad when such a thing happened to a strong man, a big healthy man. But it was not strange to anyone that he had frozen to a block during a deep winter night.

I did not say anything about it to anyone, except to Sergey, when we stood in the road together, with the woods silent and bright in moonlight. He was on his way to stay the night again. Miryem hadn't told him to stop coming, even though he couldn't do anything to stop the Staryk. She hadn't stopped paying us our pennies, either. Most of the time we were able to forget, to convince ourselves he was only coming to look after the goats. So he kept going, and ate two meals a day in their house, and we buried the pennies by the white tree on our way home.

"Do you remember?" I asked him, and he went still. We had never spoken of what had happened to him in the wood, never.

He did not want to talk of it, I could tell, but I stood with him, my silence asking for me, and at last he said, "I was cleaning a rabbit. He rode out of the trees. He told me the woods were his and I was a thief. Then he said . . ." Sergey stopped, gone strange and hollow-faced, and shook his head. He did not remember, and he did not want to remember.

"Did he ride a thing with claws on its hooves? And wear shoes with a long toe?" I asked, and Sergey nodded once.

So it was the same one: not only a Staryk, but a Staryk lord, and if he had not lied, he was lord of the whole forest. I had heard people say in the market that it went all the way to the shores of the northern sea. A great lord of the Staryk was coming to Miryem for gold, and if she could not give it to him, I knew we would find *her* dead in her yard, with curled-toe boot prints around her.

And then there would be no more debt to pay. As soon as he heard she was dead, my father would tell me I was done with payments. He would be ready to shout away Miryem's father, but he wouldn't even have to. Her mother would have eyes red with weeping, but even in her grief she would think of me. The next time I came, she would tell me that the debt was paid, that I had done enough. To keep working, I would have to tell my father they were paying me, and then he would take the coin. Every day he would come home from town drunk, and take my penny, and hit me to go and get his dinner. And it would be like that every day after, forever.

"We could tell him we were being paid, but less," I said to

Sergey, but he looked doubtful, and I understood. Our father suspected nothing now. Why would anyone pay us, when he was sending us for free, and they did not have to? But if we told him we were being paid, so he would let us keep going, then he would become suspicious. He would go and demand of Miryem's father how much we were being paid, and Panov Mandelstam would answer him honestly. We could not ask him to lie for us. He would only look at us with distress, that we wanted to lie to our father, and be sorry he could not help us.

And once our father knew we had lied about how much we were being paid, then he would ask how much we *had* been paid. And then he would know that there was money somewhere, that we had hidden. And for hiding money from him, he would not beat us with the belt or his big hand, he would beat us with the poker, and he might not even stop once we told him where it was.

The church bells ringing for Oleg, when they buried him three days later, sounded like his sleigh bells, ringing too high in a forest of white trees. They would find *me* frozen just like him, if I didn't give the Staryk his gold, but I equally had to fear what would happen if I did. Would he put me on his white stag behind him, and carry me away to that cold white forest, to live there alone forever with a crown of fairy silver of my own? I had never felt sorry for the miller's daughter before, in the story the villagers told; I'd been sorry for my father, and myself, and angry. But who would really like it, after all, to be married to a king who'd as cheerfully have cut off your head if you didn't spin his straw into gold? I didn't want to be the Staryk's queen any more than I wanted to be his slave, or frozen into ice.

I couldn't forget him anymore. He was in the corner of my

mind all the time now, creeping farther over it every day, a little more like frost on a windowpane. I started up in my bed, gasping every night, shivering with a chill inside me that my mother's arms couldn't drive away, and the memory of his silver eyes.

"Can you get him the gold?" Wanda asked me that morning, as abruptly as before.

I did not need to ask whom she meant. We were tending the goats, and my mother was in the yard, only a few feet away, so I couldn't burst into tears even if I had wanted to; she and my father were already suspicious, watching me with a puzzled and worried look. I pressed the back of my hand to my mouth to keep my noise of protest in. "Yes," I said shortly. "Yes, I can get the gold."

Wanda didn't say anything, only stared at me with her mouth a straight hard line, and my throat tightened. "If," I said to her, "if something should take me from home for a time—you'll stay on and help my father? He'll keep paying you. He'll make it double," I added, desperate suddenly. I thought of my mother and my father alone in the village without me, but with all the anger I had brewed in every house turned against them. For a moment I was in the clearing again, floundering in the snow with Oleg's twisted face above me, not frozen but flushed and red and hateful.

Wanda didn't answer me for a moment, and then she said slowly, "My father will want to keep me home." She raised her head from the trough and looked at me sideways. I stared at her in surprise, but I understood, of course. She was not giving her father the money; he would never want her to stay home if she was bringing him a penny a day. She was keeping it herself.

I kept brushing the goat, thinking this over. All this time I had thought I was bargaining with her father, not her, and all I needed to do was give him a little bit of money, more than he could get from a daughter's work on the farm. It had not occurred to me that she would want the money herself. "Do you want it for a dowry?" I asked her.

"No!" she said, very fiercely.

I couldn't understand, otherwise, why she would want to keep the money hidden. I had paid her already twelve pennies, for her and her brother, and she still wore her old ragged dress, and her basket-woven shoes, and when I had gone to Gorek's house, that first time, collecting, the whole farm had looked as poor as dirt. They could have spent twelve pennies ten times over. Slowly I asked, "What did your father do with the six kopeks he borrowed?"

So she told me. Knowing didn't help much, of course. He was her father. He had the right to borrow money from someone who would lend it to him, and the right to spend it as stupidly as he wanted, and the right to put his daughter to work to pay off his debt, and the right to take any money she earned. If she didn't want to marry, there was nothing she could do to be free of him. She didn't say what she had been doing with the money, but she couldn't have been doing anything with it, except piling it up like a dragon-hoard somewhere. He would have caught her by now, if she had spent it on anything: that was why she hadn't bought a decent dress, or boots. She was lucky her father hadn't come to town much lately: if he'd ever said anything to me, if he'd talked loudly of how we were taking advantage of a poor man, I would have answered him in heat, without ever thinking, and he'd have found out then. I didn't like to think what would have happened. It seemed to me, the kind of man who would gamble away and drink up four kopeks he had no hope of repaying was also the kind of man who would beat his daughter bloody, without ever thinking of the money she'd bring him if he kept her working.

"You can tell him I've gone to be married to a rich man," I told her. It would be true, after all. "Tell him as soon as I come

home, I'll check all the books again." And that would be true, too.
"And . . . and when the debt's paid, you can tell him that we offer
to pay him a penny a week in hard coin, for the two of you to keep
coming. To be paid once a month. And then give him the four
pennies right away. Once he's spent them, he's back in debt, and
he can't refuse to send you. And the next month, do it again."

Wanda gave me a nod, a single jerk. I put out my hand to her
suddenly without thinking, and felt foolish with it hanging in the
air between us as she stared at it, but just before I would have let
it drop, she reached back and took it in her own, big and square
with red rough fingers. She gripped my hand a little too tightly,
but I didn't mind.

"I'll go back to Vysnia tomorrow," I said, calmer. I didn't think
the city walls would keep out the Staryk, but I might as well try. At
least I wouldn't be at home. He wouldn't leave prints all over my
parents' yard, for the rest of the village to make a vicious story of.
"I'll need to be there, anyway, when he comes," and I told Wanda
about Isaac, and how I was getting the Staryk his gold.

I didn't tell my mother about it, though; I didn't remind her of
the Staryk at all, even when she said, "You're going back again so
soon?" I was glad she didn't remember, to be puzzled instead of
afraid for me.

"I want to bring back some more aprons," I said. That afternoon, I made sure the ledger was in good order, and when I finished, I went outside and looked at our house, snug now behind
shutters the carpenter had put up for me, with the small flock of
chickens and our handful of goats making a clattering mess in the
yard, and then I took my basket and walked slowly through town.
I don't know why. It wasn't a market day, and Wanda had done
the rounds. I had nothing to do in town, and nothing had changed,
except everyone scowled at me now when I passed, instead of
smirking the way they had back in the days when the sight of me
in my patched shoes and ragged clothes had been a pleasant re-

minder of the money in their pockets that they never meant to pay back.

That was why I did it, maybe: I walked all the way to the other end of town and back and when I came home again, I wasn't sorry to be leaving them. I loved nothing about the town or any of them, even now when it was at least familiar ground. I wasn't sorry they didn't like me, I wasn't sorry I had been hard to them. I was glad, fiercely glad. They had wanted me to bury my mother and leave my father behind to die alone. They had wanted me to go be a beggar in my grandfather's house, and live the rest of my days a quiet mouse in the kitchen. They would have devoured my family and picked their teeth with the bones, and never been sorry at all. Better to be turned to ice by the Staryk, who didn't pretend to be a neighbor.

There wasn't Oleg to hire anymore, so the next morning I went and stood on the market road. When a likely carter came driving past with a big sledge laden with barrels of salt herring from the sea, I waved him down, and offered him five pennies if he would take me all the way to Vysnia. I could have paid more, but I had learned my lesson. This time I had waited for an older man in an older cart, and my good dress with its fur collar and cuffs was hidden: I had put on my father's old worn-out woolen overcoat, which I had meant to use for rags now that I had bought him a good new one made of fur.

The old carter talked to me as we drove of his granddaughters, and wanted to know my age; he was pleased that his girl a year younger than I was already married when I wasn't, and asked me if I was going to town to get a husband. "We'll see," I said, and then I laughed aloud in sudden real relief, because it was so ridiculous. Me sitting in a fish cart with my muddy boots, scarecrow in my father's patched overcoat: what would a Staryk lord want with me? I wasn't a princess, or even a golden-haired peasant girl. I suppose it wouldn't make any difference to him that I was a Jew, but I was short and bony and sallow, and my nose was humped in the middle and too big for my face. In fact I wasn't married yet on purpose: my grandfather had told me judiciously to wait another two years to go to the matchmaker, so I would grow a bit fatter, and meanwhile my dowry would plump up alongside me, to help bring me a husband with the good sense to want a wife who brought more to the marriage than beauty, but not so greedy he didn't care for her appearance at all.

That was the kind of man for me, a clear-eyed sensible man who could want me honestly; I was no prize for an elven lord. Surely the Staryk had only said it as a joke, because he didn't think I could manage his task at all. He couldn't mean to marry me really. When I gave him his third sack of gold, he would only stamp himself through the ground in anger—or more likely, I thought, sobering again, he would turn me to ice anyway, for spite that I'd proved him wrong. I rubbed my arms and looked over through the woods: there was no sign of the Staryk road today, only the dark trees and the white snow and the solid ice of the river gliding away under the runners.

I came to my grandfather's house late, just before sunset. My grandmother said three times how nice it was to see me back again, so soon, and asked a little anxiously after my mother's health, and whether I had already sold all of my goods. My grandfather didn't ask any questions at all. He looked at me hard from under his eyebrows and only said, "Well, enough noise. It's almost time for dinner."

I put my things away and talked over dinner about the aprons I had sold, and the load of wool that would go with my grand- father's barge, when the river at last melted: thirty bales, not an enormous amount, but something to make a start with. I was glad to have the brick walls of my grandfather's house around us, solid and prosaic like our conversation. But that evening while I sat knitting with my grandmother in the cozy sitting room, behind us the kitchen door rattled on its hinges, and though the noise was loud, my grandmother didn't lift her head at all. I slowly put aside my own work and got up and went to the door. I pulled it open and flinched back: there was no narrow alleyway behind the Staryk, no brick wall of the house next door, and no hardened slush beneath his feet. He stood outside in a clearing ringed with pale-limbed trees, and behind him the white ice-road ran away into the distance under a grey sky washed with clear cold light, as if one step across the threshold would carry me out of all the world.

There was a box instead of a purse upon the stoop, a small chest made of pale white wood bleached as bone, bound around with thick straps of white leather and hinged and clasped with silver. I knelt and opened it. "Seven days this time I'll grant you, to return my silver changed for gold," the Staryk said in his voice like singing, as I stared at the heap of coins inside. Silver enough to make a crown to hold the moon and stars, and I didn't doubt for a moment that the tsar would marry Irina, with this to make her dowry.

The Staryk was looking down at me with his sharp silver eyes, eager and vicious as a hawk. "Did you think mortal roads could run away from me, or mortal walls keep me out?" he said, and I hadn't really, after all. "Think not to escape from me, girl, for in seven days I will come for you, wherever you have fled."

He said it smiling down at me, cruel and satisfied, as though he was sure he had set me an impossible task, and it made me angry. I stood up and raised my chin and said, coolly, "I will be here, with your gold."

His face lost its smile, which was satisfying, but I paid for it; he said in answer, "And if you do as you have said, I will take you away with me, and make you my queen," and it didn't seem like a joke here, with the stone of my grandfather's threshold patterned white with frost that crept lacelike out of his grove, and the cold silver light shining out of the chest.

"Wait!" I said, as he began to turn away. "Why would you take me? You must know I have no magic, not really: I can't change silver to gold for you in your kingdom, if you take me away."

"Of course you can, mortal girl," he said over his shoulder, as if I was the one being a fool. "A power claimed and challenged and thrice carried out is true; the proving makes it so." And then he stepped forward and the heavy door swung shut in my face, leaving me with a casket full of silver coins and a belly full of dismay.

Isaac made the crown in that one feverish week, laboring upon it in his stall in the marketplace. He dipped out cupfuls of silver and hammered out great thin sheets to make the fan-shaped crown, tall enough to double the height of a head, and then with painstaking care added droplets of melted silver in mimic of pearls, laying them in graceful spiraling patterns that turned upon themselves and vined away again. He borrowed molds from every other jeweler in the market and poured tiny flattened links by the hundreds, then hung glittering chains of them linked from one side of the crown to the other, and fringed along the rest of the wide fan's bottom edge. By the second day, men and women were coming just to watch him work. I sat by, silent and unhappy, and kept them off. Each night he took the work home with him, and I took back the lightened casket, my grandfather's two manservants carrying it for me. No one troubled us. Even the little pickpockets, with ambitions to slip a single thin silver coin off the table, were caught by the winter light; when they drifted too close their mouths softened into parted wonder, their eyes puzzled, and when I looked at them, they startled and melted away into the crowds.

By the end of the fifth day, the casket was empty and the crown was finished; when Isaac had assembled the whole, he turned and said, "Come here," and set it upon my head to see whether it was well-balanced. The crown felt cool and light as a dusting of snow upon my forehead. In his bronze mirror, I looked like a strange deep-water reflection of myself, silver stars at midnight above my brow, and all the marketplace went quiet in a rippling wave around me, silent like the clearing with the Staryk standing in it. I wanted to burst into tears, or run away; instead I took the crown off my head and put it back into Isaac's hands, and when he'd carefully swathed it with linen and black velvet, the crowds finally drifted away, murmuring to each other.

My grandfather's manservants guarded us all the way to the duke's palace. We found it full of bustle and the noise of preparations: the tsar was arriving in two days' time, and all the household was full of suppressed excitement; they all knew something of the duke's plans, and the servants' eyes followed the swathed shape of the crown as Isaac carried it through the corridors. We were put into a better antechamber to wait this time, and then the chaperone came to fetch me. "Bring it with you. The men stay here," she said, with a sharp suspicious glare at them.

She took me upstairs to a small pair of rooms, not nearly so grand as the ones below: I suppose a plain daughter hadn't merited better before now. Irina was sitting stiff as a rake handle before a mirror made of glass. She wore a silver-grey silk dress over pure white skirts, the bodice cut much lower this time to make a frame around the necklace. Her long beautiful hair had been braided into several thick ropes, ready to be put up, and her hands were gripped tightly around themselves in front of her.

Her fingers worked slightly against each other, nervous, as the chaperone pinned up the braids, and then I unwrapped the crown and carefully set it upon her head. It stood glittering beneath the light of a dozen candles, and the chaperone fell silent, her eyes wide as they rested on her charge. Irina herself slowly stood up and took a step closer to her reflection in the mirror, her hand reaching up towards the glass almost as if to touch the woman inside.

Whatever magic the silver had to enchant those around it either faded with use or couldn't touch me any longer; I wished that it could, and that my eyes could be dazzled enough to care for nothing else. Instead I watched Irina's face in the mirror, pale and thin and transported as she looked at herself in her crown, and I wondered if she would be glad to marry the tsar, to leave her quiet small rooms for a distant palace and a throne. As she dropped her hand and turned back into the room, our eyes met: we didn't speak, but for a moment I felt her a sister, our lives in the hands of others. She wasn't likely to have any more choice in the matter than I did.

Then the door opened: the duke himself come to inspect her. He paused in the doorway. Irina curtseyed to her father, then straightened again, her chin coming up a little to balance the crown; she looked like a queen already. The duke stared at her as if he could hardly recognize his own daughter; he shook himself a little, pulling free of it, before he turned to me. "Very well, Panovina," he said, without hesitation, though I hadn't said a word. "You will have your gold."

He gave us a thousand gold pieces: enough to heap the Staryk's box full again, with hundreds more left over: a fortune, for what good it would do me now. My grandfather's servants carried the chest and the sacks home for me. He came downstairs, hearing my grandmother's exclamations, and looked over all the treasure; then he took four gold coins out of the sacks, meant for the vault, and gave two each to the servants before he dismissed them. "Spend one and save one; you remember the wise man's rule," he said, and they both bowed and thanked him and dashed off to revel, elbowing each other and grinning as they went.

Then he sent my grandmother out of the room on a pretext, asking her to make her cheesecake to celebrate my good fortune; and when she was gone to the kitchens, he turned to me and said, "Now, Miryem, you'll tell me the rest of it," and I burst into tears.

I hadn't told my parents, or my grandmother, but I told him: I trusted my grandfather to bear it as I hadn't trusted them, not to break their hearts wanting to save me. I knew what my father would do, and my mother, if they found out: they would make a wall of their own bodies between me and the Staryk, and then I would see them fall cold and frozen before he took me away.

And I believed now that he would take me away. I hadn't been able to make sense of it before: what use would a mortal woman be to an elven lord, and why should boasting make me worth marrying, even if I somehow scrabbled together six hundred pieces of gold for a dowry? But of course a Staryk king would want a queen who really could make gold out of silver, mortal or not. The Staryk always came for gold.

But my grandfather only listened as I wept it out to him, and then he said, "At least he's not a fool, this Staryk, to want a wife for such a reason. It would make the fortune of any kingdom. What else do you know of him?" I stared at him, still wet-faced. He shrugged. "It's not what you would have looked for, but there's worse things in life than to be a queen."

By speaking so, he gave me a gift: making it an ordinary match, to be discussed and considered, even if it wasn't really. I gulped and wiped away my tears, and felt better. After all, in cold hard terms it *was* a catch, for a poor man's daughter. My grandfather nodded as I calmed myself. "Good. Think on it with a clear head. Lords and kings often don't ask for what they want, but they can afford to have bad manners. There's no one else, is there?"

"No," I said, with a small shake. There wasn't, although I'd walked back from the duke's house at Isaac's side, and when he had parted from me with his share, four sacks of his own full of gold, he had said to me jubilantly, "Tell your grandfather I will come and speak to him tomorrow," meaning that he had enough money not to wait any longer to be married, and I had been so jealous of Basia I could have burst into flames. It wasn't really Isaac, though: it was thinking of her married to a man with careful hands and dark brown eyes, and in her own home, where love could grow in earth made rich with gold my work had put there.

"You will go to your husband with wealth in your hands," my grandfather said, with a gesture to the casket of gold, as if he knew what was in my heart. "And he is wise enough to value what you bring him, even if he doesn't yet know the rest of your worth. That's not nothing, to be able to hold your head up." He cupped his hand under my chin and gripped it hard. "Hold your head up, Miryem," and I nodded, my mouth tight over the weeping I wouldn't let out again.

Mirnatius arrived in a vast closed sleigh painted in black and gold, drawn by four black horses steaming and stamping in the cold air, with soldiers hanging on the back and more of them riding in crisp martial ranks around it. There must have been other people, too, other sleighs, but it was hard to pay attention to anyone else when he flung open the door and climbed down in a gust of air that fogged in the cold. He wore black also, with delicate embroidery in gold thread gleaming all over the wool panels of his heavy coat. His black hair was long and curling, and everyone turned towards him a little, moths eager for the flame.

He greeted my father, perfunctorily, and when asked about his journey said something mildly complaining about the vigor of the winter, and how thin and weak the game was grown. The remark would have neatly diminished my father's entertainment, if he had then spent the tsar's visit on hunting—which of course he had intended to do, and Mirnatius plainly meant to needle him for it. But instead my father bowed and said, "Indeed, the hunting has grown sadly dull, Your Majesty, but I hope the hospitality of my hall will not disappoint you," and the tsar paused.

I was almost entirely hidden behind a curtain, but I drew back anyway when the tsar looked up and swept his gaze across the windows of the house like a hawk going over a field, trying to flush out some prey. Fortunately he looked at the main floor of the house, and not at my high-up little window. My father had not given me new chambers. There were many guests in the tsar's company whom he wanted to impress, and anyway he hoped I would be leaving soon.

Then Mirnatius smiled at my father, with the pleasure of a man who expects to be richly amused at someone else's expense, and said, "I hope so as well. Tell me, Erdivilas, how are your family? Little Irina must be a woman grown by now. A beauty, I have heard, surely?" It was more mockery: he had heard nothing of the sort, of course. I had traveled with my father; the court and his advisors knew I was nothing out of the ordinary, and hardly a girl to turn a young tsar's head—if he had been in any danger of turning his head at all, except perhaps all the way round like an owl.

"They all are well, and Irina is healthy, Sire, that is all a father can ask of God," my father said. "I would not name her a beauty to other men. But I will not lie: I think she has something in her more than most girls. You will see her while you are here, and tell me if you agree. I would welcome your counsel, for she is of an age to marry, and I would find a man worthy of her if I can arrange it."

A blunt declaration that, almost crude by the standards of

court conversation, where it was a point of honor always to speak to the side and not the heart of the thing, but it served my father's purpose: Mirnatius lost his look of easy malice. He followed my father into the house with a thoughtful frowning look instead. He had understood the message—that my father meant seriously to offer me as a bride, despite the extremely bad politics of the match, and also was not a fool who thought to sneak an ugly girl into the tsar's bed as a beauty with the help of dim lights and strong liquor; therefore, something unusual was in the offing.

Then they were all gone inside, to be greeted by my step-mother and the household, out of the cold. I stood behind the curtain without moving while the rest of the tsar's retinue were disposed of, soldiers and courtiers and servants flowing away into all the nooks and crannies of the house and stables. There was nothing more to see, and in my small crowded rooms the other women who had gone to cluster around the other window all went back to their seats and their frantic sewing, and the scullery-maids with their buckets went back to emptying out the washtubs still sitting before the fire: one to wash me and a second one just to wash my hair.

"Pardon, milady," one of them said to me timidly, by way of asking if she could use the window I was standing by, which had a useful eave below it that would catch the runoff, so it didn't just rain down onto the windows below. I stepped back, making room for her. My hair was still damp, draped all over my shoulders, long and loose down my back. It smelled faintly of myrtle, because Magreta had put branches of it in the water. "They say it protects against ill-wishing and sorcery," she had said, in a businesslike tone, "but really it's just a nice smell."

The fire had been built up, roaring to keep the chill off me, so all the other women were sweating and red-faced while they sewed urgently. I stood apart from their excited bustle. They were all half strangers to me; I knew their faces and their names, but nothing really of them. My stepmother made it her business to hire all the women of the house and know them and speak to them, so they would do good work for her, but she had never brought me into supervising the work of the household. She might have had a daughter of her own, after all.

But she had never been unkind to me; she had even sent her own best women to help with my sewing, although she would have liked to have the tsar's visit as an excuse for new gowns for herself. Of course, she saw the value of having me settled in such a place—if it could be managed. As the other women went back to their seats, from peeping at the tsar, they had all glanced at me and looked dubious. I wished I could have felt so, myself. But they hadn't seen me in the necklace, the crown. Only Magreta had, and she wrung her hands when she thought I didn't see, and gave me bright encouraging smiles when she thought I did.

The women were working on linens now. My own gowns were already finished and waiting for me, in three shades of grey, like a winter's sky. My father had ordered them made almost without ornament, of fine silk, with only a little touch of white embroidery. I had been wearing one of them for the last fitting yesterday when the jeweler's woman had brought me the crown; she had given it to Magreta, who had set it on my head, and in the mirror I had become a queen in a dark forest made of ice. I had reached towards the glass and felt cold biting at the tips of my fingers with sharp teeth. I wondered if I really could do it, run away into the white world in the mirror. The cold on my fingers felt like a warning; it didn't seem to me anything mortal could live in that frozen place.

When I had turned away, longing and afraid, the jeweler's woman—who was only my age or a bit older, although thin and hard-faced—was staring at me as if she knew what I had seen in the mirror. I would have liked to ask her a thousand questions— how the crown had been made, where the silver had come from—

but why would she have known? She was only a servant. My father came in then to inspect me, and I could not have talked to her anyway. He paid her without any haggling, but then, a throne would be cheap at the price; he had not spent half of that big chest my stepmother had brought with her.

My stepmother Galina came up to the room a little while later, after the court had been disposed of. Her carefully maintained placidity was stirred from underneath like ripples from fish darting this way and that. "Such a fuss," she said. "Piotr would not go to sleep for an hour. Is your hair dry? How long it is! I always forget when you have it up." She plainly thought of putting out her hand and stroking my head, but instead she only smiled at me. I would have been irritated if she had done it, and yet I was half sorry she hadn't. But what I was really sorry for was that she hadn't done it ten years ago, when I was small and irritating and motherless, another woman's child—the woman her husband had loved better than her, I realized, which was why she hadn't, even though it would have been sensible.

But it was just as well she hadn't loved me, and made me love her, because she couldn't have done anything to help me anyway. It wasn't that my father wouldn't listen or believe me, if I told him the tsar was a sorcerer. Everyone knew his mother had been a witch. But my father would only tell me to hurry and bear a child before the tsar spent himself in black magic, and then I would be the mother of the next tsar. Who would be his grandson—another useful tool in his hands, and all the more so if his father conveniently died off while he was still young enough to need a regent. If it was difficult or unpleasant for me to be married to such a man, very well; it had been difficult and unpleasant for him, after all, to go to war. He had brought our family this high, and it was my duty to bring us higher, if I could; he would not hesitate to spend me as he had spent himself.

And why would Galina want to defend me against such a fate?

She had spent herself so, too. She had been a widow herself, childless, who could have lived prosperous and rich alone, but instead she had brought my father that chest full of gold, so she could be a duchess. Now she might be mother-in-law to the tsar: an excellent return on her own investment.

Magreta said, "Yes, you are right, milady, Irina's hair is dry. It is time to brush it." She drew me to a chair in the corner, and she did lay her hands on my head. She was slow and gentle with the tangles, too, as she usually wasn't, and she sang very softly over my hair, the song I had always loved as a child, the clever girl escaping from Baba Yaga's house in the woods.

It took an hour for her to brush my hair as she wanted it, and then another to braid it all up, and then she wrapped the plaits around my head like a crown. My father's steward came up and knocked on the door without coming in, carrying the jewel-box. Tonight I would only wear the ring, tomorrow add the necklace, and the third night the crown, to decide matters if they had not yet been decided. I had thought of trying to slip in a substitute; my mother had left a few small silver trinkets that Galina hadn't bothered to claim, among them a ring. It was pretty and well-polished, but no one would look at it on my hand and think me beautiful because of it.

But my father would know the difference, and tomorrow there would be the necklace, for which I had no substitute. Tonight the tsar was only meant to look at me and frown and look again, and have me as an itch in the back of his head all the next day, like my father's thumb running the ring around and around on his own hand. Tomorrow night, I would really be brought to market, and the third night, my father hoped, would be a joint maneuver, him and his promised son-in-law displaying me for a shared triumph.

But the truth was, I wanted the ring. I wanted to put it on my hand, and feel the cool silver against my skin, mine. I stood up and went with Magreta into my bedroom, to put on my dress. She

tied on my sleeves and pulled through the big clouds of silk che-
mise beneath, and once I was dressed, I went back to the sitting
room and called in the steward. The ring, which my father had
worn on his big thick sword-hardened knuckle, slid easily to the
base of my right thumb, and fit there snugly. I held my hand out
before me, the cold silver shining, and the chatter of the women
sitting around me fell off, or perhaps my own hearing was muted.
Outside the sun was sinking quickly, and the world going to blue
and grey.

Chapter 9

Wednesday night in my grandfather's house, my aunts with their families all came to dinner, everyone gathered round the table in a noisy crowd. My cousin Basia was there, of course, and as we all carried dishes to the table, she caught me aside and hugged me tight and whispered, "It's all agreed! Thank you, Miryem, thank you, thank you," in my ear, and kissed my cheek, before she went back to the kitchen. And oh, why shouldn't Basia have been happy? But I would have preferred it if she'd slapped me across the face, and laughed at me, so I could hate her. I didn't want to be the good fairy in her story, scattering blessings on her hearth. Where did all those fairies come from, and how rich could they be in joy to spend their days flitting around to more-or-less deserving girls and bestowing wishes on them? The lonely old woman next door who died unlamented and left an empty house to rob, with a flock of chickens and a linen chest full of dresses to make over: that's the only kind of fairy godmother I believed in. How dare Basia thank me for it, when I didn't want to give her a thing?

At the table, I cut a big slice of the cheesecake for myself and ate it without talking, rude and starved and angry, trying to tell myself I would be glad to go away from them all and be a queen among the Staryk. I wanted to make myself cold enough to want it. But I was too much my father's daughter. I wanted to hug Basia and rejoice with her; I wanted to run home to my mother and father and beg them to save me. The cheesecake was familiar and sweet and soft down my tight throat, and when I finished, I slipped away and went up to my grandmother's bedroom and pressed water from the basin over my face. I held the cloth against it and breathed through the linen for a while.

Then there was a big joyful noise coming from downstairs, and when I went back down, Isaac had come with his mother and father to drink a glass of wine with us; Basia's parents had just announced the betrothal, although everyone in the house already knew, of course. I drank their health and tried to be glad, truly, even while I heard Isaac telling my grandfather his plans, standing before him holding Basia's hand: there was a little house that had just come for sale two doors down the street from his parents; he'd buy it outright, with that gold I'd brought to him, and in a week—a week!—they'd be married, and just so quickly as that settled; as quickly as if a magical wand had been waved over their heads.

My grandfather nodded and said since the house was small, a good size for a young family, perhaps they would care to be married from this house instead, a mark of his approval; he liked that they weren't spending too much of the money on something more grand. My grandmother had already gathered up the two mothers to begin discussing in low voices the messengers to be sent, the people to be invited, as Isaac and Basia came to me together, both of them smiling, and Basia held her hand out to me and said, "Promise us you will be there to dance at our wedding, Miryem! It is the only gift we ask of you."

I managed to smile back and said that I would. But the candles

were burning down, and it was not the only betrothal to be final-
ized that night. In the midst of their happy noise I began to hear
sleigh bells ringing, too high and with a strange tone. They grew
louder and louder until they were at the door, heavy stamping
hooves up and down, and then a thump of a fist upon the door,
knocking. No one else noticed. They kept on talking and laughing
and singing, even though their voices seemed to me muffled beneath that enormous echoing sound.

I slowly left them all in the sitting room and walked down the
hall. The casket full of gold was still standing in the entry, half
hidden beneath the coats and wraps heaped upon the rack; we
had all somehow forgotten it. I opened the door, and outside on
the white road stood an open sleigh, narrow and sleek and made
of pale wood, with four of the deerlike creatures harnessed with
white leather, with a driver on the seat and two footmen hanging
on behind, all of them bloodless-pale and tall like—*my* Staryk, I
suppose I had to think of him, although they were nothing nearly
so grand. They wore their white hair in a single braid, only a few
sparkling beads here and there, and their clothes were all in shades
of grey.

Their lord was standing on the threshold, and he had come in
ceremony: he wore a crown this time, a band of gold and silver
around his forehead with points that unfurled like the sharp leaves
of holly, with clear jewels set in the center of each one. He wore
white leather, and a white cloak trimmed in white fur, more of the
clear crystals hanging from the edge like a fringe made of glass.
He looked at me from his height with an angry and dissatisfied air,
his mouth turned down, as though he didn't like what he saw.
What was there for him to like? I was wearing my own best dress,
my sleeves embroidered around the wrists in red and my skirt in
the same color, my wool vest and apron patterned in orange, but
none of it was extravagant: the clothes of a merchant's daughter,

nothing more, even the small gold buttons on my vest and the collar of black fur only the mark of a little prosperity. Small and dark and wren-colored, and entirely absurd as a wife for him; I blurted before he even spoke, "You can't want to marry me. What will anyone think?"

His mouth grew even more displeased and his eyes knived. "What I have promised, I will do," he hissed at me, "though all the world will end for it. Have you my silver changed for gold?"

He didn't even sound malicious this time, as though he'd given up hope of my failing. I bent down and seized the lid of the casket and threw it open where it stood amid the coats and woolen wraps; I could not even have pushed it to his feet by myself. "There!" I said. "Take it, and leave me alone; it's only nonsense, to marry me when you don't want to, and I don't want to. Why didn't you just promise me a trifle?"

"Only a mortal could speak so of offering false coin, and returning little for much," he said, contempt dripping, and I glared at him, glad to be angry instead of afraid.

"*My* account books are clean," I said, "and I don't call it a reward to be dragged from my home and my family."

"Reward?" the Staryk said. "Who are you to me, that I should reward you? *You* are the one who demanded fair return for a proven gift of high magic; did you think I would degrade myself by pretending to be one of the low, unable to match it? I am the lord of the glass mountain, not some nameless wight, and I leave no debts unpaid. You are thrice proven, thrice true—no matter by what unnatural chance," he added, sounding unreasonably bitter about it, "—and I shall not prove false myself, whatever the cost."

He held his hand out to me, and I said in desperation, "I don't even know your name!"

He glared at me in outrage as enormous as if I had demanded he cut off his own head. "My *name*? You think to have my *name*?

You shall have my hand, and my crown, and content yourself therewith; how dare you demand still more of me?"

He seized my wrist, burning cold where his gloved fingers brushed me, and then he jerked me through the doorway. The cold faded out of me like a sunrise running across the wide river, even though I stood in that white forest with snow under my soft house boots and not even a shawl around my shoulders. I tried to get free of him. His grip was monstrously strong, but when I flung my whole weight against it, he only let me go. I tumbled into the snow, and scrambled up, turning at the same time, meaning to run.

But there was nowhere to go. There was only the road stretching into the white trees behind me and going on in front of me, and no sight anywhere of my grandfather's door or the city walls. Only the bone-white casket remained, standing open in front of me. In the cold light of the forest, the gold standing in it shone as though sunlight had been trapped inside every coin, and they might run like melted butter if you picked them up.

The two footmen came past me and closed the lid carefully, almost reverentially. In their faces I saw the same yearning I had seen in the market, people's eyes caught by the fairy silver. They lifted the casket with equal care, but easily, though my grandfather's two stout men had only carried it with grunting effort. I turned, following it with my eyes as they carried it to the sleigh, and came back round to my Staryk lord. He flicked a hand at me, peremptorily.

What was I to do? I went to him, graceless in the deep snow, and clambered into the sleigh after him. The only comfort I had was that he held himself rigidly straight and apart from me, as much as he could without shrinking even a finger's width from the center of the sleigh. "Go," he said sharply to the driver, and with a quick shake of the harness bells we were off down the wide white road, flying. There was a coverlet of white furs at the foot of the sleigh, and I pulled it up over my knees for the small comfort of soft fur inside my clenching fingers. I didn't feel the cold at all.

Magreta and I sat together in my father's study, waiting to be summoned. I could hear the music from downstairs already, but he meant the evening's entertainment to go on for a while before I made my entrance, not grand but subtle, coming in quietly to sit at my stepmother's side. Magreta was still sewing, talking brightly of all the linen goods that were yet necessary to my bride's chest, except her voice trailed away into silence for a few moments whenever I moved my hand and her eyes caught on the silver ring. When Galina had come to tell me to go wait in the study, even she had paused and looked at me, faintly puzzled.

I didn't try to sew. I had a book from off my father's shelf in my lap, a rare pleasure I couldn't enjoy. I stared down at the painting of the storyteller and the sultan, a thready shadow-creature taking shape out of the smoke of the brazier between her weaving hands, and I couldn't even reach the end of a sentence. Outside the window I could see the snow still coming. It had begun to fall suddenly late this afternoon, very thick, as if to taunt me by making impossible an already-absurd escape.

A roaring of laughter came faintly up through the floor, and almost covered the rattle of the doorknob, but I heard, and as it turned, I folded the book shut in my lap with my ringed hand beneath it, hidden, swiftly. It was too early for my father to have sent anyone up for me, and somehow it didn't surprise me to see Mirnatius standing in the doorway, alone in the hallway, slipped away from the feasting. Magreta went silent and rabbit-frozen next to me, her hands closed over her work. My veil wasn't even drawn over my face yet, and we were alone, so she should have chased him off. But of course, he was the tsar, and if he were not the tsar, she knew what else he was, too.

"Well, well," he said, stepping into the room. "My little protector of squirrels, grown less little. I do not think we can call you beautiful, alas," he added, smiling.

"No, Sire," I said. I couldn't make myself drop my eyes. He *was* beautiful, and even more seen close: a soft sensual mouth with his beard trimmed short like a frame around it, and his unearthly eyes like jewels. But that wasn't why I kept my eyes on his face. I was simply too wary of him to look away, the rodent watching the pacing cat.

"No?" he said softly, and took another step.

I rose from my chair so he wouldn't loom over me. Magreta, trembling, stood up next to me, and when he began to raise his hand towards me, she blurted, "Will Your Majesty have a glass of brandy?" meaning the bottle on the sideboard, with its cut-crystal glass, in a desperate defense.

"Yes," he said at once. "Not that. The brandy they are serving downstairs. Go and fetch it."

Magreta locked in place beside me, her eyes darting sideways. "She is not permitted to leave me alone," I said.

"Not permitted? Nonsense. I give her permission. I will guard your honor personally. *Go,*" he told her, the command brushing against me like a burning iron fresh from the fire, and Magreta fled the room before it.

I pressed my fingers tight on either side of my ring as he swung his eyes towards me, drawing its cold into me, gratefully. He took another step and gripped my face in his hand, jerking it up. "So what did you tell your father, my brave grey squirrel, to make him think he could force me to take you to wife?"

He thought my father meant blackmail, then. "Sire?" I said, still trying to cling to wooden formality, but his fingers tightened.

"Your father is spending gold like water on entertainments, and he has never been loose with his purse strings before." He stroked his thumb over the line of my jaw, leaning in; I thought I could smell the sorcery in him, a sharp pungent mix of cinnamon and pepper and resin of pine, and deep below it burning woodsmoke. It was as lovely and seductive as the rest of him, and I felt as though I could choke on it. "Tell me," he said softly, the words heating my face like breathing onto a cold pane of glass in winter to cover it with fog.

But my ring stayed cold, and the flush faded out of me. I didn't have to answer him. But not answering—that would be its own answer. "Nothing. I wouldn't have," I said, giving him that much honesty, trying to pry him off me.

"Why not? You don't want to be tsarina, with a golden crown?" he said mockingly.

"No," I said, and stepped back from him.

Surprise loosened his fingers and slipped them off my face. He stared at me, and then a terrifying eagerness rose up through his face, distorting the beauty for a moment like the ripple of the air above a bonfire. I thought there was almost a red glow in his eyes as he took another step towards me—and then the door opened and my father came into the room, alarmed and also angry: his plans were being spoiled, and he could do nothing to stop it.

"Sire," he said, and his lips thinned when he saw that my hand was concealed beneath my book. "I was just coming to bring Irina downstairs. You are kind to have looked for her."

He came to me and held his hand out for the book, and reluctantly I gave it to him, the silver of my ring flashing cold between us as he took it. I looked at Mirnatius, and waited grimly for a frown of puzzlement to come into his face, to see the magic catch him, but his eyes were already alight with hunger and pleasure, and his expression did not change at all. He was watching me, only me, and he had not a glance to spare for the ring.

After a moment's longer staring, he blinked once, that heat-shimmer glaze clearing from his eyes, and turned to my father. "You must forgive me, Erdivilas," he said after a moment. "Your words kindled an irresistible desire in me to see Irina again, without the noise of the hall between us. You have not spoken falsely, at all. There is indeed something most unusual in her."

My father paused, surprised; as if the rabbit had suddenly turned and leapt at the hound. But his determination carried him past this unexpected moment. "You honor my house by saying so."

"Yes," Mirnatius said. "Perhaps she might go down without us. I think we should discuss her marriage at once. She is destined for a very particular bridegroom, I think, and I must warn you that he is not inclined to patience."

Chapter 10

Every day that week, Miryem's father asked me, a little puzzled, "Wanda, have you seen Miryem?" and every day I reminded him that she had gone to Vysnia. Then he would say, "Oh, of course, how foolish of me to forget." Every day at dinner, Miryem's mother put out a fourth place, and filled it, and then they both looked surprised again to find her gone. I didn't say anything because they gave me the full plate to eat.

I did the collecting, writing the lines carefully in the book. Sergey and I looked after the goats and the chickens. We kept the yard tidy, the snow packed hard and brushed smooth. On Wednesday I went to the market and did the shopping, and a man who had come in from the north selling fish asked me if Miryem had any aprons left: he had seen others wearing them and he wanted them for his three daughters. There were three aprons left in the house. A huge daring knot rose in my throat. I told him and said, "I can go and fetch them if you want. Two kopeks for each."

"Two kopeks!" he said. "I can't pay more than one."

"I can't change the price," I said. "My mistress is away. She hasn't sold them to anyone for less," I added.

He frowned, but he said, "Well, I'll take two." When I nodded and said I would go get them, he called after me to bring all three. I went and got the aprons and I brought them back to him. He inspected them backward and forward, looking for any loose threads, faded dye. Then he took out his purse and counted out the money into my hand: one, two, three, four, five, six. Six kopeks, shining in my palm. They weren't mine, but I closed my hand on them and swallowed and said, "Thank you, Panov," and then I took the basket and walked out of the market, until no one else was looking at me, and then I ran all the way back to the house and burst in breathless. Miryem's mother was putting dinner on the table. She looked at me in surprise.

"I sold the aprons," I said. I thought I might cry. I swallowed and held the money out to her.

She reached out and took it, but she didn't even look at the coins. She put her hand on my face—so small, and thin, but warm. She smiled up at me and said, "Wanda, how did we manage without you?" She turned away to put the money into a jar on the shelf. I hid my face in my hands, and then I wiped my eyes with my apron before I sat down at the table.

She had made too much food again. "Wanda, could you eat a little more? It's a shame for food to go to waste," her father said again, sliding the fourth plate to me. Miryem's mother was looking out the window with a strange expression on her face, a little confused. "How long has Miryem been gone?" she asked slowly.

"A week," I said.

"A week," her mother repeated, as if she was trying to fix it in her head.

"She'll be home before you know it, Rakhel," her father said, in a hearty way, as though he was trying to convince himself.

"It's a long way," her mother said. That strange anxious look was still in her face. "It's so far for her to go." Then she pulled herself around and smiled at me. "Well, Wanda, I'm so glad to see you enjoy the food."

I don't know why, but the thought came into my head very clear: *Miryem is not coming back.* "It's very good," I said. My throat felt strange. "Thank you."

She gave me the day's penny and I walked slowly home. I thought, Miryem would always be about to come back. They would wait for her and wait for her. Every day they would set a place. Every day they would be puzzled she had not come. Every day they would give me her share of the food. Maybe they would give me her share of other things, too. I would take care of Miryem's work. Miryem's mother would smile at me again the way she had today. Her father would teach me more numbers. I tried not to want those things. It felt like wishing she would not come back.

I went and buried my penny at the tree, and then I went to the house and stopped near the door. There had been footprints in the road all along the way as I walked. That was not so strange. There were other people who lived along the road. But now I saw the footprints had turned off the road and gone all the way to the door of my house: two men, with leather boots, and that was very strange. It wasn't time for the tax collector. I slowly went closer. As I came near the door, I heard laughter and men's voices, making a toast. They were drinking. I didn't want to go in, but there was no help for it. I was cold from the long walk, I needed to warm my feet and hands.

I opened the door. I didn't have any idea of what I would find. Anything would have surprised me. It was Kajus and his son Lukas. They had a big jug of krupnik on the table and three cups. My father was red in the face, so they had been drinking a while already. Stepon was huddled in the corner by the fireplace, making himself small. He looked up at me. "Here she is!" Kajus said, when I came inside. "Close the door, Wanda, and come and celebrate with us. Go on, Lukas, go help her!"

Lukas got up and came to me and stretched up to try to help

me take off my shawl. I didn't understand why he bothered. I took it off myself and hung it near the fire, and my scarf with it. I turned around. Kajus was beaming at me all the time. "I'm sure it will be a sorrow to you to lose her," he said to my father, "but such is the lot of a man with a daughter! And her home will not be far." I stood still. I looked at Stepon. "Wanda," Kajus went on, "we have settled it all! You are going to marry Lukas."

I looked at Lukas. He did not look very pleased, but he did not look very sad either. He was only giving me a considering eye. I was a pig at the market he had decided to buy. He was hoping I fattened up well and gave him many piglets before it was time to make bacon.

"Of course, your father told me about this business with the debt," Kajus said. "But I have told him he will not have to pay any more. We will put it on my account instead, and you will work it off from there. And every week, you will come and bring him a jar of my best krupnik, so he won't forget what his daughter looks like. To your health and happiness!" He toasted me with his glass, and moistened his lips, and my father raised his too and drank the whole thing. Kajus filled his glass back up right away.

So my father wouldn't even get a goat for me that might make milk, or some pigs. He wouldn't get four pennies a month. He had sold me for drink. For one jug of krupnik a week. Kajus was still smiling. He must have guessed I was being paid in money. Or he thought maybe if I was in his house, Miryem would make his debt less. And if he went and talked to Miryem's father, he would be right. The debt would all go away. It would be a wedding present they made me. Then maybe Kajus would keep me working for them, but he would demand more and more money from them. Miryem was gone. She could not come and fight him. It was only her father and mother, and they could not fight Kajus. They could not fight anybody.

"No," I said.

They all looked at me. My father was blinking. "What?" he said, slurring.

"No," I said again. "I will not marry Lukas."

Kajus had stopped smiling. "Now, Wanda," he began, but my father was not waiting for him to say any words. He got up quickly and hit me so hard across the face I fell to the floor.

"You say no?" my father bellowed. "You say no? Who do you think is master in this house? You don't say no to me! Shut your mouth! You will marry him today, you stupid cow!" He was taking off his belt, trying to, but he could not get the buckle undone.

"Gorek, she was only surprised," Kajus was saying, putting out a hand, not getting up. "I'm sure she will think better of it in a moment."

"I will teach her to think better!" my father said, and grabbed me by my hair and dragged up my head. I had a glimpse of Lukas. He had backed away towards the door. He looked scared. My father was a big man, bigger than him and Kajus. "You say no?" he was repeating, again and again, hitting my face from either side, back and forth. I tried to cover my head, but he slapped my hands away.

"Gorek, she won't look good for her wedding like this," Kajus said, as if he was trying to make it all a joke. His voice was a little scared in my ringing ears.

"Who cares about her face!" my father said. "He'll have the part of a woman that matters. Don't you put up your hands to me!" he shouted at me. "You say no?" He had given up on his belt. He threw me down hard on the hearth and grabbed the poker from next to the fireplace.

And then Stepon said, "No!" and grabbed the other end of the poker. My father stopped. Even half blind with crying I picked up my head to stare. Stepon was still only small and skinny as a year-old tree. My father could have lifted him off the ground by the other end of the poker. But Stepon still grabbed the poker with both his hands and held on to it and said, "No!" again to my father.

My father was so shocked he didn't do anything for a moment. Then he tried to pull the poker away, but Stepon was holding on to it tight, and he just came along with it. My father grabbed him by the shoulder and started trying to push him off it, but the poker was longer than his arm, and he was too drunk to think of putting it down, so he began to shake it back and forth, just pushing Stepon stumbling all around the house with it, still hanging on to the other end. My father got angrier and angrier, and then he roared a noise that wasn't words and threw the poker down finally and grabbed Stepon and hit him full in the face with his big fist.

Stepon fell, with blood coming from his face, still holding the poker fast, and sobbed "No!" again.

My father was so angry he couldn't even yell anymore. He grabbed his own stool and smashed it over Stepon's back, broke it to pieces. Stepon fell flat to the ground. My father came away with a leg of it left, and whacked Stepon's hands with it, hard, until he cried out and finally his fingers sprang off the poker and my father seized it.

There was a hot red rage in my father's face. His eyes were red. His lips were pulled back from his teeth. If he started to hit Stepon with the poker now, he wouldn't stop. He would kill him. "I'll marry Lukas!" I said. "Da, I'll marry him!" But then I looked from my swollen face and Lukas was already gone, and Kajus was trying to creep to the door.

"Where are you going?" my father bellowed at him.

"Well, if the girl doesn't like it, that's the end of it!" Kajus said. "Lukas doesn't want a girl who doesn't want him." What he meant was he didn't want this in his house. He had come with his krupnik and his clever plans and got my father drunk and built this rage in him like a fire, and now it was burning everything and he wanted to run away from it.

And he could run away. He was going, and Lukas had already gone. My father could not make them do what he wanted even if he howled at them. They were rich town men who paid good taxes. If he tried to hit them, they would get the boyar to have my father whipped. My father knew it. He yelled at me, "This is because of you! What man wants a woman who doesn't know how to obey!"

He was coming to hit me with the poker, and Kajus was pulling open the door, and Sergey was there outside. He had heard us screaming. He ran inside and caught the poker before it hit my head. My father tried to pull it away from him, but he couldn't. Sergey held on to it. He was as tall as my father now, and he had already gotten a little more weight, eating twice a day at Miryem's house. And my father was thin with winter and drunk. My father tried again, and then he tried to hit Sergey with one fist, and Sergey pulled the poker away and swung it and hit *him* with it, instead.

I think it surprised Da more than anything, to be the one getting hit. Nobody ever fought him, not even in town. He was too big. He stumbled back, and tripped over Stepon still curled on the hearth, and he went over backwards. His head banged against the edge of the pot of kasha and knocked the stick loose. He went straight down past it into the fire and the whole boiling thing came down on his face.

Kajus gasped and ran out of the house while Da was still screaming and thrashing. I burned my hands getting the pot off him and we pulled him out of the ashes, but his hair was on fire and his clothes were on fire. His whole face was blistering and his eyes were swollen like big onions under their lids. We beat out the fires with our clothes. By then he had stopped screaming and moving.

The three of us stood around him. We didn't know what to do. He didn't look like a person anymore. His whole head was a big white swelled-up thing except where it was red. He wasn't saying anything or moving. "Is he dead?" Sergey said finally. Da still didn't move or say anything, and that was how we knew he was dead.

Stepon turned and looked scared between Sergey and me. His face was still bloody and his nose was all wrong. He wanted to know what we were going to do. Sergey's face was pale. He swallowed. "Kajus will tell everyone," he said. "He will tell them . . ."

Kajus would tell everyone that Sergey had killed our father. The boyar's men would come and they would take him and hang him. It would not matter that Sergey did not mean to do it. It would not matter that our father had been ready to kill us. You could not kill your father. They might take me too. Kajus would tell everyone I had refused to marry his son, and then Sergey had killed my father to stop him beating me for it. So we had done it together. Anyway, they would hang Sergey for sure. And even if they did not take me and hang me, the boyar would take the farm and give it to somebody else. Stepon was too young to farm it alone, and I was a woman.

"We have to go away," I said.

We went to the white tree. We dug up the pennies. There were only twenty-two of them, but that was all we had. We looked down at them. I knew now how much twenty-two pennies would buy. It would not buy much food or drink for three people, and we would have to go a long way to get work anywhere.

"Stepon," I said, "you must go to Panova Mandelstam." Stepon darted a look at me. He was scared. "You are little. No one will say you did it. She will let you stay."

"Why will she?" Sergey said. "He can't help her."

"He can look after their goats," I said. But I only said that to make Stepon and Sergey feel better. I knew Miryem's mother would let him stay, even if he could not do anything. But he would really be a help. Stepon was very good with goats. So even if no one went out collecting money anymore, they would not go hungry. And he would be company for them, all the days Miryem did not come home. After a moment, Stepon rubbed his eyes and nodded. He understood. Sergey and I could walk fast and for a long time. We could do work to be paid for. He couldn't yet. It would be safer for us all. But it meant saying goodbye, maybe forever. Sergey and I could not come back. And Stepon would not know where we were.

"Mama, I'm sorry," I said to the tree. The money had made trouble after all. We should have listened to her. There was a sound of wind through the white leaves like a long deep sighing. Then the tree slowly bent three low branches down towards us, each one touching us on our shoulders. It felt like someone putting a hand on my head. And the one on Stepon's shoulder had a single pale white fruit hanging off it, a ripe nut. He looked at it and at us.

"Take it," I said. It was only fair. Mama had saved me once, and Sergey, and anyway we two had made this trouble. Stepon had not asked for any of it.

So Stepon picked off the nut and put it in his pocket, and then Sergey asked me, "Where will we go?"

"We will go to Vysnia first," I said after a moment. "We can find Miryem's grandfather. Maybe he will give us work." I knew her grandfather's name was Moshel, but I didn't think we could really find Vysnia, or him. But we had to walk towards something. And I remembered that Miryem had talked of sending wool south, when the river melted. If we did that, went south on the river past Vysnia, that would be an end of people looking for us. No one would hunt for us so far away.

Sergey nodded when I told him. We went to our pen and tied

up our four thin goats that we had left on a string. Stepon took them and slowly went away down the road with them, looking back at us every few steps until he was out of sight. Then we divided the pennies between us, half and half, and each put our share into our strongest pocket. We didn't want to go into the house again, because our father was still lying there, but finally we went inside and took my father's coat from where it hung on the wall, and the empty pot out of the ashes so we could cook. Then we went into the woods.

Mirnatius and I were married the morning of the third day of his visit, me in my ring and my necklace and my crown. My father had offered the jewels as my dowry, claiming they had been my mother's. Mirnatius had perfunctorily said, "Yes, that will do," not caring. I think he would have taken me with nothing at all, but my father was a little thrown off by the ease of his own victory, made uneasy by it; he wanted to believe he had won with his machinations. The court stared at me yearningly as I came into the church, as though I carried all the stars in the world at my throat and on my brow, but the fairy silver might have been brass as far as my bridegroom cared or noticed it. For all his insistence on speed, he said his vows as if they bored him, and afterwards he dropped my hand as quickly as if it were made of coals. I could only guess he found it delightful to have a chance of marrying for spite, a girl who didn't want him, when all the maidens of the kingdom sighed at him and would have cut off their own toes to be his wife.

We left immediately after. My half-painted bride's chest was packed in a mad tumble onto the back of a sleigh painted in silver

and white—very freshly painted; it was the hasty gift of one of my
father's boyars, who had simply had one of his own done over—
and I was packed onto the seat in my turn. There was no one
coming with me. Mirnatius had told my father there was no room
in his household for another old woman, so Magreta was left behind, wretched and weeping on the stoop, hidden behind all the
other ladies of the household.

Mirnatius kissed my father's cheeks, as fitted a close relative,
and climbed in beside me. I was only grateful that I wasn't shut up
with him inside the closed sleigh; it wasn't big enough for two, if
one of them was the tsar of Lithvas. But our sleigh was almost too
hot anyway; there were heavy furs piled over us and warmers full
of hot stones at our feet and beneath the seats. He reclined back
in a lithe sprawl and held out a purse to me. "Throw coins to the
people as we go, my beloved, so all may share in our joy," he
drawled. "And look as happy as I know you must be. *Smile at them,*"
he added, another command that traveled into me like the waves
of heat rising from the warmers, but the ring sat beneath my
gloves, and the silver cooled it out of me. I only reached out warily
to take the purse, and threw out handfuls of shining kopeks and
pennies over the side of the sleigh without looking; no one in the
streets would notice that I didn't smile at them when there were
coins to be snatched up, and I couldn't make myself take my eyes
off him. He frowned and kept watching me, eyes hooded, and said
nothing more.

The sleigh flew along the frozen river road, stopping to change
horses four times, until a little while before dark we stopped for
the night with Duke Azuolas. He was a wealthy landlord with vast
fields, but his seat was a smaller town walled more for safety
against Staryk raiders than any conquest. It was a quiet place that
could not accommodate the tsar's full retinue, and Mirnatius ordered nearly his entire train to go onward and quarter themselves

with small boyars and knights along the road, to be gathered up tomorrow. I stood on the steps of the duke's house while they left, everyone who'd seen me wed, and cold went creeping along my spine. There was room in the house for some of them at least, and a great many of the knights looked sour and indignant about being sent onward. The servants were taking my chest off the sleigh and carrying it into the house. I looked at Mirnatius. It might have been only the sunset, but his eyes looked back at me with a brief red glow.

I went in to dinner with every scrap of my silver glittering in the candlelight: I didn't remove even the crown, and all around the table, men stared at me with their faces open like children, perplexed and at the same time envious of the tsar, without quite knowing why. I spoke to as many of those silver-dazzled men as I could. But I had barely eaten a few mouthfuls of the final course when Mirnatius made my excuses for me, and ordered me away to the waiting hands of the maidservants, with two of his guards to follow. "Keep close watch on my tsarina's door. I don't want her running away," he said to them, and everyone laughed at his little joke. As I left the table, he turned abruptly and caught my hand and jerked it to his mouth and kissed it, the heat of his lips burning. "I will come for you *soon*," he whispered harshly, a hot, devout promise, before he let me go.

The kiss brought a wave of color to my cheeks, and the maid-servants waiting for me tittered, thinking me eager for my beautiful bridegroom. I was grateful for their mistake. As soon as the door of my bedchamber was shut, I sent them away, instead of letting them help me undress. "My lord will help me, I think," I said, lowering my eyes demurely to keep them from seeing that it was fear and not excitement speaking. They all laughed again and slipped away without argument, leaving me alone, still dressed in my heavy gown.

Two days ago, I had said to Galina, "It's a long, cold way driving to and from Koron, and my old furs are too small." I knew there would be a mad scramble underway among the courtiers who had come with the tsar and my father's own boyars and knights, trying to find wedding gifts in a frantic hurry, and I thought it likely they would consult my stepmother. So now I had a beautiful heavy set of ermine furs, splendid enough for a tsarina to wear. I'd left them heaped white and soft in the corner of the room, and almost as soon as the maids had closed the door, I had the fur coat on, and then the heavy cloak, and the muff. I couldn't wear the fur hat and the crown together, but I didn't want to leave the hat lying there, making the rest notable for their absence, so I stuffed it into my muff.

Then I went to the tall mirror that hung upon the wall and looked at myself there, standing in the whirling snow of the dark forest. I stepped up to the glass, a bitter cold radiating against my face. I shut my eyes and took a step, terrified of every outcome: to meet only hard glass against the end of my nose, and no escape, or to go through, and find myself alone in the night, in another world, where I might never be able to get back.

But no glass met my face, only winter, biting at my cheeks. I opened my eyes again. I was alone, in a forest of dark pine trees covered with snow, surrounding me endlessly in every direction. The sky was a dark grey overhead, a late-evening twilight without any gleam of stars, and it was so bitterly cold I had to hold my muff against my lips to keep my breath from freezing my face. Thin flakes of snow drifted around me, pricking my skin like tiny needles. It wasn't merely a cold winter night, or even a blizzard; it was a gnawing, unnatural cold that tried to creep directly to my heart and lungs, that asked what I was doing here.

There was no sign of shelter anywhere—no house where I could ask for refuge. But I turned and saw that I stood on the bank of a deep river frozen almost solid, shining black as glass, and when I looked down at the surface, instead of a reflection I saw the empty room I had fled, as though I was looking in from the mirror's other side.

The door opened as I watched, and I drew taut as a bowstring, but an instant was enough to be sure: Mirnatius did not see me. He came into the room smiling wide and hungry, and only brightened when he saw the room apparently empty. He shut the door behind him and put his back to it, leaning against it. He reached down with one hand, not even looking, and locked it deliberately, the click coming to me faintly distorted, as though I heard it from underwater. "Irina, Irina, are you *hiding* from me?" he said softly, hot glee in his voice as he drew out the key and put it into his pocket. "I will find you . . ."

He began to look for me—behind the fireplace screen, underneath the bed, inside the wardrobe. He even came to the mirror, and I flinched back as he came directly towards me, but he was only looking to see if there was a space behind it. When he drew back, the smile was at last fading; he went to the window and thrust back the curtains, but he had chosen the room carefully: there was only a small window, and it was shut tightly.

He turned back with anger beginning to twist his face. I wrapped my arms around myself, the cold biting at me, while he began to tear apart the room. Finally he stopped, panting, with the curtains torn from the bed and half the furniture overturned, in baffled rage. *"Where are you?"* he shrieked, a terrible inhuman scraping in his voice. *"Come out, and let me see! You are mine, Irina, you belong to me!"* He stamped his foot so heavily the massive carved bed trembled. *"Or else I'll kill them, kill them all! Your family, your kin, to me they'll fall!* Unless you come out now . . . I won't hurt you . . ." he added, in a suddenly wheedling tone, as if he really thought I would believe him. He paused, waiting a moment longer, but when I didn't appear, he burst into a wild thrashing paroxysm, no longer searching, only smashing and tearing things like a mad beast savaging the world and itself at the same time.

It went on and on, until he screamed suddenly in fury and hurled himself into a fit on the floor, beating himself against it, his whole body convulsing with foam around his lips. The violence of it lasted only a moment, and then he just as suddenly went limp upon the floor, his mouth slack and his eyes staring empty. They seemed to look straight at me, unseeing. I stared back at them for what felt like long dragging minutes before they blinked.

Mirnatius rolled onto his belly and pushed himself first to his knees and then wincing climbed to his feet. His clothes were rent and hanging loose from his shoulders, and he looked around himself at the wrecked bed and the room he had torn apart. The hungry light had gone out of his face; he only had a look of wary confusion. "Irina?" he said, and even lifted the torn coverlet to look beneath it as though he thought I might have suddenly appeared in the meantime. He let it fall and even went to the window and looked at it again, as though he didn't remember having made sure of it only a little while before.

Still with a baffled expression in his face, Mirnatius strode across the room to the fireplace and said out loud in front of it, as though he expected an answer, "Now you've really gone and put me in it. A duke's daughter! And you didn't even leave a body. What did you *do* with her?"

The flames roared high and violently, a splash of sparks flung out into the room. He ignored them, and where they fell on his skin, the small scorched marks vanished as quickly as they marred him. *"Find her!"* the flames said, in a voice all of hiss and crackle and devouring. *"Bring her back!"*

"What?" Mirnatius said. "She wasn't here?"

"I must have her!" the fire said. *"I will have her! Find her for me!"* It

rose to the same shrieking note that had come from his lips only a few moments before.

"Oh, splendid. She must have bribed the guards to let her go. What do you want *me* to do about it? You're the one who insisted on my marrying the one girl in the world who'd run away from me! I was already going to have enough to do just placating her father for some tragic and unexpected accident; it's going to be a bit more difficult if she's *vanished*."

"Kill him!" the fire spat. *"She is mine, they gave her to me! Kill them all if they've helped her to flee!"*

Mirnatius made an impatient gesture. "Don't be foolish! He was delighted to hand her over in the first place; he won't have squirreled her away himself. She's run for it on her own. To the next kingdom by now, most likely. Or a nunnery: that would be marvelous, wouldn't it."

The fire made a noise like water splashing on hot coals. *"The old woman,"* it hissed, and horror caught in my throat. *"The old woman, you didn't want her to see. Fetch her! She knows! She will tell me!"*

Mirnatius grimaced, as if in distaste, but he only said, "Yes, yes. It'll take a day to send for her. Meanwhile I suppose you'll leave it to *me* to persuade everyone to believe a story about my darling new wife running away in the middle of the night? And what about this incredible ruin? You're going to have to give me a month's worth of power to fix it all, and I don't *care* how parched you are."

The flames roared up so high they filled the fireplace and climbed up into the chimney, orange light leaping over the tsar's face, but he crossed his arms and glared back at them, and after a moment a grudging tendril of flame broke off from the fire and stretched out towards him. He closed his eyes and tipped back his head, parting his lips, and with a sudden whiplash the tendril plunged down into his throat, a glowing heat illuminating all his body from within, so that for a moment I saw strange shapes lit from inside him and a tracework of lines shining beneath his skin.

He stood tense and shivering beneath the flow of flame, until at last it was severed from the fire and the last trailing end vanished down his throat and the light faded slowly away. He opened his eyes, swaying in a helpless, drunken ecstasy, flushed and beautiful. "Ahh," he breathed out.

The fire was dying down from that roaring height. *"Find her, find her,"* it still crackled, but low, like embers crumbling. *"I hunger, I thirst . . ."* and then it crumbled in on itself and died out into silence, the flames going out and leaving only hot coals in the hearth.

Mirnatius turned back to the room, still smiling a little, heavy-lidded. He raised his arm and lazily swept it in a wide gesture, and everywhere splinters leapt back into smashed furniture and frayed threads began to weave themselves back into whole cloth, all of it dancing and graceful beneath his hand. He was smiling as he watched it all, the way he'd smiled as he prodded the small dead squirrels in the dirt.

When he finally let his hand languidly sink to his side, as smoothly as if he'd been on a stage performing, the room might never have been touched, except by an artist's hand: the carvings on the bed had grown more intricate, and the mended coverlet had a pattern embroidered in silver and green and gold that the curtains echoed. He looked round with satisfaction and then nodded and went out of the room again, singing softly to himself beneath his breath and rubbing the fingers of his hand lightly against each other, as though he still felt the power coursing there within them.

The room stood empty and silent with him gone. The raging fire had died; there was nothing left but ordinary coals, their warm glow irresistible, even while terror lingered around them. I didn't want to go back there—how could I be sure that demon-thing wasn't still lurking in the coals? But my feet were numb in my boots, and only my thumb, with the silver ring upon it, had any feeling. I was shivering, but I wouldn't be for much longer, and there was nowhere I might go. I had to go back to warm myself for a moment, at least.

I had to, but my hand was trembling as I forced myself to kneel and reach for the smooth glass of the frozen river. My hand dipped through the surface as easily as into the water of a bath, and I saw it coming into the room on the other side. I stopped with just my fingers there, waiting, my eyes on the fire; but I couldn't wait for long. My hand was warm, so warm that it made the rest of me feel a thousand times more cold, and when no flame at once leapt up and came towards me, I took a breath and tipped myself forward into the water.

I stumbled out of the mirror and down onto the floor into lovely, lovely warmth. I sprang up at once with my hand on the mirror, ready to jump back through, but the fire didn't crackle or hiss. Whatever that thing had been, it was gone. I crept towards the hearth, and after another wary moment, I took my icy furs off, my hands clumsy and shivering, to let the warmth come back into me. But I did not take off my jewels, my silver, even through the worst of the wracking shivers that worked through me, driven by fear and not just cold. I'd known he meant me nothing good, but I hadn't imagined *this;* I hadn't feared Baba Yaga planning to put me in the oven and eat me up and pick my very bones out of the world. And I had only a cold place to hide.

When at last my body quieted, and then grew even a little too hot in my fine gown, I pressed my still-cool palms to my cheeks and forced myself to be steady, to think. I got up and turned to the room and the horror of its tidy perfection: another lie Mirnatius and his demon were telling the world, covering up the truth of ruined furniture and the torn and scorched hangings beneath this veneer of beauty. He'd taken the key, but I put a chair beneath the doorknob, so I'd at least have a moment's warning if someone tried to come inside. Then I went back to the mirror.

I took the crown off and put it carefully down on the floor. I could still see the place where I'd just been, the cold riverbank now with a small dented drift of snow where I'd been standing, already being smoothed away with more drifting snow. When I touched the glass, I felt as though I were pushing through heavy curtains, but when I leaned hard into it, at last my hands dipped through, even with only necklace and ring. So the ring and the necklace together were enough. Then I took off the necklace, and tried once more. But this time, my hands stopped at the glass, though I still saw the snow, and felt the cold seeping into the world all round my fingers. The mirror's surface had a kind of yielding softness instead of a smooth impenetrability, but it wouldn't let me through. I tried them all, and none of them would let me through alone; I needed two together to cross over. And I could keep a ring on my hand every hour of the day and wear it to bed, too, and no one would wonder, but necklaces and crowns would be odd enough to draw attention. And if Mirnatius guessed how I'd escaped him, he'd make sure I didn't have another chance.

I went and looked back into the mirror, at the snowy river-bank. I'd warmed myself through again. I could put on all my petticoats, my three new dresses one over another, all my stockings and the thick woolen ones over my boots. I could step through the mirror and be gone again. If I walked along the river, perhaps I would find some shelter. There were a handful of trinkets in my jewel-box, more wedding gifts; I could put them in my pockets, and try to buy help or shelter, if anyone lived in those woods. I didn't know how the magic would work, but I was ready to risk dying frozen in the snow to be away from that thing in the fire.

But in the morning the tsar would send for Magreta. She would come without hesitating. She'd be so happy, all the way here; her hopeful heart would think that I had persuaded my husband to let me have her for company, and that he must not be very wicked after all, and surely he had fallen in love with me already, and was ready to be kind. And then he would give her to his demon to torture knowledge out of her that she didn't have, to find out where I had gone.

The Staryk's sleigh took us flying-fast over the silver road. It ran between two ranks of tall white trees, their ash-grey bark fading to lighter branches covered with leaves the color of milk with translucent veins. Small six-pointed flowers like enormous snow-flakes drifted down upon our shoulders and into our laps as the hooves of the deer went drumming onward, the road's surface smooth as a frozen pond. I could see nothing but winter, all around. I tried to break the silence a few times, to ask where we were going and how long the journey would be, but I might as well have tried talking to the deer. The Staryk didn't even look at me.

But finally, a mountain began to rise up at the end: lost in mist and hard to see at first because of the distance, I thought, but it didn't get any easier to make it out even as it came nearer and grew great. Light passed through it and glinted on the edges, but only for a moment, and then it found a new part of the mountain to make bright, as if the whole of it was made of cut glass instead of stone and earth, and the road climbed up a ramp to its side to a tall silver gate.

The road turned strangely slow once we saw it. The hooves flashed as quickly and the trees glided as steadily past, but the mountain came no nearer, only standing there cutting out the same portion of the sky. We didn't seem to draw any closer. Beside me the Staryk sat very still, gazing always straight ahead. Then the driver turned his head just a little: he didn't look around exactly, but he made a small gesture in that direction, and the Staryk's lips tightened minutely. He made no other sign and said nothing, but the mountain suddenly began to move towards us again, as if only his will had held it off.

We emerged from the forest, and the canopy of white trees ended. The Staryk road fell in with a river running in the opposite direction, coming from the mountain and covered in a thin creaking layer of ice, large floes outlined in dark water, gradually sliding away downstream. As we came closer, I saw that a narrow waterfall from the mountain fed the river, a long thin veil falling down the side of the glass mountain that ended in a pool of blurring mist before the river ran away. I didn't understand where the waterfall came from: there was no snow resting on those strange crystalline slopes to melt and feed it, no earth that it might have drained from. But we passed close enough for me to feel a fine spray on my cheek before the road climbed up, and the silver gates swung open for us as we came.

The sleigh plunged inside the mountain without slowing, moving like a blink from one light into another, a strange glimmering that seemed caught in the walls, with twisting lines of silver veined through them, and here and there a flash of brilliant crystal in vivid colors. Darker mouths of branching tunnels split away around us, but our road kept climbing upwards and curving, gathering light until it at last emerged into a vast frost-white meadow. I thought at first we'd gone through the entire mountain and come back outside, but we hadn't: we were *inside* a great hollow space near the peak, with shining crystal facets high overhead. The pale endless grey of the sky in here was broken up into jeweled brilliance, thin dazzling rainbow lines sketched across it, and in the center of the meadow beneath that diamond roof, a grove of white trees grew.

Even sick with fear and anger and my own helplessness, the

impossible wonder of the place snagged at me. I stared up into the mountain's vault with my eyes stinging from winter glare, and I almost managed to persuade myself I was dreaming. I couldn't put myself into the picture of it. I could more easily put myself back into my narrow bed in my grandfather's house, maybe even sick with a fever. But the picture didn't let me out. The sleigh slowed and stopped instead, as the driver pulled the deer to a halt outside the ring of trees, and a crowd of Staryk faces turned to look at me from beneath the boughs.

After a single moment, my Staryk stood up and climbed out of the sleigh stiffly. He stood there with his back to me, rigid and unmoving, until I slowly and cautiously climbed out behind him. The ground crunched under my foot a little when I stepped down on it, full of silver-grey grass, crisp with white patterns of frost. It felt too real. He still didn't give me a word of explanation. He said curtly to the driver, "Take it to the storeroom," jerking his hand towards the chest of gold still sitting on the back of the sleigh. The driver nodded and turned the heads of the deer and drove away, over the meadow and around the grove of trees until he was gone out of sight. Then the Staryk lord turned and set off instantly into the grove of trees, and I had to scurry to keep up with his long strides.

The white trees of the grove were planted in widening rings, and within those rings, the other Staryk had arranged themselves by rank, or at least by splendor. The ones in the outermost rings, the most crowded, wore grey clothes and touches of silver; a few jewels in deep colors made their appearance in the next rings. As the circles grew smaller, the jewels and the clothes grew steadily lighter, and the ones in the smallest circles dazzled with jewels of palest pink and yellow and cloudy white, their clothing all in white and palest grey.

But only as we walked through the very narrowest circle did I catch even small gleams of gold, and even then, only an edge of

gilding upon a cloak clasp or a silver ring, as if it was nearly as
rare here as Staryk silver in my own world. Among them all, only
my Staryk wore clothing all in white, and clear jewels, and there
was a solid band of gold around the base of his silver crown. He
led me past all of them without stopping to a raised mound at the
very center of the grove. A great jagged cluster of frozen spars of
ice or clear crystals stood there, shining, and the tiny narrow curling of a frozen stream wound around the base and trickled away
as a silver line through the trees.

Next to the cluster, a servant stood so very still he might have
been carved from ice, his eyes downcast. He was holding a white
cushion, and upon it a tall crown made all of silver, strangely familiar to my eyes: Isaac might have used it for a pattern. The
Staryk paused when he came to it, looking down at the delicate,
fanciful thing, and when he turned out to face the crowd of his
people, his own face had also gone deathly still. He didn't look at
me, and his voice was cold. "Behold my lady, your queen," he
said.

I looked out over that glittering sea, those impossible frozen
faces staring back at me expressionless with disapproval: they
couldn't put me into this picture, either, and they didn't want to.
There *were* some smiles in the nearest circles, cruel and familiar:
they were the same smiles I'd grown up with all my life, the ones
people had worn when they told me the story of the miller's
daughter, the smiles when I'd knocked on their doors the first
time. Only this time, they weren't even smiling at *me:* I was too
small for that. They were smiling at *him,* a little incredulous, nobles pleased to see their own king brought low and marrying a
brown lump of a mortal girl.

He picked up the crown from the cushion at once: moving
quickly to get it over with and finish his humiliation. I hardly
wanted to be there myself, being smirked at by them all, but I

knew what my grandfather would have told me: those faces would smile forever if I let them. I didn't see how I could ever make them stop. The tall knights with their white cheekbones and icicle beards wore silver swords and daggers at their sides, white bows slung over their shoulders, bows they used to hunt mortal men for pleasure, and I had seen their king steal the living soul out of a man with the touch of his hand. Any one of them could surely have cut me down.

But when the king turned to me, with the crown in his hands and his face cold with discontent, I reached out boldly and took hold of it with him before he could simply plunk it on my head. He glared at me over it, startled at least into some kind of expression, and I glared determination back at him. The old anger was rising in me, but here I didn't feel cold with it; I felt hot enough for steam to rise from my cheeks, to glow through my palms. Where my hands touched the crown, it began to warm, and all around me the blade-sharp smiles began to melt away as thin lines of gold crept from beneath my fingers and went running through the silver, widening, curling over every fragile twist of lacework, every separate link.

The Staryk king stood unmoving, his mouth a straight line as he watched the silver change, until between our hands the whole crown shone gold as sunrise, strange and vivid beneath that overcast sky. All the crowd sighed together when it was done, a soft whispering noise. He held it in place another moment longer, but then together we put it on my head.

It was far heavier than the silver crown had been; I felt its weight on my neck and in my shoulders, trying to bend me. And I remembered, belatedly, that this was the very power he'd come seeking from me, what he'd wanted me for all along, and now I'd shown them all that I really had it. Surely there was no chance he'd ever let me go now. But I kept my head high and turned back to face all of them. There were no smiles among them now, and the disapproval had gone to wariness. I looked them in their cold faces and I decided I wouldn't be sorry, all over again.

We didn't exchange any vows, and there was no feasting and certainly no congratulations. A few cut-glass faces and sidelong eyes glanced at me, but mostly they all just turned and glided away out of the grove from all around us, leaving us there alone at the mound. Even the servant bowed himself away and vanished, and when they were gone, the Staryk king stood there another moment before *he* turned abruptly and walked away, too, along the glassy polished-mirror of the tiny frozen stream.

I followed him. What else was I to do? As we neared the shining glass wall of that vaulted space, I saw other Staryk stepping into openings, doorways and tunnel mouths, as if they lived within the crystal walls like houses around a meadow. The ice stream widened steadily as we walked alongside it; near the end of the vaulted grove, where we came to the shining wall, the frozen surface of it grew thinner, so I could see water moving deep beneath it, and where it reached the wall, it cracked upon the surface to show moving water beneath before it plunged into a dark tunnel mouth and vanished.

Beside that tunnel mouth a long stairway began, cut into the mountainside. The Staryk king led me up the stairs, a dizzy, leg-aching climb that took us high above the tops of the white trees. When I glanced down by accident—I did my best to avoid it, for fear of tumbling straight off; there was no railing on the stairs—I could see the rings more clearly, and the rest of the meadow spread white around them. I kept my hand on the mountain wall next to me and placed my feet carefully. He had gotten far ahead of me by the time I finally reached the top, but the staircase delivered me to a single large chamber, and he was waiting there with his fists clenched at his sides, his back to me.

It was massively long and the full thickness of the mountain wall: it ended in a thin wall of glass on the other end, perfectly clear, that looked straight out of the mountainside. I went slowly to it and looked far, far down the slope. Below me now, the waterfall was draining directly out of a large fissure in the mountainside, smoky-edged like a glass cracked in a fire. It tumbled down into a misty cloud that was all I could see from above, the half-frozen river emerging to run away into the dark forest, the fir-green trees dusted with white. I couldn't see the road of white trees anywhere. We had only driven a few hours, but there was no sign of Vysnia in the distance, no sign of any mortal village at all. Only the endless winter forest stretching away in all directions.

I didn't like seeing it, that enormous dark expanse draped with its white doilies of snow; I didn't like seeing where Vysnia should have been and wasn't, and the mortal road going back to my own village from it. Had they missed me, back at home? Or had I simply slipped out of their minds, the way the Staryk had gone out of mine whenever I wasn't looking at him? Would my mother forget why I hadn't come home yet, or forget *me*, forget she had ever had a daughter, who made too much money and bragged of it and so got herself stolen away by a king?

The walls of the chamber were hung with filmy silken hangings that had a shimmer of silver, and there was no comforting hearth, but at regular intervals great stands of icy crystals reared up higher than my head, capturing light and reflecting it inside themselves. There hadn't been any feasting below, but there was a small table of white stone set and waiting for us, and a pair of goblets already poured, silver and carved, one with a stag and one with a hind. I picked that one up, but before I could drink, the Staryk king turned and took the goblet from my hand and flung it against the wall in a noisy clamor, so hard the metal dented where it rolled away. The wine spilled in a wide puddle across the floor, and where the dregs came dribbling out there was a strange white residue foaming, from something put into the glass.

I stared at it. "You were going to *poison* me!"

"Of course I was going to poison you!" he said savagely. "Bad enough that I've had to *marry* you, but to submit myself to—" He threw a look of loathing across the room, where I realized now the filmy hangings concealed a kind of bower, a sleeping-place.

"You didn't have to marry me in the first place!" I said, for the moment almost more bewildered than afraid, but he made another sharp irritated gesture of contempt, as if I were only scraping a place already raw. So honor dictated that he had to marry me, because he'd promised he would, but it wouldn't stop him murdering me right after? He hadn't made me any vows of any kind, after all; he'd only said I was his queen, and stuck a crown on my head, no promise made to cherish or protect me.

And then he'd brought me up here to murder me, and he'd only spared me because— Slowly I went and picked up the goblet from the floor. I called back the feeling of the crown changing beneath my hands, the warming glow, and where I squeezed my hand around the stem, gold went spilling out through the silver. I turned to him with it already changed wholly in my hands, and he stared at it, bleak as if I'd shown him his doom instead of a cup of gold. He said harshly, "I do not need a further reminder. You will have your rights of me," and he reached up and flung off his white fur cloak over the chair. He unfastened his cuffs after, and the throat of his shirt; plainly he meant to undress at once, and—

I nearly said he didn't have to, but I realized in rising alarm that it wouldn't be any use: he'd already married me and crowned me because he *owed* it, no matter that I'd tried to refuse, and though he would gladly have fed me poison, he wouldn't *cheat* me. Our marriage entitled me to the pleasures of the wedding-bed, so I was getting them, whether I wanted them or not. It was as though I'd made a wish to some bad fairy for a customer who'd always pay his debts exactly on time.

"But why do you want gold so much?" I asked him desperately.

"You have silver and jewels and a mountain of diamond. Is it really worth it to you?" He ignored me as entirely as he had in the sleigh: I was only something to be endured. He had what seemed fifty silver buttons to unfasten, but the last ones were slipping quickly through his fingers. Watching them go, I blurted in a final frantic attempt, "What will you give me in exchange for my rights?"

He turned instantly towards me, his shirt hanging nearly open over his bare chest, the skin revealed as milk-pale as the marble floors in the duke's palace. "A box of jewels from my hoard."

Relief almost had me agree instantly, but I made myself take three deep breaths to consider, the way I did when someone made me an offer in the market that I wanted very much to accept. The Staryk was watching me with narrow eyes, and he wasn't stupid; though he didn't want to bed me, he knew I didn't want to bed him, either. He'd make me a low offer, one that would cost him nothing, and see if I took it quick.

Of course, I still wanted to accept—now I couldn't *stop* seeing the bed behind those hangings, and I was sure he'd be cruel; by accident and haste to be done, even if not deliberately. But I made myself think of what my grandfather would have said to me: better to make no bargain than a bad one, and be thought of forever as an easy mark. I steeled myself against the churning in my stomach and said, "I can make gold from silver. You can't pay me in *treasure*."

He frowned, but there wasn't an explosion. "What will you have, then? And think carefully before you ask too much," he added, a cold warning.

I carefully let out the breath I'd been holding. Of course now I had a new difficulty: I hadn't wanted to be taken advantage of, but now I also didn't want to ask too much, and how could I know what he would and wouldn't consider so? Besides, I knew he wouldn't let me go, and now I knew he wouldn't kill me, either, and there wasn't much else that I could think of that I wanted from him. Except answers, I realized. So I said, "Each night, in exchange for my rights, I will ask you five questions, and you will answer them, no matter how foolish they may seem to you."

"*One* question," he said, "and you may never ask my name."

"*Three,*" I said, emboldened at once: he hadn't reacted with outrage, at least. He folded his arms, his eyes narrowing, but he didn't say no. "Well? Do you need to shake to make a bargain here?"

"No," he said instantly. "Ask twice more."

I pressed my lips together in annoyance, and then I said, "Then how do you make a bargain here?" because I could see that was going to be important.

He looked at me narrowly. "An offer made and entered into."

Of course, I still didn't want to make a quarrel over it, but I could tell he was testing me again, and at three questions a night, I would be forever getting anything from him in tiny dribs and drabs like these. "That doesn't truly answer the question for me, and if your answers are useless to me, then tomorrow I won't ask," I said pointedly.

He scowled, but amended his answer. "You laid forth your terms and we bargained, until I did not seek to make you amend them further. It was therefore under those terms that you have asked your questions, and I have given answer in return; when you have asked a third, and I have answered it, the bargain will be complete, and I will owe you nothing more. What more is necessary? *We* have no need of the false trappings of your papers and gestures, and there can be no assurance in those untrustworthy to begin with."

So he'd closed the bargain by answering my first question as part of it—which seemed something of a cheat to *me*. But I wasn't willing to make a quarrel over it. That meant I had only one question left until tomorrow, and a thousand answers I wanted in return. But I asked the most important first. "What would you take to let me go?"

He gave a savage laugh. "What have I not already given to have you? My hand and my crown and my dignities, and you ask me to set a higher price upon you still? No. You shall be content with what you have gotten of me already, in return for your gift, and mortal girl, be warned," he added, with a cold hiss, his eyes narrowing to blue shadows like a deep crack in a frozen river, a warning of falling through into drowning water below, "it is that gift alone that keeps you in your place. *Remember it.*"

With that he snatched up his cloak and flung it on, and he swept out of the room and slammed the door behind him.

Chapter 11

I like goats because I know what they will do. If I leave the pen open, or there is a loose post, they get out and run away, eating the crops, and if I don't watch out for their legs they kick me when I milk them, and if I hit them with a stick they run, but if I hit them very hard they will run *always* when they see me, unless they are very hungry and I have food. I can understand goats.

I tried to understand Da, because I thought if I did, he would hit me less, but I didn't ever manage it, and for a long time I didn't understand Wanda, because she was always telling me to go away, but she would make me food along with everyone else and give me clothing sometimes. Sergey was kind to me most of the time, but sometimes he wasn't, and I didn't know why about that, either. Once I thought maybe it was because I had killed our Mama being born, but I asked Sergey and he told me I had been three years old when our Mama died and it was a different baby that killed her.

That day I went to the tree and saw her grave and the baby's grave, and I told her I was sorry she was dead. She told me she was sorry, too, and to stay out of trouble and listen to Wanda and Sergey, so I did, as much as I could.

But now Wanda and Sergey were gone and Da was dead, and it was just me and the goats and the long walk to town before us. I had only ever gone to town once before, the day the Staryk caught Sergey, and I almost didn't go then. When I found him, first I thought that no one would help me, but then I thought maybe I was wrong about that the way I was wrong about other things and so I should at least try. Then I wondered who should I ask, Da or Wanda. Da was much closer, he was just in the field working, and Wanda was all the long way away in town and wouldn't come home for hours and hours, and all that time Sergey would be lying in the woods. But I still wasn't sure, so I ran and asked Mama, and she told me to go to Wanda, so that's what I did. And that was the only time I had ever been to town.

I couldn't go as fast now, leading the goats, but I didn't really want to go fast anyway. I knew that Wanda liked Panova Mandelstam, and she gave us eggs sometimes, but she was someone else I didn't know and wouldn't understand, and I didn't know what I would do if she told me to go away. I didn't think I could go back and ask Mama in the tree for help anymore; otherwise she would not have given me the nut, because the nut was for being taken away. So I was afraid to get to town in case Panova Mandelstam didn't let me stay, and then I would just be in town with four goats and only me and I wouldn't know what to do.

But Wanda had been right, because when I did finally reach the house, Panova Mandelstam came out right away and said, "Stepon, why are you here?" as if she knew who I was, even though I had only come to the house one time, and I had never talked to her at all, only Wanda. I wondered if maybe she was a witch. "Is Sergey sick? He couldn't come tonight? But why do you have the goats?"

She was saying so many things and asking so many questions I didn't know which one to answer first. "Will you let me stay?" I said instead, desperately, because I couldn't help wanting to know that, first. I thought she could ask me all her questions afterwards. "And the goats?"

She stopped talking and looked at me and then she said, "Yes. Put them in the yard, and come inside and have some tea."

I did what Panova Mandelstam told me, and when I went inside she gave me a cup of hot tea that was much better than any tea we ever had at home, and she gave me some bread with butter and when I ate it all she gave me another piece and when I ate all of that she gave me another with *honey*. My stomach was so full I could feel it with my hand.

Panov Mandelstam came in while I was eating. I was a little worried at first because I thought by then that maybe everything was all right because Panova Mandelstam was a mother. I didn't really understand what mothers were, because mine was in a tree, but I knew they were very good things and you were very angry and sad if you lost them, because Wanda was and Sergey was too, and anyway, whenever Da came into our house I always wanted to run away, like the goats. But it was not like when Da came into the house when Panov Mandelstam came in: it did not get noisy. He only looked at me and then he went to Panova Mandelstam and said to her very softly as if he didn't want me to hear, "Did Wanda come with him?"

She shook her head. "He brought his goats. What is it, Josef? Has there been trouble?"

He nodded and put his head closer to hers so I couldn't hear the words he was whispering, but I didn't need to, because of course I knew what the trouble was already, it was Wanda and Sergey going away, because Da was dead in our house. Panova Mandelstam snatched up her apron and covered her mouth as he told her, and then she said fiercely, "I don't believe it! Not for a minute. Not our Wanda! That Kajus is as good as a thief, he always was. Making trouble for that poor girl—" Panov Mandelstam was hushing her, but she turned and said to me, "Stepon, they are saying terrible things about Wanda and your brother Sergey in town. They say that—they killed your father."

"They did," I said, and they both stared at me. They looked at each other, and then Panov Mandelstam sat down next to me at the table and said to me quietly, the way I talked to a goat when it was scared, "Stepon, will you tell us what happened?"

I was worried when I thought about having to tell him all of it, all the words it would take, because I was not good at talking. "It will take a long time for me to say it," I said. But he only nodded, so I did my best, and they didn't say anything to interrupt me, even though I did take a long time. Panova Mandelstam also sat down after a little while, her hands still over her mouth.

When I was finished they still didn't say anything for a while, and then Panov Mandelstam said, "Thank you for telling us everything, Stepon. I am very glad Wanda sent you to us. You will have a home with us as long as you want it."

"What if I want to stay forever?" I said, to make sure.

"Then you have a home with us as long as we have one ourselves," he said. Panova Mandelstam was crying, next to me, but she wiped her eyes and then she got up and gave me some more bread and tea.

It was a strange way to spend my first night as tsarina. I made a bed of my white furs in front of the mirror and slept right there upon them, so I could have snatched them in my arms and leapt through the glass in moments. I only slept fitfully, raising my head every little while to listen. But no one came in the night. I woke finally with the sky going pale and the morning bells ringing, and after a moment, I stood up and took the chair out from under the doorknob, and then I tapped on the door until the yawning guards outside opened it—two different men than the guards who had brought me upstairs the night before. I wondered what had happened to those men. Nothing good, I imagined, if Mirnatius really thought I had bribed them.

"I must go to morning prayers," I told the new guards, with as much certainty as I could put into the words: I *must* go. "Will you show me the way? I don't know the house."

With a demon wanting to devour me, I was feeling inclined to be devout, and there was no one to tell the guards that I was less so at home, so they didn't think anything of it. They took me down to the small church, and I knelt there with my head bowed, letting my lips move through the prayers. There weren't many people, only the priest and a few older women of the household who looked at me approvingly, which might be useful. The unseasonable cold blew in through the wooden walls. But I didn't mind it, a pale echo of the cold of that winter kingdom on the other side of the mirror, my refuge. It helped me to be cold, to think.

There was a statue standing in a niche next to me of Saint Sophia, bound in chains with her eyes turned up to heaven. A pagan tsar had bound her in those chains and cut off her head for preaching, but she'd won the war, if not the battle, and now the chains were kept with the sacred relics in the cathedral in Koron, and brought out when they crowned the tsars and on other special occasions. They'd been used when the late tsarina, Mirnatius's mother, had been caught trying to kill his older brother with sorcery; and even if she'd had a demon familiar of her own, they had bound her long enough to burn her at the stake.

So Mirnatius had good cause not to display his powers in front of a crowd. He hadn't simply leapt on me in the middle of the dining room, or in the sleigh for that matter, and he didn't want the inconvenience of persuading everyone that I'd run away. I tried to take heart from that, but it was precious little to take heart from. I could try to draw borders around his power, but they were terrifyingly wide: he was my husband, and he was the tsar, and he was a sorcerer with a demon of flame, a demon that *wanted* me. And the only power I had was to flee into a world of ice and die in a slightly less gruesome way.

But I couldn't stay in the church forever. The service had ended. I had to get up and go with the old women back into the house, and when we came into the hall for breakfast, Mirnatius was there, saying to the duke's wife, "Has anyone seen my beloved wife this morning?" as if he had no idea whatever might have happened to me, and there was a hard intent look in his eyes where they fixed upon her, as if he wanted to push something into her head.

The women were a gaggle around me, and there were servants laying out breakfast, and Duke Azuolas himself coming in; I took comfort from their presence and said clearly, across the room, "I was at prayers, my lord."

Mirnatius nearly leapt out of his skin and whirled round to stare at me as if I were a ghost, or a demon myself. "Where did you go last night!" he blurted out, even in front of our witnesses.

But what he didn't do was summon up his demon, or leap upon me and drag me away screaming, and I let out a breath of relief silently between my lips and lowered my eyes demurely. "I slept very well after you left, my lord," I said. "I hope you did as well."

He was staring me up and down, and then at the guards on either side of me, who were now grinning a little at him in con-gratulatory form, quite obviously unsuspecting; everyone around us hid their smiles at my newlywed enthusiasm. By the time my husband's eyes returned to my face, he had gone wary. The wreck he had made of my bedroom had included my bridal chest, and all my gowns, and his magic had repaired all of them as well. I could tell from his stare when he recognized the work of his own imagination in the elaborate vining patterns of my lace overdress. He plainly had no idea what to make of it.

I steeled myself and crossed the room to take his arm. "I am quite hungry," I added, as if I did not notice him stiffening a little bit away from me. "Shall we go in to break our fast?"

I wasn't lying. He hadn't let me make much of a wedding dinner, and the cold had left me ravenous. At the table, I ate enough for two of myself, while my husband only picked at his food and occasionally stared at me with narrowed eyes, as if to make certain I was really there. "I realize, my dear, that in my passion I was a little hasty in bringing you away from your father's house," he said to me finally. "You must feel lonely without anyone of your household with you."

I didn't look up at him, but I said in limpid tones, "Beloved husband, I can want for no companion now that I have you at my side, but I confess I do miss my dear old nurse, who has been with me since my mother died."

He opened his mouth to tell me he was sending for her, and then he paused. "Well," he said, even more warily, "when we are settled back in Koron, we will send for her—by and by," so I had won Magreta that much safety, at least, by making him think that I wanted her. I thanked him very sincerely.

Heavy snow had fallen overnight, keeping us in the house another day, and I took every chance I could to escape my husband's company the rest of the day: my old catechist would have been shocked at what a difference marriage had made in my religious habits. The duke's wife looked a little surprised when I asked to go make prayers again after breakfast, but I confided in her that my mother had died in childbirth, and I was asking the Holy Mother's intercession for me, and then she approved of my solid understanding of my duty.

No one liked, of course, that the tsar didn't have any sign of an heir yet, especially when he was so delicate-looking. At my father's table, his guests would shake their heads and say that he should have been married long ago. We could not afford a struggle over succession. If we could, there would already have been one, seven years ago, when the old tsar and his eldest died and left only a thirteen-year-old boy for heir, as suspiciously beautiful as a flower, and all the great archdukes and princes eyeing one another like lions over his head.

A few of them had even come to Vysnia over the years, courting my father's support, and I had sat silent at my father's table with my eyes on my plate, listening to his answers. They never spoke straight out, and he never answered so, but he would hand them a platter full of fresh-baked pastries made with the tart, small-berried jam that came from Svetia, and say idly, "We see a great many merchants from Svetia in the markets here. They always complain of the tariffs," by which he meant the king of Svetia had a great fleet and a hungry eye on our northern port. Or he would say, "I hear that the Khan's third son sacked Riodna last month, in the east," by which he meant that the Great Khan had seven sons eager for plunder, all of them proven warriors with large bands of raiders at their command.

Just last year we had gone on a visit ourselves to Prince Ulrich. In the evenings, after Vassilia and her whispering friends left the table, darting pleased glances at me because I wasn't threatening to be beautiful, I would stay sitting beside my father. Ulrich, whose daughter was not yet married to the tsar even though she should have been, talked of the rising price of salt, which made him rich, and how well his young knights were coming along in their horsemanship. On the last night of our visit, my father reached out his arm across the table to take some hazelnuts from the bowl, and remarked absently, "The Staryk burned a monastery a day's ride from Vysnia this winter," as he cracked them open and picked out the nutmeats and left the hollow shells scattered on his plate.

All those lords had understood his meaning: that even victory, which was unlikely to come swiftly, would leave them easy prey for the larger beasts outside our borders, or the enemy within. So far, all of them had taken that advice to heart. Only Archduke Dmitir could maybe have seized the throne without provoking a wider struggle: he had been the ruler of the Eastern Marches and five cities, with a host of Tatar horsemen in his service. But even he had cautiously settled for making himself regent, until Mirnatius was old enough to marry off to his daughter.

Naturally, as soon as an heir had been produced, the delicate tsar would have suffered a regrettable illness, and Dmitir would have gone on being regent with his grandson on the throne. But instead, three days before the wedding, he had died unexpectedly of a blistering fever—a healthy dose of dark magic, I now presumed, and the deaths of the old tsar and his son seemed remarkably convenient as well—and after the funeral, Mirnatius had announced he was too overcome with grief for his beloved regent to contemplate marriage anytime soon. The princess had vanished into a convent and never been heard from again, and the five cities had been given to five different cousins.

Since then, Mirnatius had been ruling in his own right, and no one had yet taken the risk of overthrowing him. But still great lords came to my father's table, or sent him their invitations, and more frequently of late. It had been four years since the abortive marriage, and Mirnatius hadn't married Vassilia or anyone else, and whispers said his bed was cold. I'd once heard an indiscreet baron visiting from Koron complain, late and drunk, that there wouldn't be bastards, even, the way things were going. Of course the lords didn't know the tsar had a demon to be consulted in the process. But they did know that if Mirnatius wasn't going to produce an heir, the struggle over succession would happen sooner or later. And there were enough of them willing to have it be sooner.

My father had more than one reason for wanting to see the tsar married: otherwise he would soon have to make a decision where to cast his lot, with all the risk it would entail. He wasn't the only lord, either, who saw a war on the horizon with very little chance of gain. Duke Azuolas himself was in very much the same position: not strong enough to aim for the throne himself, and too strong to be allowed to sit the struggle out. So no one in his household objected when I made my prayers over and over, and all the women were glad to help me when afterwards I asked them what the best food was to encourage fertility. By the end of the day I had a large basket full of the things that everyone had encouraged me to take from the kitchens. "You need to be fatter, dushenka," the duke's mother said, patting my cheek: her selections alone filled half the basket.

It waited next to the mirror as I put my silver on for dinner. I had a crowd of ladies trailing me, and when I put on my crown, I took it off again and complained to them that I had a headache, and that perhaps instead of coming down, I would stay quietly in my room, to be better rested when my husband joined me. They nodded approvingly and went away, and quickly I pulled on my three woolen dresses and my furs and put the crown back on my head. Then I took my basket and stepped through the mirror.

Just in time: Mirnatius had shot upstairs as soon as he'd been told I wasn't coming down. He had meant not to take his eyes off me from dinner until he'd dragged me into the bedroom with his own hands, I imagine. But I slipped through with my basket just as his key rattled in the lock, and I was safely sitting at the edge of the water with my meal of oysters and brown peasant bread and cherries when he burst through the door and found me gone again.

He looked around the empty room and threw his arms up in frustration. He didn't go into a howling fit this time, although he

went around pushing aside covers and curtains and looking beneath the bed for a few minutes; then he went and stood in the
middle of the room staring out the window at the setting sun with
his jaw and fists clenched. The last ray of orange sunlight slid off
his face, and suddenly his features twisted all at once into wild
distorted fury, thwarted rage, and I thought he might smash the
bedchamber again.

But he gasped out in a strangled voice, "Will you give me the
power to repair it all over again?" He shut his eyes tight and shuddered all over, then abruptly the fire roared up into a loud angry
crackling, and Mirnatius sank to his knees and fell forward onto
his hands on the floor. He held himself shakily there, gasping,
with his head hanging down, and then he, grimacing, pushed
himself back up onto his heels and said to the fire, "Is *this* why you
wanted her? She's a witch?"

The fire hissed, *"No! She is like the ones of winter, cold and sweet; like
a well, she runs so deep. I will drink a long time before I come to the end of
her . . . I want her! Find her!"*

"What do you expect me to do?" Mirnatius demanded. "How
is she disappearing if she's not a witch? The men on the door
weren't bribed, either last night or now. There's no other way out
of here—or in again, for that matter."

The fire crackled muttering to itself. *"I do not know, I cannot see,"*
it hissed. *"The old woman, did you get her for me?"*

"No," the tsar said after a moment, warily. "Irina wanted me
to send for her. What if she's the one who taught her all these
clever tricks?"

"Do it!" the fire said. *"Bring her! And if Irina still is fled, I will drink
the old woman in her stead . . . but oh, I do not want her! She is old, she is
frail, she will go so quick! I want* Irina*!"*

Mirnatius scowled. "And then you'll leave me to explain how
my wife and her old nurse both died mysteriously within a day of

each other? Will you see reason? I can't make everyone just forget them!"

Then he jerked back, terrified, as the fire came roaring out of the hearth. A face took horrible shape out of it, hollow mouth and eye sockets, and it swelled across the room and thrust itself towards him. *"I want her!"* it shrieked in his face, and then became a solid club of flame that lashed him violently from side to side like some monstrous big cat batting around a mouse before it withdrew again and sank back into the burning logs, leaving the tsar flung to the ground with his clothes smoking and charred away where the fire had touched him.

The fire died down slowly, hissing and muttering. Mirnatius lay there huddled and still, an arm over his head, curled protectively around himself. When at last the fire fell into dull silent embers, and he moved, it was slowly, wincingly, like someone badly beaten. But he was still perfectly beautiful: the ruins of his clothes crumbled off his skin into ash and rag-scraps as he stood up, and there wasn't a single mark upon him. The demon liked to preserve appearances all around, I suppose. He swayed with weakness, though, and after a moment looking at the door, he crawled instead into the bed—*my* bed—and fell almost at once into sleep.

On the bank of the river, I closed my hands tight around each other. My body wasn't as cold as I had been the night before, thanks to my layers of dresses and the basket of food. I'd worried it would all freeze almost at once, but instead with every bite a memory came to me like a gentle touch on the mind of the woman giving it to me, all their whispered advice and encouragement, and each taste warmed me all the way through. But it couldn't touch the ice of fear in my belly. Tomorrow Mirnatius *would* send for Magreta, no matter what clever things I said at the breakfast table, and I still didn't have a way to save her, or myself.

For a long time after the Staryk king left me, I paced my new bed-chamber in anger and in fear. The dented golden cup stood on the table, taunting me with the reminder he'd given me unneces-sarily. This was what my life was to be from now on: trapped among these ice-hearted people, filling their king's treasure-chests with gold. And if I ever refused him—there would be another cup of poison for me soon enough, surely.

I slept uneasily behind the fine silken curtains that whispered eerily when they rustled against one another, and in the morning I realized I hadn't asked the most important question after all: I didn't know how to get out of my room. The walls had no sign of any door at all. I was sure I'd come in opposite the wall of glass, and that he'd left the same way, but I ran my hands over every scrap of the surface and couldn't find a trace of any opening. I had no way to get anything to eat or drink, and no one came to me.

The only cold comfort I had was that he lusted after gold enough to marry me for it, so he wouldn't leave me here to starve to death; and I'd stipulated him answering my questions every night, but he might still leave me to be uncomfortable for a long time. And when would it be night? I paced the room in bursts until I grew tired, and then I went and sat by the wall of glass and stared out at the endless forest, waiting, but hours passed, or I thought they did, and the light outside never changed. Only a little snow was still drifting down; the blanket laid over the pines had grown thicker overnight.

I grew ever more hungry and thirsty, until I drank the liquor in his abandoned goblet, which left me light-headed and cold and furious when he finally did appear, through a doorway that hadn't been there a moment before—and I was sure it wasn't in the same place as where we'd come in yesterday. There were two servants following him, carrying a substantial chest that jingled as they set it down at my feet. But I put my foot up onto the lid when they would have opened it and folded my arms. "If you're lucky enough to catch a goose that lays golden eggs," I bit out, glaring up at the king, "and you'd like them delivered on a regular basis, you'd better see it tended to its satisfaction, *if* you have any sense: *have* you?"

The servants both flinched away in alarm, and he stiffened to a jagged looming height, glittering all over with anger of his own: icicles came prickling out of his shoulders like gleaming daggers, and his cheekbones went sharp-faceted as cut stone. But I stiffened my back with anger and kept my chin up, and abruptly he strode past me to the glass wall. He stood there looking out at the forest with his hands clenched at his sides, as if he were mastering his temper, and then he turned and said icily, "Yes—if its demands were *reasonable*."

"At the moment, what I demand is *dinner,*" I snapped. "At your side, served as you are served, as though I were a treasured queen you were overjoyed to marry. As difficult as it may be to stretch your imagination that far."

He still glittered, but he flicked his hand sharply at the servants; they bowed and quickly left the room, and soon a crowd of them came in; shortly they had laid a banquet on the table that I had to exert myself not to find impressive: silver plates and jewel-clear glass, a snowy linen cloth spread out, two dozen dishes offered, all cold, most of them nothing I could recognize, but to my relief, I could still eat them. Sharp spicy pink fish, slices of a pale white fruit with yellow-green skin, a clear jelly holding tiny squares of something hard and salty, a bowl of something that looked like snow but smelled of roses and tasted sweet. I thought I recognized the dish of green peas, but they were tiny and frozen nearly solid.

There was venison, too, raw but sliced so thin that you could eat it anyway, served on blocks of salt.

When we finished, the servants cleared the dishes, and then he picked out two of the women and told them they were to be my attendants. They both looked unhappy with the prospect, and I wasn't much happier. He didn't tell me *their* names, either, and I could hardly tell them apart from any of the others; one had very slightly longer hair, with a single very thin braid laced with small crystal beads on the left, and the other had a small white beauty mark beneath her right eye; that was all the difference I could see. Their hair was white and grey, and they wore the same grey clothes as all the other royal servants.

But with silver buttons going down the front, so I went up to them and touched the buttons with my finger, one after another, and turned them to shining gold. All the servants darted looks over as I did it. When I finished and said, coolly, "So everyone will know you're *my* servants," they looked rather more resigned to their fate, and the Staryk king looked displeased, which pleased *me*. I suppose that was petty, but I didn't care. "How do I summon you, when I need something?" I asked them, but they said nothing and darted eyes to their lord—and I realized at once, of course he'd told them not to answer my questions, to force me to use mine up with *him*. I bit my lip and then asked him coldly, "Well?"

He smiled very thinly, satisfied. "With this." He inclined his head to the one with the beauty mark, who gave me a small bell to ring. Then he dismissed them; when they had left the room, he said to me coldly, "You have one question more."

I had a thousand practical ones, especially if no one else was going to tell me anything—where was I to bathe, how was I to get clean clothes—but the urgent impractical one swelled out of my throat, the one whose answer I already knew I didn't really want. "How do I get back to Vysnia? Or my home?"

"*You?* Make a way from my kingdom to the sunlit world?" His disdain made it clear he thought I had as much chance of getting there as the moon. "You do not, save if I take you there." And then he was up and sweeping from the chamber, and I went into my bower and pulled the curtains shut against the endless twilight and buried my face into my arms with my teeth clenched and a few hot tears burning behind my eyelids.

But in the morning I got up and rang my bell, determined. My new servants did come at once, and instead of asking them questions, I tried simply issuing demands instead. It served reasonably well: they did bring me a bath, filling up an enormous and gracefully curved silver tub longer than I was tall. It had a rime of ice around the edge, and frost all over the lip of the tub, but when I warily put my hand into it, the water somehow felt just right, so I, a little wincingly, climbed in, expecting every moment to yelp, but evidently whatever the Staryk had done to bring me into his kingdom had made me able to bear the cold of it.

They also brought me food and fresh clothing, all in white and silver—every trace of which I determinedly changed to gold: I meant to go on as I'd started, and put myself in everyone's faces as much as I could. But even serving me all morning, neither of the women told me their names, and I didn't mean to give up a question to my lord for that. Instead, when I finally sat down to breakfast, I said to the one with the beauty mark, "I'll call you Flek, and her Tsop," after the braid, "unless you'd prefer me to use something else."

Flek startled so that she nearly spilled the drink she was pouring into my glass, throwing me a look of astonishment, and trading another with Tsop, who was staring at me equally taken aback. I had a moment of alarm that I'd offended them, but they both blushed a faint delicate blue-grey in their faces. Flek said, "We are honored," dropping her eyes, and she seemed to mean it. I wouldn't have thought that there was anything very nice in the names I'd given them—I hadn't tried, since I'd only been fishing for their real names.

Nevertheless, I felt reasonably satisfied, until I was finished eating and my day stretched out ahead of me, empty now except for that chest of silver, waiting in the middle of the floor. I scowled at it, but I had nothing better to do; I had nothing to do at all. And at least the king *had* met my demands. I didn't like giving him anything he wanted, much less the gold he coveted with so much greed, but I also saw plainly that this was the bargain that bought my life, and if I didn't want to make it, I might as well smash open the glass wall and hurl myself down on the waterfall rocks below.

"Tip it all out onto the floor," I grudgingly told Tsop and Flek. They did it, without any great effort, and set the empty chest back upright at the end of a torrent of silver. Then they bowed, and left me to it.

I picked up one of the silver coins. In my world they had seemed unmarked, but in the strange, brilliant light that filtered in through my walls of crystal, a picture gleamed out in pale trace-work lines: one of those slender snow-white trees on one face, and on the other side, the mountain of glass with the silver gates at its base, only in the image there was no waterfall. But in my hand, with only a faint effort of wanting, gold slid over its face, a buttery-yellow glow shining against my fingers.

It made me angry again, or I tried to have it make me angry, the contrast between that sunlit warmth caught like a prisoner in my hand, and the endless cold grey light outside. I threw it into the box, hard, and then another after it, and another. I picked up handfuls of silver coins and amused myself by letting them run out into the chest, each one tumbling into gold as they fell. It wasn't hard, but I didn't hurry. He'd only set me to changing another when I was done.

When I had filled perhaps a quarter of the chest, I went to the glass wall and sat there looking over my new kingdom. Still more snow had started falling. The thin black-silver snake of the river, winding away under its rafts of ice, was the only break in the forest anywhere, and soon the snow hid it. No sign of farms or roads or anything else I understood, and the sky was the heavy grey overcast that left no sign of individual clouds. The shining mountain was a solitary island of brightness, as if it caught all of that light reflected off the scattering of snow and ice and gathered it jealously to itself, to make its improbable sides. In the walls a thousand shifting degrees of light softly gleamed and faded, and when I pressed my fingers hard to the cold surface, for a moment they splintered into color around my touch.

"Where—point to where the food comes from," I said to Flek, after she brought me the midday meal, a simple platter of thin slices of fish and delicate fruit laid one upon the other in a circle. She hesitated with confusion on her face, but when I went to the glass wall and waved out towards the countryside, she darted one quick anxious glance out at the forest and didn't come to join me; she shook her head and then just pointed straight down.

I frowned and looked at the platter of food. "Take me where the fish come from, then." I had some half-formed thought of escaping, of swimming down a river through the mountainside, and anyway I wanted to be out of my room. I was a queen, supposedly; I ought to be allowed to go around my domain.

Flek looked very doubtful, but she went to the wall and opened it up for me. I didn't see anything she did; she touched no lever nor made any gesture nor said a magic word; she only walked towards the wall and turned towards me, and suddenly she was waiting by an archway as if it had always been there. I went out after her into a corridor that might have been a tunnel; the walls were smooth as glass, and I saw no break where panes had been joined. It sloped downwards steeply, and she led me down it very hesitantly, with many sidelong glances back; we passed chambers as we walked, what I realized were kitchens, though they didn't have a single flame: long tables with grey-clothed Staryk servants preparing dishes with careful use of knives, out of boxes of pale-colored fruits and silver-skinned fish and slabs of purplish-red meat.

I was halfway glad to see them, because they made a little more ordinary sense of the place to me: at least there were some people here doing something I could understand. But whenever one of them glanced up and saw me, they stared in open astonishment, and looked at Flek, who avoided their gaze. I suppose a queen wasn't meant to come wandering around the servants' quarters, and I was making an odd spectacle of myself. I just kept my chin up and marched along in her wake, and after another curving, we passed the last kitchen door and came to an unbroken stretch. Flek paused there and looked back at me, as if she hoped that the kitchens had been enough to satisfy me; but the tunnel traveled onward, and I was curious, so I said, "Keep going," and she turned and continued on more sharply downwards.

The light in the walls grew steadily dimmer as we went down, until it was only little flickering gleams chasing one another, a dim glow that slightly rose and ebbed, as if we'd gone below the surface of the earth and only reflections of light from above could still reach us. We walked a long time; a few times we went down narrow curving staircases, until abruptly Flek turned out of the tunnel and through another archway into a cavern room, its walls jagged crystal, with a narrow walkway around a deep pool of dark water.

The surface was as smooth and unbroken as a sheet of glass, but nets on long handles rested carefully against the wall, and after I stood looking for several minutes I caught a flickering glimpse of the silver side of some vast blind fish moving deep in the dark before it vanished away again below. I knelt and touched the surface. Even though I could now put my hand in ice-melt and think it bathwater, the water felt painfully cold to my fingertip. I watched ripples spread away from my touch in widening circles: they were the only stirring until they struck the far edge and came back to me again, breaking one another down until they faded back into perfect stillness.

I wondered how many more pools like this there were in the depths, and how many orchard groves growing within the crystal walls; how far it all went, this impossible world contained within the mountain, a fortress of jeweled light. Flek stood silently beside me, waiting. She'd done as I'd commanded, but it hadn't left me any better off. There was no escape here for me except another death, by drowning, and she wouldn't answer any of my questions. I stood up. "All right," I said. "Take me back to my chamber. By another route," I added: I wanted to see more, if I could.

She hesitated, looking anxious again, but she turned the other way after we left the pool, and led me down, as if she had to go farther in before she could find another way. The light grew even more dim, and we passed archways that looked in on more of those dark pools. Still lower down, where only the barest gleam showed, we passed another pool chamber; but when I glanced in, there was no hint of light on water. I stepped through the archway to look down: there was only an empty shaft of rough crystal going down and down with a large crack along the bottom as if a pool once here had drained away somewhere. When I looked back, Flek was standing by the door, looking at the empty pool with her arms stiff by her sides and her face blank.

We passed a few more dry chambers before we came to a junction between passageways, and Flek turned with swift eagerness into a tunnel that sloped upwards, as if she were glad to be going back above. I was soon sorry myself that I'd made her take me so far down: I had almost no sense of time passing, but my legs noticed the climb, and I was tired long before the light began to brighten in the walls again. And still we had a long way to go. Flek took me along a path running through a chamber so big I couldn't make out the sides in the dimness, full from one end to the other with a field of odd tiny pale-violet mushrooms, their heads nodding on tall stems like strange wildflowers. We passed two Staryk servants there with gathering-baskets, in clothes a single shade of grey darker than the others I'd seen. They didn't look at me in surprise; they only darted their eyes for a single look at Flek herself before looking down again. She glanced at them, just as quick, and then kept her face looking straight along the path until we left the chamber.

From there we went into a tall spiraling stair, narrow and turning around and around on a spindle-shaft of crystal. The light grew brighter, so I felt our movement upwards, but nothing else changed, and it seemed as though it might go on forever. "Take us out of this stair if you can," I said, when I couldn't bear it any longer. Flek only glanced back at me and lowered her head and kept climbing, but the very next turning brought us onto a landing.

I didn't know if it had been there ahead of us waiting or not, and I didn't care; I was just grateful to leave the confines of that stair. But we stepped off into a vineyard grove that first I thought was only another kind of strangeness, and then I understood was dead: narrow trellises of pale ash wood visible under the dry sticks of dark grey vines that had withered to the roots, standing in cracked, parched soil with small hard dark lumps of fruit that had dried on the branches, scattered among the few dark grey papery leaves left clinging. Flek hurried through the dead grove, and I was glad to hurry with her; I felt as though I were walking through a graveyard.

There were three more stairs to climb, none of them so confined, and then finally we were in a brighter passageway that sloped more gently upwards, until we were turning unexpectedly through an archway and back into my room. I'd had no sense we were anywhere near it.

I was glad to stop walking. I felt as tired as though I'd walked all the way out to the farthest villages around my home and back, miles and miles, only here I'd gone up and down instead, all inside the deep fastness of their mountain. But I couldn't be glad to come back to my chamber. It wasn't anything but a prison cell, and all this mountain was the dungeon around it. Flek brought me the glass of water that I demanded, and then bowed and left me in a visible hurry, surely glad to get away before I could order her to take me anywhere else foolish and uncomfortable, because I didn't know where I was going, and couldn't ask, and couldn't even be *warned* when I was demanding to go straight through places they avoided themselves.

A moment after she was gone, there wasn't a way out of the room anymore. But there wasn't anywhere to go anyway. I sat next to the chest and picked up handfuls of silver and flung them in as gold, resentfully. I didn't deliberately work quickly, only with the speed of dull repetition, and I found myself scraping up the last handful of silver coins to drop inside even as Tsop came in, carrying a tray with my dinner. I thought of insisting that the Staryk king come and eat with me again, just to punish him, but *I* didn't deserve that punishment, so I sat and ate my meal alone, and he made his appearance only as I was finishing.

He went past the table instantly to the chest and flung open the lid. He said nothing for a long time, only stood there looking down with the sunrise glow reflecting off his glittering-hungry eyes and limning all the lines of his icicle edges with golden light. I finished and pushed back my tray and went over to him. "The servants behaved well, and did everything I commanded," I told him sweetly: I wanted him to know that I had managed perfectly well for myself, and been comfortable, very little thanks to him.

But he didn't even look away from the chest, and only said, "As they should have. Ask your questions," utterly dismissive, and I became instantly aware that I had only made myself more convenient to *him*. Now he wouldn't have to even think of me once all day; I would sit here in my room, changing silver to gold and twiddling my thumbs, waited upon out of his sight, and a daily toll of three questions was hardly onerous.

I pressed my lips tight. "What are the duties of a Staryk queen?" I asked coldly, after a moment's thought. Of course I didn't want to be of any *more* use to him, but work made one's place in the world. If I'd improbably become the wife of an archduke, surrounded by servants, I would have had a guess at what there was for me to do—a household to manage, and children when they came; and fine embroidery and weaving and making a court. Here I had no idea what I was even meant to do, and if I didn't like it, still, I wanted to neglect my duties deliberately, and not just because I was a stupid girl who didn't know what they were.

"They depend upon her gifts, of which you have but the one," he said. "Occupy yourself with it."

"I might get so bored without any variety that I'd stop doing it," I said. "You may as well tell me what others there are, and leave it to me to decide which ones I'll try."

"Will you make a hundred years of winter in a summer's day, or wake new snow-trees from the earth?" he said, and it was jeering. "Will you raise your hand and mend the mountain's wounded face? When you have done these things, then truly will you be a Staryk queen. Until then, cease the folly of imagining yourself other than you are."

There was a deep ringing quality to his voice as he spoke, almost a chanting, and I had the unpleasant feeling he was mocking me with truth rather than nonsense. As if a Staryk queen *might* take it into her head to make winter in the midst of summer, and make that cracked mountainside whole again with a wave of her hand. And here I sat instead, in the place of some great sorceress or ice-witch, a drab mortal girl with nothing to do but make a vast river of gold for him to gloat over.

I was sure he wanted me to feel small, with his mockery, and I didn't mean for him to succeed. So when he finished jeering, I said coldly, "As I haven't yet learned to make the snow fall to suit me, I'll content myself with being what I am. And my next question is, how do I know when the sun has set, in the mortal world?"

He frowned at me. "You don't. What difference can it make, when you are not there?"

"I still need to celebrate Shabbat," I said. "It begins at sundown tonight—"

He shrugged impatiently, interrupting. "This is no concern of mine."

"Well, if you won't help me find out when Shabbat actually *is*, I'll have to treat every day as Shabbat from now on, since I'm sure to lose track of the days without sunset and sunrise to mark them," I said. "It's forbidden to do work on Shabbat, and I'm quite sure that turning silver to gold counts as work."

"Perhaps you will find a reason around it," he said, silkily, and I didn't need to work hard to find the threat in his words. Of course if I withheld my gift, I'd stop being valuable to him, and he wouldn't keep me around long.

I looked him squarely in the face. "It's a commandment of my people, and if I haven't broken it to cook food when I was hungry, or to wake a fire when I was cold, or to accept money when I was poor, you needn't expect me to break it for *you*."

Of course that was nonsense, and I *would* have done it if he put a knife to my throat. My people didn't make a special virtue of dying for our religion—we found it unnecessary—and you were supposed to break Shabbat to save a life, including your own. But he didn't need to know that. He scowled at me, and then he went out of the room again and came back a few minutes later with a mirror on a chain, a small round one in a silver frame like a pendant. Holding it cupped in his hand, he stared at it intently, and a flare of warm sunset light came out of it, not unlike the heaped gold shining out of the chest. He turned and dangled the mirror in the air in front of my face, and it was like peering out a keyhole at a slice of the horizon, orange light painting the sky with dark cold blue falling down over it, night coming on. But when I held my hand out to take it, he pulled it back and said coldly, "Ask for it, then, if you want it so badly."

"May I have the mirror?" I said through my teeth. He held it over my hands and dropped it, so there was no chance we would touch, and instantly turned and left me.

Sergey and I didn't reach the road to Vysnia. We started walking that way, through the forest, but after we walked for maybe an hour, we started to hear voices coming from the woods, and dogs barking. There were not many dogs left in the village anymore. Mostly people had eaten them because the winter was going so long. Only the best hunting dogs had been kept. Now they were hunting us. We stopped. Sergey said after a moment, "I could . . . go to them."

If they had him, probably they would stop. They would not keep chasing me alone, most of them anyway. Then at least I would get away. If we kept going together, if we had to run, I would get tired first. Sergey was taller and stronger than me, and my skirts were not good for running in the woods. But I thought of them hanging Sergey, putting a rope around his neck and pulling him up off the ground, legs kicking in the air until he was dead. I had seen them hang a thief once that they took in the market. "No," I said. So we turned back into the woods together.

For a little while it became quiet again, but then the sounds came back to our ears. First a bark far away, then another. They came closer. We hurried, and it became quiet again, but then we were tired, and we slowed down, and we heard a bark again, on one side of us, and another one on the other side. They were coming up around us like herding goats into a pen. There was snow still on the ground that had not melted yet, and we were leaving footprints. We could not help it.

Then suddenly it began to be dark. It wasn't the sun going down yet. It felt as though we had been walking a very long time, but that was only because we were tired. Instead it was a great dark grey cloud coming over the sky. A gust of wind came in our faces, smelling of snow. I did not let myself think the snow would come. It was too late for a blizzard. It was almost June. But the flakes came, first a few, and then more than a few, and then we were alone in a clearing in the forest with a curtain of white all around us.

We did not hear any more barking or noises. The snow was coming fast and thick, and there was a heavy weight in the air that said it would fall for a long time. Everyone would have gone back to the village as quick as they could. We went onward as quick as we could, even though we had nowhere to go to, only away. The new snow was covering the old snow so we could not see the icy places or the mud hollows or the loose snow. My knee was hurt when I fell upon a hard stone hidden, and once Sergey tripped and went all the way on his front in the cold and wet and then there was snow clinging to his head in clumps that grew as we kept going.

I was used to walking a long way, but we had already come much farther than it was from my house to Miryem's house, and that was on the road. But we had to just keep walking. We were not trying to walk towards the road. I didn't know which way the road was anymore. We could have been walking in circles. The cold crept from my fingers up my arms and from my toes up my legs. My shoes were wet and a few straps were breaking. I could feel it from a little way off even though my feet were getting numb. Sergey had to stop and wait for me sometimes. Finally my shoe came all the way off and I tripped again and fell, and the pot went flying off.

We took a long time finding it. We should just have kept going, but we did not think of that until after we had dug through all the snowbanks around us, and our hands were almost frozen numb. We kept looking until finally I found a hole going all the way down to the bottom of a tall snowdrift and I dug it out. There was a small dent in the side. We looked at it and it was only a pot that we had nothing to cook in. And then we both knew we should have kept going, but we did not say so out loud. Sergey took the pot and we stood up to keep going.

But then I looked at the snowdrift. Some of the snow had come off the top, and under the snow it was a wall, only as high as my waist, but a real wall that someone had built of stones. It was not very long. On the other side, it was mostly clear, except for a very big snowdrift, twice Sergey's height. It could have only been a few trees and bushes covered in snow, but when we climbed over the wall and went close, we saw that it was really a little hut, made of stones at the bottom and sticks above. An old dead curtain of ivy hung over all of it, over the walls and windows and the hole where the door had been. Ice had frozen over the dry leaves and snow had heaped on the ice. The vines broke right away and fell down when we pushed on them.

We went inside at once, without even waiting for our eyes to be able to see. It didn't matter what was inside; it was better than outside. But after a few moments we could see there was a table and a chair and a bed made out of wood, and an oven. The slats had rotted away from the chair and the bed, and also the mattress, but the oven was still good and solid. There was a pile of old firewood sitting next to it.

I brushed up some crumbled slats from under the bed and some straw from the mattress for kindling, and then I sat down next to the oven and began to work up a fire with a few small sticks. I knew how to do it well because sometimes we would run out of wood and our fire would die and we would have to start it new again. Sergey put down our dented pot and warmed himself up a little with stamping. Then he went out again. When he came back, I had gotten a little fire going. He had two armfuls of wet wood and a miracle: potatoes. "There is a garden," he said. The potatoes were small, but he had dug ten of them, and there was no one to eat them but us.

I fed the fire with the old wood until it was strong. We spread the wet wood that Sergey had brought in over the top of the oven and in front of it to dry. We put the potatoes into the oven and put our pot full of snow on to melt and get hot. We sat by the oven warming ourselves until the water boiled, and then we made cups of hot water and drank them to get warm inside. Then we boiled more water and I cut up the potatoes and put them into the water to cook the rest of the way. That way we would have the potatoes to eat, and we could drink the potato-water also. It felt like it took a long time for the potatoes to cook but then they were done and we ate them, hot and steaming and burning our tongues and so good.

We didn't think about anything all that time, and while we were eating. We were so cold and so hungry. I was used to being cold and hungry but not as bad as that. It was worse than the winter when the food ran out. So I didn't think about anything except getting warm and getting something to eat. But then we finished eating and we were warm and when I poured cups of potato-water for us out of the pot, I thought about the pot falling on Da with all the boiling-hot kasha in it, and I shook all over my body and it wasn't with cold.

After that I was thinking again. I didn't think about Da, I thought about us. They hadn't caught us, they hadn't hanged Sergey and me. We hadn't frozen to death in the forest. Instead we were here, in this little house all alone in the woods, and we were warm by a fire and we had found potatoes, and I knew it wasn't right.

Sergey knew, too. "No one lives here anymore, not for a long time," he said to me. He said it very loud, as if he wanted to be sure anyone nearby would overhear it.

I wanted to believe it. But of course no real person would ever live here. The forest belonged to the Staryk. There was no road that came here. There was no farm or field. Only a little empty house in the woods for one person to live in all alone. It had to belong to a witch, and who knew whether a witch was dead or not, and when she might come back.

"Yes" was what I said, though. "Whoever lived here is gone now. Look at the bed and the chair. They have been rotting for a long time. Anyway, we will leave soon." Sergey nodded just as eagerly as I had.

We were still afraid of sleeping in that witch hut, but we didn't have anywhere else to go, so there was no use thinking about it. We banked the fire and then we got up on the top of the oven where it was warm. I thought of telling Sergey that one of us should watch, but I was asleep before I could make the words with my tongue.

Chapter 12

lone in my chamber of glass and ice, with the sun going
down in my mirror, I broke the bread that Flek had left
me and drank a swallow of wine. I couldn't light a candle; she and Tsop had only looked at me puzzled when I'd told
them to bring me one. I sang the prayers, thin in my ears without
my father and mother singing beside me, or my grandparents. I
thought of that last night in Vysnia, the house full of people and
everyone so happy around Basia and Isaac. She would be celebrating tomorrow again with my grandmother and her mother,
my female cousins and her friends: the Shabbat before her wedding. My throat was dry with tears when I lay down.

I had nothing to read and no one to talk to. I kept Shabbat the
next day by telling myself the Torah out loud, as much as I could
remember. I confess I had never been very attached to Torah. My
father loved it, deeply; I think in his heart he had dreamed of
being a rabbi, but his parents were poor, and he didn't read very
well; he had to struggle over words and letters, though numbers
came easily. So they had apprenticed him to a moneylender instead, and the moneylender knew Panov Moshel, and his appren-

tice met Panov Moshel's youngest daughter, and so went my parents' story.

Anyway, my father had spent almost every Shabbat reading to us, the words finally made smooth to him by repetition. But I had mostly spent the time thinking of whatever work I wasn't allowed to do, or trying to imagine away a little gnaw of hunger, or in better times, coming up with the most difficult questions I could, as a game, to make my father have to work to answer them. But the memories had stuck deeper than I realized, and when I shut my eyes and tried to hear his voice, and murmur along with it, I found I could more or less stumble my way through. I was with Joseph in Pharaoh's prison cell by the time the sun went down again, and Shabbat was over, and my husband came back to me.

I didn't immediately open my eyes, glad to make him wait, but he surprised me by not saying anything, so I looked up before I'd meant to and found *satisfaction* in his face. The change from bitter resignation was remarkable. It made my jaw tighten. I sat back from the table and asked, "Why are you pleased?"

"The river stands still once more," he said, but at first that meant nothing to me. Then I stood up and went to the glass wall. The crack in the mountainside had been patched thickly over with bulging curves of ice, and the thin waterfall had frozen in its tracks. Even the river below was a solid shining road, no longer flowing at all. A heavy snow had fallen, so much of it that the trees of the dark forest were all blanketed beneath it.

I didn't know why it so pleased him, to have his world frozen, but there was something terrible and ominous in that featureless glittering white. Something deliberate, in all that green and earth wiped from the world, that made me think of all our long hard winters, of the rye killed in the fields and fruit trees withering, and as he came to stand beside me, I looked at the nearly ecstatic joy upon his face and said slowly, "When it snows in your kingdom— does it also snow in *mine*?"

"*Your* kingdom?" he said, glancing down at me, with faint contempt for such a conceit. "You mortals would like to make it so, you who build your fires and your walls to shut me out, and forget winter as soon as it is gone. But still it is *my* kingdom."

"Well," I said, "then it's *mine,* now, too," and had the satisfaction of seeing him frown with displeasure at the gruesome reminder that he'd *married me.* "But I'll reword the question if you like: is there snow in the sunlit world today, even though it should be spring?"

"Yes," he said. "The new snow comes here only when it comes in the mortal world; thus I have labored long to bring it."

I stared at him, almost too blank at first to feel the horror of it. We knew the Staryk came in winter, that storms made them strong, and they swept out of their frozen kingdom on blizzard winds; we'd known that winter made them powerful. But it hadn't occurred to me—to anyone I knew—that they could *make* the winter. "But—everyone in Lithvas will starve, if they don't freeze first!" I said. "You'll kill all the crops—"

He didn't even look at me, that was how little he cared; he was already gazing out again with those clear glittering eyes, gazing with satisfaction on the endless white blanketing his kingdom, where I saw only famine and death. And there was nothing but triumph in his face, as though that was exactly what he'd wanted. My hands clenched into fists. "I suppose you're *proud* of yourself," I said through my teeth.

"Yes," he said instantly, turning back towards me, and I realized too late it could be taken for a question. "The mountain will bleed no more while the winter holds, and I am justified in pride indeed; I have held true, though the cost was great, and all my hopes are answered."

Having completed his toll, he turned at once and was about to go sweeping from the room, and then he paused and looked down at me suddenly. "But I have gone this far amiss," he said abruptly.

"Though you are no power either of this world or your own, you are still the vessel of high magic, and I must honor that as it deserves. Henceforth you shall have whatever comforts you desire, and I shall send more fitting attendants, ladies of high station, to serve you."

It sounded extraordinarily unpleasant: to be surrounded by a flock of those smiling noblewomen, who surely either hated or despised me as much as he did. "I don't want them!" I said. "My current ones will do. You might tell them they can answer my questions, if you wanted to be kind to me."

"I do *not*," he said, with a faint grimace of distaste as if I'd suggested he might want to kick some small helpless animal. Likely he'd have done *that* with pleasure. "But you speak as though I had barred them. It was *you* chose to desire answers of me, when you might have asked nearly any other gift instead. What voice should give them to you now for nothing, when you have put so high a value on them? And how can any low servant dare set you a price?"

I could have thrown up my hands in frustration as he left. But I was just as happy for him to go away. I disliked his satisfaction and pleasure far more than I'd disliked his irritation and cold anger. I sat staring out the window at the heavy blanket of snow he'd flung over the world, even while the little mirror grew dark with night. I didn't care for the duke's sake, and I didn't care for the sake of the townspeople, very much. But I knew what would happen to *my* people, when the crops all failed, and men with debts grew desperate enough.

I thought of my mother and father alone, snow climbing to the eaves of their house, and the colder hate pressing just as close around them. Would they go to Vysnia, to my grandfather? Would they even be safe there? I'd left behind a fortune that could buy them passage south after all, but I couldn't make myself believe, now when I most wanted to, that they would forget me that far. They wouldn't leave without me. Even if my grandfather could tell them where I'd been taken, they would never go; I could send them a letter and fill it full of lies: *I'm a queen and I am happy, think no more of me,* but they wouldn't believe it. Or if they did, I'd break their hearts worse than dying, my mother who had wept to see me collect a cloak of fur from a woman who spat in the dust at her feet. She'd think I'd been frozen solid through, to choose to leave them and be a queen to a murderous Staryk, a king who would freeze the world just to make his mountain fortress strong.

The next morning when Flek and Tsop cleared away my breakfast dishes, I announced, "I want to go out driving." It was a shot in the dark at something a Staryk noblewoman might do, and yet another thin hope of escape. A lucky hit this time; Flek nodded without any hesitation, for once, and led me out of my room onto the long dizzying stair that went back to that great hollow vaulted space in the center of the mountain.

It was much more alarming to go down than up: I felt much more aware of the fragile steps that looked as though they were made of glass, and how far away below the ground was. I saw more clearly than I wanted to the delicate white trees in their perfect rings nestled inside one another, the ones in the center ring tallest and most full of leaves, and the ones on the outer edge barely saplings, some of them bare-limbed.

But at last we reached the ground, and then Flek took me through the grove along what I found a confounding maze of paths, all of them laid smooth as a frozen pond with borders of mosaic made of clear stones. I couldn't have told one turning from another if I'd had the whole day to work with. Here we passed other Staryk of higher rank, in lighter grey than Flek wore, some even in ivory and near-white, with trailing servants of their own, and they stared at me openly; a few of them with faint curious smiles for my dark hair and dark skin and shining gold: I'd put on my crown again, as it seemed worthwhile to remind anyone who saw me that I was their queen.

On the far side, we followed another tunnel into the mountain wall, but a wide one, easily big enough for a sleigh to travel down, which emerged into another inner meadow where a herd of clawed deer grazed on translucent flowers, and the sleigh stood simply out in the open—they had no need of sheds or stables, I suppose. The same coachman who'd driven us to the mountain was sitting beside it holding a few straps of harness—working on them perhaps, although I didn't see any tools in his hands. When Flek told him I wished to drive out, he silently rose and went for a pair of the deer and hitched them up swiftly. Then he opened the door of the sleigh for me, just like that.

Which was as much as to say there was no chance of my getting away by driving, and it was a waste of time. But I climbed in anyway. He spoke to the deer and flicked the reins, and they leapt lightly forward and with a lurch we plunged into another tunnel and began racing over the snowbound paths. I gripped the side of the sleigh to hold on. It seemed to me we were going much faster than when we'd come, but maybe it was because we were going down, down into the dark tunnel that led to the silver gates, the hooves of the deer making the low *tap-tap-tap* feet of dancers on the icy surface, until a dazzling-bright line of light cracked the dark ahead of me as the gates swung open out of our way and we came racing out of the gleaming side of the mountain and down the road into the snowbound forest.

I was still clutching on to the side of the railing, but as the cold air came into my face, I breathed deep and found myself still glad to be *moving*, to be getting *out*, even if I wasn't likely to get anywhere useful at all. It was still worth a try.

"Shofer," I said. The driver startled just as Flek and Tsop had, glancing around at me as if to make sure I'd been speaking to him. "I want to go to Vysnia." He stared at me blankly, so I added, "The place where you came for me, before the wedding."

He shuddered as if I'd asked him to drive me to the gates of Hell. "To the sunlit world? That is no distance to be crossed, save upon the king's road, and at his will."

When he said it, I realized only then that there was no sign of the white trees and the silver-white road that we'd traveled to reach the mountain. I turned and looked behind me. It was the same view: the glass mountain rose there tall and shining-bright, and two runner tracks ran away behind the sleigh through deep snow all the way to the silver gates. I could see the waterfall, now frozen, and the shining line of the river going towards the trees. But the Staryk road was missing as though it had never been there at all, and all the trees I could see ahead of us were dark pines, made white only with their heavy loads of snow.

I sank back into the seat, brooding, and as I didn't say anything to turn him back, the driver kept on going. There wasn't any *other* road, either: he drove onto the frozen surface of the river instead, the only path I saw between the trees. The deer didn't seem to have any trouble running even on the ice; perhaps the claws on their hooves helped them.

The Staryk kingdom seemed endless forest otherwise. I saw nothing around us, no other buildings at all, and when I forgot and asked the driver whether any of them lived outside their mountain of ice, he didn't answer, only glanced back at me as much as to say, *Ask the king.* We drove a long time and nothing changed. The day should have been going on towards noon, but instead it only grew more dim the farther we went from the mountain, the unmarked grey of the sky fading to a twilight dimness, and the trees and snow around us beginning to grow hazy and hard to see.

In the distance a line of deeper black appeared on the horizon, in the narrow opening between the trees where the river met the sky. The deer slowed, and Shofer glanced back at me. He didn't want to keep going, the same way Flek hadn't wanted to keep going, down into the mountain's depths, and my sore legs reminded me of the punishment for pushing. But if I let them decide for me where I should go, I'd certainly never make an escape.

"Should we go back?" I said, making it a question, a little maliciously, to see if he could be prodded. He hesitated, and then he turned back to the deer without answering me and spoke a sharp word to them instead. We kept moving towards the dark horizon, and soon it was full night under the branches, and I could barely see the trunks along the banks. There was no moon, no stars to break the dark sky; the leaves were only a darker shadow against the charcoal-grey of it. The deer were tossing their heads, restive; they didn't like it here, either, I could tell, and I didn't think they cared one way or another who was in the sleigh they were pulling. The frozen river kept going on into the dark, vanishing away up ahead.

"All right, turn around," I said finally, giving up, and Shofer turned their heads quickly, with enormous relief. But I looked back one more time as he turned the sleigh, and saw them: two people appearing upon the bank of the river, looming out of the dark: two people wrapped in heavy furs, and one of them a queen.

Mirnatius didn't even twitch when the cold finally drove me back through the mirror. I crept to the hearth as slowly as I could, and warmed myself at the fire, still watching him warily for any signs he might wake. His magic had made the bed into a setting for his own beauty, and even in sprawled unconsciousness he was a work of art. He sighed and shifted in his sleep, murmuring in faint unintelligible gasps, a bare arm flung out of the covers and his head turning to show the line of his neck, his lips parted.

I belonged in that bed with him, a bride afraid of ordinary things, of clumsiness and selfishness. They would have been enough to fear; I'd never imagined more than putting up with it, and finding ways outside the bedroom that I might be useful enough to earn respect, that priceless coin. But surely with such a beautiful husband I should have had the right to entertain a few wary hopes as well, for whatever it was that made women get themselves into the troubles I only overheard in whispers.

Instead that pearled shell held a monster that wanted to drink me up like a cup of good wine, drained to the dregs and put down empty, and I'd have to outwit it every day just to live. I wasn't sure who was master and who was servant anymore, but that demon had put Mirnatius on his throne seven years ago, and fed him with magic power since, and he was plainly ready and willing to hand me over in payment, with only a few minor complaints about the inconvenience of tidying up whatever ruin it left behind of me, like the rags of his half-burned clothing discarded on the floor.

I threw the scraps onto the fire and slept a little by the hearth, fitfully. As soon as morning came, I got up and hurried into my nightgown as if I'd worn it all night, and then rang the bell so the servants came in at once. Mirnatius started awake, looking around himself wildly at the unexpected noise, but they were already in the room. I asked them to ready a bath and bring us breakfast, and for another to help me dress, so they began bustling around the bedchamber without leaving us alone together, and then asked my husband in sweet tones, "Did you sleep well, my lord?"

He stared at me with baffled indignation, but there were four people in the room. "Very well," he said after a moment, without ever taking his eyes from me, and also, I could see, without thinking of what he was saying, and what it would mean to my position in his court when his servants told everyone that the tsar, so worry-ingly uninterested in the pleasures of the flesh, had definitely slept in his wife's bedchamber instead of his own, and slept well.

I don't imagine he thought much about maintaining the favor of his courtiers, since he could simply mesmerize them when they were inclined to disagree. He only preferred to ration their dis-pleasure, not to waste too much of his demon-borrowed magic. But I needed every weapon I could get hold of, anything that might be of use, and so I climbed into the bed with him—he edged back from me a little, eyeing me sidelong—and when they brought the tray I poured his tea, which I had noticed he liked to take very sweet, and added several spoonfuls of cherries before I presented the glass to him. He looked alarmed after he tasted it, as though he thought that was magic, too.

He couldn't say anything to me with all the servants there—and they weren't going anywhere when there was such gossip to be gathered, since I had given them an excuse to stay. Especially not any of the serving-maids. Mirnatius had no clothes on, after the wreck the demon had made of them last night, and the covers slipped from his bare shoulders and lean chest. The girls all darted flirtatious looks at him when they thought I wasn't looking at them, and took every excuse to hover near him. They might as well have saved the effort: he never took his eyes away from me, only took bites from my hands warily, and answered all my small conversation in kind, until the bath was filled, and then I got up and said, "I will go to prayers while you bathe, my lord," and es-caped.

But when I came out of the church this time, the sleigh was waiting in the courtyard with our baggage going onto it. "We'll be on our way to Koron, my dove," Mirnatius said to me in the hall, with narrowed eyes, and I had no choice: I was going to have to get into the sleigh alone with him and drive into the dark woods, and on to his palace, full of his own soldiers and courtiers.

I went inside and put on my silver necklace and my three wool dresses and my furs and came down carrying my own jewel-box: nothing very unusual about that; my own stepmother always kept charge of her own as well, whenever she traveled, and no one was to know that there was nothing inside but my crown, or that all the rest of my trinkets had been stuffed in among my clothes to make the box lighter. I put it between my side and the sleigh. If I had to, I would jump off with the box, and run into the forest to find a reflection of frozen water to flee through.

But the demon-hunger didn't gleam red in Mirnatius's eyes as we set off, and I remembered I had never seen it there in daylight, only after night had fallen. Instead he waited until we were well away from the house—all the women of it waving farewells to me with their kerchiefs—and then hissed at me in his own human voice, "I don't know where you're scurrying away to every night, but don't think I'll let you keep on running off."

"You'll have to forgive me, dear husband," I said, after a moment, considering carefully: what did I want him to think, or know that I knew? "I made my vows to you, but someone else keeps coming to the bedroom in your place. Squirrels run on instinct when a hunter comes too close."

He stiffened back from me into the corner of the sleigh and settled into a seething watchful silence, his eyes on me. I sat carefully ordinary, relaxed against the cushions and looking straight ahead. We were gliding swiftly through the deep hushed stillness of the forest, the tree branches bowed under the weight of the fresh snow, and I let the steady unchanging landscape soothe me; it might have been cold, but not compared with the winter kingdom where I spent my evenings, and my ring was a chill comfort on my finger.

We drove for a long time, and then abruptly Mirnatius said, "And where do squirrels run *to*, when they want to hide?"

I looked at him, a little puzzled. I'd just told him that I knew about his possessing demon and its plans for me, so he couldn't expect me to tell him anything, or cooperate with him at all. But when I didn't answer, he scowled at me as sulky as a thwarted child, and leaned in and hissed, *"Tell me where you go!"*

The heat of his power washed over me and flowed into my hungry ring, leaving me untouched. I almost asked him why he was wasting his strength: he already knew it wouldn't work. But I suppose he'd come to rely so much on his magic that he'd never learned to think. The only thing that had ever done me any good in my father's house was thinking: no one had cared what I wanted, or whether I was happy. I'd had to find my own way to anything I wanted. I'd never been grateful for that before now, when what I wanted was my life.

But I could tell that if I only sat there saying nothing, Mirnatius was likely to lose his temper. The storm clouds were already gathering on his brow, and even if his demon wasn't going to put in an appearance until after nightfall, he could still have his perfectly ordinary guards throw me into a prison cell to wait for him. People would be really shocked, of course, if he had his new wife thrown into a cell and she then disappeared without explanation, and my father would undoubtedly make use of it—but Mirnatius was giving me very little reason to think he would look far enough ahead to beware those consequences.

Unless I made him do so. "Why didn't you marry Vassilia four years ago?" I asked him sharply, even as he opened his mouth to shout at me again.

It did have the useful effect of interrupting the rise of his temper. "What?" he said, blankly, as if even the question made no sense to him.

"Prince Ulrich's daughter," I said. "He has ten thousand men and the salt mine, and the king of Niemsk would gladly let him swear fealty if you were killed. You needed to secure him, after you had Archduke Dmitir killed. Why didn't you marry her?"

Scowling and bafflement were wrestling for control of his face. "You sound like one of those old hens who cluck at me in council."

"That you never listen to, and enchant into stupors when they pester you too much?" I said, and scowling won; but it wasn't the same kind of anger: being lectured about politics must have been a familiar annoyance to him. "But they aren't wrong. Lithvas needs an heir, and if you aren't going to provide one, you might as well be overthrown sooner than later. And now that you've married *me,* instead of Vassilia, Ulrich might decide to do it before you have the chance."

"No one's going to *overthrow* me," he snapped, as if I was insulting him.

"How will you stop them?" I asked. "If Ulrich marries Vassilia to Prince Casimir, they aren't going to come visit you in Koron so you can use magic to order them not to march an army on the city. Can you control their minds from three hundred miles off? Can you stop one of a thousand archers from shooting you across a battlefield, or make ten assassins drop their swords all at once, if they burst into your chamber determined to stab you?"

He stared at me as though he'd never tried to answer any such questions even for himself. Likely he thought all his advisors fools and worrywarts who didn't know about his magic, which would save him from everything and anything that might threaten. But his demon didn't seem all-powerful, and his mother's sorcery hadn't saved *her* from the stake. He seemed to feel less invincible himself in the face of a pointed question, and he certainly didn't say I was wrong about the limits of his power.

"Why should *you* care?" he threw at me instead, as if he thought I was pretending some sort of deep concern for his welfare. "Surely you'd be delighted."

"My pleasure would last only until they stabbed me right alongside you," I said. "Ulrich and Casimir would prefer my father as an ally rather than an enemy, but they don't *have* to have him, and they won't risk me inconveniently producing an heir after they've taken your head off. Of course," I added, "that's only if *you* haven't murdered me first, in some suspicious way, and given all of them together a magnificent excuse to march on you," which was the point I *really* wanted to make.

Mirnatius subsided, brooding, back into his corner, but I took it as a small victory that he didn't sit staring at me anymore, but looked out of the sleigh, frowning over the ideas I'd shoved into his head, which he'd evidently done so well at avoiding before now.

We drove all the long cold day; a few times the coachman stopped to rest the horses, and twice changed them at the stables of one middling boyar or another, people bowing energetically. I made sure to climb out both times and walk around the courtyard and speak kindly to our hosts, saying a few favorable words about the children trotted out to make their bows. I wanted to be mem-orable to as many people as I could manage, if he was going to try making everyone forget me. Mirnatius held himself aloof and only spent the entire time staring at me with hooded eyes, which did nicely to make me look like a cherished bride.

The night was a long time in coming: strange on such a cold, wintry day, with the unnatural snow so thick on the ground. I was grateful for it, but even so, the setting of the sun was beginning to light the red glow in Mirnatius's eyes as we drew into the courtyard of his palace in Koron. The walls were bristling with his soldiers, and Magreta was standing on the steps, her hands gripped tight at her breast, small and old in her dark cloak between the guards on either side of her, as if he'd sent men back to Vysnia last night, and had them drag her pell-mell to get here before dark.

When I climbed the steps, she put her arms around me and wept a little, saying, "Dushenka, dushenka." She did thank me for remembering an old woman and sending for her, but I had been unfair to her: her voice trembled, and her hands gripped too hard at me. She understood that we were in mortal danger.

I made a show of my own, thanking my husband for his kindness and the wonderful surprise of finding her here, and I steeled myself and kissed him on the steps in front of his guards, startling him; he only thought of it as a weapon for *him* to use, I suppose. So he didn't move when I brushed his warm mouth with mine and then quickly darted away from him again, as though I were embarrassed by my own daring. I turned to the guards, and asked Magreta if they'd taken good care of her, and thanked them when she nodded and said she'd felt so safe, even on the long road from Vysnia.

"Tell me your names, so I will remember them," I said, and took my hand out of my muff to give to them, with my ring gleaming upon it, and they fumbled over it and stammered back at me, although they had surely been ordered to go and get the old woman no matter what anyone said to them, or how she wailed, and had thought of themselves as jailers, not as escort. Some of the stammering was the ring's magic, but the rest, I suspected, was the subtler magic of contrast; I didn't imagine Mirnatius showed much courtesy to his servants. "Matas and Vladas," I repeated. "Thank you for your care of my old nanushka, and now let us go inside: you must have a drink of hot krupnik in the kitchen after your long trip."

Mirnatius could hardly take back such a small kindness without looking peculiar as well as petty, but of course he didn't like his men taking any sort of order from me. "You and your nurse will go up to my rooms and wait for me," he said coldly, as soon as he followed me into the halls, and he beckoned sharply to two other guardsmen at the door. "Take them upstairs and wait in the room with them until I arrive," he ordered, the very trap I'd feared, and stalked away himself into the great hall. I gripped Magreta's hand tight as we went up the stairs. She held on with equal force, and didn't ask me if my husband was kind to me, or if I was happy.

"Will you tell me, did I do something wrong, to tell the guards to go have krupnik?" I asked one of the guards, as we went upstairs. "Does my lord disapprove of drink?"

"No, my lady," the guard said, darting a look at me.

"Oh," I said, with a show of being a little downcast, disappointed in my husband's mercurial mood. "I suppose some affairs of state must be worrying him. Well, I will try and take his mind off it tonight. Perhaps we will have dinner in the room. Magreta, you will brush out my hair, and put it up fresh."

The bedchamber was as large as my father's ballroom and absurd in its gilded and impractical splendor. I hardly had to study to look wide-eyed all around myself, at the vast mural nearly twenty feet overhead—of Eve tempted by the serpent, which struck me as particularly unjust under the circumstances—and the bed itself, which could have served nicely as a bedroom on its own, being built into a large alcove in the wall and framed with golden scrollwork and pillars and rich curtains of silk damask subtly patterned with lighter threads. The windows were set in doorframes that could be swung open to a balcony outside of delicate wrought-iron. Trees from the garden overhung the edge of the balcony, covered presently with snow.

There were four separate fireplaces in the room, which were all blackened with smoke and roaring even in the middle of the day, in May: there was a servant feeding them even when I came in. It was a room for a duke in Salvia, or in Longines, some country where winter only glanced in briefly and in passing. No one of sense would have built this room here in Lithvas, and indeed I could see no one of sense *had:* there were faint cracks in the walls where Mirnatius himself had surely ordered them to knock out the floors above and the rooms beside, to make this ridiculous space.

But for all its excess, the chamber was still beautiful—extravagant and inconvenient and uncomfortable, yes, but taken all together it somehow skirted the edge of taste to be lush and not simply ludicrous. It was out of a book of fairy-stories painted by an inventive hand, and everything harmonized. Just barely, but that only made it somehow more impressive, like watching a juggler keep seven sharp knives in the air at once, knowing one slip would bring them all down in disaster. I think anyone would have found it difficult to stand in that room and not however grudgingly be won over by it. The guards themselves stood looking around it when they came in with us, forgetting to look stern and unyielding.

They didn't say anything when I took my jewel-case and led Magreta behind the bathing-screen. Another fireplace was going on the other side, too, warming the air around a truly magnificent bath—that was also gilded, and so large I could have stretched in it my full length. But more important, beside it stood an even more magnificent mirror, as though Mirnatius liked to admire the work of art he was when he stepped from his bath.

I called to the guards from behind the screen to ask them to send down for tea, while Magreta quickly in response to my motioning hands put the necklace and the crown upon me. She looked puzzled even as she obeyed, and still more when I wrapped my spare cloak around her, and knelt down to drag up the heavy fur before the fireplace, to wrap around her shoulders. She clutched it around herself when I put the ends into her hands, and didn't say anything out loud, but her mouth opened and moved, silently forming the questions she wanted to utter. I put my finger to my lips to keep her silent, and beckoned her over to the mirror.

The dark forest stood on the other side, blanketed white with deep snow. I didn't know if it would work, if I could bring her through with me, but I had no other hope at all. Even as I reached

for Magreta's hand, I heard a noise in the corridor, footsteps coming, and as the door banged open violently I heard the demon
hiss, in Mirnatius's voice, *"Where is Irina, where is my sweet?"*

But Magreta had given a small gasp: I had taken her hand,
and she was staring at the mirror, her face pale, and pulling against
my grip instinctively. I held on tighter. "Don't let go of me," I
whispered to her, and after a single frightened look behind her
shoulder, she jerked her head in a nod. I turned to the mirror and
stepped through, pulling her with me, out onto the frozen bank of
the river.

Chapter 13

In the morning Panov Mandelstam came in and stamped snow off his boots and told Panova Mandelstam quietly, "They didn't catch them. The snow came first." So I was glad for the snow. Although then I didn't know if I should be glad for the snow, because what if Wanda and Sergey were frozen to death somewhere, but then I decided I would be glad for the snow, because I had been cold sometimes working out in the snow and sleepy and Da would smack me on the head to wake me up and say did I want to freeze to death, and I didn't, but it was only falling asleep, and that didn't hurt and you wouldn't be scared. I wondered if Da was scared when he died. It had sounded like he was scared.

For breakfast Panova Mandelstam gave me two bowls of porridge with some milk on top and some dry blueberries and she put a little bit of brown sugar on top, and I ate it and it was very good and sweet. Then I went to take care of the goats, because that was what Wanda had said to do. "They should have a hot breakfast, too, on such a cold day," Panova Mandelstam said, and helped me cook up a big pot of mash. I made sure to give my goats big helpings. They looked skinny next to the Mandelstams' goats, and the other goats had been butting them and biting them yesterday. But now the other goats were glad for more company because their coats had already been cut, and my goats still had theirs although theirs were full of burs and dirt. They all huddled together in the shed after they ate up all the hot mash.

There was a lot of snow in the yard. I shoveled some of it into big heaps so the goats and chickens could get to the grass. The ground was frozen, but I took out the nut from the white tree and looked at it and wondered if maybe I should plant it here. But I wasn't sure, and I didn't want to make a mistake, so I put it back in my pocket instead and went back inside. For lunch Panova Mandelstam gave me three pieces of bread with butter and jam and two eggs and some carrots and dried plums cooked together. That was very good too.

Then it was the afternoon, and I didn't know what to do. Panova Mandelstam sat down at her spinning wheel, but I didn't know how to do that, and Panov Mandelstam was reading a book, and I didn't know how to do that. "What should I do?" I asked.

"Why don't you go out and play, Stepon?" Panova Mandelstam said, but I didn't know how to do that either, and anyway Panov Mandelstam said to her, "The other boys . . ." and she pressed her mouth together and nodded back to him, and they meant that the boys in town would be mean to me, because I had maybe helped kill my father, or just because I was a new goat.

"What did Wanda do when she was here?" I asked, but I remembered as soon as I asked. "She did the collecting."

"But you are too young to do that," Panova Mandelstam said. "Why don't you go and see if you can find some good mushrooms in the forest. Do you know how to tell good ones to eat?"

"Yes," I said, and she gave me the basket, but there was a lot of snow in the forest today, so it didn't really make sense to go picking mushrooms. And I went outside and looked at all the snow and I didn't see any mushrooms. Then I thought I would try to do the collecting even though I was too young, because if the Mandelstams weren't doing it, and Wanda wasn't doing it, then I didn't see who else there was to do it. Someone else had lived in the house also, I remembered Wanda talking about them, but I couldn't remember their name. It made me feel strange trying to remember when the name didn't come, because names always came when I wanted them to. But anyway I was sure there was no one else in the house or the barn now, because I looked around all over for them. If I found them then I could just have asked them what their name was and I would stop feeling strange. I even looked inside the chicken coop in case maybe someone had crawled in there, but there were only chickens. So there was really no one else but me.

It was the day after market day in the fourth week of the month, so that meant Wanda was going to collect from the two villages down the cart-track going southeast from town and the names to collect from were Rybernik, Hurol, Gnadys, Provna, Tsumil, and Dvuri. I said the names over to myself on the way because they made a nice song in my head. When I got there I knocked on all the doors I saw and asked their name and if they said it was one of those names then I held out the basket. They looked at me and then they put things into it. Panova Tsumil said to me, softly, "Poor child!" and put her hand on my head. "And the Jews are already putting you to work!"

"No?" I said, but she only shook her head and put some balls of yarn in the basket and then gave me a thing to eat that was called a cookie. Wanda had brought some home once that Panova Mandelstam gave her and they were very nice. So I didn't argue with Panova Tsumil, I just ate the cookie, which was also very good and said, "Thank you," and then I went on.

Then I brought back the basket to Panova Mandelstam and told her, "I am not too young after all." She looked in the basket and then she was very upset. I didn't know why, but then Panov Mandelstam put his hand on my shoulder very gently and said, "Stepon, we should have explained. It is very important not to make any mistakes when collecting, and to keep a careful account. Do you think if you try very hard you can remember and tell us exactly where you went, and exactly who gave you each thing?"

"Yes," I said. "This day of the month Wanda goes to Rybernik, Hurol, Gnadys, Provna, Tsumil, and Dvuri," and then I pointed to each thing and told him who gave it to me. I thought Panova Mandelstam was still unhappy afterwards, but she gave me some dumplings with a thick sauce with carrots and potatoes and real chicken meat in it, and a cup of tea with two big spoons of honey, so I must have been wrong.

Sergey and I did not like staying in the little house, but we couldn't leave right away. The first day when we woke up, there was snow drifted over the threshold, and on all the windowsills and beneath them in big heaps. When we went outside, all the forest was white and white, only little bits of dark trunks showing and all the trees bent low. They had started to put out leaves before the snow came, so now they were weighed down. We didn't know where the road was.

We looked all around the house. We found many things. There were potatoes and carrots in the garden, and a shed where goats had lived with one heap of old straw and another heap of shorn wool as tall as my head. It had not been washed, and the bottom layers were stained and had mold, but there was still good wool at the top. Up on a shelf there was a basket and in a corner a shovel that would make it easier to dig potatoes. Inside the house we found a folded blanket on a shelf.

The sun was out all that day and it was warm even though the snow was still on the ground. It began to melt quickly. Sergey went out to get firewood and I put the potatoes and carrots to cook and then I started to make us new shoes out of the straw. One of mine was already lost, and the rest were falling apart. I used some of the wool, too, so the shoes wouldn't be so hard, since we didn't have any real shoe bark. The wool was full of burs and nettles and thorns. I made a pot of water and washed it in there, but I had no comb. The spines stuck my hands and made them sting as I worked, but we had to have shoes.

I finished a pair for Sergey by the time he came back with the firewood. He tried them on and they weren't too bad. I put more wool inside them and that helped. We ate the potatoes and carrots. After that I made my shoes, and when those were done I made covers for the windows. Sergey found a bird nest in a tree with eggs that were speckled brown, so we could take them. We ate those and then it was dark, so we went to sleep again.

In the morning we found a grain box, because the snow had melted off its sides, half full of oats. We looked inside it. There was enough for us to stay and eat for a long time. Sergey and I looked at each other. The witch had not come back, and that made me think maybe she would never come back. But I didn't like the way we were finding so many things.

"Maybe we should go," I said to Sergey reluctantly. I did and did not want to. Who knew if we would find the road? But then Sergey looked up, and I looked up, too, and the sun was going away. It had already started to snow again. We could not go anywhere.

Sergey did not say anything for a moment. He was unhappy, too. Then he said, "We could fix the chair and the bed. In case anyone ever comes back."

That seemed like a very good idea to me. If we were only taking potatoes and carrots and wool and oats and staying in this
house without giving anything back, then we would be thieves.
Someone who came back here would be angry and they would be
right to be angry. We had to pay it back.

So I took the oats inside, and while they cooked we made a
new seat for the chair: Sergey went out in the snow and pulled
some thin branches off young trees and made a frame and I wove
the straw and wool around it, the way I had done our shoes, until
it was good enough to tie onto the chair to sit on. Then the chair
was fixed.

All we meant to do was put new mats like that on the bed, but
when Sergey went out to look for firewood after we ate, he came
back almost right away. He had found a small load of wood buried under the snow behind the house, next to a chopping block,
and there was an axe someone had just left sticking in it. It was
rusted and the handle was a little rotten and full of splinters, but
Sergey scraped off the rust with a stone and then he could use it
to cut wood, even though it hurt his hands. So now we could
make a whole new frame for the bed, not just a new mat.

We were afraid to stay, but now we were also afraid to go away
and leave the work undone. It seemed we were meant to do what
we had promised. Anyway, it was still snowing. So Sergey began
on the frame while I worked on the mats.

By the morning the snow was two feet deep again. At least we
had food and the house was warm. Sergey worked on the bed and
I wove six big mats like the chair seat to rest on them. We heaped
them with straw and clean wool. Then I thought at last we were
finished, and we could go if we wanted to. All that day it had been
sunny again and more snow melted. Sergey and I agreed we
would go the next day.

The next morning we went outside to look for some more food

in the garden to take with us and we found a whole patch of strawberries. The plants were dying from the frost, and the berries were frozen solid, but they would still be good to eat. I went inside and looked for something to carry them in, and on a shelf in a dark corner next to the oven, I found some old jars that I hadn't noticed before, though I was almost sure I had looked there. One big one was empty and just right to hold the strawberries. One was full of salt and one had a little bit of honey that still tasted all right.

That was bad enough, but on the shelf next to the biggest jar, there was an old wooden spindle and some knitting needles. So that meant we weren't done, because now I could spin the wool and knit the yarn I made, and that meant we could make a real mattress like the one that had been on the bed and rotted away. I showed it to Sergey. "How long will it take?" he asked me, uneasily. I shook my head. I didn't know.

I spent all the rest of that day spinning yarn while Sergey washed some more wool for me. I made six big balls of yarn, as fast as I could, but I thought it would take more to make a mattress cover. Then Sergey went out and got more firewood. He got a lot, and I made a big pot of porridge, so the next day we would not have to go out at all. We could just eat from the pot all day. Then we went to sleep on the oven again.

"Wanda," Sergey said the next morning. He was looking at the table. I looked at it, too. Everything seemed all right. The table was cleared off. The chair was neatly tucked in against it to keep it out of the way. Then I thought, but we had put it against the wall yesterday. Maybe we had moved it back before we went to bed. But I did not think we had. "Let's eat," I said, finally.

The pot of porridge was still warm in the oven. I took off the lid and I stopped, looking inside. I had made the whole pot full. It was not a very big pot and we would eat all of it in one day. But someone had already eaten a big helping of it. I couldn't even think to myself that maybe they hadn't, or maybe Sergey had taken some, because there was a big wooden spoon sticking in the pot, and last night I had thought to myself, I wish I had a big spoon, and there had not been a spoon like that anywhere in the house.

When I said "Stop!" Shofer pulled the deer to a halt, but he looked back in alarm over his shoulder at the two figures on the riverbank, and he said, urgent and low, "Only wights would come to this place."

But I knew who she was, the girl standing there in her white furs with the familiar crown of silver on her head, the crown that had brought me my own: Irina, the duke's daughter. And if she had found a way here, there was a way back. "Go to them, or answer me, why can't we?" I said, ruthlessly, and after a moment Shofer reluctantly turned us back around and drove along the river until we drew up beside them. Irina wore the crown, and the necklace gleaming, and her silver ring on her finger, and her breath didn't frost in the air. She had her arms around the other, an old woman who was shivering terribly though she had a heavy fur wrapped all around her, her breath hanging in thick mists around her head.

"How did you get here?" I demanded.

Irina looked up at me, without any recognition in her face. "We mean no trespass," she said. "Will you give us shelter? My nurse cannot stand in the cold."

"Come in the sleigh," I said, though Shofer flinched, and I put out my hand. Irina hesitated only a moment, glancing down at the river, then she urged the old woman up into the sleigh and

climbed up after her. I took off my own cloak, and put it over
the old woman like a blanket. She was trembling even more, and
her lips were going blue. "Take us to the nearest shelter," I told
Shofer.

He flinched again, but after a moment he turned the deer and
drove up over the bank and into the dark trees. On our left there
was solid night, and on the right the pale twilight brightened in
the distance, as if we were on the very border of the dark. Irina
had turned her head to look behind at the river disappearing behind us, and then she looked at me. Her long dark hair was stark
against the white of her furs and beneath the silver crown, and
snowflakes drifted onto it from the trees and gleamed on its length
like small clear jewels. The twilight behind her caught in her pale
skin, and she gleamed with it so I realized suddenly she must have
Staryk blood, somewhere in her line; in her glittering silver she
could have changed places with me, and fit into this kingdom as
though it were her own. "How did you get here?" I asked her
again.

But she was staring back at me, frowning, and she said slowly,
"I know you. You're the jeweler's wife."

Of course she didn't know better: no one would have told her
my name, or Isaac's. She was a princess, and we didn't matter. I
wished bitterly that I still didn't, that she was right; that I was
home in Basia's place or in my own. "No," I said. "I only gave
him the silver. My name is Miryem."

Shofar flinched on the seat ahead of me, his eyes darting back
shocked a moment. Irina only nodded a little, still frowning in
thought, and she reached up to touch the necklace at her throat.
"Silver from *here*," she said.

"That's how," I said, understanding. "The silver brought you?"

"Through the mirror," Irina said. "It saved me, saved us—"
but then she was leaning over the old woman. "Magra! Magra,
don't fall asleep."

"Irinushka," the old woman muttered. Her eyes were half closed, and she had stopped shivering.

The sleigh jerked to a halt: Shofer had pulled hard on the reins, and the deer threw their heads up, restive. He was staring ahead of us, his back very straight and his shoulders rigid. We'd come to a low garden wall, almost buried in the snow, and on the other side I saw a faint, familiar orange glow: the flickering of an oven's fire from inside a house, warm and welcoming. From his face it might have been the coming of an angry mob.

"Who lives there?" I asked without thinking, but Shofer only threw me an anguished look, and anyway I didn't see what else there was for it; the old woman was sinking quickly. "Help us get her out," I said, and with enormous reluctance he hooked the reins over the seat and climbed down. He lifted Magra as easily as if she were a small child, although she whimpered at his touch even through the layers of her clothing and fur.

He walked away with her, lightly, over the top of the snow, but Irina and I both floundered through the crust and into the deep drifts beneath. We struggled on after him until suddenly it thinned as we came to the wall of the garden. It was only a very little house, barely a peasant's hut and nearly all oven, but there was a smell of warm porridge cooking and the oven's glow was coming through thin cracks in the window covers and the door. Shofer had stopped well back from the hut, and his fear made me wary, but Irina went straight to the door and pushed it open without hesitation: it was only a thin panel of slats and straw woven over them, to keep out the wind, and it fell in onto the floor with a bang.

"There's no one here," Irina said, after a moment, looking back at us.

I went inside after her: it was easy to see it was all empty. There was only one room, with a single small cot heaped with a pile of straw. Irina covered it with the cloak I had put on Magra, and

Shofer very reluctantly came in and put the old woman down on it, his eyes always on the oven's shut door, the tiny flicker of light around it, and as soon as he had laid her down, he retreated back to the threshold in a rush. There was a box heaped with firewood beside the oven, and I opened the oven door and found a pot inside, full of fresh hot porridge.

"Let me give her some," Irina said, and on a shelf we found a wooden bowl and spoon. She put a good helping of the porridge inside, steam rising off it into the air, and knelt by the cot. She fed it to Magra, who stirred and roused with the smell, enough to eat it in small spoonfuls. Shofer was flinching with every bite, as if he were watching someone deliberately eat poison. He looked at me and his mouth worked, as though he wanted to say something and only a worse fear stopped his tongue. I kept waiting for something dreadful to happen: I looked in every corner of the room to make sure there was nothing hiding there, and then I went outside and looked all around the yard, too. Someone *should* have been nearby, with a fire going and hot food ready, but I didn't even see a footprint in the snow all around the house, except the trail going back to the sleigh where Irina and I had gone floundering through the drifts. A Staryk wouldn't have left a trail, of course. But . . .

"This isn't a Staryk house," I said to Shofer, a statement and not a question. He didn't nod, but he also didn't look at me puzzled or surprised, the way Flek and Tsop did when I'd gotten something wrong. I looked down at the garden again. The house stood directly upon the line: one half of the garden was in twilight, and the other in full night, caught between the two. I looked at him and said, "I'm going to close the door."

"I will stay outside," he said instantly, which gave me hope. I went inside and picked up the door and propped it back into place, and then I waited a little while and then with a quick jerk pulled it aside again—

But I was only looking back out onto the empty yard, with

Shofer standing there waiting and anxious. He had retreated even farther, to the other side of the garden wall. I turned back inside, disappointed. Magra had opened her eyes, and she was holding Irina's hands in hers. "You are safe, Irinushka," she whispered. "I prayed you would be safe."

Irina looked at me. "Can we stay here?"

"I don't know if it's safe," I said.

"It's not less safe than where we were."

"Did the tsar refuse to marry you?" I asked. I thought the duke might have been angry with her if he had: he hadn't seemed like a man to be satisfied if his plans went awry.

"No," she said. "I am tsarina. For as long as I live." She said it dryly, as if she didn't expect that to last long. "The tsar is a black sorcerer. He is possessed by a demon of flame that wants to devour me."

I laughed; I couldn't help it. It wasn't mirth, it was bitterness. "So the fairy silver brought you a monster of fire for a husband, and me a monster of ice. We should put them in a room together and let them make us both widows."

I said it savagely, an angry joke, but then Irina said slowly, "The demon said I would quench its thirst a long time. It wants me because . . . I am *cold*."

"Because you have Staryk blood, and Staryk silver," I said, just as slowly. She nodded. I leaned into the door and peered through a crack: Shofer was still far back from the house, well out of earshot, with no sign at all that he was inclined to come any closer. I took a deep breath and turned back. "Do you think the demon would bargain? For the chance to devour a Staryk king instead?"

Irina showed me how the Staryk silver let her go back and forth: together we went out back and found a big washtub behind the house. We poured hot water into it, over the snow heaped inside, to make a pool with a reflection in it. She stared down into it and said, "I see the same place we came from: a bedroom in the palace. Do you see it?" she asked me, but I only saw our faces floating pale in the shifting water, and when she took my hand and tried to put it through, I got wet to the wrist, even as Irina drew her own hand out dry and without a drop. She shook her head. "I can't bring you through with me." As if I had stopped existing in the real world at all, as if the Staryk king had ripped me out of it by the roots.

"I'll need to persuade *him* to bring me over," I said grimly: just as he'd told me. I didn't care to be on this side of the water when and if my husband was successfully introduced to his untimely end. I didn't think the rest of the Staryk would accept me as queen in his stead, at least not until I'd learned to make endless winters myself and pop up snow-trees out of the earth or whatever else he'd demanded.

We finished our planning quickly: there wasn't much *to* plan, only a time and place, and all the rest just a desperate lunge at the only hope either one of us had. "The demon can't come during the day," Irina said. "He only appears at night. I don't know why, but if he could, he'd surely have tried to take me before now: he had me alone today, or close enough." She paused and added, thoughtfully, "When the tsar's mother was condemned for sorcery, they took her and burned her all in one day, before the sun set."

"At night, then." I was silent, thinking what excuse I could give a Staryk king that he'd accept, for why I wanted him to take me back. "Could you persuade the tsar to go back to Vysnia?" I asked slowly. "In three days' time?"

"If I can persuade him to do anything at all but kill me," she said.

When we were done, Irina went back inside to her nurse, and I walked back to the sleigh. Shofer asked no questions; he was too eager to be gone. I sat unseeing for the whole drive back, my head running in circles and my stomach churning and hot with gall.

Of course I was terrified. Of trying, of failing, of success. It felt like murder—no, I wouldn't lie to myself; it *was* murder, if it worked. But after all, the Staryk seemed to think it perfectly reasonable to murder *me,* and I hadn't made him any promises, either; I wasn't sure I was even really married. He'd given me a crown, but there certainly hadn't been a marriage contract, and we hadn't known each other. I'd ask a rabbi, if I ever had the chance to talk to one again. But married or not, I was reasonably sure that the rabbis would tell me that I might justly take Judith for my model, and take off the Staryk's head if he gave me the opportunity. He was the enemy of my people, not just me alone. But that only left me the enormous difficulty of doing it.

Shofer stopped the sleigh at the foot of the steep walkway to my chambers: Tsop was sitting on a low stone there, as if she'd been all day waiting for me to come back—anxiously, judging by the look of relief that crossed her face when she saw me. I climbed out stiffly: it had been a long time driving, and my whole body was sore. Tsop led me back up to my room at a pace quick enough to make me out of breath, and flinched back and forth with visible impatience when she had to pause. She kept looking downwards, and I followed the line of her gaze to the grove of trees: the white blooms were all closing softly, as if that was what marked the night coming on. I suppose the king would have been upset if I hadn't been home in time for him to deliver his three answers. Then it occurred to me he might feel obligated to provide marital services after all, if he missed his nightly chance, so I quickened my steps as much as I could.

He was waiting in my chamber with his arms folded and anger bright in his face, light gleaming along the edges of his cheekbones and in his eyes. *"Ask,"* he bit out, the instant I came in: the sun was halfway down in the mirror he'd given me.

"Who lives in the house on the edge of the night?" I said. There hadn't been much choice about it, but I hoped I hadn't left Magreta there to be devoured by someone coming back later.

"No one," he said instantly. "Ask."

"That's not true," I said, and Tsop, who'd been bowing her way out of the room, startled like a horse that had been struck with a whip out of nowhere. The Staryk's eyes widened with shock, and his fists closed; he took a step towards me, as if he meant to *hit* me. "There was porridge in the oven!" I blurted out in an instinctive alarm.

He stopped short. His lips pressed together hard, and then after a moment he said, *"that I know of,"* finishing off his sentence. *"Ask."*

I almost did ask again. He was *shimmering* with anger, a faint iridescence shifting back and forth across his skin, and I couldn't help thinking of Shofer picking up Magreta like she was a sack of wool and not a person, of Tsop and Flek easily turning over the chest full of silver; if any ordinary Staryk could do that, what could *he* do to me? I wanted to ease the moment past. The temptation was familiar: to go along, to make myself small enough to slip past a looming danger. For a moment I was back in the snow with Oleg coming at me, his face contorted and his big fists clenched. I wanted to scramble away, to ask for mercy, fear running hot all along my spine.

But it was all the same choice, every time. The choice between the one death and all the little ones. The Staryk was glaring at me, unearthly and terrifying. But what was the use of being afraid of him? For all his magic and all his strength, he couldn't kill me any more thoroughly than Oleg would have, crushing the breath from my throat in the snow. And if I made him angry enough to do it, he wouldn't hold back for all the pleading in the world, any more than Oleg would have stopped because I'd begged for mercy in the woods. I couldn't buy my life in the last moment, with hands around my throat. I could only buy it by giving in sooner, giving in all the time; like Scheherazade, humbly asking my murderous husband to go on sparing me night after night. And I knew perfectly well even that wasn't guaranteed to work.

I wouldn't make that bargain. I was going to try and kill him, even if I was almost certain to fail, and I wouldn't be afraid of him now, either. I straightened my shoulders and looked him in his glittering eyes. "I'd say that I'm owed an educated guess if you can make one. If you knew who built it, for instance."

"*Owed?*" he spat. Out of the corner of my eye, Tsop had very slowly and carefully been maneuvering herself farther back by inches, and now she eased the rest of the way out of the chamber. "*Owed?*"

In a sudden lurch he was standing right before me, as if he'd moved so quickly my eyes couldn't see him do it; he put his hand on my throat, his thumb in the hollow beneath my chin, pushing it up so I still looked him in the face, my neck bent back. "And if I say all I *owe* you is two answers more?" he said softly, glittering down at me.

"You can say what you like," I said without yielding, my voice pressed up against the skin of my throat, forcing its way through.

"One more time I will ask: are you *certain?*" he hissed.

There was a deep ominous warning in his voice, as if I was pushing him to a hard limit. But I'd already made the choice. I'd made it the winter before last, sitting at my mother's bedside, hearing her cough away her life. I'd made it standing in a hundred half-frozen doorways, demanding what I was owed. I swallowed the sharp taste of bile back down my throat. "Yes," I said, as cold as any lord of winter could have been.

He gave a snarl of rage and whirled away from me. He stalked to the edge of the chamber and stood there with his back to me and his fists clenched. "You *dare*," he said to the wall, not turning to look at me. "You *dare* set yourself against me, to make a pretense of being my equal—"

"*You* did that, when you put a crown on my head!" I said. My hands wanted to shake, with triumph or anger or both at once. I held them clenched tight. "I am not your subject or your servant, and if you want a cowering mouse for a wife, go find someone *else* who can turn silver to gold for you."

He gave a hiss of frustration and displeasure, and stood there a moment longer just breathing in furious heaves, his shoulders rising and falling. But then he said, "A mighty witch grew tired of mortals asking her for favors and built for herself a house on the border of the sunlit world, that they might not find her at home when she did not desire company. But she went away long ago and has not returned, for I would know if so great a power came back into my realm."

I was breathing just as hard, still enraged, and it didn't make sense to me at first as victory, as an answer to my question; it felt as though it came out of nowhere. "What is *long ago*?" I said, too hastily.

"Do you think I care for the mayfly moments with which you count the passage of your lives in the sunlit world, save when I must?" he said. "Mortal children born then have long since died, and their children's children now are old, that is all I can say. Ask *once more*."

A good answer as far as it went: at least I could hope that no monstrously powerful witch was going to appear and decide to make Magreta her dinner in place of the porridge she'd eaten. I would have liked to know a bit more about where the food might have come from, and who had laid the fire, but I couldn't afford to ask; I had a more pressing question. "I promised my cousin that

I would dance at her wedding," I said. "And she will be married in three days' time."

I thought I'd have to go on from there, but he'd already turned round to look at me, a gleam coming into his eye: I suppose as seriously as they took their given word here, he knew at once that he had me over a barrel. Which he did, if not quite the way he thought he did. "Then it seems you must ask my aid," he said softly, with visible glee. "And hope that I don't refuse it."

"Well, you won't do it to help me," I said, and he gave a small snort, amused. "And you've made clear there's only one thing I'm good for in your eyes. So how much gold do you want me to make, in exchange for escorting me to Basia's wedding?"

He scowled with a hint of regret, as if he'd looked forward to my prostrating myself and begging for his help, but he was practical enough not to let that stop him. "I have three storerooms of silver," he said, "each larger than the last, and you shall turn every coin therein to gold, ere I take you thence: and you must work swiftly, for if you have not finished the work in time, neither shall I convey you, and you will be foresworn." He finished in triumph, as if he were threatening me with an axe over my head, which maybe he was; I had the bad suspicion that if I was foresworn and he knew it, he would consider that a mortal crime.

"Fine," I said.

He jerked and stared at me in sudden dismay. *"What?"*

"Fine!" I said. "You just demanded—"

"And *now*, for the first time, you make no effort to negotiate—" He pulled himself up short, his face glitter-flushed again, and I had a deeply sinking feeling even as he said, bitterly, "We are agreed. And may you complete as much of your task as you can."

"Exactly how big are these storerooms?" I demanded, but he was already going out of the room, without a pause.

I didn't pause, either. I rang my bell urgently, and Tsop came timidly back inside, darting her eyes over me to see if I'd been, I don't know, strangled or beaten or otherwise chastised for my dreadful temerity. "There are three storerooms of silver in the palace," I said. "I need you to take me to them."

"Now?" she said doubtfully.

"Now," I said.

Chapter 14

watched Miryem leave, and then I went back inside. Magra was huddled by the oven, wrapped in all her things and the cloaks and the fur. I asked her to lie down, but she shook her head: there was nothing on the cot but a pile of straw, and she said it was too hard for her old bones. "Sleep, dushenka," she said. She had already found some work for her hands, a spindle and a ball of wool; she never liked to be idle. "Lie down and rest, and I will sing to you."

The cot was narrow and stiff and uncomfortable, but I hadn't slept well since my wedding night, and my bones weren't old. With Magreta's familiar creaky voice in my ears, I fell deeply asleep. It was still dark outside the little hut when I sat up again, but I felt too much refreshed to have woken in the middle of the night. Magra was drowsing half asleep in the chair. I put on my fur coat and went outside.

The shading line between night and twilight hadn't moved from where it crossed the garden. The woods stood thick and silent on the other side of the wall, without even any signs of living things; I missed the sounds of birds and animals in the heavy hush. I went around the back to look into the big washtub. Miryem had helped me push it up against the back of the oven, on the outside of the house, and it hadn't frozen all the way through. I broke the crust with a stick, and there in the dark water I saw sunlight in the tsar's bedroom, gleaming on all the expanses of gilt. Mirnatius was awake and dressed and pacing the room, limping a little as if he was sore. Servants with their heads bent and shoulders hunched were hurrying to lay out his breakfast. I didn't know what they imagined had become of me.

I went back inside and kissed Magra's cheek: she was still spinning by the fire. "Irinushka, you shouldn't go back," she said tremulously, clinging to my hands. "It's too dangerous, this plan you've made. That unholy thing wants to devour your soul."

"We can't stay here forever," I said.

"Then wait until he isn't watching," Magra urged. "Wait and we'll go back and run away."

"Away from the tsar? Sneak all the way out of the palace with no one seeing us?" I shook my head. "And then what?"

"We'll go back to your father . . ." Magra said, but her voice trailed off. My father could avenge my murder, but he couldn't keep me from my husband. He wouldn't try.

I didn't pull my hands away; I was thinking. "If I disappear now, whatever the cause," I said, "it will be war. Father will go to Ulrich and Casimir, and give them their excuse. And Mirnatius and his demon won't go easily. They'll burn down half of Lithvas without a second thought, *either* of them. No matter who wins, the kingdom will be in ruins. And the Staryk will bury us all in ice."

Magra said uneasily, "Dushenka, this isn't anything for you to worry about, to think of."

"Who else is there to think of it? I am tsarina." Which technically meant that I was to produce a tsarevitch and otherwise stay quiet and unobtrusive, but few tsarinas did, and it wasn't a choice open to me anyway. "I have to go back."

"And if the demon doesn't want this Staryk king?" she said. "You shouldn't even try to make bargains with such a creature."

I didn't disagree with her, but I gently freed my hands and said softly, "Do my hair up again, Magreta." I took off the crown and turned my back to her and sat down on the floor, to make it easy for her to work. She put her hands on my shoulders for a moment. Then she took out the silver comb and brush from her purse and went to work on it, the pull and weight of her hands as familiar as bread. When she was done, together we put my crown back on my head, and then I went out to the water.

The servants had left Mirnatius. For the moment he was sitting there alone and seething with his back to the water, only drinking angry gulps from his cup at intervals; his plate was untouched. I stepped into the tub of water as slowly and carefully as I could, and I came out of one of the enormous gilt-framed mirrors on the wall behind him. I took a few steps away from it and softly reached behind me to open one of those balcony doors, as if I'd just stepped inside. "Good morning, husband," I said, at the same time, and he crashed out of his chair, dropping his cup in a steaming red-wine smear across the floor as he whirled to stare at me.

I was a good distance away from him: I could thank his extravagantly massive room for that, which saved my neck from being instantly wrung; by the time he'd reached me, I'd put my hand back on the door and said sharply, "Shall I just leave for good, and you can see how your demon likes *that*, or are you willing to discuss the situation?"

He pulled up and looked out the balcony doors—the snow had drifted in around my feet already, like I'd been blown in by the winter wind out of nowhere, and could go back into it as easily. "What exactly is there to *discuss*?" he bit out savagely. "Why do you keep coming back at all?"

"My father's tax rolls," I said. I'd thought a little what would move him—him, and not his demon; I needed him as a go-between, and I was reasonably certain he only wanted his angry demon fed, so it wouldn't erupt and beat him. "Do you know what they are? Do you know what *yours* are?" I added, in case.

"Of course I know what mine are!" he snapped, which meant he hadn't any idea what my father's were, although he should have. "I'm supposed to believe you want me to cut your father's *taxes*—"

"What's been happening to your rolls?" I broke in on him, sharply. "Have they been going down?"

"Yes, of course, they've sunk year over year. I was going to raise the rates, but the council made such an infernal noise about it—why are we talking about *taxes*?" he burst out. "Are you trying to make a fool of me?"

"No," I said. "*Why* are your rolls sinking? Why didn't the council let you raise the rates?"

He started shouting at me, "Because the—" He stopped, and finished out more slowly, "Because the winters are getting worse."

He wasn't stupid, at least. Even as he spoke, he was looking past me out onto the balcony, piled thick with snow on the last day before June, with a few flurrying flakes still coming in behind me to vanish into the white of my furs, and he wasn't seeing a freak accident of the weather anymore. And as soon as he stopped see-ing it as a single unlucky chance, he began to see the rest, too: more blizzards, and failed crops; starving peasants, lords raising rebellion; his neighbors' well-fed armies coming upon him, his glittering palace torn down around his ears while he tumbled into the hungry fire waiting for him. I saw them creeping one by one over his face, and he began to be afraid, as I wanted him to be.

"It's the Staryk," I said. "The Staryk are making the winter last."

He still wasn't pleased, but he did listen to me after that. He flung himself onto one of his gilt-and-velvet divans as I seated myself on one across from him. Between us a large table with a silvered mirror top shone with deep night sky and falling snow, a square pool I could have dived into. When I leaned back, so my own reflection didn't catch in the glass, the image faded into the ceiling above, the gleam of the green serpent winding around the apple between us while Mirnatius reclined with a hand posed over his lips and listened to my careful proposal in sullen silence.

I'd agreed with Miryem, on the other side: we needed to bring the Staryk king here, and not the other way. On this side of the mirror, I had my father's name and power at my back, and a tsarina's crown on my head. If we were lucky, and our two monsters destroyed each other, most likely even Mirnatius's soldiers would listen to me at first, for lack of anyone else to obey, and my father had two thousand men of his own to stand behind me. He still wouldn't care what I wanted any more than he ever had, but we would want the same thing, then: to preserve my neck.

I didn't share those details of my planning with Mirnatius. I only told him a little more, of how the Staryk were stretching the winter to strengthen their own kingdom. "Your demon wants me for my Staryk blood," I finished. "How much more would it like a pure-blood Staryk, and their king? If it agrees, I'll bring him to you, and you can save your kingdom and feed your demon all at once."

"And why precisely should I believe you?"

"Why do *you* think I keep coming back? It should be clear to you by now that I don't have to, and that you can't stop me from going, either. Do you really think piling still more guards on me will do any better? If it would, why would I take the risk?"

He flicked his fingers out long and dismissive into the air. "I have no idea why you would do any of this anyway! Why do *you* care if the Staryk freeze the kingdom? You're nearly one of them."

It was a good question: Magreta had asked it, too. I hadn't had an answer for her. "The squirrels will starve, too, when the trees die," I said.

"Squirrels!" He glared at me, but though I'd meant to say it flippantly, the words felt strangely true when they came out of my mouth.

"Yes, squirrels," I said, and meant it. "And peasants, and children, and old women, and all the people you don't even see because they're useless to you, all those who'll die before you and your soldiers do." I didn't know what I was feeling, that made those words come. Angry, I think. I didn't remember ever being angry before. Anger had always seemed pointless to me, a dog circling after its own tail. What good was it to be angry at my father, or my stepmother, or angry at the servants who were rude to me? People were angry at the weather sometimes, too, or when they stubbed their toe on a stone or cut their hand on a knife, as if it had done it to them on purpose. It had all seemed equally useless to me. Anger was a fire in a grate, and I'd never had any wood to burn. Until now, it seemed.

Mirnatius was scowling at me exactly as petulantly as he had in the garden seven years ago, when I'd told him to leave the dead squirrels alone. How dare I think they were worth anything next to his pleasure? It made me still more angry, and my voice sharpened. "Do you really care what my reasons are? You're no worse off than you are now if I'm lying."

"I *might* be, if you're not telling me all the truth, and you aren't," he shot back. "You still haven't told me how you vanish, or where you go—or where you've stashed away that old crone of yours. And you certainly aren't being forthcoming about the details of how you're going to provide this Staryk lord."

"Of course not," I said. "Why would I trust you? You've done nothing since we exchanged vows but try to stuff me down your demon's gullet."

"As though I had any say in it. Do you really think I wanted to marry *you*? *He* wanted you, so off to the altar I went."

"And my father wanted me on a throne, so off to the altar *I* went. You can't excuse yourself to me by pleading that you were forced to it."

"What, you didn't do it all on purpose to save the squirrels and mud-stained peasantry?" he sneered, but he didn't meet my eyes, and after a moment he said, "Fine. Tonight I'll ask him if he'll take a Staryk king, and leave you be in exchange."

"Good. And in the meantime," I added, "you'll write to your dukes and command them all to come and celebrate our wedding with us. And when you write to Prince Ulrich, you'll make sure to tell him I insist on seeing my dear friend Vassilia. When she comes, I'll make her my chief lady-in-waiting."

He frowned at me. "What does that have to do with—"

"We can't let her marry Casimir," I reminded him, a little impatient; we'd even *spoken* of this already.

"If Casimir and Ulrich want to steal my throne, do you think they'll care that his daughter's your lady-in-waiting?" he demanded.

"They'll care that they haven't a blood tie to bind them together," I said. "And all the better if there's one that binds Ulrich to *you*, instead. We'll marry her off as soon as she arrives. Do you have any suitable relatives at court—someone young and handsome, if possible? Never mind," I added, seeing his blankness. He had two aunts, and I knew they'd produced a dozen offspring. I hadn't met all of them to remember, but at least one of them would hopefully be unmarried or a convenient widower. "*I'll* look for someone. You need to present me to the court today anyway."

"And why, exactly? I assure you that you won't enjoy the experience. My court has quite an elevated standard of beauty."

It was plain he hadn't expected me to last long enough to be presented. Perhaps he still didn't. "I'm your tsarina, so they'll have to get used to my deficiencies," I said. "We need to quash any rumors before they begin. The servants must already have it all over the castle that I vanished during the night, and we can't *afford* whispers. The crops are going to be bad this year, even if we do manage to stop the winter. And you've already made a great many of your nobles angry."

He wanted to keep protesting, I could see it, but he glanced uneasily at the snow heaped on the balcony, and said nothing. He wasn't stupid, after all; only as far as I could tell, he'd never given a moment's thought to politics. I imagine that all he'd ever wanted were the trappings of rule, the wealth and luxury and beauty, and none of the work of it: he wasn't ambitious at all.

Of course, if he *had* ever thought about politics, he'd be asking the far more important question of whom we were going to have *Casimir* marry. And the answer to that was *me*—as soon as Mirnatius and his demon had either been frozen solid or burned at the stake or at least exposed to the entire court and forced to flee, and I'd been granted an annulment of my thoroughly unconsummated marriage.

I didn't particularly like Prince Casimir. He'd come to stay at my father's house once, and I'd been beneath his notice at the time, so he hadn't been on his best behavior. He'd made a serving-girl sit upon his lap and smile for him as if she liked it when he squeezed her breast and slapped her rear; but when he'd left three days later, she'd had a necklace of gold she couldn't have bought on her wages, so at least he'd given her some return for it. He was nearly my father's age, and a man who lived almost entirely on the surface. But he wasn't a fool, or cruel. And more to the point,

I was reasonably certain he wasn't going to try and devour my soul. My expectations for a husband had lowered.

I'd weave a net out of us to hold all Lithvas. Casimir married to me and on the throne would satisfy him. Vassilia married to a nephew of the late tsar would at least balk Ulrich, and I'd put a whisper in his ear that it would be just as well for my dear friend to start having her children at the same time as I had mine, and promise him a grandchild on the throne after all. That would satisfy him and Mirnatius's kindred both. All I needed to arrange it was a space where Mirnatius now stood, and conveniently, he'd put himself on top of a trapdoor going directly to the bowels of Hell, if I could only find the way to unlatch it.

But first, I needed his demon to kill a Staryk king for me, or there wouldn't be any Lithvas to save. I stood up from the divan and paused, frowning slightly, as if I were having a fresh idea. "Wait," I added abruptly. "We should go back to my father's house for the celebration. When you write to the princes and archdukes, tell them to come to Vysnia instead of here."

"Why should—oh, never mind," he muttered, throwing his hand up in the air, graceful as a bird taking flight, his lace cuff its long feathered tail. I was gratified; I'd had a few excuses ready, but they were a bit thin, and all the better if I didn't have to use them. I didn't mean to tell him in advance that the Staryk king would hopefully be in Vysnia in three days' time himself, to be a guest at a different celebration.

On Monday afternoon, when I was walking back to Panova Mandelstam's house after the collecting, I met two boys from town playing in the woods. I was not big the way Sergey was, but I was still bigger than them, so they didn't try to fight with me, but

Panov Mandelstam was right anyway because they didn't want to play with me either. One of them yelled at me, "How does it feel to have killed your own father?"

They ran away into the trees and didn't wait for me to answer, but I thought about it the rest of the way. I wasn't sure if I had killed my father, because I had only wanted him to not hit Wanda with the poker; I hadn't wanted him to fall over me. But he *had* fallen over me and that was part of why he was dead, so maybe it didn't matter that I hadn't wanted it. I didn't know.

I did know that it felt good to be living with Panov and Panova Mandelstam. I had stopped feeling hungry even a little bit. But anytime I thought about Sergey and Wanda, even if I was sitting at the table, I felt like I had swallowed stones instead of food. I would have felt very good if Sergey and Wanda and me were all living with Panov and Panova Mandelstam. The house was small, but me and Sergey could sleep in the barn. But we couldn't, because Sergey had pushed my father and he was dead.

Then I thought whether it was better for me only to be living with the Mandelstams or for all of us to be living with my father. I decided it would be better to be living with my father after all, if Sergey and Wanda were there and all right. Only we could not have been doing that, either, even if my father was not killed, because he was going to make Wanda marry Kajus's son. Then I had to think whether it would feel better to be here with the Mandelstams or better to be somewhere else that might not be as good, but with Sergey and Wanda. It was hard to think about that because I didn't know what the somewhere else would be like, but after I thought about it a long time, I decided slowly that still I wanted to be with Sergey and Wanda. I could not be happy with stones in my stomach.

The nut from the white tree was in my pocket. I had kept thinking about planting it in the Mandelstams' yard, but I still hadn't done it. I took it out and I looked at it and then I said out loud, "Mama, I cannot plant the nut here, because Sergey and Wanda cannot come here ever again. I will not plant it until I find a place where me and Sergey and Wanda can all live together and be safe." Then I put it away again. I was sorry not to be able to plant the nut, because I missed feeling that Mama was near, but still it felt like the right decision. Sergey and Wanda had given me the nut to plant, but Mama would want them to be able to visit.

I got back to the house with the basket. While Panov Mandelstam was carefully writing everything down, I asked him, "Does anyone know where Sergey and Wanda are?"

He stopped and looked up at me. "The men went out to look for them again today. They did not find anything."

I was glad for that, but then I thought about it and I realized it was bad, too. "But *I* have to find them," I said. If no one else could, even a lot of big men, then how was I going to do it?

Panov Mandelstam laid his hand on my head. "Maybe they will send word to you when they are somewhere safe," he said, but he said it too kindly, the way you say nice things to a goat when you are trying to get it to come so you can tie it up. It did not mean he wanted to hurt me. He only wanted to keep me in a good safe warm place so I wouldn't die in the snow somewhere. But if I stayed in this safe warm place, I would never be able to see Sergey and Wanda again.

"They cannot send word," I said. "If they did then everyone here would know where they were, and they would go and get them."

Panov Mandelstam did not say anything back, only looked up at Panova Mandelstam, who had stopped her spinning and was looking back at him. So I knew I was right, because if I was not right, they would have told me so.

I said, "Sergey and Wanda were going to go to Vysnia. They wanted to ask someone for work." I had to think about it because he was someone's grandfather, and I didn't know who the someone was, which was strange. But I did know the grandfather's name. "Panov Moshel."

"That is my father," Panova Mandelstam said. Then she said to Panov Mandelstam, "Basia's wedding is on Wednesday. We could go. And . . ." She trailed off frowning in a puzzled way. "And . . ." she said again, as though she expected something to come out of her mouth, only it wasn't coming. He was frowning at her, puzzled too. She stood up from the spinning wheel and walked around the room with her hands gripping each other, looking out into nothing, until she came to a stop in front of the shelf over the oven. She stared at a little group of carved wooden dolls standing there. "*Miryem* is there," she said suddenly. "*Miryem* is visiting my father."

She said it like she was pushing against a wall to make the name come out. Panov Mandelstam stood up so quickly his pen fell to the ground, his face going pale. I was going to ask them who that was, but by the time I opened my mouth to ask, I couldn't remember the name she had said anymore. Panova Mandelstam turned, putting her hand out. "Josef," she said. Her voice went up and down. "Josef—how long—?" She stopped talking, and I didn't like looking at her face. It made me think of my father on the floor making noises and then being dead.

"I will go hire a sleigh," Panov Mandelstam said. It was already getting late, but he was putting on his coat anyway as if he meant we would go right away. Panova Mandelstam hurried to the secret jar in the fireplace and counted out six silver coins into a bag to give to him. He took the bag and went out.

Panova Mandelstam snatched up a sack and went into the bedroom and started packing as soon as he left. I was glad that we were going to go look for Sergey and Wanda, but I didn't like the hurry. It felt like she was afraid something bad would happen if she stopped moving. She knelt down and started taking clothing out of the clothing box. I helped her by holding the bag open for each piece to lay inside, but then she stopped putting things inside. She was sitting on her heels staring into her box. There were some dresses in there that were too small for her, and a pair of small black leather boots. They were worn and had some patches but they were still mostly good. She touched them with her hand and it was trembling.

"Were those yours?" I asked her. She didn't say anything, only shook her head. She put a few more things in the bag and closed the box. I thought we were finished but she kept kneeling there with her hands on the top of the box, and then she looked at me and opened the box again. She took out the boots and gave them to me. I tried them on. They were a little big on my feet but they felt so soft. I had never had leather shoes before.

"Put on another pair of socks," she said, and gave me a pair out of the box, knitted and thick, also small. The boots fit so nicely afterwards. My feet were very warm even when I went outside to take care of the goats. I could walk right through the snow and not feel it.

"Who will feed the goats and the chickens while we are away?" I asked her, when I came back in.

"I will go and talk to Panova Gavelyte," she said, and she put on her coat and her kerchief and took some pennies from the jar and went out. I watched from the doorway when she went to the house across the street and knocked on the door. Panova Gavelyte did not ask her inside. She folded her arms across her chest like making herself into a wall, and kept her on the doorstep talking. She did not bring the wall down until Panova Mandelstam held out the pennies, and then she took them and quickly went inside and shut the door in her face.

Panova Mandelstam looked tired when she came back to the house, as if she had been traveling very far or working all day hard in the fields, but she didn't say anything. She took out a basket and packed it with food for traveling. Then she stirred the coals in the oven and turned ash over them until the fire went dark and cold. When she was done, the sleigh was already pulling up to the door. Panov Mandelstam was sitting on the seat. He came out and got the basket and the sack and helped her get into the back of the sleigh. I sat next to her and he put two fur cloaks and some thick blankets over us, and then he shut the door of the house, and shut the gate after that, and he got into the sleigh on my other side.

The driver was a skinny young man about Sergey's age. He was wearing a coat for a big man and I think two other coats underneath it, though, so he looked big on the seat. He clucked to his big horses and the sleigh lurched forward and we started going. We went down the road through town. It was crowded. I think everyone had finished working for the day. There would not be much to do in the fields anyway because the snow had not melted yet. People watched us going by with hard angry faces. At the end of the road a few men came out of a very big house with a big chimney and a sign that had a picture of a big mug of steaming krupnik painted on it. They stopped the sleigh in the road and said to Panov Mandelstam, "Don't think we won't hear about it, Jew, if you help murderers escape justice."

"We are going to Vysnia for a wedding," Panov Mandelstam said quietly.

The man snorted. He looked up at our driver. "You're Oleg's boy, aren't you? Algis?" he said. The driver nodded. "You stay with the Jews. Keep your eye on them. You understand?" Algis nodded again.

I looked over at the house. Kajus was standing in the doorway with his arms crossed over his chest and his chin raised, as if he was proud of something. I wondered what. I stared at him. He glanced at me and scowled, but he stopped looking so proud. He turned and went inside very quickly. Algis shook his reins and the horses set off again. We were all quiet in the back of the sleigh behind him. We had been quiet before, too, but now it was not a nice kind of quiet. Even though we were in a sleigh and it was open, I felt like we were shut in with him. The trees came up all around us quickly when we left town. When I turned my head to watch them going by, they all came together into a wooden wall built around the road, keeping us out.

I already half knew what I would see when Tsop took me down to the storerooms, but there was something dreadful about seeing the doors open to the first small chamber, itself already three times the size of my grandfather's vault, chests and sacks of silver heaped to the ceiling along each wall. Grimly I walked down the path left open between them to the second room, which was three times again the size of the first, although at least there were small paths left between the stacks, and wooden shelves to hold the treasure.

But the doorway to the third room stood at the other end: two heavy doors made of white wood bound with silver, and when I pushed them open, on the other side I found a chamber that surely a thousand years had slowly chiseled out of the mountain; enormous, with sloping foothills of sacks and loose gleaming coin piled taller than my head. The river itself snaked through the middle of the room, a shining frozen road coming in from one dark archway and leaving through the other: as if it wound through the depths of the mountain all the way here from the grove of white trees, and went on all the way out to the mountainside waterfall. I had spent a day changing a single chest. I couldn't imagine how much magic it would take to turn all of this into gold, and how much time. More than I had.

Tsop was standing next to me, eyeing me sidelong. "Go bring

me something to eat and drink," I said grimly, and then I went back out to the first room.

I'd had a long day already, and what I wanted was my bed. Instead I emptied sacks and filled my hands with silver coins, and poured them back in, gold. I did try to thrust my hands into a bag and change it all at once, but it didn't work properly: the coins changed unevenly, and when I poured it out, there were a dozen of them still silver. I wasn't going to change every coin in the place and then have the king slit my throat for one that had rolled away into a corner. I was perfectly certain that if I did by some mistake leave one unchanged, he'd *find* it. It went quicker to do them carefully than to have to check carefully afterwards. Which isn't to say it went quickly at all. I had only done a few sacks when Tsop came back with a tray of food and drink.

When I finished gulping down a few mouthfuls, I looked at the napkin on the tray and spread it out over the ground. I took the next sack and poured half of it out onto the napkin, the silver spread one layer thick, so I could see which ones had changed. After a few tries, I found a way to change them just by brushing my hand over them—not too quickly, or the change didn't go all the way through, but if I moved at a steady even pace, keeping my will on them, they all went.

"Bring me a large dark tablecloth, the biggest you can find," I told Tsop, and when she brought it, I started dumping out the sacks and chests onto it. I could fit two or three at once on the cloth, and when I finished with one batch, I pulled the cloth from beneath, spilling the golden pieces off, and spread the cloth again on top of them.

It became boring, which seems ridiculous to say. I was pouring out magic by the bucketful, turning silver into shining gold with my very fingers, but it quickly stopped being magical. I would have liked to turn some of it into birds, or just set it on fire. It stopped even being a fortune, the way you could say a word too many times in a row and turn it into nonsense. I was tired and stiff and my feet and fingers ached, but I kept working. I sat on gold and slipped on gold underfoot as I took more silver from the shelves and left empty ghosts of sacks and upturned chests in a growing heap in the corner. Time slipped away unmarked, until I dumped out the final chest in that first room, and I changed the very last pieces of silver in it. I went staggering to all the shelves in the room, looking for anything left to change, and when I didn't find anything after going round three times, I just stood there stupidly for a few more moments, and then I lay down on my mountain of gold like an improbable dragon and fell asleep without meaning to do so.

I woke with a jerk and looked up to find the Staryk lord standing over me, surveying the hoard I'd made him; he had cupped a handful of the coins and was staring at the warm gleam of it with bright avaricious hunger in his face. I struggled up to my feet in alarm, stumbling on the shifting gold. *He* didn't have any trouble keeping his footing. He even put out his hand to catch my arm and steady me, although the gesture was less a kindness than to keep me from thrashing around next to him. "What time is it?" I blurted.

He ignored me instead of answering my question, which meant at least it wasn't evening; I hadn't lost an entire day. I didn't feel like I'd slept long, either: my eyes were still gritty and tired. I drew a deep breath. He had gone away to make a survey of the room, glancing into emptied chests and sacks, still holding that shining handful. "Well?" I challenged him. "If I missed any, say so now."

"No," he said, letting the coins run out of his hand to go clinking and jingling among the rest on the floor. "You have changed every coin in this first storeroom. Two storerooms yet remain." He sounded almost polite about it, and he actually inclined his head to me, which surprised me enough that I only stared after him until he had gone out again. Then with a jerk I scrambled and slid down the golden heap to the door, and ran back upstairs to my own chambers.

But there on my bed I found the mirror he'd made me with sunrise climbing pink and gold inside it. I sat down on the bed with a hopeless thump and stared at it in my hand. I'd spent one whole night or nearly all of it just on the smallest chamber. I could hope to finish the second one, if I didn't sleep again, but I'd barely be able to change a single coin in the third before my time ran out.

I thought of running away. I could get as far as the hut in the woods, maybe, but what good would that do me? I couldn't get out of his kingdom. But I didn't go back downstairs, either. Instead I rang the bell, and told Tsop and Flek to bring me breakfast, and I didn't hurry over it. I sat resentfully eating platters full of fish and cold fruit as if I didn't have a care in the world, much less an enormous silver sword hanging over my head. My husband's politeness had made me even more certain that it was going to mean my death if I didn't succeed, and Tsop and Flek even traded glances when they thought I wasn't looking, as if they were wondering what I was doing. But why even try, if all I could do was leave a larger pile of gold behind for him to cut my head off over? Their law didn't seem to allow for mistakes, and if you couldn't make what you said true, they'd repair the fault in the world by putting you out of it.

I had been about to tip back another glass of wine—why not be drunk until the end, for that matter—but then I stopped abruptly and put it down again. I stood up and told Tsop and Flek, "Come down to the storerooms with me. And send for Shofer to meet us there. Tell him to get the biggest sledge in the stables, and I want him to bring it there."

Tsop stared at me. "*Into* the storeroom?"

"Yes," I said. "The river's frozen now, after all. So tell him to just drive the whole way down from the grove until he gets there."

The deer looked fairly dubious coming out of the tunnel and picking their way delicately between the vast hills of silver: he'd had to come and lead them by their heads. Flek and Tsop and Shofer looked even more dubious than that when I told them what I wanted them to do. I carefully didn't ask them to do it, just told them. "But . . . where do you want us to *take* it?" Tsop said after a moment.

I pointed to the dark mouth of the river tunnel on the other side of the chamber. "Drive the sledge into there and dump it out. Make sure you leave enough room for all of it."

"Just—*leave* it?" Flek said. "In the tunnel?"

"Is anyone going to steal it from there?" I asked coolly. They all flinched, and then hurriedly avoided even looking at me, in case I should read an answer in their faces. I didn't actually care if it was safe. What I cared about was: I had promised to change every piece of silver *within these three storerooms*. So there had to be a lot less of it in here, very quickly. And if my husband didn't like the new location of his money, he could move it back after I was done.

After a moment, Shofer silently took three sacks in each hand and tossed them into the sledge. The deer twitched their ears backwards at the thumps. After another moment, Flek and Tsop started helping him.

Once I saw they were really doing it, I turned and went back out into the second room and set to work with my dark cloth again. It was even more tedious than yesterday: I was sore and aching in every limb, and I wasn't quite as exhausted, so it was more boring as well as more painful. But I kept dumping out one sack after another and changing them silver to gold, silver to gold, and shoving the golden pieces away into the empty aisles while I worked. I didn't stop to eat or drink again; I'd hung the mirror on its chain around my neck, and the sun was brightening in it with now-alarming speed. There were six enormous racks holding countless chests of silver, and I hadn't even finished one halfway before the golden brilliance of noon began to fade again. I'd just started the second rack when the first gleam of sunset began to glow orange out of the edge of the glass. The first of my three days was gone.

My husband appeared a few moments later, on his murderous clockwork schedule. He picked up a handful of golden pieces from the messy heap in the doorway and let them run out of his fingers as he looked around at my progress; he compressed his lips and shook his head, as if he was annoyed to see how much was left to do. "At what hour is the wedding?" he demanded of me.

I was concentrating hard—I'd found I could reliably manage the pieces two deep, if I worked at it—but the question interrupted me. I sat back with a huff of breath. "What I promised was to dance at their wedding, and the musicians will be going until midnight," I said coldly. "I have until then." For all my bravado, it didn't feel like very much time: two nights left and two days, to dig my way through a mountain with a spoon.

"You have not finished here, and there is all the third storeroom yet to change," he said—bitterly, when it was his fault for demanding the impossible in the first place. I was glad that the doors were shut, so he couldn't see what was going on inside the last room of his treasury. "Well, you will change what you can, before you fail." I glared at him. If I hadn't had any prospect of succeeding, I certainly would have stopped even trying that instant.

He ignored my glares and only said coldly, "Ask your questions."

I wanted time more than answers. I suppose I could have asked him what he would do to me if I didn't succeed, but I didn't much want to know, and have something more to fear in advance. "How can I make this go quicker, if you know of any way?" I asked. I didn't have much hope of it, but he certainly knew more about magic than I did.

"You can only do it as quickly as you can," he said, eyeing me almost suspiciously, as if the question were so ridiculous he couldn't quite believe I'd asked it. "Why would I know, if you do not?"

I shook my head in frustration and rubbed the back of my hand across my forehead. "What's past the edge of your kingdom? Where the light ends."

"Darkness," he said.

"I could see that much for myself!" I said with asperity.

"Then why do you ask?" he said, in equal answering irritation.

"Because I want to know what's *in* the dark!" I said.

He made an impatient gesture. "My kingdom! My people and our deep strength, that makes the mountain strong. Through ages of your mortal lives we have raised high our shining walls, and together we have won this fastness from the dark, that we may ever dwell in winter. Do you think it is so lightly done, that you can wander blindly past the borders of my realm and find your way into another?" Then he looked around the room and the silver heap in downturned sourness. "Perhaps you now regret your mortal-hasty promise, and wonder where you might *flee*, from an oath broken in my kingdom? Do not imagine you will find some way into the dwarrowrealms, or that they would shelter you against retribution."

He sneered it at me, as if I should have been ashamed to flee from him. Well, I would have made a dash for escape without the least hesitation, but I had no more notion how I would find these dwarrowrealms than I did the moon, and I was sure he was entirely right about the welcome I would receive from whoever lived there. But that left me without a question to ask him. I didn't care about his customs or his kingdom anymore: one way or another, I was leaving it, and the only thing I wanted was to get on with my work. "Is there any use you can be to me at all in this?" I said.

He made an impatient gesture. "None I can see, and if there were, you have naught left to barter for my aid in any case," he said. "You have pledged your gift too high in folly, and I have little hope you can redeem it."

He turned and left me, and I looked at the poisonous mountains of silver around me, and thought he was very likely right.

Chapter 15

It was so cold in that little house after Irina left, and outside the white trees seemed to have crept closer to the windows, as if they wanted to reach their branches in. I kept the heavy fur rug clutched around my shoulders and dragged the chair to the oven and sat there shivering while I ate another helping of the porridge, my bones sore so that I could feel them rub one against the other at every joint, a little pain every time I moved. But worst of all was to be there alone, with the terrible winter outside. I put another stick on the fire and stirred it to have a brighter flame leaping, like a little bit of company, and to chase away that cold dark outside that would not change. It was no place for an old woman to be, a tired old woman. "Stay out of the woods or the Staryk will snatch you, and take you away to their kingdom," my mother would say, when I was a little girl. And now here I was hiding in their kingdom like a mouse, and what when the fire went out, and what when the porridge was gone? At least there was a great deal of wood in the box next to the oven.

It was a peculiar housekeeper who lived there. While Irina had talked to that strange Jew girl, I found strawberries and honey and salt and oats, and six enormous balls of rough yarn, uneven as lumpy porridge, beside an old-fashioned spindle. It caught on my fingers, but the wool underneath was good; it had only been spun without carding or care, by someone in too much of a hurry to do it properly. My lady the duchess would have cracked my hand across the knuckles with her stick if I had made such a mess in her sight. Not the duchess now, of course—Galina was a good manager, but she spun very indifferent; nor Irina's mother before her, who when she would spin at all made thread that shone like alabaster off her spindle while she stared out the window and sang softly to herself, and never looked at the work of anyone else's hands. But the duchess that was, before either of them.

She had gone to the convent long ago, of course; ten years dead now I had heard, God keep her in his sight. I had seen her last on that terrible day when Irina's father broke the city wall, in the battle that had made him the duke and helped to put the tsar's father on his throne. We watched the smoke of the fighting together from the palace, all of us her women close together, until the smoke began to move into the city. Then she turned away from the window and said, "Come," to me and to the other girls, the six of us not married, and took us down into the cellars to a little room far in the back, with a door fitted out of the stones of the wall, and locked us into it. That was the last time I saw her.

It was so cold and dark and close. That place felt near again to me now, in the cold dark little hut with the deadly winter pressing in. We held to each other and wept and trembled. And they found us anyway there, the soldiers. They found everything in the house—jewels, furniture, the sweet little golden harp that Lady Ania had played, before she died of the fever; I saw it smashed in the hall. There were so many of them, like ants that find any crumb anyone has left unswept.

But by the time they broke open the door to that little room, it was very late in the night; they were already tired out, and it was only a few of them; most of the men had fallen asleep. They only

found us because we were all so frightened by then, we thought it
had been days, though it was only hours, and one of the girls had
begun to rock and say that no one would ever find us and we
would die there walled up. We all caught the terror from her, so
that when we heard voices passing, first one and then the rest of
us began to scream for help. So when they brought us out we fell
into their arms weeping, and they were kind to us, and gave us
some water when we begged them for it, and one of them was a
sergeant, who took us up to his lord and told him we had been
locked up in the cellars.

Erdivilas, Baron Erdivilas he was then, was in the duke's study,
already at home there, his own papers everywhere and his own
men coming in and out. It didn't seem very different to me, either.
I had only once or twice been there. I was not so pretty that the
duke would send for me, and not so ugly that the duchess would
have me go, when she wanted to send him a message. The new
duke had a harder face than the old. But after he looked us over
he said, "Just as well. Take them up to the women's quarters and
tell the men to leave them alone; we don't always need to be
brutes. Do what you can for the others," he told us. I tried as best
I could, and when I couldn't do anything more, I went and spun
the wool that was left in my lady's rooms, and made many skeins
of fine thread while in the city they put out the fires, and so when
things were settled a little more, he kept me on in his household,
as he did not keep anyone who did not make themselves useful
enough.

I was grateful for it, like I was grateful to be let out of that cellar room even by enemy soldiers. I had no husband and no dowry
and no friends. My mother had been the wife of a poor knight
who lost his little land to gambling and the Jews. He had gotten
her a place with the duchess and went out on Crusade to die, and
the duchess had kept me with her women out of kindness when
my mother also passed—the same fever, that winter year, and she

was sorrowful over Ania; I was only a few years younger. But I was no longer young when the city fell, and she went to the holy sisters even before I was out of the cellar.

There was no one else left for me. There was not anyone for me, there had not been since my mother died. I stayed on in the women's quarters and spun, and still the years went by and by, and my hands began to ache if I spun too much, and my eyes began to see less well for fine sewing. So when Silvija, Irina's mother, died with the stillborn boy, I did not stay with the other ladies dutifully weeping. I crept away into the nursery where the little one slept. No one liked her, as no one had liked her mother, because they did not seem to care to be liked. She was too quiet, all the time, and though she did not have her mother's strange eyes, still she seemed to be thinking too much behind them. Irina was sitting up in the bed when I came in, as if she had been woken by the wailing. She was not crying. She only looked up at me with those dark eyes and I felt uneasy, but I sat down beside her and I sang to her and I told her everything would be all right, so that when Erdivilas came to the room he found me already tending her, and told me to keep doing it.

I was glad for it, to have a place secure again, but after he left the room, Irina still looked at me too thoughtfully, as if she understood why I had come to look after her. Of course I came to love her very soon anyway. I had no one else to love, and even if she was not mine, I had been let to borrow her. But I had never been quite sure what she felt for me. Other little children would go running to their nurses and their mamas with open arms and kisses. She never did. I told myself all these years that it was only her way, cool and quiet as new-fallen snow, but still in my secret heart I had not been truly sure, not until the tsar sent men to bring me to hurt her with, and I saw that it would have worked. Oh, it was a strange way to be happy.

She had slept on the cot here in the hut for a little while, and I had sung over her, over my girl, sitting by the fire like all these years, and now I knew she was mine, and not just borrowed for a little while. The yarn I had found was loose enough I could pull the wool apart easily, even now with my big-knuckled hands, and I had the silver comb and brush, the comb and brush that were all Irina's mother had left for her daughter. I combed the wool out soft and spun it over from the beginning, and coiled it into skeins, and after each one was done I put another log in the oven, and so sat spinning away the time, until Irina had woken.

But she had gone back to him now, to that monstrous creature crouching in the palace, black evil disguised as beauty. If he hurt her, if he did not listen . . . But what use was it to worry? I could not do anything, an old woman carried so long here and there on life's stream and washed now to this strange shore; what could I do? I loved her and I had taken care of her as well as I could, but I could not protect her from men or fiends. I braided her hair for her again, and put the crown upon her head, and I let her go. And when she left I did what I could, which was to sit and wait and spin, until my hands grew heavy and I rested them in my lap and shut my eyes for a little while.

I woke with a start and the last log cracking. Outside there was a step, and I was afraid and lost from myself, trying to remember where I was, why was it so cold, while the steps came closer and Irina opened the door. For a single dreadful moment more I still didn't know her—she was so strange and silver in the opening, with that wide crown on her brow and the winter outside crowding close behind her, and she seemed part of it. But it was still her face, and the moment passed. She came in and shut the door and then stopped and looked at it. "Did you do this, Magra?" she asked me.

"Do what?" I said, confused.

"The door," Irina said. "It's properly fastened to the wall now."

I still didn't understand: it hadn't been, before? "I've only been spinning," I said, and I meant to show her the yarn, but I couldn't remember where I had put the skeins; they weren't on the table. But it wasn't important. I stood and went to my girl and held her hands, her cold hands; she had brought in a basket full of things for me. "You're all right, dushenka? He didn't hurt you?" She was safe for another moment, one more moment, and all of life was only moments, after all.

Sergey and I looked into the porridge pot together and we did not say anything. Then we turned and looked at the rest of the house. I remembered suddenly I had put my yarn away on the shelf with the spindle and the knitting needles, but now it was all in a heap on the table. Or I thought it was my yarn, but it was not. It had been wound into skeins and when I picked one up it was different, smooth and soft and much more fine. There was a silver comb lying next to them, a beautiful silver comb that looked like something a tsarina would have, with a picture on it of two deer with antlers drawing a sleigh in snowy woods.

I looked on the shelves for my yarn, but it was gone. The fine smooth yarn was the same color. When I looked very closely it was the same wool. It had only been spun differently, as if to show me what was wanted.

Sergey was looking into the fire box. It was half empty. We looked at each other. It had grown very cold again during the night, so one of us might have climbed down to put more wood on the fire. But I knew I had not done it, and I could see from Sergey's face that he had not done it. Then Sergey said, "I will go see if I can get a squirrel or a rabbit. And I will fetch more wood while I am at it."

There was still plenty of the wool that Sergey had washed for me. I had never spun yarn so fine as the yarn here, but now I tried to do it better. I combed the wool for a long time with the silver comb, carefully so as not to break the teeth, and when at last I began to spin, I remembered suddenly my mother telling me to make the yarn tighter. *Try to go a little faster than that, Wanda.* I had forgotten. I had stopped being careful how I spun after she was dead. There was no one in our house who knew better than I how it was supposed to be. I looked down at my own skirt, which was knitted roughly of my lumpy yarn. Before she died my mother would make big balls of yarn from our goats and take them to our neighbor three houses away who had a loom, and come back with cloth. But the weaver would not take my yarn, so I had always had to knit our clothes instead.

It took me a long time, hours, just to spin one ball of good yarn. Sergey came back as I was finished. He had caught a rabbit, brown and grey. I made another pot of porridge for us while he skinned it. I put all the meat and the bones into the pot to make a stew with the porridge, and some carrots. I made it as much as our pot could hold, more than the two of us would eat. Sergey saw me doing it and he did not say anything and I did not say anything, but we were both thinking the same thing: we did not want whoever was eating our porridge and spinning the yarn to be hungry. If they did not eat the porridge, who knew what they might want to eat instead.

While it was cooking I thought I would start knitting. I wanted to see how much of the bed I could cover with what I already had, so I did not waste time spinning more yarn than we needed. I knitted a strip twice the width of the bed, measuring it until it was long enough, and then I went on from there. The work did not go quickly. I tried to be careful and keep it even and smooth. But I was not used to knitting so carefully either. It was hard to remember not to make it so loose. And then in one place I made it too tight instead, and I did not notice at first until I had already knitted three rows onward and I started having to push hard to get the needles in. Then I tried to keep going and just make it better from there on, but I had made that last row so tight that I was going very slow, like trying to walk through thick mud, and finally I gave up and unraveled those three big rows and did the wrong part all over again.

Once I had finished up the first skein, I stopped and looked at how much I had made. It was a piece as long as my hand. It was so nicely spun and wound up that there was more yarn than I thought there could be. I measured the length of the bed with my hands and counted ten. I had five skeins left and the ball of yarn I had made today. So if I made only three more balls of yarn, that would be enough. I folded up my knitting carefully and I put it on the shelf and I went back to spinning.

I spun all the afternoon. It was still getting colder and colder. All around the door and windows there were little clouds of fog where the air from outside came in through the cracks, and there was starting to be frost creeping inside. Sergey could not help me, so instead he made wooden hinges to hang the door. He had found some old nails and a little rusted saw in a corner of the shed to make them. On the inside of the house, he nailed on some more branches around the edges of the doorway, making the opening smaller than the door, to block the wind. He did the same thing around each window. Then he plastered it all with straw and mud. After that the cold air could not come in and we were warm and cozy in the house. The oven and the porridge filled it with a good smell. It felt strange to be in that warm quiet place with food. It felt strange because I was already used to it. It was so easy to be used to it.

We stopped to eat after I finished spinning. "I think I can finish in three days more," I told Sergey, while we ate the good meat porridge. We left plenty over in the pot.

"How long have we been here?" Sergey asked me.

I had to stop and count it in my head. I started from market day. I had sold the aprons in the market. I did that in the morning and then I went home and Kajus was there waiting. Even in my head, I hurried past the rest of that, but it was all still one day. Then we had run into the woods and we had kept going a long time into the night. Until we found the house. We had found the house that day. It didn't feel as though it could all have been the same day, but it had been. "It is Monday," I said finally. "Today is Monday. We have been here five days."

After I said it out loud, we were both quiet over our bowls. It did not feel as though we had been in that house five days. But that was not because it felt as if we had just arrived. It felt as if we had always been here.

Then Sergey said, "Maybe they have sent word on to Vysnia, about us."

I stopped eating and looked up at him. He meant, maybe we should not go ever. He meant we should stay here. "It would have been hard to send with all the snow," I said slowly. I didn't want to leave either. But also I was still afraid of this place where things came out of nowhere and someone did my spinning over for me and ate our porridge and burned our wood. And I did not see why it was all right for us to stay. It was all right for us to stay when we would freeze to death otherwise. We had to do that. And we had paid back for the food. We had fixed the chair and we would fix the bed. We had made the windows and doors tight. But that did not make it *our* house, that we could stay in forever. Someone had built this house and it was not us. We didn't know who they were. We couldn't ask them if we could stay, even if they would let us.

"We cannot leave for three days anyway," Sergey said. "Maybe the snow will melt by then."

"Let us see," I said after a moment. "Maybe the knitting will not take me so long."

But after we cleared the table I went back to the shelf where I had left my knitting and it was not there. Instead on the shelf there was half a loaf of still-fresh bread, and underneath a beautiful fine napkin there was a small ham and a round of cheese and a lump of butter, with only a little bit cut off of each. There was a big box of tea and even a jar of cherries in syrup, like Miryem had bought to eat once at the market. There was even a basket big enough to hold all of it.

I stood looking at the things so long that Sergey got worried and came to see also. We didn't know what to do. It wasn't something we could even make believe had happened in some real way. We could not pretend that we had just not seen all that food. We could not pretend someone had come into the house and put that food there and went away again. We had not been asleep.

Of course we wanted to eat some of that beautiful food. My mouth remembered the taste of those cherries, the thick sweet syrup like the smell of summer. We were afraid, though, even more than we had been about the oats, and the honey. It was food that did not even pretend to go with the house. And we had just eaten, so we were not even really hungry.

"We should save it for later," I said after a moment. "We don't need it now."

Sergey nodded. Then he took the axe. "I will go break up some logs," he said, and went out into the yard, even though it was dark. We needed more wood. We had not put any wood on the fire all day, but the box was almost empty.

I found the knitting lying on the cot. It felt different, and when I unfolded it, the piece was the same size as I had made, but it had all been done over from the beginning. It had a pattern in it now, a beautiful design like a raised vine with flowers that I could feel with my fingers. I had never seen anything like it except for sale in the market for money, and not so fine, either.

I unraveled some of it to try and see how the picture was

made, but each line was so different, the stitches changed so much from one to another, and I couldn't see how to remember which one was next. Then I thought, of course, it was magic. I took a stick out of the fireplace with one end charred, and I used the magic that Miryem had taught me. I started at the beginning of the vine in the first row, and I counted how many of a stitch there was in a row, and I wrote down that number, and if it was a forward stitch, I put a mark above it, and if it was a backwards stitch, I put a mark below. I had to make some other marks too, when stitches were brought together, or added. I had to make my numbers small as if I were writing in Miryem's book. There were thirty rows all different before I came back to the first one.

But when I was done, I had the whole picture there on the floor, turned into numbers. It looked very different. I was not sure I believed it could really be the same thing. But I remembered how those little marks in Miryem's book became silver and gold, and I took the knitting and I began to add on another row. I did not look back at the picture while I worked. I thought I had to trust the numbers. So I did, and I followed them, for all those thirty rows, and then I stopped and I looked at what I had done, and there were all the vines and leaves, just as beautiful, and I had made it. The magic had worked for me.

Sergey came back in, stamping off his feet. There was a dusting of white across his shoulders. He put his big armful of wood into the box, but it only filled it halfway. "I must go get more," he said. "It is snowing again."

"Are you warm enough, Stepon?" Panova Mandelstam asked me. I said I was because however warm I was, that had to be warm enough, because there was nothing to do about it if I wasn't. I was in the best place in the sleigh, huddled between Panov and Panova Mandelstam under the blankets and furs, but I was getting colder the whole time. At first I thought I was feeling so cold because Algis was there spying on us, but that wasn't why. It got colder and colder all that afternoon, and overhead there were dark grey clouds getting thicker and thicker. We were not halfway to Vysnia when it finally began snowing. It was only a little bit at the beginning, but then it began to come faster and faster, until we could not see what was in front of the horses' heads. After a while Panova Mandelstam said, "Perhaps we should stop at the next village for the rest of the night. It should not be far."

But we did not come to any houses, even though the sleigh kept going a long time. "Algis," Panov Mandelstam said to the driver finally, "are you sure we are still on the road?"

Algis hunched a little in his coats and darted a look back at us. He didn't say anything, but his face was scared. So he knew he had lost the road. Sometime ago, when the road had turned, the horses had gone between two trees that were not on either side of the road, they were just far apart from each other. The snow was covering the road and the bushes, so Algis had not noticed. He had just kept going. Now we were lost in the forest. The forest was very big and there were not any houses in it away from the road and the river. The Staryk killed anyone who made a house away from the river.

The horses were not going very fast anymore. They were tired and they plodded. Their big feet were digging into the new snow and they had to pull them up again each step. Soon they would stop. "What do we do?" I asked.

Algis had turned around again and was just sitting hunched over the reins. Panov Mandelstam looked at his back, and then he said, "It is all right, Stepon. We will stop somewhere there is not too much wind and get the horses under blankets and give them their grain and any grass we can find. We will stay between them and under blankets and keep warm until it is light. Once the sun comes up we can tell where we are. I am sure you can find some-place good, Algis."

Algis did not say anything, but in a little while he turned the horses' heads and stopped near a very big tree. If we did not know we were in the forest before, we knew then, because there were no trees so big anywhere near the road. Someone would have cut it down to use it if it was close enough to get it out of the forest. It was as big across as one of the horses almost, and there was a rot-ting hole on one side of the tree that made a little sheltered hol-low.

Panova Mandelstam and I held the reins of the horses while Panov Mandelstam and Algis stamped down the snow next to the tree and made a wall of snow around an open place. Horses are much bigger than goats. I was a little scared of them, but I had to help hold them, and they only stayed still and did not jump like goats did, and I could tell they were very tired. Finally we led the horses in the open place and then we took all the blankets from the sleigh and covered them with the blankets. Panov Mandels-tam took the bags out of the sleigh and put them in the little hol-low, and then he helped Panova Mandelstam climb down from the sleigh and over the snow to sit on them.

Then he straightened up and looked at Algis. Algis was stand-ing next to the back of the sleigh. His head was hanging. He said, low, "I didn't fill the bucket." He meant the grain bucket. So there was no food for the horses.

Panov Mandelstam didn't say anything for a minute. The si-lence felt very long. Finally he said, "It is lucky this is a late snow. There will still be some fresh growth under. We must dig and get them some grass and whatever else we can find for them to eat."

He was still kind, but I thought that he had not *felt* kind, and that was why he had been quiet. I thought that meant he must be very worried. So then I was very worried. I did my best to help to dig. Because Panova Mandelstam had given me the boots, I could kick away snow and get down to the ground. But it was mostly dry pine needles here under the big old tree.

We all went in different directions. "Do not go so far that you cannot see the big tree," Panov Mandelstam told me. "The snow will cover your steps and you will not find the way back. Every ten steps turn around and look."

The big tree was so big that I could see it for a long way. I counted and looked every ten steps until I came to a place that was open to the sky. There was a big dead tree under the snow making a lump. It had been here and then it had fallen over. Now there was an open place. I dug under the snow with my boots and a broken branch and I found some grass. It was dying because of the snow, but it was not all the way dead, and also there was old dry grass under it. I pulled up as much of it as I could get to. It did not seem like a lot, but even a little bit of food is very good when you are very hungry. I thought maybe it was the same for horses as people. When I had an armful I carried it back. Panova Mandelstam had stayed with the horses. She was petting their heads and singing to them softly. Their heads were hanging low. She had given them water at least. I didn't know where she had found water that wasn't snow, but then I saw she was shivering and then I knew. She had put snow into the water bucket and wrapped herself around it so it would melt for them.

I gave them each half of the grass I had found. They did not start to eat it right away, but Panova Mandelstam took it and gave it to them by hand. Then they ate, and they ate it all up very fast. Panov Mandelstam and Algis came back too. They had not found any grass, but Algis had brought some wood to try to make a fire with. It was wet and I didn't think it would work to start a fire, though.

"There was more grass where I got this," I said.

"I will go with him," Algis said to Panov Mandelstam. He still did not look up. I think he was ashamed he had gotten lost and had not filled the grain bucket, and now he was trying to say he was sorry. I did not really want to listen to him saying sorry, but I couldn't say I didn't want him to come with me so we went back to the clearing. Algis spread his topcoat out on the snow, and we dug up more grass until we made a big heap on top of the coat, and then Algis took the heap back while I kept finding more grass until he came back to help again.

It was easier with Algis than if I was alone, because he was taller and stronger than me. But I wished Sergey and Wanda were with us instead. They were both taller than Algis and stronger than him, and they would get more grass, and also they would not forget to fill the grain bucket in the first place. Maybe they would not fill the grain bucket, but that would only be if there was no grain to put into it, they would not just forget. Also they would not be spies on us.

I was not feeling kind at all. I thought maybe we would all die of cold. I thought maybe if we did not die of cold, but the horses died of being worked so hard without enough food, and we were in the forest with no horses and not traveling, then it would be like we were making a house. Then maybe the Staryk would come after us. I did not like to think about what the Staryk had done to Sergey, but I could not help thinking about it sometimes at night. I was thinking about it now.

Finally Algis and I had gotten to all the grass we could find. Now when we kicked away the snow we only found places where we had already pulled up all the grass. We went back. The horses ate up all the grass, but their heads were hanging afterwards, and they were still hungry. They were cold too because there was no fire. Panov Mandelstam had tried, but the wood and kindling was too wet to make a spark. There was some food for us, because Panova Mandelstam had packed the basket. She would not forget to fill a grain bucket either. But she shared the food with Algis anyway, and she even gave him as big a portion as she gave to Panov Mandelstam.

After we finished eating one of the horses gave a very big sigh and slowly got down on the ground. It was very cold on the ground, but it was too tired to get up again even though Panov Mandelstam and Algis both tried to get it back up. Panova Mandelstam was holding the other one and trying to coax it to stay up, but after a little while it got down, too. Their heads were even lower. I thought maybe they would die. And then even if we did not die, in the morning we would be alone deep in the woods. Like Sergey and Wanda had been, but we were not as strong as Sergey and Wanda. They had left me behind because they could go for a long time in the woods and I could not. Unless maybe they had not gone on. Maybe they had stopped in the woods and died in the snow like we were going to.

There was nothing I could do. I was not even tall enough to pull up on the horses' reins. When the others gave up, Panova Mandelstam had me sit down next to her up against the side of one horse, and we covered ourselves with a blanket and a fur cape. The horse's body blocked the wind, and the tree blocked it some too. It was still cold, but that was all we could do. Panov Mandelstam and Algis sat next to the other horse the same way. I put my hands in my pockets and huddled next to Panova Mandelstam. The nut was still in my pocket and I wrapped my fingers around it and held it tight.

After the Staryk king left me, I got up and went back to the big storeroom to see how the work was going. I didn't have enormous hope—there was so much silver. It was just a little better than *no* hope, and also had the benefit of being an annoyance to my husband, even if he disposed of me, too.

But Tsop and Flek and Shofer had done more than I'd expected. It certainly went quicker to throw money away than to make it, and Staryk strength made light of the work: they'd already opened a large circle in the middle of the room, and the sledge was half full again. They'd gotten almost all the sacks out, and only loose coin was left. There was a great deal of loose coin, however. They all straightened up when I came in; magical strength or not, they looked tired, too. I didn't feel badly for throwing away my lord's silver, but I was making them slave away to do it, and to have any chance at all I'd need them to keep at it for me to the very end. All through this night and the coming day, and then another night and day after, every last hour I could eke out before the dancing had ended. Luckily Basia's wedding wouldn't begin until late, since she was a city girl. Without sleep or rest, for them as much as me, except I'd gotten myself into the mess, and why should they care?

"I need something to eat and drink," I said. "Bring something for yourselves, too. And if I'm alive at the end of this," I added, "you'll bring me all the silver you own yourselves, or can borrow, and I'll make it gold for you in thanks for the work you're doing."

They all three went perfectly silent and still. After a moment, they looked at one another—making certain I'd said it?—and then Tsop burst out, "We are *servants*."

"I'd rather you had a better reason than that to help me," I said, warily. It didn't help. They still looked as uneasy as if I'd invited them to walk through a room full of snakes. Flek had her hands twisting together before her, staring down at them.

Then Shofer abruptly said to me, "Open-Handed," saying it like a name, "though you know not what you do, I accept your promise, and will return myself for it as fair measure, if you will accept the exchange." He clenched his fist to his collarbone, and bowed to me. Tsop swallowed and said, "And I too," and bowed as well. She looked at Flek, whose face was wrenched and unhappy. After a moment, Flek whispered, barely audible, "I will as well," and clasping both her hands against her chest bowed, too.

Well, Shofer wasn't wrong, I *didn't* know what I'd done, but I'd certainly done *something*, and it had been worth doing. "Yes," I said at once, and Flek ran out of the room to go and bring us food, and in the meantime Tsop and Shofer began to hurl the last sacks into the sleigh as if their own lives depended on it now, and not just mine. Perhaps they did, for all I knew. It didn't seem that gold would be enough of a reward for that, but if they thought it was, I wasn't going to complain.

"I must change the deer," Shofer told me when Flek came back, and I joined them in the big storeroom to eat. I nodded. We all wolfed down a few bites, and I took a drink of the cold water and went back to work in the second storeroom alone.

I think I did fall asleep once or twice during that night, but not for long; I only drowsed off drooping as I sat, and jerked back awake a little bit later when I heard the clattering of hooves in the room beyond, another load being taken away to dump into the tunnel. My eyes were burning and tired, my back and my shoulders ached, and I finished sweeping my hand over the coins on the cloth, and spilled them away again.

The hours dragged away at once too slowly and too quickly. It was an agony that I only wanted to be over, except when the line of sunrise appeared in the mirror, my heart started pounding. I'd gotten quicker once I'd mastered the trick of doing them two deep: I was a good way into the third rack. But there were three more left: I'd have to keep working this fast all the way to the end, to manage it. I had to stop and eat: Tsop brought me some food on a plate and a cup of water, and my hands shook so that the water nearly slopped up over the sides. I swallowed everything she'd brought me without tasting it, and went back to the endless grinding terrible work.

My husband appeared again just as the sunset vanished out of my mirror. I sat back on my heels and wiped my arm across my forehead. I wasn't sweating, but I felt as though I *should* have been. He looked around the room with cold displeasure, measuring how much I had left to do. I'd nearly finished the fourth rack by then, but there was only one night and day left, and as far as he knew, there was that monstrous third room still to do.

"What does it mean among you to give someone a gift?" I said. I very much wanted to know what I *had* done, with my servants.

He frowned at me. "A *gift*? Something given without return?" He made it sound like murder.

I tried to think how to describe what I'd done. "Something given in thanks for what might have been demanded instead."

His contemptuous expression didn't change. "Only the worthless would imagine such a thing. A return must be made."

He'd been perfectly happy to make me change silver to gold for him without any return at all until I'd prodded him, but I didn't point that out. "You've given me things without return," I said.

His silver eyes widened. "I have given you that to which you are entitled by right and have demanded of me, nothing more," he said hastily, as if he thought I was going to be violently offended, and added, "You are already my wife; you cannot imagine I meant you to become my bondswoman."

So a gift that couldn't be repaid, had to be repaid with—that? "What is a bondswoman?"

He paused, once more overcome by my appalling ignorance of perfectly obvious things. "One whose fate is bound to another," he said very slowly, as if speaking to a child.

"That's not enough to explain it to me," I said with asperity.

He raised his hands in impatience. "One whose fate is bound

to another! Where a lord rises, so do his bondsmen; where a lord falls low, so too his bondsmen; when a lord is stained, so are they, and as he, so too must they cleanse their names with their life's blood."

I stared at him, queasily. I hadn't *really* thought that Flek and Tsop and Shofer were putting their own lives on the line, and as much as I'd suspected it would mean my death to fail, there was something worse about hearing it plainly out of his mouth. *Stained,* like a ruined cloth, only to be repaired by dyeing it all the way through red with blood. "That sounds like a terrible arrangement," I said through my tight throat, trying to coax some more out of him; perhaps I was misunderstanding. "I can't imagine why anyone would agree to become one."

He folded his arms. "If your imagination fails you, that is no sign I have failed to answer the question."

I pressed my lips tight, but I'd walked into that one too squarely. I worded my final question more carefully. "All right. Then what are several illuminating reasons why anyone would either accept or refuse such an opportunity?"

"To rise beyond their station, of course," he said immediately. "A bondsman stands always but one rank removed from their lord. Their children inherit both bond and rank, but their children's children inherit rank alone, and whatever standing the bondsman holds, at the time of their birth, they have it in their own right. As for who would refuse, those whose rank already stands high, or who suspect the lord who asks their bond is likely to fall: only a fool would bind their fate for little gain." He'd been visibly pleased to win his point on the question, but he paused, suddenly going wary. "What concerns you so of bondsmen?" he demanded.

"Do *I* owe *you* answers?" I asked, in the most dulcet tones I could manage, careful to make it a question. He opened his mouth and then shut it again and glared at me in irritation before sweeping out without another word to me: he couldn't give me a free answer, after all.

But I sat there alone and silent after he'd left, instead of getting back to the work. I hadn't known what I'd done with Shofer and Tsop and Flek, and now that I did know, I tried to convince myself I'd have done it anyway. I'd only made them the offer, after all, and they'd chosen to accept, knowing better than I did the risk they took.

But I couldn't help thinking of those circles within circles at the wedding, and all the grey-clad servants standing far distant in the outer rings, silent and their heads bowed. I hadn't just promised them wealth. I'd suddenly thrust open a golden path all the way from that outer ring and straight to the highest rank of the nobility, like a fairy with a poisoned fruit in one hand and a dream come true in the other. Who could turn away from such a chance, even if the risk was your life? Then a slow cold shudder ran up my back: Flek almost *had* turned away. Shofer and Tsop were afraid, but they'd done it; she'd really hesitated.

I didn't want to know why. I didn't want to think about it. I couldn't ask her; I tried to make that my excuse, but my hands were shaking when I put them out over the silver coins, and they wouldn't change. Finally I stood up and pushed open the doors to the other room, the room where Shofer and Tsop and Flek were all heaving silver into the sledge as fast as they could go, even though the sharp edges of their faces were dull with weariness and the blue-ice of their eyes clouded like a pane of glass fogged over with breath. They'd emptied nearly half of the room. There was still a chance, a chance for me: a chance I'd wrung out of their strength and courage. They stopped to look at me. I didn't want to say the words. I didn't want to care.

I said, through my tight throat, "If you have children, tell me how many."

Tsop and Shofer were silent, but they looked at Flek. She didn't look in my face. She whispered, "I have one daughter, only one," very softly, and then she turned away blindly and began shoveling again, silver spilling over the blade and ringing on the floor like a dreadful metallic rain.

Chapter 16

I did not want to wake up, but I thought I heard Mama calling me in a voice that sounded like a bell ringing, so I opened my eyes. The horses had snow on their backs and there was snow in the hollows of the fur coat that Panova Mandelstam had covered us with. Everyone else had fallen asleep, too. I thought maybe I should wake them, but it was still snowing and very cold, and I thought we would probably not live until morning anyway. It did not seem to be worth waking them up only for them to be afraid. I was afraid, too, but then I heard a sound. It was the ringing sound that had woken me up. It was not far away.

After a minute I made myself get out from under the fur coat. It was very cold and I was shivering right away, but I went to the ringing sound, and in a little while I knew it was an axe, and then I stopped. Someone was cutting wood, and I could not think who would be cutting wood in the middle of the night in the forest when it was snowing, because that was very strange. But if they were cutting wood with an axe then they probably wanted the wood for a fire, and if they had a fire and they would let us come sit by the fire, then we would not die.

So I kept going. The ringing got louder until I saw the man cutting wood and first I thought it was Sergey, but then of course I knew it was not Sergey, it only looked like Sergey. Then I said, "Sergey?" and he turned around, and it *was* Sergey, and I ran to him. I thought for a moment maybe we were all dead and this was Heaven, like the priest talked about in church when Da took us, which he did once in a while if the priest saw him in town. But I did not think I would be cold or hungry in Heaven. I hoped we were not in Hell for killing Da.

"No, we are alive!" Sergey said. "Where did you come from?"

I took him by the hand and led him back to the big tree and showed him everyone else asleep. "But he is a spy," I said, pointing at Algis. "The men in the village told him to tell them if we saw you."

Sergey shrugged after a moment. He meant we could not leave Algis to freeze anyway, even if he was a spy, and even if he had forgotten to fill the grain bucket, and gotten us lost. I supposed that was true. Also, if he had not gotten us lost, I would not have found Sergey, so maybe I could not be angry at Algis anymore.

We woke up the Mandelstams and Algis, and they were all very surprised to see Sergey, but of course they were glad, although Algis was afraid also, but even he was glad that there was somewhere warm to go. Sergey went to the horses. One of them was dead, and the other one did not want to get up, but Sergey got his arms under the horse's front legs and pushed up while Algis pulled on the reins and Panov Mandelstam and Panova Mandelstam and me all helped push from under, and finally the horse got up.

Sergey took us through the forest back to where he was chopping wood and then he kept going, and in a few steps more I could see a little firelight up ahead. We all walked quicker once we saw it, even the horse. There was a little house there with a chimney and a big shed with a heap of straw. Sergey put the horse in the shed and it started eating the straw right away. "There are oats inside," Sergey said. "Go in."

Wanda was inside the house, but she opened the door because she heard us. Panova Mandelstam made a glad noise when she saw her and ran to Wanda and put her arms around her and kissed her cheeks. I could tell that Wanda did not know what to do but she looked happy anyway, and she said, "Come in," so we went into the house and it was very warm and there was a good smell of porridge. There was only one chair and a log stump to sit on, but there was also a cot and a pallet on the top of the stove. We gave Panova Mandelstam the chair and put her by the fire, and Wanda put a big blanket over her. Panov Mandelstam sat on the stump next to her. Algis sat down on the floor near the fire and huddled up. Wanda told me to climb up on top of the oven and I did and I felt very warm.

"I will make tea," Wanda said, and I wondered how she would make tea, and where the house had come from, but mostly I thought about how good it would be to drink hot tea, but I fell asleep again before it was ready. I didn't wake up again until it was early morning, and I heard a noise of wood rubbing against itself and felt cold air sweeping in on my head. I picked up my head. I was still on top of the oven and Panova Mandelstam and Panov Mandelstam were sleeping on either side of me. Wanda and Sergey were sleeping on the floor in front of the oven.

The sound was the door scraping shut. Algis was going out into the snow. I put my head down again. Then I picked it up again and said, "Sergey!" but it was too late. When we went outside, Algis was already gone. He had taken the horse. Sergey had fed it oats and rubbed its legs and given it warm water to drink so it had gotten better by morning. It was a big strong horse meant for pulling a sleigh. With just Algis on its back I thought it would be fast. Probably if he just let the horse lead him, it would go back home to its stable. He would tell everyone in the village where we were.

"We must try to get to Vysnia before the snow melts," Panova Mandelstam said, while we sat around the table. Wanda had made tea, and she was cooking porridge now for us all to eat before we left. Sergey and Panov Mandelstam had brought in a few more stumps to sit on. "We have food and warm coats. We will get out to the road and get someone to take us on to the city. No one will tell on us in the quarter, and there is some money in the bank. We will bribe someone to clear your names if we can. My father will know who to go to."

"I must finish the mattress before we go," Wanda said. She went and picked up the big blanket she had been knitting, and I saw it was not a blanket but a mattress cover. It was very pretty. There was a beautiful pattern in it of leaves.

"Wanda, this is beautiful work," Panova Mandelstam even said, touching it. "You should bring it with you."

But Wanda shook her head. "We need to fix the bed."

I didn't know why, but if she said so, then she had to. I looked at the cot and the mattress cover. "It is almost done, isn't it?" I asked. "It is the right size."

Wanda held up the blanket and it was the right size. It was longer than she was. When she held up her hands over her head it still reached almost all the way to the floor. She put it down again and I thought she looked a little scared even though I didn't know why she would be scared because it was done, when she wanted it to be done. "Yes," she said. "I can finish it quickly now."

"Wanda," Panov Mandelstam said slowly, as if he wanted to ask a question, but Wanda shook her head fiercely, because she did not want to talk about it, and even though Panov Mandelstam liked words so much, he saw that she did not want to talk, so he stopped.

"It is all right, Wanda," Panova Mandelstam said after a moment. "Go ahead and do what you need to do. I will make some more porridge."

Wanda quickly sewed up two open sides of the mattress, and then she stuffed it with a big pile of wool, and then she sewed up the last bit of the mattress and put it on the cot. The cot looked very pretty with the mattress on it. Meanwhile Panov Mandelstam and I helped Sergey tidy up the yard and the shed. We filled the woodbox again. It had gone empty overnight. I didn't know why the oven took so much wood, but now I knew why Sergey was cutting wood in the forest at night, and it was just as well he had been doing that. Panova Mandelstam asked me to bring her a long stick, and she tied some straw around the bottom and swept the house.

The porridge was ready so we ate it. We went outside with our plates, which were just pieces of wood that Sergey had cut off a tree, and rubbed them with snow until they were clean. We put them on a shelf inside the house. Wanda made up another pot of porridge and put it into the ashes to cook, even though we were leaving. She closed the door of the oven and we looked around. The house looked nice and tidy. It was almost as big as our old house, but I liked it more. The boards were close together and the oven was very solid and the roof was snug. I was sorry to go away from it, and I thought Sergey and Wanda were sorry to go away too.

"Thank you for giving us shelter," Wanda said to the house, as if it were a person. Then she picked up the basket and went outside. We all followed her out.

Minutes went slipping through my fingers with silver coins, vanishing as they changed to gold. I was close enough to the doors now that I could hear the shovels ringing faintly in the other room, going quickly, whipped along by the same fatal deadline, but I didn't allow myself to go and look and see how far they'd gotten. We worked all through the night without stopping. When the disk of the mirror began to glow with morning, I had to make myself keep changing them systematically: my head swam, nauseated, when I looked up and saw it. There was still an entire rack left to change, and my first flinching terrified instinct was to madly turn out every last chest and try to change them all at once. I closed my hands and eyes for a moment before I could go on.

I didn't stop to eat any breakfast. I was distantly grateful that my husband didn't come to inspect my progress again that morning, as much as I could be grateful for anything. I felt sore as if I really were being beaten. But the horror kept me at it. I kept thinking how they would do it, what they would do. Would they put a knife in the hand of a small child and expect her to put it to her own throat, or would they kill the child themselves? Would they make her watch her mother die first, or the other way around? Would they make *Flek* do it? I knew that no matter what there would be no mercy to it, no kindness allowed. You couldn't return a kindness after you were dead.

In the middle storeroom I spilled the chests out one after the other and changed them, until I finally poured out the very last one, and made all of it go to gold. I spilled the final heap off the tablecloth and staggered up. The blue of the mirror's sky was just starting to go dim with the approach of sunset. I had perhaps an hour until my time expired. Dragging the cloth behind me, I opened the doors.

The storeroom was nearly empty. The sledge was all the way at the far opening, nearly full again, and inside the mouth of the tunnel I could see the gleam of silver packed from the surface of the ice all the way to the ceiling. Flek and Tsop were working in the last corner on the nearer side of the river, and Shofer was

on the other side. I ran to them. "Go help him!" I told Flek and
Tsop. They didn't even nod; they only went to the other one
where Shofer was working and joined him. I put down my cloth
and shoved silver onto it with my bare hands and changed it. All
that was left was a tiny pile, almost pathetic in that enormous
space, only the crust of honey you would scrape from around
the edges of an empty jar when you had nothing else left. But it
was a big jar, and even this little scraping still had to be gold, not
silver.

My hands were trembling by the time I changed the last coins.
Shofer had gone and emptied another load into the tunnel, and
while he had done it, Flek and Tsop had shoveled the last of the
final corner into a pile by the river's edge, so when Shofer brought
the sledge back, they could load it quickly. I let them do it, and
went around the room searching in every corner for any gleam of
silver, any last coin left. My mirror was almost gone full dark.

But they had cleared the room. Only on one little ledge jutting
from the wall, I found a single silver coin caught. The hooves of
the deer clattered on the ice behind my back as Shofer turned the
sledge, with only one small mound in the bottom. They had
packed the tunnel so full that he had to back it up to have room to
dump the last heap out onto the ice. Flek and Tsop came slowly
towards me. I picked the one coin up and held it up, and between
my thumb and forefinger gold swept across its face, just as the
great double doors of the storeroom were thrust open, and my
husband came into the room.

He had a grim anger-clenched look on his face that fell away
instantly. He stopped open-mouthed, gazing on his emptied storeroom. I was shaking with weariness and reaction, but I dragged
myself straight and said with hoarse defiance, "There. I have
changed every coin within your storerooms to gold."

He jerked his head to stare at me. I'd expected him to be furious; instead he looked almost—bewildered, as if he had no idea

what to make of it, of me. He slowly turned his head to look: at the silver piled inside the tunnel, at Shofer standing there sagging, holding the heads of the deer on the sledge, at Flek and Tsop both wavering like willow saplings in a high wind, and at last at me again. He walked slowly across the room and took the final coin out of my fingers and looked at it, and broke it in half with his bare hands.

"It's gold all the way through!" I snapped at him.

"Yes," he said, blankly. "It is." He stood there still a while longer before he lifted his head at last out of a daze. He put the two halves of the coin on the ledge and bowed to me, formal and courtly. "The task I set is accomplished. I will take you to the sun-lit world, as I have promised, that you shall dance at your cousin's wedding. Ask your questions now, my lady."

The courtesy confused me; I'd been pulling myself together to do battle with him. I stared at him blankly instead. I couldn't think of a single question. After a moment, I said, "Do I have time to bathe?" I was a bedraggled mess, after three days and three nights more or less entire spent staggering around changing the silver.

"Make ready as you will. You shall have as much time as you require," he said. It didn't seem exactly an answer, but if he was that certain, I wouldn't argue. "Ask twice more."

I looked at Flek and Tsop and Shofer and said, "I promised to turn all their own silver to gold for them, in exchange for their help. They accepted, and made return of themselves. Are they my bondsmen now?"

"Yes," he said, and inclined his head to them, as if he hadn't the slightest trouble thinking of three servants as nobility, just like that. The three of them had a bit more difficulty with it; they all started to bob low curtseys, and had to stop themselves partway down, and when Flek came back up she seemed to suddenly real-ize we'd finished, it was all over, and she jerked like a doll and turned around and put her hands over her face with a stifled cry somewhere between agony and relief.

I would have liked to sit down and weep myself. "Do I have time to change their silver for them now?" I asked. I wasn't planning to come back here if I could help it.

"That you have already asked and been answered," he said. "Ask again."

That was annoying, when for once I had been trying to use my questions *up*. "What does that mean?" I demanded. "Why is it the same whether I want to go take a bath or change their silver, too?"

He frowned at me. "As you have been true, so will I be, and in no lesser degree," he said, a bit huffily. "I will lay my hand upon the flow of time, if need be, that you shall have however much of it you seek. Go therefore and make ready however you wish, and when you are ready to depart, we shall go."

He paused to look around the storeroom once more, while I sluggishly puzzled through what he'd said, but by the time I burst out belatedly, "You could have taken me there in time, then, no matter what!" I was saying it to an empty doorway, which cared about as much as he would have, I suppose.

I was glaring at the space where he'd been when Tsop said a little timidly, "But he couldn't have."

"What?" I said.

Tsop moved her hand around the storeroom. "You have done a great working. So now he can do another in return. But high magic never comes without a price."

"Why is it a great working that we shoved more than half his treasure into a tunnel?" I said, exasperated.

"You were challenged beyond the bounds of what could be done, and found a path to make it true," Tsop said.

"Oh," I said, and then I realized—"You answered me! Twice!"

"I am bondswoman to you now, Open-Handed," she said, sounding a little taken aback. "You need not make me bargains."

"So now you *will* answer my questions?" I said, trying to understand, and they all three nodded. All when I couldn't think of anything to ask. Or rather, there were any number of questions I wanted to ask, but they seemed unwise to say out loud, even under the circumstances: how do you kill a Staryk king, what magic does he have, will he win if he fights a demon? Instead I said, "Well, if I have all the time in the world, now, I *do* want a bath. And then I will change your silver before I go."

I wrote the letters to Prince Ulrich and Prince Casimir myself, but Mirnatius did sign them, and he even grudgingly took me down to his own table for dinner—after certain preparations. "You wore that two days ago," Mirnatius said sharply, when I came out from the dressing alcove, and for a moment my heart stopped. I thought he had finally noticed my Staryk jewels, but then I realized he was complaining of my pale grey gown, the finest work of all my stepmother's women, which yes, I meant to wear again, without even thinking about it. Not even archduchesses were rich enough to have a gown for every ordinary day.

But *he* evidently insisted on wearing an entirely new ensemble each and every single day, an extravagance so outrageous he must surely have been spending magic on his councillors just to keep them from howling every time they looked at his accounts. And apparently he now meant me to follow suit. "You *should* know more about the tax rolls," I said, while he rummaged scowling through my entire bridal chest, evidently to prove to himself that I only—*only*—had three suitable gowns, all of which had already seen too much use to be acceptable for *his* tsarina.

He straightened up and glared at me, and then he abruptly put his hands on my shoulders, and beneath them my dress unfolded itself into green velvet and pale blue brocade like a gaudy butterfly fighting its way out of a grey cocoon, bannered sleeves unfurling all the way to the ground with a silver-tasseled thump. He was wearing pale blue himself, and a cloak lined in deep green, so we made a matched pair as we descended on the court. He was still far from content with my appearance. "At least your *hair's* handsome," he muttered, with a tone of dissatisfaction, looking down at the back of my intricately braided head; he plainly expected to be sniggered at for his choice.

I hadn't been to Koron in four years, but I'd heard enough grumbles at my father's table to know what to expect. Mirnatius had made the court his own mirror, as much as he could: of course many of the most powerful nobles of Lithvas kept houses in the city, and they were the most important, but the rest, the courtiers and hangers-on who were there by his sufferance, were one and all the beautiful and the glittering. Half the women were bare-shouldered and collarless, even with a foot of snow on the windowsills outside, and the men all wore silks and velvets as impractical for riding as his own, without the benefit of magic to keep them pristine or change them over again. They eyed one another like hungry wolves looking for something wrong, and I would have felt sorry for any girl Mirnatius *had* chosen to throw before them, no matter how beautiful.

But they grew less judgmental in the dazzle of Staryk silver. As we made our entrance, they looked me over with their narrowed eyes from all the corners of the room, and first they smirked, and then they looked again, and then they looked puzzled, and then they stared at me lost and half bewildered, and forgot that they had to make polite conversation. Some of the men looked at me like dragons, covetous, and they kept looking at me even when they were speaking to Mirnatius himself. After the fourth one tripped off the royal dais because he couldn't stop staring, Mirnatius turned his own bewildered look at me. "Are you enchanting them?" he demanded, during a short break between courtesies; there were two callow young noblemen of precisely equal rank arguing violently with the herald over which one of them should be presented to me first.

I didn't particularly want him thinking of what I might be using to make myself more beautiful. I leaned conspiratorially close. "My mother had enough magic to give me three blessings before she died," I said, and he instinctively bent in to hear it. "The first was wit; the second beauty, and the third—that fools should recognize neither."

He flushed. "My court is full of fools," he snapped. "So it seems she had it the wrong way round."

I shrugged. "Well, even if I were, surely it's no more than you're doing. Witches always lose their looks at the end, don't they, when their power begins to fade? I've always thought that's how they looked all along, and they only covered it with spells."

His eyes widened. "I am not *covering* anything!" But when he thought I was looking elsewhere, he surreptitiously touched his own face over with his fingertips, as if he feared an ugly troll hiding somewhere under the mask of his own beauty. It distracted him, at any rate.

"Which of these men is your relation?" I asked, to keep him so, and he irritably pointed out half a dozen cousins. They were mostly of the late tsar's stamp: big and vigorously bearded with dirty boots and an air of having been grudgingly forced into their court elegance. They were all older than Mirnatius, of course; he'd been the son of his father's second wife. But there was one pouting and rather splendid young man standing at the side of Mirnatius's aunt, an old woman in lavish brocade drowsing by the fire. He was very evidently the cosseted child of her age, and if he wasn't as beautiful as Mirnatius, at least he'd taken his tsar and cousin for a model when it came to dress, and he was tall and broad-shouldered. "Is he married?"

"Ilias? I haven't the faintest idea," Mirnatius said, but to give him a little credit, he stood up and took me over to present me to his aunt, who remedied our lack of knowledge very quickly.

"Who is your father?" she asked me loudly. "Erdivilas—Erdivilas—What? Oh, the Duke of Vysnia?" She peered at me a bit dubiously at that—not even an archduke?—but after a moment's consideration she shook her head and told Mirnatius, "Well enough, well enough. It is high time you married. Perhaps next *this* one will give his old mother the joy of a wedding," she added, poking the annoyed Ilias with a ring-encrusted knuckle.

Ilias bowed over my hand with remarkable coldness, despite my silver, which was quite obviously explained when he looked at Mirnatius next. Mirnatius was more interested in a critical examination of the wide panels of Ilias's coat, which were embroidered with two peacocks with tiny glittering jeweled eyes. "A handsome design," he told his cousin, who glowed with appreciation, and threw me another look of violent and miserable jealousy.

"He'd be loyal to you, at least," I said, when we went back to our chairs. That wasn't a recommendation to me, of course, but his shrewd-eyed mother was: every nobleman of real substance was stopping to pay her his respects, and half of the cousins Mirnatius had pointed out were her sons. Ilias might be unhappy to see Mirnatius fall, but she would be delighted to get her beloved son into Vassilia's bed—however little he liked it there—and I thought she might well accept her son's advancement as repayment for her nephew's fall.

"Why do you imagine so?" Mirnatius said sourly. "No one here is loyal five minutes past their own interest."

"He *is* interested," I said dryly.

I thought he might be offended, but he only flicked his eyes heavenwards in impatience. "They're *all* interested in *that*," he sneered. It sounded odd to me, and after a moment I realized I'd heard the same thing many times before, but always in a woman's mouth, and most often a servant's: two of the younger maids talking as they polished the silver at the cabinet next to the back stairway, which was the easiest way for me to climb to the attic, or another chaperone speaking to Magreta at a ball, the mother of a prettier girl with a less powerful father. There was a resentment in it that didn't fit with his crown: as if he'd felt the weight of hungry eyes on him and the sense of having to be wary.

But his mother had been executed for her sorcery when he was still young, and his brother had still been alive at the time, a promising young man by court opinion; I vaguely remembered him, a great deal more like those big burly men scattered around the room. Mirnatius would have been a court discard after that, the too-pretty son of a condemned witch—until a convenient wasting fever had carried his father and brother off from one day to the next, and made him the tsar instead. Perhaps he'd had more cause than simple greed to make his bargain, and hand himself over in exchange for his crown.

If so, I could feel a little sympathy for him after all, but only a little. His own father, his brother, too, and Archduke Dmitir: the demon hadn't taken *them* for a mere snack. Mirnatius had deliberately bought their deaths, his crown, his comfort. And he'd bought them with all the nameless people he'd fed to the demon in the years since he'd let it crawl down his throat and take up residence inside his belly. I knew with cold certainty that I wasn't the first meal he'd offered to that seething creature in the fireplace, whining of its endless thirst and hunger.

I rose from my chair while the dancing was still going. With the overcast sky, I couldn't tell when exactly the sunset was coming. I didn't want to be another of those meals, and I still didn't have the *demon's* agreement, even if Mirnatius had agreed to the plan. I didn't particularly trust either of them. "I mean to go and meet with the household before bed—unless you mean to lock me up in our bedchamber yet again?" I said to him, making it sound as though I spoke of a childish folly.

"Yes, very well," he said very shortly, distracted over his cup of wine. He was staring past me out the tall impractical windows of his ballroom: fresh snowflakes were gently drifting past their length, to add themselves to the frozen white ground.

In the kitchens, I ordered the slightly puzzled but obedient servants to make me a basket of food. I took it with me back into the presentation rooms and found one of them empty, a harp standing alone among velvet divans waiting for an occasion. In the gilt-edged mirror on the wall, I saw the low garden wall and the dark trees beyond, the same place I had left, and I stepped through to the little hut in the woods with my heavy basket on my arm.

It wasn't snowing, at least for this one moment, but new snow had fallen since I'd gone, here just as in Lithvas: it was creeping up the sides of the house. My feet crunched alone on a thick layer of ice frozen atop the drifts. I stopped in the lonely yard at the edge of the twilight, where it cut the house in half, and on an impulse I took a piece of bread from the basket and crumbled it over the snow. Perhaps there were living things here, and it didn't seem they would find much more to eat than the squirrels back in Lithvas.

Magreta was sleeping when I came in, deep wrinkles shadowed in her old face and silver lines in her hair. Her hands were lying idle in her lap for once, as if someone had taken her knitting away from her. The fire was very low, but the wood box was still full, at least. As I was adding another log and stirring up the fire, she muttered, "It's still dark. Go back to sleep, Irinushka," the way she did when I was a little girl and woke up too early in the morning and wanted to get out of bed. Then she woke up, and scolded me away from the fire, and insisted on herself putting on water to boil for tea, and cutting the cheese and ham. She never liked me to get too close to the fire, or to chance cutting myself with a knife.

I drowsed on the cot through the dark hours again, watching Magreta's knitting needles move in the firelight the way I had used to as a child in the small room I grew up in, near the top of the house: cold in winter, stifling in summer. The cold of the Staryk kingdom crept into the hut the way it had slid like a knife around the windowsills and under the eaves of my father's house. I still preferred it to the tsar's palace.

Chapter 17

My darling tsarina vanished again after dinner, somewhere between the kitchens and my bedchamber. I was hardly surprised by now. I didn't object, either. After several unbroken years of lecturing me on the importance of choosing my bride and all the many tedious factors to consider, all the old dotards on my council had fallen over one another to congratulate me for having shackled myself to a girl with none of the dowry or political value they'd been insisting on, which was irritating enough, but all the *young* dotards in my court had also fallen over one another to congratulate me on the astonishing beauty of my pale mousey rake of a bride.

Even my most reliable cynic, Lord Reynauld, on whom I'd have confidently wagered a thousand pieces of gold to find something viciously insulting to say about any new wife I'd presented—in his magnificently polite way, naturally—wandered up to my throne late in the evening and told me coolly that I'd made quite a clever and unexpected choice, and *then* he looked round the room and asked where she'd gone to, in a tone so artfully uninterested that I realized with enormous indignation that he was *passionately* interested in looking at her some more.

It was enough to make me wonder if she'd been telling the *truth* about that enchantment from her mother. Blinding fools to her beauty seemed rather more like a curse than a blessing, given the number of fools among the nobility, but as I'd ample cause to know, mothers weren't necessarily to be relied upon to deliver those, whatever song and story like to say about it. Or perhaps I'd been right, and the blessing really was the other way round.

Except my Aunt Felitzja, who very decidedly was not a fool— I'd found her impossible to muddle without expending really enormous amounts of power—made Ilias help her dodder over to me before leaving, and told me in resigned tones, "Well, you've married the way most men do, for a pretty face, so now make it worthwhile, and see to it there's a christening before another year is gone." And this while Ilias, who has been trying his best to worm his way into my bed since even before he'd worked out what he wanted to do once he got there—the quantities of horrible poetry he's inflicted on me don't bear describing—stood there and looked as though he wanted to burst into tears.

I wanted to stand up and shout at them all that my wife not only wasn't divinely beautiful, she wasn't even interestingly ugly; her conversation consisted entirely of insults, dire warnings, and tedious lectures I couldn't even ignore; and *they* were all extraordinary idiots for imagining I could possibly have had the bad taste to fall in love with a dull, prosing, long-faced harridan. The only reason I didn't yield to the temptation was that I'd have been put to the awkward necessity of explaining just why I *had* married her. "Because my demon told me to" isn't a generally accepted reason, even if you have a crown on your head. And I *would* have raised more objections if I'd known what I was getting into.

Under normal circumstances, when my friend wants itself a meal, it doesn't usually last long. I just hold my nose and dive deep until the screaming is all over, then cover things over and occasionally send a compensatory purse to the appropriate destination. I *have* had words with it about snatching up awkward people like noblemen and parents of small children, to a little grudging effect, but that's only because it's not very picky. Unless I do something stupid like smile encouragingly at a serving-maid or a well-turned footman, even in broad daylight, in which case I'm sure to find their staring corpse in my bed a few nights later. "Why didn't you marry Prince Ulrich's daughter?" indeed. It delights in doing that sort of thing—the added pleasure of surprising the poor fool who thinks they're about to have an evening's delight and a handsome reward in the morning. I'm dreading the night Ilias finally gets really enterprising and bribes his way into my bedchamber. My aunt will not be happy in the least. As for Ulrich's daughter, if I *had* let my councillors shove me into bed with her, she'd have had a great many objections afterwards, if she didn't before.

But not sweet innocent Irina, who evidently doesn't bat an eye at flaming horrors. In hindsight, I shouldn't have thought for an instant she'd have trouble with the court; a woman who can coolly bargain with a demon that wants to gnaw on her soul is hardly to be intimidated by Lord Reynauld D'Estaigne. Or, more to the point, by her *husband*.

I could already see the freshly hideous future taking shape ahead of me. I was going to be *stuck* with her. My blasted demon was going to snatch at her offer with both clawed hands, Aunt Felitzja was going to be delighted at the chance to marry Ilias off to a rich princess, my entire court already thought her enchantingly beautiful, and my councillors were really going to *adore* my having a wife who would listen to them prose on about tax rolls and then come and harangue me for hours in their stead, since I couldn't send her away. And everyone would love her as absolutely no one did *me*.

Oh, and five minutes from now she'd undoubtedly inform me that she expected me to *consummate* this relationship, so she could pop out an heir or two to still more general acclaim. After which

I wouldn't be the least surprised to find a knife sticking out of my back some morning. There was a gruesome inevitability to it all. My life has been a sequence of monsters one after another tossing me about to suit their whims; I've got a finely tuned sense for when another round of buffeting has arrived.

And one was certainly on the way *now*. I drank half of a bottle of brandy as the sun began coming sideways through the windows of the ballroom, and took the rest of it along with me to my chambers. I hadn't any idea what the servants thought had become of Irina *this* time, and I didn't care, either. She could worry about the rumors she was starting herself, if she cared so much.

Except—a morose realization—the rumors would undoubtedly all end up being about *me*. I'd be the hobgoblin locking my poor innocent wife in a closet somewhere, and if I refused to lie back and be mounted when she decided it was time to take possession, I'd be the pathetic impotent who couldn't get a child on what everyone else seemed to think was the most beautiful woman in the world.

I was in a fine mood by the time I reached the privacy of my chambers, and to improve it, I only just had time to down a final gulp of brandy as the fire climbed out of the knot at the base of my skull and jerked me puppetlike to my feet. *"Where has she gone?"* it hissed with my tongue and throat, clawing through my mind and memories just enough to find that she was gone again, and then it screamed with fury and spun out of me into the open air, a firespout twisting around my body.

"Why did you let her go?" it snarled, and didn't let me answer. It shoved a flaming brand down my throat, scorching up my screams before they could emerge into the air, and flung me to the floor and beat me savagely with whips of fire, every blow a shock of bright pain against my skin. There was nothing to be done but endure it. Fortunately it had thrown me on my back: I find it helps somewhat to follow the endless up-and-down pattern of the gilt

line bordering the ceiling, all the way around the full length of the room. The demon was in fine form tonight: I had gone around five times before the beating finally wound to a halt and it hurled me away with sulky finality onto the floor beneath the fireplace. It went slouching into the crackling flames and spat at me, *"What bargain?"* So it had picked that much out of my head already, not that it had felt the need to let that get in the way of finishing up a proper thrashing.

I couldn't so much as twitch without agony, and my throat was raw as though I'd drunk broken glass, but of course that had nothing to do with anything truly being wrong. The demon seems to feel the need to keep the terms of the original bargain for beauty, crown, and power, no matter how the circumstances have changed, and I suppose leaving me festooned with scars wouldn't fit. But it's grown quite adept over the years at managing to produce the sensation of lingering damage without leaving any actual marks behind.

"The king of the Staryk, instead of her," I said, and my voice sounded perfectly normal. A considerable effort was required not to let it waver, but the demon likes tears and misery, so I do my best not to produce them; the last thing I want is to encourage it to extend its entertainments. These days I've become more of a boring convenience than an exciting toy. I've found the line to tread between servility, which it enjoys too much, and provocation, which makes it fly into rages. It had been almost a year since it had bothered to beat me. Until darling Irina appeared on the scene, that is. If something *else* drives it into a frenzy, and I'm the nearest target to hand—as I rather inevitably am—then there's not much I can do about it.

I was more than a little reluctant to risk prodding it further, but Irina's offer had a remarkable effect: the demon came flowing back out of the fireplace and went coiling around me like a purring cat. Its flames still came licking at my skin, but only incidentally; it wasn't trying to hurt me anymore. Still, there was nothing to shield me from the stinging tendrils, as it had done very permanent damage to my *clothes*. Irina had sniffed quite censoriously when I made a point of ensuring she didn't wear the same gown twice. I suppose she'd rather scatter alms to the poor or endow a bunch of droning monks somewhere; it would go far better with the holier-than-thou drivel she attempted to feed me. But I've gone to great lengths to ensure everyone knows that *I* never appear in the same ensemble twice. The last thing I need is for anyone to start wondering what's happened to my favorite pair of trousers or those expensive riding boots I wore three days ago. I'd rather be thought a mad spendthrift than a sorcerer—and it would look odd if I didn't insist on my tsarina matching me for style.

"How?" the demon breathed out over my ear, claws of flame curling around my shoulder, a grip that shot fresh agony down my back. I clenched my teeth down over a howl; it would let go of me in a moment if I didn't stir up its interest. *"How will she give him to me . . . ?"*

"She was thin on the details," I managed to force out. "She says he's making the winters longer."

The demon made a low roaring noise in its throat and prowled away from me again, leaving smoking trails in the carpets on its way back to the fireplace. I shut my eyes and breathed a few times before gathering myself to push back up. "She's certainly lying about any number of things, but she's been hiding *somewhere*," I said. "And two blizzards since Spring Day does rather stretch the bounds of chance."

"Yes, yes," it crackled to itself, gnawing idly on a log. *"He has locked them away beneath the snow, and there she flees where I cannot go . . . but can she bring him to me?"*

As little as I cared to trust Irina's too-clever explanations—not for a second did I imagine she had *my* welfare anywhere remotely near at heart—she had made a few excellent arguments. "If she can't, we're no worse off for her trying," I said. "Are you sure you can defeat him, if she *does* manage it?"

It made its sputtering crackle of laughter. *"Oh, I will slake my thirst, I will drink so deep,"* it muttered. *"Only he must be held fast! A chain of silver to bind him tight, a ring of fire to quench his might . . . bring him to me!"* it hissed at me. *"Bring him to me and make ready!"*

"She wants your promise, of course," I said. Irina seemed rather eager to rely on the word of an unholy creature, for all her cleverness and sanctimony, but then she'd plainly decided that I'd made a bargain with it myself to get the throne, and fair enough, here I was upon it, for all the delights it afforded me. I would have thought my situation rather an object lesson in being careful what you wished for.

"Yes, yes," the demon said. *"She will be tsarina with a golden crown, and whatever she desires will be hers, only let her bring him to me!"*

So I'd been quite right: I *was* going to be stuck with delightful darling Irina for the rest of my days, and much say I was going to get in any aspect of the matter.

My Irina went back to the demon in the morning. I had knitted away the night too quickly. After she had gone, I smoothed my hands over the wool, my fingers trembling as they had not done while I worked. I had made flowers and vines, a cover for a wedding-bed, and it seemed to me that whenever I closed my eyes, they kept growing on their own, quicker than my hands could have made them. I drowsed beneath the heavy weight of the cover in my lap by the fire, until the door swung shut and Irina's hand was on my shoulder again. "Irinushka, you gave me a fright. Is it night again already?" I said.

"No," she said. "The bargain is made, Magreta. He will leave me alone, and take the Staryk king in my place. Come. We're leaving for Vysnia right away. We have to be there in two days' time."

I left the knitting on the bed when I went with her. Maybe someone else would come to this little house and need it someday. I didn't argue. Her father was in her face, then, though she did not know it, and I knew there wasn't any use. He had looked so in the old duke's study, and he had looked so when he had taken Irina down to the chapel to be married to the tsar: his feet were on a path and he was walking, and if there were turns, he would not take them aside. That was how she looked, now.

I only hoped not to be so cold anymore, when she brought me out into the palace, in a room full of shining mirrors and silence and a golden harp no one was playing. But there was snow high on the windowsills, and there was no fire in that dark room to warm my hands. There was no chance to find another one lit. The household was all in a frenzy when we came out, servants running in the halls, except when they saw Irina, and then they stopped and bowed to her. She asked each one of them their name, and when they were gone she said it over to herself three times—a trick her father used also, whenever new men came to his army. But what good would scullery-maids and footmen do her, with a demon and a devil on either side?

I followed after her to the courtyard: a royal sleigh was made ready, a great chariot of gilt and white painted fresh, perhaps that morning, and the tsar stood beside it in black furs with golden tassels and gloves of red wool and black fur; oh that vain boy, and his eyes were on my girl, and I could not hide her from him anymore.

"Magra, the tsar is a sorcerer," she had said to me: ten years old, with her hair already a flowing dark river under the silver brush as we sat by the fire in a small room in the old tsar's palace.

"The tsar is a sorcerer," just in such a way she said it, calmly out loud, as if that were a thing anyone might say at any time with nothing ill to come of it, as if a girl might say it at the dinner table in front of the whole court just as easily as she said it fresh out of her bath to only her old nanusha; a girl who was only the daughter of a duke whose new wife already had a great belly.

But it was even worse than that: after I slapped her cheek with the brush and told her not to say such things, she put her hand up to her cheek where the color was already fading, and stared at me, and said, "But it's true," as though that mattered, and added, "He is leaving dead squirrels for me."

I did not let her out into the gardens again while we were in Koron, though her skin grew even more pale, and she listless and tired from sitting all day by the fire, helping me spin. With those skeins of yarn I bribed the girl who scrubbed our floor to tell me every day when the tsar left the tables: she knew from her sister, who was two years older and trusted to carry plates, and for fine-spun yarn she would carry away the tsar's plate and then run up half the stairs quickly and call to her sister, who would run back up to us in the attic rooms, and only then I would take Irina down to eat, in the last minutes of cold food before the platters were taken away.

It was seven weeks like that, seven hard weeks, for the tsar came always very late to the table and lingered there very long; but every morning as we sat hungry and cold waiting upstairs, I brushed Irina's hair until the serving-girl came and told us he had gone, and every evening I kept her busy carding the wool and giving it to me in clouds, until it was safe to creep downstairs for whatever was left to glean.

At last one morning, thin and white, she burst from the chair and ran to the window: a cold wind was blowing in, the first frost of the year, and she cried out, "Winter will be here soon, and I want to go outside," and wept. My heart broke, but I was not a young girl anymore, afraid of being trapped behind a door forever. I knew the door was safety, I knew the door would not always be closed, and I did not let her out. That evening her father's servant came, impatient after climbing the stairs because we were not at the tables for him to find us; he told us sharply the roads had frozen hard, so we would be going in the morning. I thanked the saints after he had gone.

The seven years of safety since then I had won for her, with those seven hard weeks of patience: that was not nothing. But they felt as nothing when I saw him look at her with eyes as hard as stone. Seven years were gone, gone so quickly, and I could not close a door against him anymore. Someone stronger than I had pulled it open. He held out his gloved hand, and she let go of my arm; she murmured to me, "Go in the sledge there with the guards, Magra. They'll look after you."

They were young men, soldiers, but she was right anyway; I was an old woman, white-haired, and my lady was their own tsarina now. Those rough boys helped me into the sledge, and put blankets over me and a warmer at my feet, and called me baba kindly, and old nanusha, and paid no attention to me otherwise; they were talking to each other about good places to drink in Vysnia, and grumbling because the duke's kitchens were not generous, and when they thought I was drowsing they talked of this girl and that.

They prodded and jostled one of them, a strapping young fellow with a mustache, handsome enough that he should have had girls sighing for him, and who did not speak of anyone, until another one laughed and said, "Ah, leave Timur alone, I know where his heart is: in the tsarina's jewel-box." They all laughed, but only a little, and they did not keep teasing him; when I sat up and yawned to let them believe I had really been asleep, I saw him,

eyes wounded as if he had been caught by an arrow. He was looking ahead past the driver, at the white sleigh in the distance running, and I, too, could see Irina's dark hair beneath the white fur
of her hat.

Mirnatius did not speak to me more than he needed to on the
journey, his face as close to sour as expression could make it.
"Please yourself," he'd said shortly, when I told him we should
leave for Vysnia at once. "And when precisely is this Staryk going
to materialize? There isn't an infinite store of patience to be had,
as I trust you realize."

"Tomorrow night, in Vysnia," I said.

He grimaced, but didn't argue. In the sleigh he put me beside
him on the seat and looked elsewhere, except when we stopped at
another nobleman's house to break our journey. The household
came out and bowed to us, and Prince Gabrielius himself, proud
and white-haired. He had fought alongside the old tsar, and he'd
had a granddaughter in the running for tsarina, too, so he had
ample cause for the cold offended resentment in his face when I
was first presented to him, but it faded out as he stood too long
with my hand clasped in his, staring at me, and then he said in low
tones, "My lady," and bowed too deeply.

Mirnatius spent all dinner looking at me with angry desperation, as if it was near driving him mad wondering what the rest of
the world saw in me. "No, we're *not* staying the night," he said
with savage rudeness to the prince afterwards, all but dragging me
away to the sleigh in what I suppose looked like a jealous ferment.
He threw himself into the corner violently, his jaw clenched, and
snapped at the driver to get the horses moving, and as we went he

darted quick, half-unwilling glances at me, as if he thought maybe he could surprise my mysterious beauty and catch it unawares before it fled his eyes.

Not quite an hour passed, and then he abruptly called a halt mid-forest and ordered a footman to bring him a drawing-box: a beautiful confection of inlaid wood and gold that folded into a sort of small easel, and a book of fine paper inside. He waved the sleigh onward and opened it. I caught glimpses from within as he turned the pages, designs and patterns and faces glancing back out at me, some of them beautiful and familiar from the dazzle of his court, but on one page a brief flicker of another face went by, strange and terrible. Not even a face, I thought after it had vanished; it was formed only roughly with a few shadows here and there, like wisps of smoke, but that was enough to leave the suggestion of horror.

He stopped at a blank page, near the end. "Sit up and look at me," he said sharply, and I obeyed without arguing, a little curious myself; I wondered if the magic would hold, when men looked at a picture of me. He drew with a swift sure hand, looking more at me than at his paper. Even while we glided onward, my face took shape quickly on his page, and when he finished, he stared at it and then tore it out with a furious jerk and held it out to me. "What do they *see*?" he demanded.

I took it and saw myself for the first time with my crown. More myself on the page in his few lines, it seemed to me, than I had ever seen in a mirror. He hadn't been unkind, though utterly without flattery, and he had put me together somehow out of pieces: a thin mouth and a thin face, my thick brows and my father's hatchet nose only not twice broken, and my eyes one of them a little higher than the other. My necklace was a scribble in the hollow of my throat and my crown on my head and the thick doubled braid of my hair resting on my shoulder, a suggestion of weight and luster in the strokes. It was an ordinary unbeautiful face, but it was certainly mine and no other's, though there were only a handful of lines on the page.

"Me," I said, and offered it back to him, but he wouldn't take it. He was watching me, and the sun going down was red in his eyes, and as it lowered, he leaned in and said to me in a voice of smoke, *"Yes, Irina; you they see, sweet and cold as ice,"* caressing and horrible. *"Will you keep your promise? Bring me the winter king, and I will make you a summer queen."*

My hands closed, crumpling the paper, and I steadied my voice before I spoke. "I will take you to the Staryk king, and put him in your power," I said. "And you will swear to leave me be, after, and all those I love as well."

"Yes, yes, yes," the demon said, sounding almost impatient. *"You will have beauty and power and wealth, all three; a golden crown and a castle high; I will give you all you desire, only bring him soon to me . . ."*

"I don't want your promises or gifts, and I have a crown and a castle already," I said. "I'll bring him to you to break the winter, for Lithvas, but my desires I'll manage on my own once you've left me and mine alone."

He didn't like it. That glimpse from the notebook, the shadow of horror, looked out of Mirnatius's face at me scowling, and I had a struggle not to flinch back. *"But what will you have, what will I give you in return,"* he said, complainingly. *"Will you take youth forever, or a flame of magic in your hand? The power to cloud the minds of men and bend them to your will?"*

"No, and no, and no again," I said. "I'll take nothing. Do you refuse?"

He made a spiteful hissing noise and curled himself up unnaturally in the seat of the sleigh, drawing Mirnatius's legs up and wrapping his arms over them, his head swaying back and forth, like a fire clinging around a log. He muttered, *"But she will bring him . . . she will bring him to me . . ."* and he glared at me again, red-eyed, and hissed, *"Agreed! Agreed! But if you bring him not, a feast still I will have, of you and all your loves."*

"Threaten me again, and I'll go and take them all to live with me in the Staryk lands," I said, a show of purest bravado, "and you can hunger alone in a winter without an end, until your food vanishes and your fire dwindles to embers and ash. Tomorrow night you will have your Staryk king. Now leave until then. I care for your company even less than *his,* and that's saying a great deal."

It hissed at me, but I'd struck on some threat it didn't care for, or else it didn't like *my* company, either; it shrank back into Mirnatius like a spark dying out, the red gleam gone, and he sank back gasping against the cushions with his eyes shut until he caught his breath. When he had it again, he turned his head to stare at me. "You *refused* him," he said to me, almost angrily.

"I'm not a fool, to take gifts from monsters," I said. "Where do you think its power comes from? Nothing like that comes without a price."

He laughed, a little shrill and sharp. "Yes, the trick is to have someone else pay it for you," he said, and shouted ahead to the driver, "Koshik! Find us a house to stop for the night!" and sank back again with his hand over his face.

He hadn't thought the situation through well enough when rushing us back onto the road, and neither had I, while I was making my grandiose speeches to his demon. The only shelter to be found was a modest boyar's house, nothing so grand as if we'd stayed with Prince Gabrielius. Naturally the boyar gave up his own bedroom to the tsar and tsarina, and a well-curtained bed in it, but everyone else was crammed in only with difficulty. It was bitterly cold again, enough that all the horses and livestock had to be gotten under cover; no one could sleep outside at all, and there was little enough room in the stables. It meant a few servants had to sleep on the floor in our room, so I couldn't take flight, and though the demon wasn't there, my *husband* still was.

My wedding night had been so long a thing of hideous and unnatural dread that I'd forgotten to be alarmed by the ordinary horror of having to lie down with a stranger. I told myself with relief that at least he didn't *want* me, no matter how unpleasant it would be even just to lie in a bed together. When the servants began to undress him, and he noticed I was still there, he also looked over at the bed in a kind of blank resignation. And then, after the candles were put out and we were lying stiffly beside each other with the bedcurtains drawn around us, the winter chill still creeping in around them despite the wooden walls and the fire in the grate, he heaved out an angry breath and turned over towards me, with his mouth tight as a prisoner going to the block.

I stopped him with my hands on his chest, staring at him in the dim rose light with my heart thundering suddenly fast. "Well, my beloved wife?" he said bitterly, and too loud, a mockery of tenderness performed for our audience, and I realized he meant to have me after all. I couldn't think; I was as blank as a page. There were four servants outside listening: if I said *no*, if I said *not yet*, if they heard me—and then his hand bunched my gown and drew the thin fine linen of it up over my thighs, and his fingers trailed over my skin.

It made me jump, an involuntary shiver, and my cheeks went painfully red and hot. Then I said too loudly, "Oh, *beloved*," and put my hands on his chest and shoved him back from me, as hard as I could.

He wasn't expecting it, and he was only propped up in the bed on his arms, so he fell over; he pushed himself up with a half-outraged expression, for all he'd been doing it as a man condemned, and I leaned in and whispered fiercely, "Bounce the bed!"

He stared at me. I moved on the bed myself, enough to make the old wood groan audibly, to demonstrate, and with a half-bewildered look he joined me, until I gave another small cry for the benefit of our audience, and he abruptly seized a pillow and thrust his face into it and began shaking with a laughter so violent I thought for a moment he'd been possessed again into a fit.

And then suddenly he was weeping instead, so stifled I didn't hear a sound even there behind the curtains with him; only when he had to break away just long enough to snatch one breath between agonies. If they had heard him out in the room, there would have been nothing to make them doubt our theater; he only made the small gasps, all other sound silenced.

I sat there wooden as a doll; I didn't know what to do. I didn't want to feel anything, and at first I only resented it, that he had the bad taste to weep in front of me as if he had the right to expect me to care, but I'd never heard anyone weep so. I had been afraid, and I had been hurt, and I had sorrowed, but I didn't have cries like that inside me. *He* would have filled me with them, if he'd fed me to his demon. As he was being devoured himself, perhaps.

His own fault, I would have said, and I did say to myself, fiercely, over and over, as I sat there with his body softening beside me like melting snow as he sank into the limp quietness of exhaustion. But I still felt sorry for him, even though I didn't want to, as if he was conjuring sympathy out of me. I sat with my knees drawn up under my shift and my arms wrapped around them tight, trying to hold it in, until I thought maybe he was asleep. I risked a look over his shoulder: his eyes were open and dull, but the bloodshot red was fading out of them already, and he closed them and turned his face a little farther into the pillow.

Chapter 18

I was afraid that Stepon and Miryem's mother would have a hard time walking, after we left the house, with all the snow. But the snow had frozen hard, and we stayed on top of it. Only Sergey fell through, twice, and we beat the snow off his clothes so it didn't melt and make him cold. And it was not for a long time. We were walking for only half an hour maybe, even with him falling through the snow, when suddenly Sergey said, "I think I see the road," and he was right. We came out of the trees and there was the river, frozen hard, and the road next to it, with sleigh tracks already in the snow.

There were houses and villages on the road all the rest of the day while we were walking. They came very close together because we were getting nearer to Vysnia, Miryem's mother said. I didn't understand how we could have been so close to so many houses. We had been so far from the road, so deep into the forest, when we found the little house. It was strange that we had not heard any sounds of people, and that Sergey had never seen anyone while he was going out for wood. But the houses and villages were there. I was a little afraid when we saw people, but nobody paid any attention to us. When it was getting dark, Miryem's father told us to wait on the road, and he went ahead to the next house up ahead, a farmhouse. He came back with a basket of food, and said he had given them money to let us sleep in their barn above the animals that night. In the morning we went the rest of the way to Vysnia, and it was only a few hours walking.

I thought Vysnia would be like town only bigger, but really it was like a building. All we could see of it was a wall that went as far as you could see in either direction. It was made out of red bricks built one on top of another so high that you could not see over it, and then higher than that, too. There were no windows in the wall except little very narrow windows up at the very top, that looked so small that you would have to put the side of your face up to them and peer through with one eye. The only way through was a door at the end of the road, so big that a big sledge pulled with four horses and loaded all the way with wool could go right through it.

There was no other way to get close to the wall. A big ditch had been dug all around the bottom of the wall. It was full of snow, but we could tell it was there because the snow was lower there, and there were sharp points poking out of it: big trees that had been stripped of branches with their ends made sharp. It looked like they did not want anyone to come in, ever.

But there were many, many people waiting at the city door to come in. I had never seen so many people. They stretched out along the road like chickens walking in a line. When we got close enough to see that wall and the line of people, I drew close to Sergey, and Stepon slipped his hand into mine and tugged on it. He wouldn't say anything until I put my head down close so he could whisper right into my ear, "Couldn't we go back to the house?"

But Miryem's parents did not seem to be worried. "It will be a long wait today," Miryem's mother said. "Someone important must be coming to see the duke. See, they are keeping the gate clear until they arrive."

"The tsar's coming, I heard," a woman ahead of us in line said, turning around. She was wearing a good wool dress, brown, embroidered at the hem, with a red shawl over her head and a basket on her arm; her son was a tall silent young man with curls behind his ears like Panov Mandelstam wore, so they were Jews also.

"The tsar!" Miryem's mother said.

The other woman nodded. "He married the duke's daughter, last week. And back for a visit already! I hope it's not a bad sign."

"The poor girl must be homesick," Miryem's mother said. "How old is she?"

"Oh, she's old enough to be married," the woman said. "My sister pointed her out to me in the city last year, walking with her servants. Not much to look at, I would have said, but they say the tsar fell in love with her at first sight."

"Well, the heart knows what it wants," Panova Mandelstam said.

I had never heard her talk with anyone like that. I thought they must know each other, but after a while, Miryem's mother asked, "Do you have family in the city?" and the woman said, "My sister lives there, with her husband. We have a farm in Hamsk. Where are you from?"

"From Pavys," Miryem's mother said. "A day's journey. We've come for a wedding: my niece, Basia."

The woman uttered a glad cry and took her by the shoulders. "My nephew Isaac!" she said. They kissed each other on the cheeks, and embraced, and then were talking of names of people I didn't know: they were friends, as easily as that. I did not understand how they had found each other standing in that long line of all those many people. It seemed like magic.

We were waiting for a long time. I would have thought it would be easier to stand than to walk, but it wasn't. The woman had food in her basket, and she insisted that we eat some of it, and I still had some in mine also, and we shared it all out. We brushed snow off some stumps and bigger stones along the side of the road so we could sit for a little while at least.

While we were eating a drumming began to come through the ground under us, and then a jingling sound faintly off. Men came out of the city gate and walked down the line pushing everyone even more back off the road, and when they came to us they told us in sharp voices to get up and be ready to bow. They had swords on their belts, real swords, not toys. We were still standing for a long time again waiting as the jingling got louder little by little, and then it was very suddenly there next to us. I saw black horses with gold and red, and a long low sleigh carved with big swoops and shining with gold, and a girl with a silver crown sitting in it. They went so fast that they were there just for a moment and they were gone. That big sleigh went through the door and inside the big building of the city and disappeared without even slowing down. "The tsarina, the tsarina!" I heard some people shout, but we forgot to bow, until they were gone, and then we bowed too late, but it was all right because there were still people to bow to: sledges full of bags and boxes and people, enough people to make a village of their own, all following after the tsar, like he was not really one person but all of them together, something made out of people.

After at last they were all gone, the whole tsar inside the city, the men started letting us through. All that time we had been waiting just so the tsar could get into the city without having to wait. The line was even longer behind us than in front of us. But once they began letting us come in, it only took maybe half an hour before we reached the door, even though they had kept us there for hours already. I was so tired of waiting; I only wanted to get to the door, but Stepon walked very slowly, so slowly that the people behind us began to crowd on our heels, impatient. He was looking at the door.

"What if we can't get out again?" he said to me.

I didn't know the answer. Then we got closer and I saw that people were not just walking through the door. The men with the swords were asking them questions and writing things down. I suddenly felt afraid. What if they asked us who we were and where we were from and why we were there? I didn't know what I would say.

But Panova Mandelstam reached out and took my other hand that Stepon wasn't holding and squeezed it and said softly, "Just don't say anything," and when we came up to the door, Panov Mandelstam spoke to a man with a sword, and then I saw him give that man a silver coin, and the man said, "All right, all right," waving us on through.

I was so glad and easy with relief that I just kept going without thinking about it, and then I was inside the city. The wall was so big that it took twenty steps from the start of the door to the end of the door. A noise got bigger and bigger the whole way we went. Then we got to the other side and the sky was open over us, and all around us there were other buildings, like the city had swallowed them up into its belly along with us and all the other people.

Stepon stopped and put his hands over his ears and didn't want to go anywhere. He was trembling when I touched him. Panova Mandelstam said, "Come, it will be more quiet when we get out of the busy streets," but he couldn't move, so finally Sergey said, "Come on, Stepon, I'll carry you on my back," even though he hadn't done that for a long time, not since Stepon was very little, and Stepon was big enough now that his legs with the boots that Panova Mandelstam gave him dangled down Sergey's sides and hung long and kicking while Sergey walked. But he put his face down against Sergey's back and did not look up the whole time.

It was not easy to walk. The streets had been full of snow for some time, and so that people could walk, they had pushed the snow out of the middle, into two big walls on either side of the street, with holes dug out going to the doors of each house. But the streets were not very big, and then it had snowed again just yesterday, and now the walls were bigger than our heads, and there was some snow in the road that there was no room for on the walls and it was black with dirt and half frozen and slippery under our feet. There were big houses everywhere, all pushed up against each other with no room on either side, going up so high that I felt they were leaning over, looking down at us in the street beneath them. There were people everywhere you looked. There was nowhere that didn't have anyone in it.

We followed Panova Mandelstam. She knew where she was going. I didn't know how. Every corner she turned looked just like the other corners. But she walked very steady and sure as though she did not have to think about which way to turn, and she was right, because we finally came to another big wall, not so big as the first one, with a door in it, and two more men with swords. Panov Mandelstam gave them a coin, too, and they let us through the door. I thought maybe now we would be leaving, but there was more city on the other side of that wall, too. Only in this part, everyone around us was a Jew.

I had never seen any Jew but Miryem's family before, except the woman on the line and her son. Now I did not see anyone else. It was a strange feeling. I thought that when Miryem had to go to the Staryk kingdom maybe it was like this for her. All of a sudden everyone around you was the same as each other but not like you. And then I thought, but it was like that for Miryem already. It was like that for her all the time, in town. So maybe it hadn't been so strange.

So I was thinking about Miryem, and wondering how it was for her, and that was why suddenly I realized, Panova Mandelstam had come here for Miryem. I stopped in the street. I had not asked why they had come. I had been so full of gladness to see them in the woods, and Stepon, that I had only had room for the gladness and not for any questions. But of course that was why they had come. She was looking for Miryem. But Miryem would not be here.

I had to keep walking because Panova Mandelstam was still going onward, and if we got lost, Sergey and Stepon and I would not know what to do. I didn't know how to get back out of this city. It was like being in a house that had a thousand rooms and all the doors were the same. We went through a big noisy market-place in a square, full of people buying and selling, and then we turned down a street into what felt like quiet after the noise of the market but was still very loud next to the forest. Soon it got even quieter and the houses began to get big and wide with big windows full of glass, and here the snow was in neater piles and stairs went up to the houses coming out of the snow. Finally we came to a very big house with an arch and a courtyard next to it, and there were horses there and people carrying things around, very busy.

Miryem's mother stopped at the steps of that house. She had her arm in Panov Mandelstam's arm, and he looked up at the door, and I thought that he did not want to go inside that house, but then they climbed up the stairs together, and she turned and beckoned to say, *Come along,* so we climbed up behind them and inside. "Rakhel!" a woman was saying; she had hair that was mostly grey and silver and white, and there was something about her face that made me think of Panova Mandelstam, and they were kissing and I thought, this was Miryem's grandmother. Miryem's mother had a mother, too, who was still alive. "And Josef! It has been too long. Come in, come in, take off your things," she was saying, and kissing Panov Mandelstam's cheeks.

I was afraid that Panova Mandelstam would ask her about Miryem right away, but she didn't. More women came out of the kitchen and there was a big noise of greeting and talk among them. I thought at first they were just talking so fast that I couldn't understand, but then I realized they were saying words that I didn't understand at all, mixed up with words that I did know. It made me want suddenly to go away, to go back to that little house in the forest. Sitting at the table in Panova Mandelstam's house, eating off Miryem's plate, I had thought a little bit secretly in my heart, without really meaning to, that maybe I could slip into Miryem's place, but now I felt I had not really known Miryem's place. I had seen a part of it, but not all of it. This was Miryem's place too, and it was not a place for me. I was not wanted here at all.

I would have left if I knew where to go. Sergey was next to me, and Stepon had come off his back and was huddled up against me with his head in my side and was pulling my apron up over his face. They would have left with me. But we didn't know any way to go. And then I heard my own name: Panova Mandelstam had taken her mother to one side out of all the noise and talking, and she was saying something about me, about us, softly to her mother, who was listening and worried and looking over at us. I wanted to know what they were saying, to make her so worried, and I wondered what we would do if she said she did not want us here even to sleep. There was trouble with us, and she did not know us.

But she did not say that. She said something to Miryem's mother, and then Miryem's mother came to us with a smile that felt like it was saying everything will be all right but wasn't sure if it would, and then she took us deeper into that big house. There was a staircase going up and we followed her to a big hallway with a carpet in the middle of it, and at the end of that hallway there was another staircase, and we climbed that one, and then there was *another*, wooden steps, and then we were in a small hallway that did not have a carpet, only plain wooden boards, and there were only two doors on either side of it and a door in the ceiling with a cord hanging down from it. She opened the door on the left and took us into a room that was the size of the room of the little house in the forest, that was how big that house was, that you could climb and climb up through it and then you found another whole house at the top of it, and that was how big the city was, that it had so many of these houses in it that you couldn't tell them from each other.

But there was a window in the room in the wall across from the door, and Stepon pulled his hand away from me and ran to the window and pressed his whole face to it with a cry. I thought he was upset, but he said, "We're birds! Wanda, Sergey, look, we're birds," and I went to him a little bit afraid and we looked out through the glass and Stepon was right: we were birds. We had climbed so high up in that house that we were looking down at the roofs of other houses, and looking down at the streets. From up there I could see the marketplace we had been in, only it was so small I could cover it with my hand if I put it on the window, and I could see the big wall of the city and it was only a thin little line like an orange snake going around the outside, an orange snake with snow on its back, and on the other side of it there was the forest with all the trees turned into one big dark thing, and a heavy blanket of white snow all over it that hurt my eyes to look at. There was white snow on the roofs of all the houses, too, but in the streets it was all dirty and black, but from this high even that did not look bad.

"Come, sit down and rest," Miryem's mother said. I had not even looked at the room, because of the window. There were three beds, real beds made out of wood, each one with a mattress, and blankets, and pillows. There was a little fireplace with no fire in it, but the room was very warm anyway, and there was a little table in front of the window and there was a chair at the little table and there were two other chairs in front of the fire. They had cushions on their seats that were only a little worn out. "I know you must be hungry. I'll have some food brought up. I'm sorry to put you so far up, in servants' rooms: all the other bedrooms downstairs are full of guests already. But some of them will leave tomorrow after the wedding, and then it won't be so crowded."

We didn't know what to say so we didn't say anything, and then she left us there and each of us sat down on a bed and we looked across the room at each other. I had known that Miryem's grandfather was rich, but I had not known what rich meant before. Rich meant that this room with three beds and a table and chairs and a window filled with glass was something to say sorry for. It was even bigger than I first thought it was because when we sat down there was a big open place of the floor between us where there was nothing to cook with and no big firewood pile and no pots and no axe or broom on the walls. There was a little picture on the wall above my bed that someone had made of the town outside the window, only it was a picture of spring, with the trees green and birds in the air.

After a while Panova Mandelstam came back up, and there was a girl with her, a tall strong young girl with her hair under a kerchief, carrying a big heavy tray with food on it, and she put it down on the table and then she nodded her head to Panova Mandelstam and went away. I looked after her and I thought, that girl was me; there wasn't even room here for me to carry things and bring things. They already had someone in that place, too.

Stepon and Sergey went to eat right away, but I couldn't feel hungry. I was hungry, but there was a pain in my stomach when I looked at the food, and I said to Panova Mandelstam, "We are not any good to you here," and I almost said, *We should go,* but I couldn't, because we didn't have anywhere to go, unless we did turn into birds and fly away.

Panova Mandelstam looked at me surprised. "Wanda!" she said. "After all the help you have been to us? Am I to say, *Oh, but what good is she to me now?*" She reached out and took my face in her hands and shook me a little back and forth. "You are a good girl with a good heart. So much work you've done without a word of complaint. Since you came into my house, I did not have to lift a hand. Before I thought of doing a thing it was done. I was sick, but because you were there helping, I grew well again. And you never ask for a thing. It's only what we press into your hands that you take. So now you must let me do it."

"What you press in my hands is more than all I have!" I said, because it hurt to hear her saying those things that were not true, as if I had only come and helped her to be good, and not because I wanted silver, and wanted to be safe.

"Then you don't have enough, and I have more than I need," she said. "Hush, sweetheart. You don't have a mother anymore, but let me speak to you with her voice a minute. Listen. Stepon told us what happened in your house. There are men who are wolves inside, and want to eat up other people to fill their bellies. That is what was in your house with you, all your life. But here you are with your brothers, and you are not eaten up, and there is not a wolf inside you. You have fed each other, and you kept the wolf away. That is all we can do for each other in the world, to keep the wolf away. And if there has been food in my house for you, then I am glad, glad with all my heart. I hope there will always be.

"Hush, don't cry," she said, and her thumbs were wiping tears from my face, though they were coming faster than she could take them away. "I know you are afraid and worried. But there will be a wedding here today. It is a time to rejoice. For today we don't let sorrow come into this house. All right? Sit and eat, now. Rest a little while. If you want, when you are not tired, come down and help me. There is still work to be done, and it is happy work. We

will raise the canopy for the bride and groom, we will put food on
the tables, and we will eat together and dance, and the wolf will
not come in. Tomorrow, we will think of other things."

I nodded without saying anything. I couldn't say anything. She
smiled at me, and wiped more of my tears, and then she gave up
trying to wipe them and just gave me a handkerchief out of her
skirt and touched my cheek again and went out. Sergey and Stepon were sitting at the table staring at the food on it. There was
soup, and bread, and eggs, and when I sat next to them, Stepon
said, "I didn't know it was magic, when you brought it home. I
thought it was just food."

I reached out my hands to them, suddenly: I put out my hand
to Sergey on one side, and to Stepon on the other, and they put
out their hands to me, and to each other, and we held tight, tight;
we made a circle together, my brothers and me, around the food
that we had been given, and there was no wolf in the room.

In the morning Mirnatius thrust back the curtains early and set
the servants scurrying before I had even sat up in bed; they
brought us hot tea on a tray and warm bread with butter and jam,
another plate of thick slices of ham and cheese: hearty food that
was surely their best, though only a step up from peasant fare. He
made a face at it and only picked. I forced myself to eat, keeping
my eyes downcast so as not to look at him in his luxuriously embroidered dressing gown, his hands and his mouth. The fire was
warm against my cheek, but my other cheek was hot also. I kept
remembering his fingers on my thigh, and my ring wouldn't swallow up that heat.

He demanded a bath, and I had to endure that: they put it
before the fire, and two serving-girls washed him while I tried not

to watch their hands moving over his body, tried not to feel something like jealousy. I wasn't jealous over him, but over what he'd made me feel, that stirring that should have belonged to a man I would have *let* touch me; a man who would have *wanted* to touch me, who could really be my husband. I wanted that shiver along my leg to be a gift I'd never expected; I wanted to be able to look at him in his bath and blush and be *glad* for it. And instead I had to deliberately look away, because if I had my way, tonight I'd throw him down into a pit with a Staryk king, and bury them both, and marry myself off to a brutish man as old as my father.

Magreta crept in timid-brave, with her comb and brush, to do my hair; her hands on my shoulders asked a trembling question I couldn't answer anymore. She'd told me some time ago, in quick prosaic terms, the way between a man and a woman, when I was still young enough to think it sounded silly and to promise without hesitation never to let a man do it until we were married. "Not that *you'll* be left alone with any men, dushenka," she'd added, belatedly, stroking my hair: she'd been passing on a speech that someone had given to her, a long time ago; a speech she'd listened to and obeyed for all her days.

Some years later on from there, when I'd been old enough to understand what *marriage* meant for a duke's daughter, and why I would never be left alone with any man long enough to choose anything at all until my choices were gone, she'd told me of it all over again comfortingly, as something to be endured: not too bad, it's only a few minutes, it won't hurt much, and only the first time. I had been too old to be comforted so, however. I understood that she was lying, without knowing exactly *how* she was lying; perhaps it would hurt every time and perhaps it would hurt a great deal and perhaps it would go on for ages—a wide array of unpleasant possibilities. I'd even asked her how she knew, and she'd gone pink and embarrassed and said, "Everyone knows, Irinushka, everyone knows," and that meant she didn't really know at all.

But she'd never told me about other possibilities, about why she'd made me promise in the first place. Now I wondered if she'd ever been hungry this way, and how she'd stifled that hunger; what crust of bread she had pressed into her mouth to keep from swallowing up the seeds of a disaster. I sat with her hands slowly braiding my hair and my hands were clasped in my lap, the silver of my ring lit gold by flame-reflections, like my husband's skin, sheened with amber light as he stepped dripping wet from the bath.

He stood like a statue before the wide fireplace before me as the serving-girls wiped the droplets from him with soft cloths: a little too lovingly, which I tried not to notice. They were both very pretty, of course, chosen to please the tsar's eye. But he only twitched his shoulders like a horse shivering away flies and said with sharp impatience, "My clothes." They left off hurriedly as his own body servants from the palace shooed them away and brought him his garments, silk and velvet laid on in layers as carefully as my father's armor, under a sharp critical commentary from him all the while, dissatisfied with this crease or that bulge.

I was already dressed. The servants bowed to Mirnatius when he dismissed them, and then turned to me as Magreta set the crown upon my newly braided hair. They stood in silence a moment before me, looking, and then they all bowed again, lower; the two serving-girls curtseyed deep, and slipped out of the room hand in hand with their baskets of cloths and soap on their other arms, whispering to each other wistfully. Mirnatius watched them all with more baffled indignation and then abruptly seized his book from where the satchel lay against the wall. Without even sitting down, he roughly drew my face again in quick furious lines and turned to catch one of the servants still going back and forth emptying buckets out of the tub. "Look at this! Is this a beautiful face?" he demanded.

The poor man was very alarmed, of course, and looked at the

picture only trying to divine what answer the tsar wanted; he stared at it and said, "It's the tsarina?" at once, and then he looked up at me, and looked back down at it, and looked helplessly at the tsar.

"*Well?*" Mirnatius snapped. "Is it beautiful or not?"

"Yes?" the man said faintly, in desperation.

Mirnatius ground his teeth. "*Why?* What about it is beautiful? *Look* at it and tell me, don't just bleat whatever you think I want to hear!"

The man swallowed, terrified, and said, "It's a good likeness?"

"*Is* it?" Mirnatius said.

"Yes? Yes, very good," the man said, hastily more definite as Mirnatius stepped towards him. "But I am no judge, Majesty! Forgive me!" He bent his head.

"Let him go," I said, in pity, "and ask the boyar instead."

Mirnatius scowled at me, but waved the servant off, and he did take the picture to the boyar and thrust it in his hands at the door, as all our retinue crammed into the sledges and sleighs again. The boyar and his wife looked at it, and she touched it with her fingers and said, "How beautiful, Your Majesty."

"Why?" he snapped, instantly turning on her. "Which features please you, what about it?"

She looked at him in surprise and looked back and said, "Why—none alone, I suppose, Your Majesty. But I see the tsarina's face again when I look at it." She smiled at him suddenly. "Perhaps I see what your eyes see," she said, gentle and well meant, and he whirled away almost breathless with rage and threw himself into the sleigh, leaving the loose page still in her hands.

He drew me a dozen times more that day, one picture after another from every angle he could arrange; he seized my chin and pushed my head in one direction and another in mad frustration. I let him do it without complaint. I kept thinking, unwillingly, of his silent weeping. His book filled with pictures, and he made the servants look at them, and the boyar whose house we stopped at to break the morning. We came into Vysnia a little while after noon, and the sleigh drew up before the steps of my father's house. We hadn't quite stopped moving before Mirnatius leapt out; without even saying a word of greeting, he thrust the book into my own father's hands and said, almost savagely, "Well?"

My father looked through the pictures slowly, turning the pages with his thick callused fingertip; a strange expression was coming into his face. I had climbed out, with a servant's help, and my stepmother Galina was holding out her hands to me in greeting. We kissed cheeks, and I straightened, and my father was still lingering on the last drawing, a sketch of my face looking out at trees heavy with snow, a single curve for the sleigh's edge and only the far side of my face visible, just eyelashes and the corner of my mouth and the line of my hair. He said, "She has a look of her mother in these," and handed the book back to Mirnatius abruptly, his mouth pressed into a line, and turned to kiss my cheeks.

I had never slept in the grandest chamber of my father's house. I had peeked into it a few times as a daring game, when there were no honored guests in the house and Magreta would let me. It had always seemed to me an imposing, massive room. The windowsills were carved stone, as was the one heavy imprudent balcony that looked away over the forest and the river. "It was the old duchess's chambers," Magreta once told me. There were tapestries on the walls: Magreta had helped mend a few, but my own sewing was not good enough to be allowed; I had done a little of the embroidery on two of the velvet pillows that littered the bed, with its funny big clawed feet that I had always liked: the last duke's crest had been a bear, and there were half a dozen old pieces of furniture still left with the carved feet.

But now the room seemed suddenly small and close and too hot for me after the delicate beauty of the tsar's palace. I went to stand on the balcony while the servants brought in our things, bustling around me, with the cold wind welcome on my face. It was a little way into the afternoon, the sun going low. Magreta came in scolding along the servants who brought in my box of dresses, but then she came to stand with me silently, pressing my hand between hers, stroking the back of it.

When the others went out and we were alone for a moment, I said quietly, "Will you get one of the other servants to find out where the house of Panov Moshel stands? It's in the Jewish quarter somewhere. There's going to be a wedding there tonight, and the driver will need to know the way. And find me a gift to take."

"Oh, dushenka," she said, softly, afraid. She brought my hand to her cheek and then she kissed it and went away to do as I'd asked.

One of Mirnatius's guardsmen came in, one of the soldiers who had come with us from the palace. He wasn't really a footman, but unlike the other servants bustling in the room, I was not the duke's daughter to him; I was the tsarina, and when I looked at him, he bowed deeply to me and stopped there in his place, waiting. I said, "Will you go tell my father I would like to see him?"

"At once, Your Majesty," he said, a note in his voice like the deepest humming string on an instrument, and he went out.

My father came to me. He stopped in the doorway and I turned, still on the balcony, and looked at him with my back straight. His eyes were on me, heavy and assessing as they always had been, measuring my worth, and after a moment he crossed the room and came to join me on the cold stone. Below us, the near-unbroken white of the forest and the frozen river rolled into the blanketed countryside. "It won't be a good harvest this year," I said.

I half expected him to be irritated or even angry at being summoned, to speak sharply to me: to him surely I was only the unexpectedly useful pawn. I was not meant to begin sweeping independently around on the board. But he only said, "No. The rye is blighted in the fields."

"I'm sorry to put you to the expense, but there's going to be a wedding while we're here," I told him. "We're marrying Vassilia to Mirnatius's cousin Ilias."

He paused and looked at me from under his brows for a long moment. He said slowly, "We can manage. How soon after she comes?"

"In the same hour," I said, and we looked at each other, and I knew that he understood me perfectly.

He rubbed his hand across his mouth thoughtfully. "I'll make sure Father Idoros is ready and waiting in the chapel when Ulrich's horses come through the gate. The house will be crowded, but your mother and I will leave our bedroom for them. She'll sleep upstairs with her women, and I'll take the one next door, with your cousin Darius. A few other men of your husband's household can share with us to make room."

I nodded, and I knew I wouldn't have to worry about Ulrich finding a way to spirit his own valuable daughter out from under her new bridegroom.

"Will Prince Casimir be visiting?" my father asked after a moment, still studying me.

"He may not come until the day after, I am afraid," I said. "Our messenger to him was late getting started, some trouble with his horse."

My father glanced back into the room. The servants were still working, but none of them were near the balcony. "How is your husband's health?"

"Mostly good. But he has . . . a nervous complaint," I said. "A trouble his mother had, I think."

My father paused and his brows drew hard together. "Does it give him . . . difficulty?"

"So far, yes," I said.

He was silent, and then he said, "I'll have a quiet word with Casimir when he comes. He's not a fool. A sensible man, and a good soldier."

"I'm glad you think well of him," I said.

My father put his hand up and held my cheek for a moment, so unexpected I held still beneath it, startled. He said low, fiercely, "I am proud of you, Irina," and then he let go again. "Will you and your husband come down to dinner tonight?"

"Not tonight," I said after a moment. It was an effort to speak, at first. I hadn't thought that I wanted my father to be proud of me. It had never seemed possible at all, but I hadn't known it mattered to me. I had to force myself to find words again. "There's one more thing. Something . . . else."

He studied my face and nodded. "Tell me."

I waited in silence, until the room had emptied of servants again for a moment. "The winter's being made by the Staryk. They mean to freeze us all." He stiffened, and instinctively reached his finger halfway towards the hanging chains of my silver crown, looking at it. "Their king means to bring the snow all summer."

His eyes were hard and intent upon me. "Why?"

I shook my head. "I don't know. But there's a way to stop it."

I told him of the plan in those few private moments, plain and brutally quick. When I had spoken of politics, I knew just how to tell him a thousand things without saying a single betraying word that anyone else would understand, never fearing that he wouldn't know what I meant, but not when I spoke of winter lords and demons of flame. They moved through our words like they moved through our world, disasters beyond its boundaries. I spoke quickly not just to keep from being overheard, but because I wanted to hurry through: the story made no sense beside the hard reality of stone walls and murder, and the sun shining on the snow-bright rail.

But my father listened intently, and he didn't say *Don't be foolish*, or *This is madness*. When I finished, he said, "There was a tower once in the southern end of the city walls, near the Jewish quarter. We broke it in the siege when we came into the city. We rebuilt the wall straight afterwards, and left the cellar and the foundations of the tower outside, covered over with dirt, and my two best men and I dug a tunnel to it all the way out of the palace cellars, while the city was still half burned." I was nodding swiftly, understanding: he'd made a back way out of the city, a way to escape a siege, like the old duke hadn't had to use. "Once a year, in the night, I go down the tunnel and back to check it. I'll dig it out tonight with my own hands, and wait for you there, outside the walls. You have the chain?"

"Yes," I said. "In my jewel-box. And twelve great candles, to make a ring of fire."

He nodded. More servants came in and we fell silent together. He said nothing while they unpacked another two boxes of rich clothing, velvet and silk and brocades. His eyes were on the work, but he was not really seeing it; I could see his mind unwinding a tangled thread with slow careful patience, following it from one end to another through a thicket. "What is it?" I asked, when they had gone away again.

He said after a moment, "Men have lived here a long time, Irina. My great-grandfather had a farmhouse near the city. The Staryk rule the forest, and lust for gold, and they ride out in winter storms to get it, but they have never before stood in the way of the spring." My father looked at me with his cold clear eyes, and I knew he was warning me when he said, "It would be well to know: *Why?*"

I had the Staryk king's promise, but I didn't want to trust it; the panic of the storerooms still filled me. But I was so tired that I drifted to sleep in my bath as soon as they put me in it. I suppose I might have slept however long I wanted, but as I lay there drowsing, I had a half dream of standing on the threshold of the ballroom in my grandfather's house, the whole room empty and the lights dimmed and the Staryk jeering next to me, "You mistook the date."

I jerked up in sudden terror, wide-awake, my heart pounding. I stared for a moment in confusion at the wall of my room in front of me, which wasn't clear anymore but solid white, and then I clumsily dragged myself out of the bath, wrapping a sheet around me as I stumbled over. It wasn't the wall that had changed: it was the whole world that had gone all to white; the forest buried so deep that the nearest pines were under up to their small pointed tops, coated thickly, with not a single dark green needle visible anywhere. The river had vanished completely beneath the blanket, and the sky had gone almost pearl-white above.

I stood staring out at it with the sheet clenched in my fists against me, thinking of all that snow falling on my home, falling on Vysnia, until one of the servants behind me said timidly, "My lady, will you dress?"

Flek and Tsop and Shofer had all vanished, mere servants' work evidently beneath them now, but they'd arranged everything I needed before they went. Shofer had gone to order one of the other drivers to make the sleigh ready for my journey, and a crowd of other servants had been summoned, who obeyed me with a different kind of silence and swiftness, as though some word and whisper had already gone through the kingdom, and changed me in all their sight.

They brought me a gown of heavy white silk with a coat of white brocade embroidered in silver, and a high-necked collar of silver lace and clear jewels to go around my shoulders. They put the heavy golden crown above it all—mismatched at first, but I barely glanced at myself in the mirror and noticed, and gold shot suddenly down every line of silver all the way to the embroidered hem. Around me the women dropped their hands from the silk and their eyes from my face.

I would be far more mismatched at Basia's wedding, a fantastical doll that someone had imagined unrestrained by cost or sense. But I didn't tell them to bring another dress. I was bringing a Staryk king as a wedding guest, and hoping to kill him in the midst of the festivities; my clothes would be the least of it. And if I was lucky enough to escape this night with my life and dress intact, I'd sell it to some noblewoman to make a dowry for a real marriage. I didn't believe silver would turn to gold for me in the sunlit world, but I'd still be a rich woman to the end of my days off the one ensemble.

So I held my head high under the weight of my crown and let the burden of it make me glide with stately pace to the front of the chamber. Tsop and Shofer had come back and were waiting there for me, each of them with a small box full of silver: mostly small pieces of jewelry, a cup or two, some scattered forks and knives and plates and loose coins filling in around them. They had changed their clothing, too, to garments of palest ivory. Tsop had put the gold buttons from her old clothes onto the new ones. The other servants bowed to them and looked at them sideways at the same time.

Then Flek came in, also in ivory and carrying a box of her own, and at her side a little girl followed, a Staryk girl. She was the first child I'd seen here, and even stranger to my eye than the grown Staryk were: she was as thin and reedy as an icicle and almost as translucent, and shades and veins of deep blue were visible beneath her skin, a thin clear layer of ice. Beside her the other Staryk looked like snowy hillsides, and she a frozen core that snow had yet to settle on. She looked up at me with silent wide curiosity.

"Open-Handed, this is my daughter, who now is your bonds-woman, too," Flek said softly, and touched her shoulder, and the little girl made me a careful leaning bow. She was carrying a small fine necklace of silver across her hands, a simple adornment she evidently hadn't wanted to put into the box with the rest, and I reached down and touched it first of all.

Warm gold blushed through the whole length of it with the slightest push of my will, and the child gave a soft delighted tinkling sigh that made it feel more like magic than all the work I'd done in the treasury below. Slowly, I turned to Flek's box and touched the top of the small pile of silver inside. Everything blazed into gold at once, the same quick and easy way, as if I'd somehow stretched the muscles of my gift to new lengths—as if now I *could* have gone and changed three storerooms packed full of silver into gold, without any trick involved. I changed Tsop's silver and Shofer's also; neither of them seemed surprised at how easily it went. I finished and then asked them, "Is it permissible to say thank you here, or is that rude somehow?"

"My lady, we would not refuse anything you wished to give us," Tsop said a little helplessly, after they all three exchanged a look. "But we have always heard that in the sunlit world, mortals give *thanks* to one another to fill the hollowness where they fail to make return, and you have already given us so much that we shall only answer it with our lives' service: you have given us names in your voice, and raised us high, and filled our hands with gold. What are your thanks besides that?"

When she put it that way—although I hadn't thought of the names as a *gift* I was making them—I had to think about what I would have *meant* by saying thank you, instead of just the automatic politeness. I had to grope a while; I'd been jolted out of being sleepy, but I still felt dulled, as if my head had been padded with wool inside. "What I mean—what we mean by it is—it's like credit," I said, suddenly thinking of my grandfather. "Gifts, and thanks—we'll accept from someone what they can give then, and make return to them when it's wanted, if we can. And there are some cheats, and some debts aren't paid, but others are paid with interest to make up for it, and we can all do the more for not having to pay as we go. So I do thank you," I added abruptly, "because you risked all you had to help me, and even if you count the return fair, I'll still remember the chance you took and be glad to do more for you if I can."

They stared at me, and after a moment Flek reached out a hand and put it on her daughter's head and said, "My lady, then I will ask, if you do not think it beyond what you owe: will you give my child her true name?" I must have looked as baffled as I felt; Flek lowered her eyes. "The one who sired her would not accept the burden when she was born, and left her nameless," she said softly. "And if I ask him again now, he will agree, but he has the right to demand my hand in return, and I no longer wish to give it."

I didn't know what the laws among the Staryk were, about marriage, but I knew exactly what I thought of a man who'd sire a child and refuse to own it: I wouldn't have wanted him, either. "Yes. How do I do it?" I asked, and after she told me, I held out my hand to the little girl, and she came with me to the far end of the balcony, and I bent down and whispered in her ear, "Your name is Rebekah bat Flek," which I thought would certainly give any Staryk trying to guess it a significant degree of difficulty.

She brightened up all throughout her body, as if someone had lit a flame inside her. She ran back to her mother and said, "Mama, Mama, I have a name! I have a name! Can I tell you?" and Flek knelt and pulled her into her arms and kissed her and said, "Sleep with it in your heart alone tonight, little snowflake, and tell me in the morning."

It made me glad looking on their joy: I felt in that moment that I *had* given fair return, even for that day and night of terror they had all lived with me, and if I never saw them again, I still hoped that they'd do well for themselves. I did feel a pang of guilt, because I didn't know exactly what would happen if my plan succeeded and I left their king's throne vacant for someone else to claim. Would that mean my own rank had fallen, and theirs with mine? But I hoped that would only put them in some lower rank of nobility at worst. I had to take the chance, anyway, for the sake of my own people, being buried alive under that endless snow outside my window.

I took a deep breath. "I'm ready to go," I said, and almost instantly the glass wall parted and my husband came in: my husband, whom I meant to murder. For just cause and more, but still I felt a little queasy, and I didn't look him in his face. I'd avoided looking at him before because he'd seemed so terrible and strange, a glittering of icicles brought to life; now I avoided it because he looked suddenly too much like *someone*, like a person. I had held the hand of that frozen little ice-statue of a girl, and she was my goddaughter now or something close to it, and when I looked at Flek and Tsop and Shofer, their faces were warmed by the reflection off the gold in the chests at their feet, and they were the faces of my friends, my friends who had helped me, and would help me again if they could. What did it matter that they didn't *speak* of kindness, here; they had *done* me a kindness with their hands. I knew which one of those I would choose.

But they made it suddenly harder to see only winter in *his* face. He wasn't my friend; he was all monstrous sharp edges of ice, wanting to cut me open and spill gold out of me while he swallowed up my world. But he was a satisfied monster for the moment: I *had* cut myself open, and I'd filled him two storerooms of gold, and he had to *match* my accomplishment to fulfill his own sense of dignity, so he came to me dressed in splendor equal to my own, as if he meant to do courtesy to the occasion, and he bowed to me as courtly as if I really *was* his queen. "Come, then, my lady, and let us to the wedding," he said, even suddenly polite to me, now when I most wanted him to be cold and grudging and resentful. I suppose I shouldn't have been surprised: he'd never given me anything I wanted unless I'd bound him to it beforehand.

I looked at my friends one last time and inclined my head to them, saying farewell, and walked out beside him. We went down together to the courtyard. The sleigh was waiting, heaped with white furs without a mark. My dress and my crown were so heavy on me that I reached for the sides to haul myself up into it, but before I could, he took me by the waist and lifted me without effort inside before taking his own seat next to me.

The deer leapt away at the twitch of the driver's reins, and the mountain went flashing away around us. The wind was strong and sweet in my face, not too cold, as we rushed down the passage to the silver gates and back out into the world, the sleigh runners whispering over the road and the hooves of the deer a light drumming. It was only a few minutes before we were running quick towards the forest. The deer and the sleigh flew over the top of the new-fallen snow without leaving more than light tracks, and the half-buried trees looked oddly small as we drove through them.

I watched to see what the Staryk would do, what spell or incantation he'd use to open a path to the sunlit world, but all he did was turn and look back at me in very nearly the same speculating way, as if he was wondering whether *I* might not fling out some unexpected magic. And then he said to me abruptly, "I will answer no questions for you tonight."

"What?" My voice nearly cracked with alarm; for an instant I thought he'd *guessed*, he knew what I'd planned and we weren't going to any wedding but to my execution. Then I understood what he *really* meant. "We have a bargain!"

"In exchange for your rights only. You have given me nothing in exchange for *mine*. I set no value upon them, and now see I

bargained falsely—" He cut himself off abruptly, turning to face
forward, and then he said slowly, "Is that why you demanded answers to fool's questions as your return? To show your disdain for
my insult?" He sat there for a moment of silence, and before I
could correct him, suddenly he laughed, like a chorus full of bells
singing a long way over snow, a baffling noise; I'd never even
imagined him laughing. I stopped open-mouthed, half startled
and half outraged, and then he turned and seized my hand and
kissed it, the brush of his lips against my skin something like
breathing out onto frostbitten glass.

He took me so much by surprise that I didn't say anything at
first, or even pull my hand free, and then he said to me fiercely, "I
will make you amends tonight, my lady, and show you that I have
learned better how to value you; I will not require another lesson
beyond this one," with a wave of his arm out of the sleigh, over
the wide landscape smothered in the snow.

At first I looked in confusion, wondering what he meant, but
there was nothing around us, nothing to be seen, except his depth-
less winter. A hundred years of winter that had somehow come all
at once on a summer's day, when the Staryk should have been
shut up behind the glass walls of their mountain, waiting for the
winter to come again. Though the Staryk had never before been
able to hold back the spring so long.

A hundred years of winter, on a summer's day. I said through
a throat suddenly choked and tight, "*You* didn't make this winter."

"No, my lady," he said, still looking at me with all the vast self-
congratulation of a man who'd found a treasure hidden in a dirty
trough. A treasure of gold, like the Staryk ever coveted; and when
they'd begun to raid us more, when they'd begun to come for that
gold more often—that was when the winters had begun to grow
steadily worse. And now—and now—there were two vast storerooms heaped with shining, sunlit gold; the warmth of the sum-

mer sun trapped into cold metal for the Staryk to hoard deep inside his walls, while he buried my home under a wall of winter.

He *smiled* at me, still holding my hand; he smiled at me, and then turned to the driver and said, "Go!" and with a lurch we were onto the white road; the king's road, Shofer had called it; the Staryk road I had known and glimpsed in the dark woods all my life. It was running on ahead of us as if it had always been there, and stretched away behind us too, as far as I could see, an endless vaulted passageway. The strange unearthly-white trees lined it on both sides, their limbs hung with clear ice-drops and white leaves, and the surface of it was smooth blue-white ice, clouded. The sleigh flew over it, and all at once a sudden strong smell of pine needles and sap came into my nose, a desperate struggling of life. Through the canopy of white branches overhead, the sky began to change: the grey flushed slowly through on one side with blue, and on the other with golden and orange, a summer evening's sky over winter woods, and I knew that we'd slid out of his kingdom and back into my own world.

He was still holding my hand in his. I left it there deliberately, thinking of Judith singing in her sweet voice to make Holofernes's eyes go heavy in his tent, and what else she'd endured there first. I could bear this. I was so angry I had gone cold straight through. *Let* him think he had me, and could have my heart for the lifting of his finger. *Let* him think I would betray my people and my home just to be a queen beside him. He could hold my hand the rest of the way if he wanted to, as a fair return for the gift he'd given me, the one thing I'd wanted from him after all: I'd lost even the slightest qualm about killing him.

ℰChapter 19

There were a few servants who went to the Jewish quarter sometimes: Galina's maid Palmira, when her mistress wanted some jewelry, would go and look at their stalls. She had been too high to talk to me before with anything but impatience, when my lady was the little-wanted daughter of the wife who'd come before; all the dance that went on in the great ballrooms and bedrooms, we danced over again among ourselves in our narrow halls. But now I was servant to the tsarina, who valued me enough to have sent for me, so when I went knocking at the duchess's dressing room, Palmira got up from where she sat polishing jewelry and came and kissed me on both cheeks, and asked me if I wasn't tired from the journey, and had me sit in her own chair next to the wall that was on the other side of the fireplace in the bedroom; she sent the under-maid to bring a cup of tea. I sat gladly before the warm wall and drank the tea: oh, I was tired.

"The banker?" she said at once, when I told her the name Moshel. "I don't know where he lives, but the steward will. Ula," she said to the girl, "go bring us some kruschiki and some cherries, and then go tell Panov Nolius that dear Magreta is here and ask if he won't join us for a cup of tea: we shouldn't make her run all over the house after so much traveling." Another little dancing step there, because she liked to make the steward come to *her*, which he would not do, except that here I was. And here I was, and the wall was warm at my back, and I was too old to keep dancing anymore. I only sat and drank my tea and took another cup with cherries and ate a sweet crisp melting kruschik and said thank you to Panov Nolius when he did deign to come and sit and have tea with us.

"Panov Moshel lives in the fourth house on Varenka Street," he said cool and stiff, when I asked him the name. "Does Her Majesty want to arrange a loan? I would be glad to be of service."

"A loan? The tsarina?" I said, confused; Irina had said a man in the Jewish quarter, and I had thought of those moneylenders in their little stalls who looked through their small round glasses at a silver ring that had come from your mother, and then gave you money for it. A little nothing of money, compared with what it was worth to you, but the little money that you had to have just then, because one of the girls who had sat in that dark room with you, for hours, had snuck out to see one of those soldiers who'd let you out, and now she needed a doctor who wouldn't come except for silver and in the middle of the night. That was what it meant to me, someone who lent money in the Jewish quarter. That was not someone for a duke or a tsarina to deal with.

Nolius liked that I didn't know any better; I might be the tsarina's servant, but I was still a silly old woman who thought the world was made of small things, and he was the trusted steward of the duke. So then he unbent a little and took a kruschik and told me, pleased and full of knowledge, "No, no, Panov Moshel has a bank: a man of solid worth, most reputable. He helped to arrange the loans for the rebuilding of the city wall after the war, with great discretion. His Grace has had him here to the house eight times on business, and all times ordered that he be treated with great respect. And never once has Moshel tried to trade upon it. He comes always on foot, not in a carriage; the women of his family dress soberly, and he keeps a modest house. Never has he asked a favor in return."

I had always thought of the city wall as something built by soldiers, and not with money, but of course you would have to pay for it somehow; for stones and mortar and food for men to eat and clothes for them to wear while they built it for you, but even if I had imagined it so far, I would have thought only that the money must have come from a strongroom somewhere, a chest full of gold like a duke would have or a tsar. I wouldn't have thought of it coming from quiet men in plain coats who didn't ride in carriages.

Nolius leaned in so he could be sure I would understand he was telling me a private thing only a man of his importance would know, and added with much significance, "He has been given to know that if he converted, doors might be opened for him." Then he sat back and shrugged, opening a hand. "But he did not choose it, and His Grace was satisfied. I have heard him say, 'I would rather have my affairs in the hands of a man who is content than a man who is hungry. I prefer to take my risks on the battlefield.' I would certainly recommend him if Her Majesty desired to make any financial arrangements."

"Oh, no," I said. "No, it's a different matter, a woman's matter. His granddaughter gave her a gift, one that she treasures, and she wants to make a return on the occasion of her wedding. She asked me to arrange a gift."

Nolius looked puzzled, and glanced at Palmira: of course they thought I had muddled the story, and they were right, I knew I had gotten something in it wrong. But it didn't matter. Let that be the story. It was strange enough already. "It was a gift given before her wedding," I added, though, to make it a little less strange to them.

Palmira said, "Ah!" very delicately, and they both decided at once they wouldn't press the question more, after all. There wasn't any sense bringing up the old days when they might have been rude to me in the hallways when we passed; the days when Irina and I lived in two cold rooms a little too high in the house for a duke's daughter, and when she might have been glad for whatever present a Jew's granddaughter might send her: a farsighted Jew's granddaughter, who had been wiser than they, and planted a seed of gratitude that now would come to flower.

"Well, of course it must be something notable," Nolius said firmly: anyone who *had* recognized my lady must be rewarded, since otherwise those who had neglected her must be punished. "No jewels, of course, or money. Perhaps something for her household . . ."

"We should ask Edita's advice," Palmira said, meaning the housekeeper, and Nolius was also happy to have her come, since *he* had lowered himself, so a few minutes later she came, too, and had tea with cherries and asked me questions about the tsar's palace.

"It's too cold for an old woman," I said. "Such windows everywhere! Taller twice over than this whole wall," I showed them with my hand, "and the wall as long as the ballroom, and that is only the bedchamber. Six fireplaces going at once, to keep from freezing alive, and everything in gold, everything: the windows and the table legs and the bath, everything. Six women to clean the room."

They all sighed with pleasure, and Edita said to Nolius, "I don't envy whoever runs his household! So many to manage!" and he nodded seriously back to her, both of them of course full of glowing envy, but since they could not have the trouble of it themselves, they would at least content themselves by reminding each other with pleasure that they, too, had a great household to manage, and understood as others could not how difficult it was.

But the conversation wasn't foolish really: it gave us all an excuse to sit a little while longer and rest together, in the room that was warm with the fire behind me and the four of us sitting close and the hot tea, an excuse that we had to have, or else be bad servants neglecting our work. The duchess did not keep bad servants. Edita took another small sip of her cup and said to me, in a thoughtful tone, "What about that tablecloth, dear Magreta? Do you remember, the present for the wedding of the boyar's daughter, and then nothing came of it? It was such lovely work."

I remembered it, I remembered it very well. That boyar was a man who had fought for the duke, and so the duke wanted a handsome gift given. And everyone else had as much work as they could hold, the duchess and her ladies, and over the years I'd little by little slowed my pace and spared my hands, cautiously, as Irina grew; I'd said, oh, I have all her things to sew, and apologized, and did the tasks Edita sent me a bit slower than she liked, so she gave me a little less. But Irina was fourteen that year, so they had brought up the baskets of silk wool to our little rooms, and Edita had smiling said it was time for Irina to be learning how to do fine work; I could teach her. And it must be done in a month, dear Magreta.

So in the end, she got back all the work I had tried to save out of my hands. I had spun the silk alone with my eyes and fingers aching into the hours of the night while my girl slept, because she already wasn't beautiful, with her thin pallid face and sharp nose, and I was afraid to make her ugly with squinting and bending over work by the fire and not enough sleep. There wouldn't be a great marriage for her, I thought then, but there might be a house somewhere at least; maybe an older man who wouldn't trouble her very much, and she would have a bedroom that was not at the top of the stairs, and be the mistress there. And there would be a corner for me, where I could rock by the cradle if a child came, and knit only small things.

I had spun the silk and then I had knitted it with the finest needles in the vines and flowers of the duke's crest, so that every feast day when they laid it down on their table they would look at it and think of their patron, who showed them such favor. And then, yes, nothing came of it; a fever came instead. The boyar's daughter died before the wedding, the boy married some girl less well-connected, and all my hours and pain were folded in paper and put away into the duchess's cupboard for when she needed another gift to give.

"Thank you, Edita, if you can spare it," I said. It *was* a kindness, a kindness and an apology both, because she had not been wise enough to give me a little help herself, and make it *our* work. So when next the duchess needed a notable gift, she would not have a tablecloth folded in paper to take out, and it was Edita who would have to see a gift made, without a pair of spare hands upstairs that she could easily put to use. And now Irina had a gift to give, a gift she needed because I had saved her looks enough that her father had not just left her upstairs to become a pair of spare hands for her brothers' wives; her father had put a crown on her shining dark hair that I had combed, and given her to a demon for his wife.

"Well, of course, after all your pains on it," Edita said, more easily now that I had accepted her apology; they all smiled at me, relieved, because I was too old and tired to dance with them and be haughty as I should have been with the tsarina as a mistress, and I would not take too much from them to pay the old debts they had laid up with me; it was too hard to collect. And oh, I wanted to creep back upstairs to the little rooms and put my hard chair close to the small fire and shut the door again. But it was too late.

We finished our tea and she brought me the tablecloth, and Nolius made me a little drawing of the streets where the house was, and I took them upstairs. The duke was out on the balcony with Irina. Their faces looking at each other were dark shapes with the grey sky behind them, a pattern knitted mirror-fashion;

she was tall as he was, and she had his nose. I kept my head down and hurried into a corner for the few minutes until he left her. "Thank you, Magra," she said absently when she came back inside afterwards, looking at the tablecloth in its paper half unfolded on the bed. She took her small wooden jewel-box and opened it: a heavy silver chain and twelve squat candles of pure white wax lay in the bottom of it, and she put the tablecloth in atop the rest. She touched it with her fingers, but she did not see it really; she was not thinking of tablecloths and thread and the time that made them one. She did not have to. I had let her sleep, and so now she could think of crowns and demons instead, and she had to, or she would die.

She closed the box as the tsar came into the room on a wave of servants: he had come to change his clothes. He looked at Irina coldly. "Have you anything else to wear?" he demanded, even as he threw himself into a chair and held out his legs one after another; the servants drew off his boots, and then he stood and put himself in the middle of the room and did nothing while they sprang to take off his coat, his belt, his shirt, and his trousers, everything.

"There's the blue dress," I whispered to Irina, which I had been sewing for her. It had been put aside in the rush before the wedding: it could not have been finished in time to go into her box, and it was not grand enough truly for a tsarina; I had been making it for her to wear at her father's table, to set off the thick braid and give a little color to her face. But then she had driven away with her box in a sleigh with the tsar, and I had been left behind alone in the cold rooms. And I knew soon they would at least put some other maids in there with me, but I hoped at least they would let me stay in them, so I took the blue dress out and worked upon it though it hurt my hands, meaning to make it for the duchess instead, something I would have crept downstairs and given to Palmira where the duchess could see, and I hoped like the dress enough to keep me sewing for her. So it was finished.

Irina nodded to me. I did not go for it myself. I went out and found one of the other maids and told her to go bring the dress down from the cold rooms, and she did it because I was important now enough to spend an hour having tea with Palmira and Nolius and Edita. I went back inside and Irina was standing by the balcony again, staring at the forest while the tsar stood all naked before the fire, dismissing this coat and that shirt and this waistcoat, out of the bags and boxes piled like a small fort made in the room. None of us mattered, of course, but it was not that he did not care because we were servants: even Galina or the duke would not stand there forever naked before a mirror while they picked through every shirt of their wardrobe, as if they did not need to be ashamed of their nakedness in their own heart and cover themselves. But the tsar stood as though he might go out of the room and put himself just so before everyone's eyes as easily as put anything on; as though he only troubled himself with clothing for the pleasure of its beauty, and if nothing satisfied him, he wouldn't bother, and would put everyone else to the trouble of looking away from him, or having to pretend he wasn't naked before them.

But for Irina, I opened a screen to make a hidden place in the corner of the room, and then the girl came down with the blue dress, and we helped Irina to put it on there in the small dark corner. When we had finished putting it on her, we folded the screen away, and the tsar was dressed at last or nearly: he wore a coat of red velvet and a waistcoat of red embroidered in silver, and they were putting on fine shoes for him with lines of glittering red jewels sewn along the seams. He stood and turned and looked at Irina with cold displeasure, and said, "Get out," to all of us, and I had to go. I looked back at her for a moment from the door, but she did not look afraid; she stood looking steadily back at him, my cool quiet girl with nothing showing in her face.

They came out again a little while later, and the dress wasn't what it had been; it was wider and more full, and the blue shaded from deep strong color at the waist out to pale grey at the hem with a waterfall of petticoats spilling out beneath it, and silver embroidery tracing every edge with red jewels winking out of it at me that I had never sewn onto it. She was carrying her jewel-box in her arms, and the long sleeves had become gauze thin as a summer veil with more red jewels in twisting lines drawn over them, as though he had sprinkled drops of blood upon her, bled out of his red coat. I closed my hands on each other and dropped my eyes as they passed, not to see. I had made the dress like I had made the tablecloth, out of pain and long work, and I knew how much of both it had taken to make it. And so I knew how much that dress would have cost, that he had put her in, and I did not want to think of how it had been paid.

Wanda and Sergey went downstairs to help with the wedding. "Will you come, Stepon?" Sergey asked me, but I shivered, remembering all those people crammed together, in the rooms and in the streets, more people than I knew there were in the whole world. So I said, "No, no, no," and they didn't make me, but they went, and after a while the sun started to go down, and I started to not like being alone in the room. I was all alone with nobody, not even goats, and Wanda and Sergey were gone. What if they had really gone again? What if someone had come looking for them and they had to run away? I opened the window and stuck my head out and looked down, and when I did that I could hear noise from all the way down on the ground. There were a lot of people outside the house and some horses too, but it was dark down on the ground already, even though the sun was still coming in the window, and I couldn't see anyone's faces. I couldn't see Wanda or Sergey. There was one woman with yellow hair but I wasn't sure if it was her.

I pulled my head back inside, but the house was getting so loud and full of people that I heard some of that same noise even when I closed the window. It came up through the fireplace and under the door. It got louder and louder and then music started playing. It was loud music and people were dancing to it. I felt it in my feet not just in my ears. I sat on the bed and covered my ears and I still felt it coming up all the way through the house.

It kept going on and on. It was all the way dark outside and I was really afraid now because why would Wanda and Sergey stay down in all that noise unless something bad made them. I had my face pressed up against my knees and my arms over my head, and then there was a knock on the door. I didn't say to come in because I would have to take my arms from over my head, but Panova Mandelstam came inside anyway. "Stepon, are you all right?" she said. She meant it but she didn't really mean it, I could tell. She was thinking about something else. But when I didn't say anything back and didn't pick my head up, she started to really mean it, and then she went and got the candle she had left on the table for us and she took out a couple of big lumps of wax from it and blew on them until they weren't hot, and she said, "Here, Stepon, put the wax in your ears."

I thought I would try. I took my hand away for just a little bit and took the wax. It was still warm and soft. I pushed it into my ear and it squished into the little spots and then it stopped being so warm, and the noise stopped being so loud on that side. I could still feel it in my body but I couldn't hear it so much. So then I was very glad and I took the other lump of wax and that helped too.

Panova Mandelstam put her hand on my head and stroked it.

I liked how it felt. But she was already thinking about something else again. She looked around the room as if she was looking for it and being worried about it. "Are Wanda and Sergey all right?" I asked, because it made me remember I was worried. I was so glad about the noise being so much better that I had forgotten for a second.

"Yes, they are downstairs," Panova Mandelstam said. She sounded funny and far away because of the wax in my ears but I could still understand her.

So then I was glad again and not worried, but she was still worried, so I asked her, "What are you looking for?"

She stood there looking around the room and then she looked at me. "Do you know, I have forgotten. Isn't that silly?" She smiled, but she didn't mean the smile. It was not a real smile. "Do you want to come down and have some macaroons?"

I didn't know what a macaroon was but I thought, if anyone would go down to the noise to eat them then they must be good, and I was sorry I couldn't help her find what she had forgotten. "All right," I said. "I'll try."

She put out her hand to me and I took it and we went downstairs together. The noise got bigger but not as much bigger as I was afraid it would. The closer we got the more it stopped being just thumping in my teeth. Now I could hear music and people singing words even though the wax stopped me hearing what the words were. They sounded happy. Panova Mandelstam brought me into a big room: big and crowded with many men. I was afraid again, because some of them were red-faced and loud and smelled of drink, but they were not angry. They were smiling and shouting laughter and dancing all together, holding hands and making a circle although it was not really a circle because the room was not big enough so they were mostly crammed in and stepping on each other, but they didn't seem to mind. I thought of being upstairs and holding hands with Wanda and Sergey: that was how it felt. Sergey was with them, and in the middle of that circle there was a young man dancing and everyone else was taking turns going into the middle and dancing with him.

We went into the next room, and it was full of women dancing, with a woman in the middle in a dress that was red and had patterns on it in shiny silver, and she had on a veil hanging all the way almost to the floor and she was laughing and very pretty. Panova Mandelstam took me to a table next to the wall with empty chairs and there was a plate on it full of cookies that were light and sweet and like a cloud someone had baked, and she put it in front of me and gave me some other food, too, so much food: thick slices of soft meat I had never eaten before that she said was beef, and roast chicken and fish and potatoes and carrots and dumplings and little green vegetables, and a big torn hunk of yellow soft sweet bread. I sat there and I ate and ate and everyone was happy and I was happy, too, except Panova Mandelstam was sitting next to me and she was not happy. She kept looking around the room for whatever she was trying to find, and it was not there. People kept coming and talking to her, and when they talked to her, she would be distracted for a little while, and forget she was looking for something, but when they went away she would remember and start looking again.

"Where is Wanda?" I asked her.

"Wanda is in the kitchen, sweetheart, she has been helping carry the food," Panova Mandelstam said, and I saw her then when she pointed, so it was not Wanda she was looking for. She was looking at the bride, dancing in the middle again, and she was trying to smile, but she kept stopping.

Everyone started clapping all together, and the men were coming into the room with the groom in front. Everyone started to get up from their chairs and push all the chairs and tables out to the very edges of the room, and the women in their circle were making room so the men could be there in their circle also. One of the men took a chair no one was sitting in and put it in the middle of their circle, and the groom sat down on it, and one of the women was putting down a chair for the bride in the middle of their circle, too. I was waiting to see what they would do, but they didn't do anything. They stopped, suddenly, because someone knocked on the door.

It was so noisy in the room. Everyone had been singing and laughing and talking so loud it was almost shouting, because otherwise they couldn't hear each other, and there was music playing. But the knock was louder than all of it. It was so loud and hard that it came in through the wax in my ears and the two lumps of it fell out to the floor. But the noise of the room didn't bother me anymore without the wax because after that knock, there was no noise left. Nobody was talking and the music had stopped.

There were two big doors in the side of the room, which went out into the courtyard, and that was where the knock had come from. After a moment another knock came. It felt the way the music had felt upstairs coming through the house. It thumped like that. It thumped in my bones and it made me afraid.

Then Panova Mandelstam stood up and ran across the room suddenly, pushing through everyone else, and Panov Mandelstam was pushing from out of the men, and they took hold of the doors and pulled them open. Nobody stopped them. I wanted to say *No, no, no*, but I couldn't say anything. I wanted to hide my head, but I thought I would imagine something worse than whatever it was.

But I wouldn't have. It was the Staryk.

Sergey and Wanda were next to me. They had come to me when they heard the knocking and now they were standing with me, and Sergey had a hand on the back of my chair. He was so tall he could see over everyone's heads, and I heard him draw a breath and I thought he was afraid. I was afraid too. Everyone was scared. It was the Staryk. There were two of them with crowns on their heads, a king and queen. They were holding hands, too. The king was as tall as Sergey. The queen wasn't, but her crown was so tall it almost made up for it. It was all gold and she was in a dress of white and gold. They stood there in the doorway and nobody moved.

Then a man stepped forward out of the crowd. He was old and he had a white beard and white hair. He stopped in front of the Staryk and said, "I am Aron Moshel. This is my house. What do you want here?"

The Staryk had drawn back when the old man said his name, and was looking down at him. I was afraid that the Staryk was going to do something bad to him. I thought he might put his hand on him and touch him and the old man would fall down and be lying on the floor the way Sergey had been lying in the woods, like there was nobody left inside him. But instead the Staryk answered him, "We are come by invitation and by true promise given, to dance at the wedding of my lady's cousin."

His voice sounded like a tree creaking when it is covered with ice. Then he turned his head towards the queen, and then Panova Mandelstam made a noise, and the queen turned her head and looked at her, and I realized, she was not a Staryk after all. She was just a girl in a crown, and she was crying, and so was Panova Mandelstam, and then I thought, that is her daughter, and I finally remembered after all: Panova Mandelstam had a daughter. She had a daughter and her name was Miryem.

Everyone was still quiet, and then that old man Panov Moshel said, "Then come in and be welcome and rejoice with us," and I thought *No no no* again, but it was not my house, it was his house, and the Staryk came inside with Miryem. There were two empty chairs facing onto the dancing there, and they sat down in the chairs. Even after that nobody was talking or moving. But Panov Moshel turned back to the musicians and said, "This is a wedding! Play! Play the hora!" very hard and fierce. Then the musicians started to play a little, and he began to clap with them, turning to face the rest of the room and showing us all his clapping, and then little by little everyone else started to clap, too, and stamp, like they were trying to make a noise big enough to stand up to that knocking on the door.

I didn't think anything could do that. We were only people. But the musicians started to play louder and everyone started to sing, and the song got bigger and bigger, and everyone around us was getting up to join the people already standing. They took hands and they all started to dance again, everybody: children who were not as big as me got up and went to dance and so did very old people: they stayed on the outside mostly clapping, but everybody else was making big circles again dancing fast, one circle of men and one circle of women. The bride and the groom were inside the circles, like everyone was keeping them safe.

The people in the circles all went into the middle, everyone putting up their hands at the same time, and then they came back out again. Everyone was dancing except for me and Wanda and Sergey: we were outside watching and afraid, and on the other side of the circle, the Staryk king and Miryem were just sitting there in the chairs watching also. He was still holding her hand in his. The circle was going by us full of strange people I didn't know, but then I saw Panova Mandelstam coming towards us, and she let go of the woman next to her to reach out, and Wanda reached back to her.

Panov Mandelstam was coming towards us in the other circle. But I didn't want to go into a circle. I wanted to crawl under the table and keep out. But Panova Mandelstam was asking us; she wanted us to come in and help make those circles, and I was scared and I didn't want to but Wanda got up and went in, and I couldn't let her go alone, so when Panov Mandelstam held out his hand I took it, and I gave Sergey my hand, and we went into the dancing, too.

Then everyone in the whole house was dancing, except for the Staryk and Miryem. But the circle kept going, and then Panova Mandelstam reached out one hand to Miryem. I didn't want her to, I didn't want to be dancing with the Staryk and his queen even if she was Panova Mandelstam's daughter. But she held out her hand and Miryem took it, and then she got up and was being pulled into the circle, and the Staryk king didn't let go of her hand. He got up, too, and came dancing along with her.

Something strange happened when he started dancing. We were in two circles, but somehow after he joined the dancing there was only one circle, with all of us in it, and I was holding Wanda's hand, even though I had never let go of Panov Mandelstam. And as we kept going, all the old people on the outside of the circle started to come into it, and they were dancing even though they were old, and the children were dancing even if they were not tall enough to reach up to our hands from the ground.

And there was room for everyone, even though we had already been crowded in. We were not inside anymore. There was no ceiling over our heads. We were outside, in a snowy clearing with white trees all around us, white trees that were just like Mama's tree, and a big grey circle of sky over our heads that didn't know if it was day or night. I was too busy dancing to be scared or cold. I didn't know how to dance or how to sing the song but that didn't matter because everyone else in the circle was helping me, and pulling me along, and what mattered was that we had decided to be there.

The bride and groom were still in the middle of the circle on their chairs. They were holding tight to each other's hands. We danced in towards them, and then we danced out again, and then some men came out of the circle, but not to stop dancing. They came into the middle, and they bent down and took hold of the chairs and picked them up off the ground with the bride and groom still on them, and they started to carry them around to-

gether, moving them up and down, still singing that song. It was
so big and loud that it did get bigger than the Staryk knocking. It
was so big I felt it all through me on and on, but it didn't scare me
the way the noise had scared me before. I didn't mind feeling it
inside me now. It felt like my heart was beating with it at the same
time, and I couldn't breathe but I was happy. Everything was
dancing. The trees were dancing, too, their branches swaying,
and their leaves made a noise like singing.

We kept dancing, and we were going fast, but I wasn't getting
tired. The men did get tired carrying the chairs, but other men
ran in to help instead of them, and they kept carrying the bride
and groom around. Even Sergey went in to help once, I saw him
go, and then he came back after. We all kept going, and none of
us wanted to stop. We kept dancing under that grey sky, and dancing, and I thought maybe we would just be dancing forever, but
the sky began to get dark.

It didn't get darker like the sun was setting. It got darker like
clouds clearing on a winter night, and first a little bit of them blew
away and left a little glimpse of clear sky, and then a little more of
them, and more after that, until overhead it was all just the big
clear night sky, and in it all the stars were shining all above our
heads, but it was not the right stars for spring; it was the winter
stars, very bright and glittering in that clear sky, and all the snow
beneath us and the white flowers on the trees glittered back to
them. We all stopped dancing and stood there looking up at them
together, and then we weren't outside anymore, we were back inside the house, and everyone was laughing and clapping, because
we had made a song. Despite the Staryk, despite winter, we had
made a song.

But then there was a big loud clanging noise like a church bell,
only close by, just through the door, and we all stopped laughing.
It was a bell that had started to ring midnight. The day was over
and so was the song. The music had stopped. The wedding was

finished, and the Staryk was still there. We had made the song despite him, but it hadn't made him go away. He was standing in the middle of the room, and he was still holding Miryem's hand.

He turned and said to her, "Come, my lady, the dancing is done." When he spoke, everyone all moved away from him, as far as they could get in that room. Me and Sergey wanted to move away, too, but when we tried, we stopped, because Wanda pulled back on our hands and didn't move away.

Panova Mandelstam still had Miryem's other hand, and she was holding it tight, and she was not moving away. She stayed there with Miryem and wouldn't let go, and Panov Mandelstam was holding her, and Miryem did not want to let go of them either. The Staryk looked at them and he was frowning with his whole face and his eyebrows were like sharp icicles glittering. He said, "Let go, mortals, let go. A night's dancing alone did she buy of me. You shall not keep her. She is my lady now, and belongs no more to the sunlit world."

But Panov Mandelstam didn't let go and Panova Mandelstam didn't. She was staring at the Staryk, and her face was white and sick, and she didn't say anything; but she shook her head a little. He raised his hand, and Miryem cried out, "No!" and tried to pull her own hand free from Panova Mandelstam's, but Panova Mandelstam still wouldn't let go, and then the doors in the side of the room flew open again, so hard that everyone near them had to jump or run out of the way. They banged into the walls with a crash.

There was another king and queen standing in the doorway. Only the queen was wearing a crown, but I knew he was a king, because it was the tsar and tsarina that we had seen that same day in the sleigh, going in the gate before us after we had waited and waited. And the tsar looked into the room at the Staryk and he laughed out loud, a laugh like a fire makes, and the Staryk went very still.

"Irina, Irina," the tsar said, "you have kept your promise and he is here! Give me the chain!"

The tsarina opened the box and took out a silver chain and gave it to him, and he came into the room grinning his teeth bare. None of us got in his way. We were all pressed up against the walls, as far away as we could be.

But the Staryk said suddenly, fiercely, "Do you think to catch me so easily, devourer? I have never seen your face before, but I know your name, *Chernobog.*" He jumped forward and took hold of the chain in the middle with both his hands. Ice went suddenly shooting along its length, long sharp points of icicles growing out of it like a whole blizzard happening at once, and the ice went all the way to the tsar's hands and climbed over them. He howled and let go of the chain. The Staryk threw it to the floor behind him with a crash, and then he struck the tsar with the back of his hand.

Da would hit me sometimes like that, or Wanda or even Sergey, and Da was very big and strong, but even when he hit just me, I only just fell down on the floor. But when the Staryk hit the tsar, it was like he was hitting a straw doll. The tsar's feet came off the ground and even after he landed hard on the floor his whole body went sliding all the way across the floor until he smashed into the stage and some of the instruments went over with a big awful twanging sound around him.

I thought he must be dead, when he was hit like that. When Da took the poker to hit Wanda, I thought he was going to kill her if he hit her with it, but he could not hit her hard enough even with the poker to make her whole body go across the room. But the tsar was not dead. He didn't even just lie there on the ground being glad not to be dead and trying to hide from being hit again. Instead he got back on his feet. He didn't just stand up, he came up in a strange twisting way, and there was blood coming from his mouth and red all over his teeth, and he hissed at the Staryk, and when he hissed, the blood started to smoke and burn out of his mouth, and his eyes were red.

"Get out!" the tsarina called suddenly. "Everyone, all of you, run, get out of the house!"

It was like she had let everybody loose. Everyone started to go out of the room. Some people ran past her and out the open doors into the courtyard and some people ran back through the door to the other room where the men had been dancing and some people ran out through the kitchen door. The bride and groom ran that way hand in hand. The children were being picked up and the old people were being helped. Everyone was going.

I thought we should go, too, but Wanda wouldn't. Miryem was trying to make Panova Mandelstam go with everyone else, but she was not going either. She was holding on to Miryem's hand with both her hands and she was not letting go.

"Father, please! Mama, he'll kill you!" Miryem said.

"Better we should die!" Panova Mandelstam cried to her.

"*You* go, *you* run," Panov Mandelstam was saying. He was trying to put his arm around her.

And Miryem shook her head and turned and cried out, "Wanda! Wanda, please, help me!"

So Sergey and I couldn't go, because Wanda ran to her. Miryem pushed her mother towards Wanda and said, "Please, get her away!"

"No!" Panova Mandelstam said, still holding tight.

I could tell that Wanda did not know what to do. She wanted to do what Miryem wanted and she wanted to do what Panova Mandelstam wanted. She wanted to do both things so much that she couldn't leave that room, and then I couldn't leave either, because I couldn't leave Wanda and Sergey in there.

All the time they were arguing, the tsar and the Staryk were fighting. But the tsar was not fighting like a tsar. I thought a tsar would fight with a sword. Sergey told me stories sometimes about knights that killed monsters that Mama had told him. Once a knight rode down our road. I was with the goats and I saw him coming from a long way off. I didn't see him use his sword but I walked along the road as far as I could to keep seeing him. I could do it for a long time because he didn't go very fast. He had a sword and he had armor and two boys that walked with him leading a spare horse and a mule with baggage. After I saw him and I knew what a knight was, sometimes I fought with a sword in the field when I was with the goats, except it was just a stick, except I pretended it was a sword.

I thought a tsar would be like a knight only his armor would be more splendid and his sword would be bigger, but the tsar did not have armor at all. He was wearing a coat of red velvet and it had been splendid but it was torn and wet and burned now. And he did not have a sword. He was fighting with his hands, trying to catch the Staryk, but he kept missing. I didn't know how he was missing because the Staryk was right there, but he would grab and then the Staryk wouldn't be where he had grabbed anymore. And if he grabbed a chair or a table that was in the way or put his hand on the floor, there was a smell of smoke, and when he took his hand away there was a burned mark in the shape of his hand left behind. There was something in his face that I couldn't look at for too long or else it made me feel as if he was putting that burning hand on me, inside my head.

I thought, he was not really a tsar. He was Chernobog, that name the Staryk had said, and that was a name of something that was like the Staryk, just another monster. And I didn't want the Staryk to win, but also I didn't want Chernobog to win. I hoped maybe they would go on fighting forever, or at least long enough so we could all just get away. But I could see the Staryk was going to win. Chernobog was a monster, but he was still inside a person. Each time he missed, the Staryk hit him back, like taking turns, and the tsar was starting to be all bloody. His face was getting strange and swelled up, and it made me think of when the kasha came on Da's face. I didn't want to look at his face but I couldn't stop. I was afraid if I hid my face the Staryk would win when I wasn't looking. Then the Staryk would come and kill Panova Mandelstam and Panov Mandelstam. I didn't think I could stop him from doing it by looking, and I didn't want to watch if it happened, but I didn't want to look back and see that it had happened, either.

The tsarina had run around the fighting to Miryem. "The silver chain!" she said. "We need a silver chain to bind him!"

So then Panov Mandelstam turned and got the silver chain from the floor. It was broken into two pieces and those pieces looked too short to go all around the Staryk. But the tsarina put her hands up around her neck and took off her necklace. It was made of silver and it was shining and beautiful like snowflakes going past a window. She put one end of it through the first half of the chain and then she put the other end of it through the second half of the chain, and then she clasped the necklace, and it was one long chain again, from start to finish. Then Panov Mandelstam took that chain from her.

The tsar went at the Staryk hissing again, even though his face was all red now with blood, and not just his face. Some of his fingers were the wrong way around, and his legs were sagging like a twig that was broken part of the way, but he still flung his arms forward. The Staryk darted out of his way like if you try and catch a fly and you think you have it, but you open your hand and it's not there, and then it buzzes next to your ear again. But he was not a fly. He was standing by the fireplace. When they had started fighting they were all the way in the middle of that big room, but now they had moved all the way across it. The whole time they were fighting the Staryk had been making the tsar chase him closer and closer to the fireplace. He did all that on purpose and now they were there, and when the tsar missed him this time, the Staryk grabbed *him*.

A big hissing cloud of steam came off the Staryk's hands, and he looked like it hurt him, but he still grabbed the tsar, and then he threw him down into the fireplace, and said, "Stay where you belong, Chernobog! By your name I command you!"

A horrible roaring crackling sound came out of the tsar's mouth and where his mouth was open and his eyes were open there was fire inside them, but he went all limp everywhere else. The crackling sound made a voice and said, *"Get up! Get up!"* like he was talking to himself, but he didn't listen to himself. He didn't get up. He just lay there in the fireplace and didn't move.

The Staryk was standing over him holding his hands together and watching to see if he would get out of the fireplace. And then Panov Mandelstam ran at him and tried to throw the chain around him.

I didn't see it because I stopped looking right when he started running. I thought the Staryk was going to kill him and I didn't want to see after all. So I put my head down and wrapped my arms around it and then Panova Mandelstam cried out, "Josef!" and Miryem said, "No!" and I couldn't keep from looking. Panov Mandelstam was lying on the floor and he was not moving. I thought he was dead, but then he moved, so he wasn't dead, but the chain was not around the Staryk, either. It was on the floor far away from him. Panova Mandelstam had run to Panov Mandelstam and was kneeling next to him. Miryem had run to stand in front of the Staryk, and suddenly she took the crown off her head and threw it onto the ground with a big crash of metal, and she said very loud, "I'll never go back with you if you hurt them! I'll die first! I swear it!"

The Staryk had his hand up as if he was going to do something to Panov Mandelstam, but he stopped when she said that. He did not want to stop; he was angry. "You trouble me like summer rain!" he shouted at Miryem. "He came at me with a chain to bind me! Am I to make no answer?"

"You came first!" she shouted back. "You came first and took me!"

The Staryk was still angry, but after a moment he made a grumbling noise and he dropped his hand. "Oh, very well!" He said it as if he still did not like it very much, but maybe he would not bother to kill Panov Mandelstam, and then he put out his hand to Miryem. "Now come! The hour is late, and the time is done, and never again will I bring you hence, to be insulted by weak hands who dare think they can keep you from me!"

He waved his other hand at the doors. They opened again, and outside it was not the courtyard. It was that forest where we were dancing, but now there were no stars. There was only that grey sky and the sleigh with the monsters pulling it, waiting for them.

Miryem did not want to go with him. I would not want to go with him either, so I was sorry for her, but I still wanted her to go. I wanted her to take his hand because then he would take only her and go and not come back. Then Chernobog would be stuck in the fireplace and the Staryk would be gone and we would all be safe. Panov Mandelstam and Panova Mandelstam would not die. I wished and wished she would go.

She looked around at her parents so that I saw her face, and I felt a big swelling relief in me because I could see she was going to go. I felt sorry because she was crying, and it made my stomach go sick and knotted inside to think about what if it was me and Panova Mandelstam was my mother and I had to go away from her with the Staryk, but I was still glad. I was also afraid because what if she changed her mind, but she didn't. She was only looking around for one last time to see them, and then she turned back to the Staryk, even though she was crying, and she took a step towards him.

"No!" Panova Mandelstam cried, but she was not holding Miryem's hand anymore, she was kneeling on the floor with Panov Mandelstam's head in her lap too far away. She reached out her hand anyway and called, "Miryem, Miryem!"

The Staryk made an angry noise. "And still you dare!" he hissed at Panova Mandelstam. "Think you to bind her? Victory has come to my hands this night, and the devourer is cast down! Now for a lifetime of men I will close the white road and keep my kingdom fast, until all who know my lady's name have died, and I will leave you not even scraps of memory to try and catch her with!"

Then he reached out to grab Miryem's hand, and pulled her away towards the door, and I was so glad that he was going that I didn't even notice what Wanda was doing in time to be afraid or to look away, and so I was looking when she threw the chain around him.

I saw what he had done to get away from it last time because he almost did it again. He twisted to get out from under the chain, but this time when he did it, Miryem threw herself to the floor, and because he had her hand, she pulled him off his feet a little, and Wanda brought her arms down fast and kept the chain around him. So when he stood up again, he was still inside the chain. His face was so angry a white light came into it. He did not let go of Miryem's hand, but he reached out with his other hand and grabbed the ends of the chain and pulled them.

He almost dragged Wanda off her feet, but Sergey ran to her across the room and grabbed the chain too. He grabbed one end of the chain and Wanda grabbed one end of the chain and then they were both holding tight with their feet hard like trying to pull a stump out of the ground, except the stump was pulling back at them, and it was about to pull them down instead of them pulling it up. And I was scared, I was so scared, but I thought, it was the same as the dancing, and I climbed out from under the table and

I ran across the room and I grabbed hold of the knot of Wanda's apron and the back of Sergey's old rope belt and I made the circle with them.

When I did that, the Staryk made a shriek that was like the sound when the ice on the river broke at the end of winter. It was a terrible noise and it made my ears hurt, but I kept holding on and he stopped making it. He stood there and stamped his foot and said to Wanda angrily, "Very well, you have bound me! What will you have to let me go?"

We stood there and then Wanda said, "Leave Miryem and go!" Miryem was still on the floor trying to pull free from him, but he was still holding her hand.

The Staryk glared back at her, glittering. "No! You have caught me with silver, but your arms have not the strength to hold me. I will not surrender my lady!"

Then he threw himself against the chains again, and tried to break our hands loose. But it was not just us holding anymore: Panov Mandelstam had climbed up from the ground and he had come and grabbed the chain with Wanda, and Panova Mandelstam was pulling on Sergey's side, and she and Panov Mandelstam were holding hands behind my back to help me be strong. We were all pulling tight, and he nearly dragged loose anyway, but he didn't, and then he stopped and was angry again, and he said to Wanda, "What will you have to loose your bond? Ask for something else, or fear what I shall do when you tire!"

But Wanda shook her head and said, "Let Miryem go!" and he shrieked that awful ice-breaking noise again and hissed, "Never! I will not leave you, my queen, my golden lady; once I was a fool, twice I will not be!" and he fought again, so hard he pulled us across the floor, all of us with our feet sliding and almost falling. I thought, I thought, we could not hold him for much longer. I could see that Wanda's hands and Sergey's hands were slipping on the chain. They had put their fingers into the links, but their hands were getting sweaty and the chain had slid through one link at a time and they could not risk letting go of it long enough to grab it higher again, or else he would pull free at once.

But this one more time we held on to him, and he stopped. He breathed hard, three times. Big clouds of frost streamed away from his lips when he panted. Then he stood up very tall, and ice started to grow on him. It crept out from his edges in a thin layer that you could see through and then a little more crept over it and then there was another thin edge poking out but the first one was thicker, and that kept happening over and over and the ice was getting sharp and prickly and I could feel the terrible cold of it on my face. Sergey and Wanda were both leaning away from it, and it was climbing down the chain towards their fingers.

The Staryk did not shriek at Wanda again. When he spoke this time, he sounded soft instead, like when deep snow has stopped falling and you go outside and everything is very quiet. "Let go, mortal, let go, and ask a different boon of me," he said. "I will give you a treasure of jewels or elixir of long life; I will even give you back the spring, in fair return for holding fast. But you reach too far, and dare too high, when you ask me for my queen. Try me thus once again, and know I will lay winter in your flesh and flay your hearts open to freeze in red blood upon that snow: you have no high powers, no gift of magic true, and love alone cannot give you strength to hold me."

When he said that, I knew he was not lying. We all knew it. And Miryem got up on her feet again. She had stopped pulling on his hand where it was around her wrist. She said, "Wanda," and she meant that we should let the Staryk go.

But Wanda looked at Miryem and she said, "No," and it was the no she had said to our father, in our house, when he wanted to eat her up.

I didn't mean to say no to him that day. I had never said no to him before, because I knew if we did he would hurt us, and he hurt us anyway already, and so I knew he would hurt us even worse if we said no. I would not have even thought of saying no to him no matter what he did, because he could always do something worse. And when Wanda said no to him, I said no too, but I didn't really decide to say no, I just said it. But now, I thought, I had said it because there wasn't anything worse he could do to me than hit Wanda with that poker over and over and make her dead while I was there just watching. If he was going to do that then I could be dead too, and that would not be as bad as just standing there.

Now Wanda was saying no because there wasn't anything worse that the Staryk could do to her but take Miryem away. And I wasn't sure if I thought so myself, but then I thought, I could not let go without making Panova Mandelstam and Panov Mandelstam let go too, because their arms were around me. And being dead would not be as bad as having to look at Panova Mandelstam after I did that to her.

But the Staryk was not lying either. It was not like with Da where there was Sergey to come in and be stronger than him and push him into the fire. Sergey was already helping as much as he could, and none of us were as big and strong as the Staryk. So we were going to all be dead. There was nothing we could do about it except let go. And we were not going to let go.

And then a hoarse awful wet voice said, *"A chain of silver to bind him tight, a ring of fire to quench his might,"* and all around us twelve great candles lit in flame. I looked around and the tsar was standing again: the tsarina had put those candles in a big circle all around us, while we were trying to hold the Staryk, and then she had gone to the tsar and helped him stand up in the fireplace. She was holding him up, and he had said those words out of his broken mouth even though they came out in popping red bubbles of blood. He was pointing his hand out: it was shaking and the fingers were bent in terrible ways, but with one finger he was pointing, and all the candles burst into tall hot flames almost as long as the candles were tall.

Inside the chain, the Staryk gave a choking gasp, and the armor of ice around him broke off in great chunks and fell to the ground with small tinkling sounds. He went white all the way through. And then the tsar laughed aloud, except it was not the tsar laughing, it was Chernobog, it was the monster. It was a terrible sound like fire crackling up, and then he took a dragging step out of the fireplace, and when he did, a few of those fingers that were bent all wrong straightened out. When he took another step, his shoulder that was turned in a bad way jerked itself right, and then his nose that was broken fixed itself too, and little by little as he came closer all of him went right again, until his face was perfect and even his torn red coat was smooth and not even wet anymore. But he wasn't right at all, there was nothing right about anything in him, and he was coming towards us.

He reached up and spun his hand in the air, and the chain pulled itself out of Wanda and Sergey's hands and wrapped tight around the Staryk, pulling his arms against his sides. Miryem pulled her hand out of his grip and jumped back from him, and then we all scrambled back, as fast as we could, to get away from Chernobog. But he wasn't paying any attention to us. He was going to stand in front of the Staryk and smiling at him. The last link of the chain on the left side opened up like a jaw and closed itself around a link far along on the other, and the last link of the chain on the right side bound itself to a link on that side, and it was tight and tight around him.

"I have you, I have you," Chernobog crooned. He reached up and touched the Staryk's face with one finger and drew it down his cheek and over his throat, and steam rose off into the air and the Staryk had his jaw tight and it was hurting him. Chernobog half closed his eyes and gave a little crackling noise that was happy, only it was happy about something horrible. I wanted the wax back in my ears but I didn't know where it was. I was holding tight to Wanda's hand, and Sergey was standing in front of us, and Miryem and her mother and father were all holding each other tight.

"Tell me," Chernobog said to the Staryk. "Tell me your name." And he reached up and touched him again.

The Staryk shuddered all over, but he whispered, "Never."

Chernobog made a crackling of anger and laid his whole hand flat down against the Staryk's chest. A horrible white cloud burst out around his hand and went writhing around them, and the Staryk cried out aloud. "Your name, your name!" Chernobog hissed. "You are bound, I have you; I will have you whole! Tell me your name! By the binding I command you!"

The Staryk had shut his terrible eyes and was shaking in the silver chain, and his face was drawn up and looked very sharp on all the edges like it was pulled tight. He was breathing like he could not do anything but breathe, and that was all he could think about, but when he stopped having just to breathe, he opened his eyes again and said in a thin faint voice, "*You* have not bound me, Chernobog; you hold my chains, but I owe you no surrender. Neither by your hand nor by your cunning am I bound. You have not paid for this victory, false one, cheat, and I will *give* you nothing."

Chernobog made a vast snarling hiss and whirled on us—on the tsarina. "Irina, Irina, what will you have? Name a gift, it shall be yours, name even two or three! Only take a payment from my hands and *give him true to me.*"

But the tsarina shook her head. "No," she said. "I brought him to you, as I promised, and that is all I promised. I will not take anything from you. I have done this for Lithvas and not for greed. Is he not bound? Can you not break his winter?"

Chernobog was very angry, and he went prowling in a big circle around the Staryk muttering and crackling and hissing to himself, but he didn't say no. "I will feast upon you every day," he muttered as he coiled around the Staryk, and he put up his hand and dragged his fingers across the Staryk's face, leaving more deep steaming lines. "Sweet and cold will each draught be. Each one will burn you to the quick. How long will you say no to me?"

"Forever," the Staryk whispered. "Though you feast upon me to the end of days, I will never unlock my kingdom's gates, and you will have nothing of me you do not steal."

"I will steal everything!" Chernobog said. "I have you chained, I have you held fast. I will steal all the fruit of your white trees and devour them whole; I will drink your servants and your crown, I will bring all your mountain down!"

"And even then," the Staryk said. "Even then will I refuse you. My people will go into the flame with their names locked fast in their hearts; you will not have that of them, nor me."

Chernobog roared in fury and seized him with both his hands on either side of the Staryk's face, and the Staryk shrieked like before only worse, like the sound Da made when the kasha came on his head, and I put my face in Wanda's skirt and covered my ears but I couldn't keep the sound out, even though she put her hands over my ears also and pressed with me. When it stopped I was shaking. The Staryk was on his knees on the ground with the chain still wrapped around him, and Chernobog was standing over him and his hands were dripping wet, and he put one to his mouth and licked it with his tongue, and where his tongue went over it, his hand was dry after. "Oh, how sweet the taste, how the cold lingers!" he said. "Winter king, king of ice, I will suck you until you are so small I can crunch you with my teeth, and what will your name be worth then? Will you not give it to me now and go into the flame while you are still great?"

The Staryk trembled all over, and then he said, very faintly, only, "No," and it was the same as our *no* had been, it was a no that said no matter what Chernobog did to him, it was not as bad as if the Staryk gave him his name.

Chernobog made a disappointed crackling noise. "Then I will keep you bound in silver and bound in flame, until you change your mind and give me your name! Call them!" he shrieked. "Call them and take him and hide him away!" and suddenly he lurched over and nearly fell, staggering so he knocked chairs over and grabbed at them until he had one that didn't fall over, and held him up even though he was shaking, and his head was hanging down. The tsarina suddenly went across the room to him, and he looked at her, and it was the way a person looks at someone, it was not Chernobog there anymore. He said after a moment, almost a whisper, "The guards," and his voice was very beautiful, like music even though he was only talking very softly.

He turned and pointed his hand at the doors, the way he had pointed it at the candles, except now his hand was straight and perfect, and they opened. The sleigh was not out there anymore. It was just the empty courtyard. "Guards!" the tsar called loud, and men came running into the courtyard. They were men who did have swords and armor, but when they saw the Staryk they stopped, afraid, and stared. They made signs in front of themselves.

The tsar started to point his hand at them, the same way he had pointed it at the door and at the candles, but suddenly the tsarina reached out and put her hand on his arm and pushed it down. She said to those men, "Have courage!" They all looked up at her. "This is the lord of the Staryk, who brought this evil cursed winter to our land, and with the blessing of God he has been captured. We must lock him away to bring spring back to Lithvas. Are you all God-fearing men? Bless yourselves, and each of you take a candle in your hands, and keep them around him! And we must find a rope to tie to the chain that binds him, and draw him along."

Those guards all looked very afraid, but one of them who was very tall, as tall as Sergey, and had a big mustache, said to the tsarina, "Your Majesty, I will dare it, for your sake," and he went and brought a rope out of the courtyard and he went straight up to the Staryk and tied the rope to the chain very fast, and then he stepped back, wincing, and I saw his hands were hurt at the tips of the fingers, all white and blanched as if they were frostbitten. But he had the rope, and some other men came and helped him now and pulled on it. The Staryk stood up on his feet so that they would not just drag him along the floor. The other guards had come and taken the candles and were all around him.

But when they tried to pull him, he did not just go with them. Instead he turned around and looked at Miryem. She was standing with her parents and staring at him. They had their arms around her, and her face was all sick and worried as if she was still afraid, even though the Staryk was bound up. But he did not try to get to her. He only said, as if he was very surprised, "My lady, I did not think you could answer it, when I took you from your home without your leave, and set value only on your gift. But I am answered truly. You have given fair return for insult thrice over and set your worth: higher than my life and all my kingdom and all who live therein, and though you send my people to the fire, I can claim no debt to repay. It is justly done."

He bowed to her, very deeply, and then turned and he went with the guards where they were pulling him, and Miryem put her hands on her forehead and made a sound like she wanted to cry and said, "What can I do? What am I going to do?"

Chapter 20

It wasn't really much of a surprise to discover that my beloved tsarina's father had a secret dungeon hidden outside the city walls, buried under a mat of grass and straw. It was the same sort of careful, well-thought-out advance preparation I was beginning to expect from my darling queen; he'd certainly trained her well.

There was a door in the wall around the Jewish quarter, a narrow door at the end of an alleyway tucked between two houses, not far from the one where the wedding had been. Irina led us all to it, the Staryk a silent figure that might have been carved of salt among the guards with their candles, while I brought up the rear of the procession. We must have made quite a picture of hellish sorcery underway. In my belly the demon—Chernobog, and how delightful to finally have a name for my passenger; we were finally growing familiar after all these years—still writhed around itself and purred with joy. It was just as well that the hour was late, and no one left in the streets but drunkards and beggars.

At the wall, Irina pushed aside a curtain of ivy and opened the door with a key from her purse, and at her direction half the guardsmen carefully stepped out one after another, keeping the ring of candles around our silent prisoner, before the tall, handsome, excessively brave one at the head tugged on the rope and pulled him through. The Staryk went unresisting, even though he couldn't possibly have been pulled by force. I still felt phantom echoes all over my body from everywhere that the Staryk's hands had struck me, every blow like being hammered on an anvil, as if I'd been well-heated metal to be beaten flat.

But the demon had kept hurling me at him, grabbing my shattered hands furiously on open air even while my ribs pierced into my lungs, my hips cracked apart so that my legs dangled, my jaw hung loose with teeth falling out of it like loose pebbles. I could have been crushed into wine-pulp and still I think Chernobog would have been oozing me over the floor to glaze his boots with my blood. When the Staryk finally pushed us into the fireplace and told the demon to stay there, I would have wept with gratitude, with relief, if only he'd done me the kindness of one final parting kick to crush my skull and end the agony.

But he left me there. And then my sweet Irina came and put her arms around me like some grotesque parody of comfort. If she'd wanted to comfort me, she could have slit my throat. But she had a use for me, she too had a use for me, I'm so *endlessly* useful; she knelt and said to me urgently, "The ring of fire. Can you light the candles?" At first I think I only wept at her a little, or maybe laughed, as much as I could make any sound at all come out of my mouth. The experience was rather cloudy in my memory. But then she took me by the shoulders and said fiercely, "You'll be trapped here forever if we don't stop him!" and I woke to the gruesome horrified certainty that she was right.

Oh, I thought I already knew a fate worse than death; how absurdly, ridiculously naïve I'd been. I wasn't broken enough to die, only to lie there in the cinders and the ash. I imagined the household fled, everyone in the neighboring houses fled, from the horror of the twisted wreck of me in the fireplace. They'd board up the windows and the doors, and maybe they'd burn the whole building down and bury me in a mountain of blackened timbers, and I'd be lying underneath it forever with the demon still howling in my ears, devouring me because it couldn't get to anyone else.

So I did get up, and with a feeble croaking spell and a trickle of the magic my demon had given me, a ragged scrap of meat tossed to an adequately obedient dog, I captured the Staryk king for my beloved queen and my beloved master. And now here I was rewarded: I was whole again! I could breathe without a fountain of blood gurgling in my throat! I could stand and walk and see out of both my eyes, and oh, how grateful I was for it, except I understood that I hadn't escaped anything. I'd only deferred it for a while. That fate was waiting for me, sooner or later. Chernobog would never let me go, not even to death. Why would it? It didn't have to. I'd been signed over comprehensively; no fine print or limitations on my term. All I would ever be able to do about it was what I'd ever been able to do about it: nothing. Nothing but to catch at those scraps of life when they came, and devour them, and lick my greasy fingers, and try to make life endurable when I had the chance.

So I let myself breathe in the night air, and I looked at my once-again beautiful well-formed hands, and I followed my queen and my guardsmen through the streets and through the narrow door, because as long as Chernobog had a Staryk to feast upon, I wouldn't need to fear. It felt heavy and replete inside my belly, a well-fed monster, almost somnolent with satisfaction. Long might it sleep so.

Outside the wall, Irina took us out onto the hill, to a place beside a small wizened tree, and told the guards to put down the candles in a circle around the Staryk, and then she said, "You have served Lithvas and God tonight. You will be rewarded for what you have done. Now go back to the city, and before you return to the palace, go straight to the church and give thanks, and speak to no one of what you have seen tonight."

They all fled promptly, the obviously sensible men they were, except for our one brave hero, who set down the rope carefully inside the ring of candles, and asked Irina, "Your Majesty, may I not stay and serve you?"

Irina looked at him and asked, "What is your name?"

"Timur Karimov, Your Majesty," he said. Yes, *very* eager to serve her, that was patently obvious, although he'd want payment for it sooner or later, I imagined. However, as soon as I'd had the thought, it occurred to me—he had a Tatar strain himself: dark-skinned and handsome and broad-shouldered, and judging by that mustache he had dark hair to go with his light eyes. And if Irina didn't insist on my providing stud services, *someone* was going to have to do the work.

"Timur Karimov, you have shown your worth," I said, and startled him into noticing that yes, that was her *husband* standing right there, her husband the tsar of Lithvas who could have his eyes put out and his tongue slit and his head and hands cut off and nailed over the castle gate, and all for the effort of saying a word. I would have taken some small satisfaction in seeing him look a little nervous, but instead he only saw me and then looked— *crumpled*, with miserable envy, as if he didn't actually hope to enjoy any favors after all, he only dreamed longingly of his shining ideal from afar, and had temporarily forgotten that she was out of his reach. Well, perhaps he could be cured of that lack of ambition. "I hereby appoint you captain of the tsarina's personal guard, and may you ever show as much courage in protecting my great-est treasure as you have this night."

Evidently I overdid it; he lunged forward to fall down on one knee at my feet and seized my hand and kissed it. "Your Majesty, I swear it on my life," he said, in throbbing tones, as if he thought he were acting in a play, only it sounded as though he really was on the verge of bursting into tears.

"Yes, very well," I said, drawing my hand away. Irina was looking at me with a little frown, as if she didn't understand my motives; I gave a pointed look down at the charming young gallant's bowed head and then her cheeks darkened in a completely unwarranted maidenly flush as lo, the sudden light dawned! As though she had grounds at all for not understanding in the first place after those lectures to me on dynastic succession. "Well?" I added to her. I felt quite comfortable keeping Timur around; he wasn't going to be telling our secrets to anyone, not to betray her beautiful beloved Majesty.

Irina must have worked that out herself as well, because after a moment she pointed him to a spot in the ground in front of the Staryk's feet and said, "Dig there."

Not much work was required to uncover the stones and the trapdoor; as soon as we had cleared it off, Irina knocked on it, and a moment later it was swung down and open, and I saw my father-in-law's face swimming up out of the dark below. He nodded to Irina, and made room for us to bring the Staryk down. He'd been busy to some purpose himself: he'd pickaxed out a round channel in the floor, among the stones, and he'd filled it up with coals. There was another ring of candles burning down around the channel as a second row of fortifications, and more stacked up in a wheelbarrow waiting against the wall to replenish the supply. Everything so very tidily organized.

Timur pulled the Staryk on his leash into the ring of coals, and then climbed back over and tossed the rope back to pool at his feet. The Staryk ignored it; he stood in the circle looking out at us with his cold gleaming icicle of a face, his head high and proud even with the silver chain still wrapped around him, impossibly strange: that was *winter* we had locked up in the cellar there among us. He didn't entirely seem a living creature. There was something odd in his face that didn't stay the same whenever you looked at him twice, as if his edges were constantly melting and re-formed. He wasn't beautiful, he was terrifying; and then he was beautiful, and then he was both, and I couldn't decide from one moment to the next which it was.

It made something in my head itch; I would have liked to draw him, to catch him with pen and ink, and not just fire and silver. I looked over at Irina there in the dark pit: some of his cold blue light was reflecting on her face, on her silver crown and the red rubies of her silver gown, and it occurred to me that *this* was what they saw when they looked at her: they saw her like a Staryk, but close enough to mortal to be touched.

Inside, Chernobog stirred and gave a small internal belch, nothing I'd ever felt before and gruesomely unpleasant, and lashed me a little; I gritted my teeth and flicked my fingers at the circle of coals, and set it glowing red with flame. Timur flinched back from it. The Staryk didn't *quite* flinch, but I got the impression he would have rather liked to, if that weren't far beyond his dignity. I repressed the urge to tell him to enjoy flinching as much as he wanted to. Chernobog never took much notice of anyone's dignity or lack thereof so far as I'd ever seen. It pleased itself either way.

"Shall we be off?" I said to Irina. "I'm sorry to forsake the manifest charms of this place, but we *do* have another wedding to attend tomorrow, I believe? A busy season for them."

Irina turned away from the Staryk. "Yes," she said somberly. She didn't seem particularly happy with the final outcome of her excellently laid plans, although as far as I could tell they'd gone off without a hitch. Unless of course there had been a corollary to them she hadn't shared with me—for instance, one where I *had* been left tucked safely in the fireplace forever, perhaps chained in gold and ringed with ice; that seemed the poetic mirror. Yes, the more I thought of it, the more I was certain something like that had been on the agenda. Ha, how silly of me—*had been*. That knife in the back was still very much on its way.

"A trusted man?" the duke said to Irina, gesturing at Timur. She nodded. "Good. He will come up with me and help to cover the door again, and keep guard. Walk straight down the tunnel. Take no turns. It crosses a few old sewers along the way."

That rather nicely conveyed the prospective scenic quality of our walk. I smiled at Irina with every last ounce of the sincere affection that was blooming in my heart for her, and put out my arm formally. She looked at me, once more dull and expressionless as glass, and set her hand on the curve of my arm. We left the Staryk standing silently and alone behind us in his bonds of flame and silver, and set off together down a stinking impenetrable-dark rat tunnel full of squeaks and dangling-maggot tree roots. I cupped a fire in my hand while we walked, red light dancing over the earthen walls.

"What a convenient bolt-hole this is," I said. "Shall I keep it in mind if your father ever rebels against the crown? I suppose that's hardly likely anymore—or is it?" She only looked at me. "I suppose you think I'm an idiot," I snapped at her. Her silence was more infuriating than her lectures. I hadn't asked for any of this: I hadn't wanted to marry her, I hadn't wanted to help her survive, I hadn't wanted to be smashed like eggshells for her sake. Chernobog was sitting in my belly like swallowed coals, a thick sated presence, *pleased* with itself—and her, too, no doubt. I couldn't even shove her into one of these dark tunnels and run away, leaving her behind.

"Are you all right?" she asked me abruptly.

I laughed; it was so absurd. "What's a little agony and mortal injury here and there," I jeered at her. "Really, I don't mind. I'm delighted to be of service anytime. Hm, *delighted*—do I mean that, or is there another word for it? I'll have to give it some thought. What exactly do you expect from me? Should I be *grateful* to you?"

She paused. After a moment, she said, "The winter will break. Lithvas will—"

"Shut up about *Lithvas*," I spat at her. "Are we playacting for the worms now, or is this something you do to keep your hand in for public appearances? As though *Lithvas* means anything but the lines where the last round of people finished killing each other. What do I care about Lithvas? The nobles would gladly slit my throat, the peasants don't know who rules them, the dirt doesn't care, and I don't owe a thing to any of them *or* you. I can't stop you dancing me around the chessboard, but I'm not going to thank you humbly for permitting me to be useful to you, my lady, like that groveling monkey up there. Stop trying to pretend you wouldn't have been delighted to leave me there in bloody pieces on the floor. Don't you have the next tsar waiting in the wings? It seems like the sort of thing you'd have ready just in case."

She fell blessedly silent for a while, but not long enough to suit me. We reached the end of the tunnel and came through an archway cut into a wall of stone: it let us into a small dark cramped closet of a room, with a cleverly designed bit of the wall that swung out into the wine cellars. When we came out and I pushed it shut again, you could hardly even have told that the place was there. I ran my fingers over the bricks and could barely find the edges, and that only because the mortar was missing. Chernobog hummed drowsily in satisfaction: it would go tomorrow, it would feast again . . .

I turned and found Irina looking at me in the dark; I'd closed my hand on the flame, and there was only a little bit of lamplight shining off the stairs, reflected in the solid black pools of her eyes, to show her face to me.

"You don't care about any of it," she said. "And yet you bargained to be tsar anyway, in your brother's place—"

It was very much like having a monster crush your ribs straight into your heart. Oh, how I hated her. "I'm afraid *you* wouldn't have liked Karolis very much, darling girl," I said, through my teeth. "Who do you think taught me to kill squirrels? No one else had a minute for the witch's get, until he was—"

I stopped; I still couldn't be clever about it. Not about that. Chernobog even stirred a bit and put out its tongue through my head, lazily lapping up the unexpected delicious treat of my pain. How nice to know I could still give satisfaction, even when it was so well-fed.

She was staring at me. "You loved him. And you bargained anyway?"

"Oh, no," I said, thick with rage. "I've never had the chance to bargain for a thing. You see, my mother wasn't as lucky as you, sweet Irina. She didn't already have a crown, and she didn't have magical beauty, and she didn't have a Staryk king to buy them with. So instead she paid for them with a promissory note, and the ink on my contract was dry before I even came wet out of the womb."

When Irina came back, I was sewing in the corner of her bedroom, as fast as I could. I had gone to Palmira and told her that the tsar would not let Irina wear the same dress twice, and if she had a gown I could make over for Irina to wear tomorrow, I would give her the blue with rubies to make over for Galina. Galina would not know where they came from; Palmira would not. Better not to know. To them they could be jewels, rich and fine, that someone had bought and paid for with gold and not with blood. They would have gone far enough away from the cruelty that made them, and then they could be only beautiful. And I would have work to do during the night, the long night, sitting by a lamp and wondering if Irina would ever come back.

"But it must be splendid," I said. "Otherwise it won't do: you see how *he* dresses! He will not have her less fine." So Palmira gave me a gown of deep emerald-green brocade and palest leaf-green silk, embroidered so thickly in silver that I needed to get a young maid to help carry it back to the room, with tiny beads of emeralds knotted upon it: not as valuable as the rubies, but there were so many of them that the gown glittered in the light. Galina had worn it as a girl, before her first marriage. It was too small for her now, but still it had been kept put by, for a daughter or a son's wife. Not a stepdaughter, before now, but it would fit Irina without too much work. She was only more narrow in the chest. I was almost done bringing in the bodice when she came back to the room, and her face was white and blind above those shining ruby drops of blood.

The tsar went to the fire and snapped to his servants as they scrambled awake to bring him hot wine, and he held out his arms for them to take off his red coat of velvet, as if nothing much had happened. I went and tried to take my girl's thin hands, but she would not let me see them, or open her cloak. But I put my arm around her and I drew her to my own chair and put her in it. She was not cold, she did not tremble. But she was as blank as a field of snow, and there was a thick terrible smell of smoke in her hair, and when she sat I saw there was blood on the blue dress, real blood, dried dark, and on her palms and under her nails, as though she had been butchering meat in that gown. I stroked her head. "I will draw a bath," I whispered to her. "I will wash your hair." She said nothing, so I spoke to the footmen and sent them to bring the bath, and cold water to wash the dress.

The tsar was already in his shift and drinking his wine while they warmed the bed over again fresh for him. By the time the bath was brought up and ready, he had gone into it and the curtains were drawn. I sent all the other servants out and I took the crown off Irina's hair—she flinched and reached a hand for it and only then looked at the bed to see that he slept, and then she let me. Her necklace was gone, and I didn't ask her what had happened to it.

First I washed her hands and arms clean in the basin. It was dark, so the water only looked dirty and cloudy, not red. I took the basin and went shivering out onto the balcony to throw the water out, down onto the stones far down there. The duke's men drilled in that square. They would not notice a little more blood on the stones. I took the blue dress off her and put it to soak in the basin in cold water. The stains were not so old; they would come out.

Then I helped Irina into the bath, and there I washed her hair with dried myrtle I had gone and taken from the closet in our old room: a smell of sweet branches and leaves, and when I had washed it three times, at last when I put her hair to my nose I smelled only myrtle and not smoke. I took her from the bath and dried her with a sheet and put her sitting by the fire while I combed her hair. The fire was getting low, but I did not put on another log, because it was not too cold in the room yet. She sat in the chair and her eyes were drifting closed. I sang to her while I combed her hair and after I drew the last strokes from the very crown of her head all the way to the end, she put her head against the side of the chair and slept there.

The blood had come out of the blue dress. I took it dripping out and took the basin to the balcony to throw the water out again. But I was not cold when I went outside this time. Warm air came into my face and a smell of fresh trees and earth, a smell of spring that I had almost forgotten because it had been so long since it had come. I stood there with the basin full of red water and breathed that smell without thinking until my arms trembled; the basin was too heavy for me to hold for so long. I managed to get it to the stone railing and tipped it over, and then I went back inside. I did not close the doors, but let the spring come into the room. My girl, my brave girl had done this. She had gone and come back bloody and she had brought us back the spring. And she had come back, she had come back, which was worth all the spring and more for me.

I scrubbed the blue dress until the last marks came out of it; I was careful of course, but anyway the rubies were sewn on so tightly they did not come off. I took the dress and I put it over a chair and stood it outside to dry; later I could give it to Palmira, and she would never know it had been stained. When I turned to go back in, Irina was standing next to the chair, holding the sheet around her body, looking out at the window; her hair was hanging long in a pool around her, already almost dry. It was growing light outside, the sun was coming, and she came out on the balcony in her bare feet. I almost said, *You will catch cold, dushenka,* but I held the words in my mouth and moved the chair instead, so she could come and stand at the railing. I stood next to her and put my arms around her to keep her thin body warm. A great noise of birds and chattering animals was coming from a distance, coming nearer with every moment, nearer and nearer, until suddenly it was around us, all around us; I saw the squirrels leaping as shadows in the trees of the garden below for another moment before the sunlight touched the leaves, the soft new leaves, and together Irina and I and the joyous birds watched the sun climb into the world over green fields instead of snow.

I stroked her head and said softly, "All is well, Irinushka, all is well."

"Magreta," she said, without looking at me, "was he always so beautiful, Mirnatius, even as a boy?"

"Yes, always," I said. I didn't have to think about that; I remembered. "Always. Such a beautiful child, even in his cradle. We went for the christening. His eyes were like jewels. Your father hoped to ask for the fostering of him—your mother had no children yet, and he thought perhaps the tsar could be persuaded to think it was better than the house of a man with many sons. But your mother wouldn't hold the baby. She only stood there like she was made of stone and didn't lift up her hands. The nurse couldn't even set him in her arms. Oh, how angry your father was."

I shook my head, remembering it: how the duke had shouted, telling her that in the morning she would go and hold the child, and speak of his beauty, and say how sad she was not to have one of her own; and all the time Silvija had only stood silently with her eyes downcast before him, saying nothing—

And then it came back to me suddenly, as a drop of oil floating up to the surface of water, that he had shouted and shouted, and when he finished, Silvija had looked up at him with her silver eyes and said very softly, "No. There is another child coming to our house who will wear a winter crown," and he had stopped shouting and taken her hands and kissed them, and he had said nothing more of fostering the prince. But then Irina had not been born for another four years. I had forgotten all about it by the time she came.

Irina stood looking out at spring, my tsarina with her winter crown and her hawk father's eyes, and her face was still so very pale. I squeezed her a little, trying to comfort her, whatever had wounded her so. "Come inside, dushenka," I whispered softly. "Your hair is dry. I'll braid it, and you should sleep a little. Come lie down on the couch. I won't let anyone come in. You don't need to go into the bed with him."

"No," she said. "I know. I don't have to lie down with him."

She came inside, and after I braided her hair, she lay down on the couch and I covered her. Then I went into the hallway and I told the footmen out there that the tsar and tsarina were very tired from their gaiety and were not to be disturbed, and I went inside and took the green dress to the window, to finish my sewing in the spring air.

When I woke in my grandfather's house the next morning, the room was stifling-hot. I stumbled still half asleep to the window to let in some air. My mother and father were still in bed, and as I went I stepped barefoot on the gold-encrusted gown lying crumpled on the floor. Last night I'd clawed it off my body like a snakeskin and crawled onto the foot of the bed, even while my parents were still talking to me. Their words had stopped making any sense. Then they'd stopped speaking and only put their hands on my head. I fell away into slumber while they sang softly over me, with the familiar smells of woodsmoke and wool in my nose, warm again, warm again at last.

I unlatched the window and warm air blew into my face. I was high enough in my grandfather's house to see over the city wall and into the fields and the forest on the other side, and all the fields were green, green, green: green with rye standing as tall as if it had already had four months of spring to grow in, green with new leaves already going dark with summer, and all the wildflowers open at once. The fruit trees down in my grandmother's garden were full of flowers, too, plum and cherry and apple blossoming together, and even in the window-box there were flowers open, and a faint low humming in the air as if all the bees in the world had rushed to work together. There was not a trace of snow anywhere on the ground at all.

After a breakfast that was tasteless in my mouth, I folded up the gold-and-silver gown and wrapped it in paper. There were crowds of people in the street when I went out carrying my parcel. In the synagogue as I passed the doors I heard singing, and it was full even though it was halfway through the morning and the middle of the week. In the market no one was doing any work. They were all telling each other stories about what had happened: about how God had stretched out his hand and given the Staryk into the tsar's hand, and broken the sorcerous winter.

The dress got me through the gates of the duke's house, when I showed a corner of it to a servant, but I still had to wait sitting outside the servants' entrance for an hour before someone finally took a message and Irina had me brought up—because she was tsarina, the tsarina who had saved the kingdom, and I was only a small moneylender from the Jewish quarter in my brown wool dress. But when the message reached her, she did send someone for me at once, her old chaperone Magreta, who looked at me anxiously and sidelong as if she thought my dress and my plain braided hair were a disguise, but took me upstairs anyway.

Irina was in her bedchamber. Four women were sitting together near the fire, sewing frantically to make over a gown almost as splendid as the monstrosity I had brought; she was going to another wedding that very day, it seemed. But she was on the balcony, scattering bread for a feasting of birds and squirrels: they had all come out again, too, just like the people into the streets, lean and hungry after the long winter and willing to dare human company in exchange for food. As she threw out a handful, they darted in close to her feet to snatch up hunks and then darted back away to eat it before rushing in for another helping.

"I need to see him," I told her.

"Why?" she asked me, slowly.

"We've done more than just stopped him!" I said. "If you keep him for—" I glanced over my shoulder into the bustle of the room, and didn't say the name. "—that one to devour, it won't just end the winter, it will destroy his kingdom. *All* of the Staryk will die, not just him!"

Irina finished scattering her bread and then spread her empty hand out to me: unadorned, except for the ring of Staryk silver gleaming upon it, a thin band of cold light even in the bright sun. "But what else would you have us do?" I stared at her. "Miryem, the Staryk have raided in this kingdom ever since men first settled here. They treat us like vermin skulking among their trees, only with more cruelty."

"A handful of them!" I said. "Most of them can't come here, any more than we can cross to their kingdom whenever we like. Only the powerful among them can open a path . . ." I stopped, realizing I wasn't making matters any better, and maybe worse.

"And those also have the power to decide for the rest," Irina said. "I don't think with pleasure of the death of all the Staryk people, but their king began this war. He stole the spring; he would have let all *our* people, all of Lithvas, starve to death. Do you tell me he didn't know what he was doing?"

"No," I said grimly. "He knew."

Irina nodded slightly. "My hands don't feel clean, either, after last night. But I won't wash them in my people's blood. And I see nothing else we can do."

"If they offered us a treaty, in exchange for his life, they'd hold to it. They never break their word."

"Who would that treaty come from?" Irina said. "And even if one came . . ." She looked into the bedchamber, her bedchamber: a room she shared with the tsar and a black thing of smoke and hunger that lived inside him. Her face was bleak. "I don't pretend to be glad of the bargain we've made. But there is spring in Lithvas today, and there will be bread on the table in every peasant's house this winter." She looked back at me. "I will buy that for them," she said quietly. "Even if it costs more than I would like to pay."

So I left with nothing to show for my visit but a sick hollow emptiness in my stomach. Her chaperone stopped me in the room as I left and asked me what I wanted for the dress, but I only shook my head and went. But leaving it didn't help. I could slough off the dress of a Staryk queen, but I had been one for too long to just forget. And yet I couldn't tell Irina she was wrong, and I couldn't even tell her she was selfish. She *was* going to pay, the price I hadn't been willing to pay myself: she was going to lie down with that demon next to her, and even if she hadn't let it put its fingers into her soul, she'd feel them crawling over her skin.

And with that payment, she would buy us more than spring. She would buy us spring, and summer, and winter, too; a winter where no Staryk road would gleam between the trees and no white-cloaked raiders would come out to steal our gold. Instead our woodsmen and our hunters and our farmers would go into the forest, with axes and traps for the white-furred animals. She'd buy us the forest and the frozen river, and it would all go to crops and timber, and in ten years Lithvas would be a rich kingdom instead of a small, poor one, while somewhere in a dark room far below, Chernobog crunched up the Staryk children in his teeth one bite at a time, to keep all the rest of us warm.

I went back to my grandfather's house. My mother was waiting for me anxiously outside, sitting on the steps, as if she hadn't been able to bear having me out of her sight. I went and sat beside her, and she put her arms around me and kissed my forehead and held my head against her shoulder, stroking her hand over my hair. There were many other people going in and out of the house around us: wedding guests leaving with ordinary smiling faces. They were already forgetting a night of dancing under white trees, with all winter and a burning shadow coming into the house among us.

Only my grandfather remembered a little. I'd crept down from the bedroom that morning, leaving my parents asleep, to take a cup of tea and a crust of bread in the kitchen, bewildered and trying to fill the cold hollow inside me. It was still early, and only a couple of servants had been stirring in the house, beginning to put food out on the tables for the guests who would soon be waking up. But after a little while, one of them came and told me my grandfather wanted me. I'd gone up to his study. He was standing by the window frowning out at spring, and he looked me in the face and said abruptly, "Well, Miryem?" the same way he did when I came to show him my books. He was asking if they were clean and balanced, and I had found I couldn't answer him.

So I'd gone to the duke's palace, and now I'd come back with no better answer than when I'd gone. It should have been easy. The Staryk himself had told me yes: he'd bowed to me without hatred or even reproach, as though I had the right to do just as he'd done, and set fire to his kingdom for trying to bury mine in ice. And maybe I did, but I wasn't a Staryk myself. I'd said *thank you* to Flek and Tsop and Shofer, and I'd named that little girl I didn't want to think about. She had a claim on me, surely, if no one else in that kingdom did.

"We'll go home tomorrow," my mother said softly into my hair. "We'll go home, Miryem." It was all I'd wanted, the only hope I'd had to give me courage, but I couldn't imagine it anymore. It seemed as unreal to me as a mountain of glass and a silver road. Would I really go back to my narrow town and feed my chickens and my goats, with the scowls of the people I'd saved on my back every day? They didn't have a right to hate me, but they would anyway. The Staryk was a tale for a winter's night. *I* was their monster, the one they could see and understand and imagine tearing down. They wouldn't believe I'd done anything to help them even if they heard a story of it.

And they were right, because I hadn't done it for them at all. Irina had saved them, and they'd love her for it. I'd done it for myself, and for my parents, and for these people: for my grandfather, for Basia, for my second cousin Ilena coming down the stairs and kissing us on our cheeks before she climbed into the waiting cart to set off for her own home in another narrow village where she lived with seven other houses around hers and every village around them hating them all. I'd done it for the men and women going by in the street in front of my grandfather's house. *Lithvas* didn't mean home to me; it was just the water we lived beside, my people huddled together on the riverbanks, and sometimes the wave came rolling up the slope and dragged some of us down into the depths for the fish to devour.

I didn't have a country to do it for. I only had people, so what about *those* people: what about Flek, and Tsop, and Shofer, whose lives I'd bound to mine, and a little girl I'd given a Jewish name like a gift, before I'd gone away to destroy her home?

But I'd already done it, and it seemed past my power to undo. I wasn't anyone here that mattered. I was just a girl, a money-lender from a small town with a little gold in the bank, and what had once seemed a fortune to me now looked like a scant handful of coins, not even a single chest out of my Staryk king's store-room. I'd picked up a silver fork that morning and held it in my hand, not sure what I wanted to happen. But what I wanted didn't matter. Nothing happened. The fork stayed silver, and whatever magic I had was back in that winter kingdom I would never see again. A kingdom that would fade away forever soon, beneath that same rolling wave. And I had nothing left to say about it.

So I went inside with my mother. In our bedroom we made a parcel of the few things my parents had brought from home, and then we went downstairs to help: there were still so many people in the house, people I'd never met, but who were still my family and friends, and there was cooking to be done and dishes to be washed, tables to be laid and cleaned again, children to be fed and crying babies to be held. A crowd of women around me doing the ocean of women's work that never subsided and never changed and always swallowed whatever time you gave it and wanted more, another hungry body of water. I submerged into it

like a ritual bath and let it close over my head gladly. I wanted to
stop my ears and my eyes and my mouth with it. I could worry
about this, whether there was enough food, whether the bread
was rising well, whether the beef had cooked long enough,
whether there were enough chairs at the table; I could do something about these things.

No one was surprised to see me. No one asked me where I'd
been. They all kissed me when they saw me for the first time and
told me I'd gotten so tall, and some of them asked me when they'd
be dancing at *my* wedding. They were happy that I was there, and
happy I was helping, but at the same time I didn't really matter. I
could have been any of my cousins. There wasn't anything special
about me, and I was glad, so glad, to be ordinary again.

I finally sat down at the tables to fill my own plate, tired out at
last with carrying and cooking, tired enough not to think. Guests
were leaving as the meal wound to a close, already saying goodbye
and flowing out the door. I was still deep underwater, a fish in a
school, indistinguishable. But then suddenly the flow was checked.
People cleared out of the doorway, and a footman came into it in
the livery of the tsar, red and gold and black, and looked around
us down his nose with the faint disdain of borrowed superiority.

And when he came in, I stood up. It wasn't my place, it wasn't
the place of an unmarried girl in my grandfather's house, but I
stood and said to him sharply from across the table, "What are
you here for?"

He paused and looked at me and frowned, and then he said,
very coolly, "I have a letter for Wanda Vitkus: are you she?"

All that afternoon, Wanda had been swimming alongside me
in that crowd of women; she had carried heavy stacks of plates
and brought large buckets of water, and we'd barely talked, but
we'd looked at each other and we'd been together in the work, the
safe and simple work. She was standing in the back of the room,
just inside the kitchen, and after a moment she came forward,

wiping her wet red hands in her apron, and the footman turned and gave her the letter into her hands: a thick folded sheet of heavy parchment sealed with a great lump of smoke-blackened red wax, with a few runny drops like blood that had trickled away before it hardened.

She took it in her hands and opened it and looked inside it for a long time, and then she put her apron up to cover her mouth, her lips pressed tight, and she jerked her head twice in a nod and then she folded the letter back up and held it tight, pressed against her chest, and she turned and went away into the back of the house, towards the stairs. The footman threw a dismissive look over us—we did not matter, we were not important—and he turned and left the house as quickly as he had come.

I was still standing at the table. Around me the conversation resumed, the flow resumed; *When will you be in town again, How old is your eldest now, How is your husband's business,* the steady lapping waves, but I didn't go back into the water. I pushed my chair back from the table and I went upstairs to my grandfather's study. He was there with a few other old men, all of them talking in their deep voices; they were smoking pipes and cigars and speaking of work. They looked at me frowning: I didn't belong there, unless I was coming to bring them more brandy and tea and food.

But my grandfather didn't frown. He only looked at me and put his glass and his cigar aside and said, "Come," and took me into the small room next to the study where he kept his important papers locked behind glass doors, and he shut the door behind us and looked down at me.

"I owe a debt," I said. "And I have to find a way to pay it."

Chapter 21

In the morning, there were red blistered marks across my palms where I had held the silver chain with Sergey and Stepon. Last night before the tsarina left, she had said to me, "How can I repay you?" I had not known what to say to her, because it was me doing that; I was repaying. Miryem had taken me out of my father's house for six kopeks, when I was only worth three pigs to my father, who stole money from hers with lies. Her mother had put bread on my plate and love in my heart. Her father had sung blessings on that bread before he gave it to me to eat. It did not matter I did not know the words. They had given it to me even when I didn't know what they meant by it and thought they were devils. Miryem had given me silver for my work. She had put her hand out to me and taken mine, like I was someone who could make a bargain for myself, instead of just someone stealing from my father. There had been food in her house for me.

And that Staryk wanted to take her for nothing. He made her give him gold just to live, as if she belonged to him because he was strong enough to kill her. My father was strong enough to kill me but that did not mean I belonged to him. He sold me for six kopeks, for three pigs, for a jug of krupnik. He tried to sell me again and again like I was still his no matter how many times he sold me. And that was how that Staryk thought. He wanted to keep her and make more gold out of her forever, and it did not matter what she wanted, because he was strong.

But I was strong, too. I was strong enough to make Panova Mandelstam well, and I was strong enough to learn magic, Miryem's magic, and use it to turn three aprons into six kopeks. I was strong enough, with Sergey and Stepon, to stop my father selling me or killing me. And last night I did not know if I was strong enough to stop the Staryk, even with a silver chain, even with Sergey and Stepon, even with Miryem's mother and father. But I had not known that I was strong enough to do any of those things until they were over and I had done them. I had to do the work first, not knowing. Afterwards, Stepon put his face in my apron and cried because he was still feeling afraid, and he asked me how I knew the tsarina would make magic and stop the Staryk from killing us, and I had to tell him that I did not know. I only knew the work had to come first.

So when the tsarina asked me how she could pay me, I did not know what to say. I did not do it for her. I did not know her. Maybe she was the tsarina, but I did not even know what her name was. One day when I was ten one of our neighbors came to the house and said the tsar was dead and when I asked what it meant they said that there would be a new tsar. So I did not really see why a tsar mattered. And now that I had seen a tsar, I did not want anything to do with one. He was terrible and full of fire. I would have told her that to repay me, she could make the tsar go away, but he had already gone out of the house with the guards who were leading the Staryk.

But Miryem's father heard her asking me, and he saw I did not know what to say. He had a big bruise all on the side of his face, and his hands were all hurt and shaking where he had been holding tight on that silver chain with me, and he was sitting with

Panova Mandelstam and they had their arms wrapped around Miryem and they were kissing her head and touching her face like she was worth more to them than silver kopeks, more to them than gold, more than everything they had. But when he saw I did not know what to do, he kissed Miryem's forehead and he got up and he came limping over the floor to the tsarina and said to her, "This brave girl and her brothers came to the city with us because they are in trouble at home." Then he put his hand on my shoulder and he said to me softly, "Go and sit down and rest, Wanda, I will tell her about it."

So I went away and sat down with Sergey and Stepon and put my arms around them, and they put their arms around me. We were too far away to hear what Panov Mandelstam was saying because he said it very quietly. But he talked to the tsarina for a little time, and then he came limping over to us and told us that everything would be all right. We believed him. The tsarina was going out of the house then. She walked out those big doors into the courtyard where some more of the guards were waiting for her. Two of them reached inside and took hold of the doors and they pulled them shut. And we were inside the house without them.

There was a big mess in the room. Around the edges of the room there was still some food on the tables going bad and flies were already buzzing around it. Chairs were knocked over everywhere and coming out of the fireplace over the floor there were black scorch marks like the footprints a man leaves walking through snow in heavy boots. The big golden crown Miryem had been wearing was on the floor near the fireplace and it was all bent out of shape and almost melted. Nobody could have put it back on. But it did not matter. We looked at Miryem's family, and they looked at us, and we all got up and Panov Mandelstam put his arm around Sergey's back, and I put my arm around Panova Mandelstam's, and we were a circle all together, the six of us: we were a family, and we had kept the wolf away again; for another day we had kept the wolf away.

Then we went upstairs and went to sleep. We did not clean up the mess. I slept a long time in that beautiful big quiet room up at the top of the stairs, and when I woke up there was spring outside, spring everywhere, and it felt like that spring outside was inside me, too. Even though my hands had blisters, I felt so strong that I did not even worry a little about what would happen to us. I kissed Sergey and Stepon and I went downstairs to help the other women in the house, and I did not care anymore that I did not understand what they were saying. When someone said something to me that I did not know, I only smiled at her, and she smiled at me and said, "Oh, I forget!" and told me over again what she was saying except in the words I knew.

I carried dishes to the tables: there were tables in all the rooms for people to sit and eat, not as many people as yesterday but still so many that they had tables in every room and chairs crammed tight around them. There were tables in the other dancing room, too. Somebody else had cleaned up the mess, and I could not see the black marks on the floor anymore because someone had unrolled a big carpet over the floor and brought in tables, and there was no fire in the fireplace because it was so warm that instead they had opened the windows to the air. The smell of smoke was gone.

And there was food everywhere, so much food that we could almost not find places to put food down because already every spot had food on it. When I was hungry myself, I sat down at the table and ate until I was full, and afterwards I helped again to put out more food for more people. I kept doing it. Later on in the day, Miryem and her mother came, too, and still we all worked together.

But I had just put down a pair of buckets, with water that I carried from the fountain down in the city, when I heard a noise out in the room with the tables, and then I heard Miryem asking, hard and clear, "What are you here for?" as if someone had come again to hurt us. I pushed out of the kitchen and came into the doorway and there was a guard with a sword and fine clothing in the room who said my name. He said he had a letter for me. Then I was afraid for a moment, but I was in this house, with all these people, and I thought, I was strong enough for this too; so I stepped forward and I held my hand out and I let him put the letter into it.

On that letter there was a heavy thing of wax as red as blood, pressed with a shape of a great crown. I broke it open and I looked at the words. I knew how to say them, because Miryem had taught me, so in my mouth I silently made the words with my tongue one after another, and what it said in that letter was, *Be it known to any who come into Our domain of Lithvas that by Our imperial command the woman Wanda Vitkus and her brother Sergey Vitkus and her brother Stepon Vitkus are pardoned of any and all crimes of which they stand accused. Let no man's hand be raised against them, and every one of Our people do them honor for the great and courageous service which they have done for Us and Lithvas. And they are furthermore granted by Our will permission to go into the Great Forest and therein take freehold wherever they so choose, in any untenanted property, and there claim from Our hand title to whatever land they can put into crops, or enclose for herding, in three years' time, and they shall have it for themselves and their heirs.*

And underneath those words there was a great scrawling of ink that was not a word, it was a name, *Mirnatius,* and then after it *Tsar of Lithvas and Roson, Grand Duke of Koron, of Irkun, of Tomonyets, of Serveno, Prince of Maralia, of Roverna, of Samatonia, Lord of Markan and the Eastern Marches,* and last after all that list, *Lord and Master of the Great Northern Forest.*

I looked at that letter and then I understood why a tsar mattered. It was magic like Miryem's magic. That tsar, that terrible tsar, could give me this letter and now we were safe. I did not have to be afraid anymore at all. Nobody from town would look at that letter and try to hang Sergey or me. They would look at the tsar's name on that paper and be afraid of him, even if he was far away.

But we did not even have to go back to town at all. We did not have to go back to our father's house, where maybe he was still lying on the floor, and we did not have to go back to that farm where nothing much would grow and the tax collector came every year. That letter said that we could go into the forest and take any land that we wanted. It could be the best land we found. It could be full of big trees that we could cut down and sell for lots of money. I knew a big tree was worth a lot because the year before my mother died, there was a tree on our neighbor's property and one year it fell down and he worked very hard and cut it up quick before the boyar's men came to take it, and he hid two big pieces of it in the woods. Da saw it and came in and said at dinnertime what he saw and said sourly, "That's a clever man, he will make ten kopeks off that wood."

But Mama shook her head and said, "It's not his property, there will be trouble," and he slapped her and said, "What do you know," but the next day the boyar's men came with a big wagon and they put the pieces of the tree in it, and there was a man with them who looked at those pieces and somehow knew that some of the tree was missing, and they beat our neighbor hard until he told them where he hid the pieces, and they put the pieces in the wagon and left him on the ground bloody. He was sick for a long time because of it, and his wife had to try and sow the crops alone because he could not walk. One day that winter she came to beg for food, and Mama gave her some. Da beat her for it that night even though her belly was already getting big.

But nobody would beat us for cutting down trees, because in this letter the tsar said we could. He said they were ours. He said all that land, as much land as we could take care of, would be ours. We could have goats and chickens and we could plant rye.

And we did not even have to build a house. We could go to the little house, the house that had saved us, where there was already a garden and a barn, and we could make a farm all around it. This paper said that it was all right because there was no one living in it. I thought we would go there and we would go into the house and promise to take care of it, and we would promise that if anyone who had ever lived there wanted to come back, we would give them the best bed, and all the food they wanted, and they could stay there with us as long as they wanted.

And then I thought, if anyone came to the house at all—if anyone came to the house who was hungry and in trouble—we would let them stay. There would be food in our house for them, and we would be glad. Like Panova Mandelstam. That is what that letter said. We could make a house like her house and we could feed anyone who came.

I took the letter upstairs to Sergey and Stepon. Sergey had helped with the horses and Stepon had helped him for a while also even though it was still very noisy, but then he had to go upstairs and he was still afraid, so Sergey went upstairs with him. I went upstairs and I came into the room and I showed them the letter, and they did not know how to read the letters, but they saw the big red seal, and they touched the heavy soft paper, and I told them carefully out loud what it said, and then I asked them if they wanted to do what I wanted to do, I asked if they wanted to go to the little house in the woods and make a farm there, and let anyone come to us in trouble. I did not say, *We are going to do that,* even though it was what I wanted. I asked them if they wanted it also.

Sergey carefully reached out and took the paper in his hands. I let him have it. He very lightly touched the shape of one of the letters on the paper with his finger just to see if it would come off. It did not come off even a little. "Yes," he said softly. "Yes."

Stepon said, "Can we ask them to come live with us?" He meant Miryem's family. "Can we ask them to come? And I can plant the nut, and then Mama will be there too. Then it will be all of us together, and that would be the very best thing."

When he said it, I started to cry because he was right, it would be the very best thing, it would be so good that I had not even been able to think of it. Sergey put his arm around my shoulders, and he said to Stepon, "Yes. We will ask them to come," and I wiped the tears away from my face, carefully, so I would not get any of them on the letter.

When I left my grandfather's study, I went to my parents' room. They were sitting by the fire together, and Wanda and her brothers had come down to them; Wanda had brought the tsar's letter, and had given it to my father, who was looking at it surprised. "We can go and fetch the goats," Wanda was saying, to him and my mother, "and the chickens. It is warm now. We can build more of the house by winter. We can cut down some trees. There will be room," and as I came around and looked at the letter, where the tsar had signed himself *Lord and Master of the Great Northern Forest*, I understood: Irina was already stretching out her hand. She had given Wanda a farm in exchange for taking her brothers and her strong arms into the forest to clear trees and plant crops and build a house and a barn, the first of many to come.

"Leave our house?" my mother said slowly. "But we've lived there so long," and then I understood also that Wanda was asking my parents to come and live with them, there on the farm the tsar had given them; she wanted them to leave our town, our house, our little narrow island in the river that was always in danger of being flooded.

"And what is there to stay for?" I said. "It's not ours. It's the boyar's. Everything we've ever done to improve it, we've done for him, for nothing; we're not even allowed to buy it if we wanted to. But with help in the house, Sergey and Wanda can clear more land and make the farm richer. Of course you should go."

My mother stilled; they all looked at me and heard what I hadn't said, and she reached for my hand. "Miryem!"

I swallowed hard. The words were on my lips: *Go tomorrow, stay one day more,* but I thought of Rebekah, thin as a sliver of blue ice. How long before she would melt away? "You should go now," I said. "Today, before the sun goes down."

"No," my father said flatly, standing up: my kind, gentle father, angry at last. "Miryem, no. This Staryk—he was right! He *deserves* what has come to him! It is the reward of the wicked."

"There's a child," I said, my throat choked and sore. My mother's hand tightened on mine. "I gave her a name. Will I let a demon feast on her, because *he* was wicked?"

"Every winter they come from their kingdom of ice, to steal and murder among the innocent," my father said after a moment, just as Irina had said, but then he asked me, as a plea: "Are there even ten righteous among them?"

I drew a breath, still afraid but half relieved, too: it made the answer so clear. "I know that there are three," I said. I put my other hand around my mother's and squeezed back. "I have to. You know I have to."

I took the deformed golden crown to Isaac's stall, where his younger brother was minding things for him, and he carefully melted the whole thing down for me into flat gold bars, and then I went out with them hidden in a sack, out to the great market in the center of the city. One after another I traded them, not caring if I made a good bargain, so long as I made a quick one. I traded for a cart, for two strong horses to pull it, for a crate full of chickens, for an axe, a saw, hammers, and nails. I bought a plow and furrows and two sharp scythes, and sacks of seed for rye and beans. Sergey and Wanda came with me; they loaded everything into the cart and piled it high. And last at the end, I bought two long hooded cloaks, exactly the same, a dull grey: those *were* a good bargain, their price come down far from what they'd been yesterday, on a table full of others.

It took us a long time to drive the heaped cart back to my grandfather's house: the streets were crammed full of traffic and moving almost not at all. As we crawled along, Wanda said, "There is a wedding," and looking down a side street towards the great cathedral I glimpsed a princess coming down the steps, wearing my Staryk dress of gold and white with a thin crown upon her head; she was smiling and triumphant, and her husband beside her equally so, among a crowd of splendid nobles. The dress fit better there than it had in my grandfather's house. I looked for Irina: she was already at the foot of the stairs, with the tsar beside her, climbing into an open carriage. The sunlight caught on her silver crown, and he only sat leaning on an elbow, looking irritated with boredom, and no sign of the demon lurking beneath his skin. I looked quickly away.

It was beginning to be late by the time we got back, but the sun had not gone down: it was almost summer, after all. We didn't wait to eat supper. It was our turn to be the ones leaving, saying our goodbyes to a thinning crowd. I kissed my grandfather and my grandmother at the table, and my grandfather drew me down and kissed my forehead. "You remember?" he said quietly.

"Yes," I said. "In the street behind Amtal's house, next to the synagogue." He nodded.

We climbed into the cart and drove away from the house in front of everyone, waving. Sergey and my father sat up on the front seat: the horses had been expensive, but they were good, well-trained horses; it wasn't hard to drive them. I wore the cloak and pulled the hood up over my head in the back. Even at this hour, the streets were still bustling: the eating-houses were putting tables and chairs outside in the street so people could sit in the

warm air together, and we had to turn down a narrower street of
only houses, where children had been called inside for supper.
Halfway through the street, a moment came when there was no
one there; my mother spread the second cloak over a couple of
sacks of grain in the bottom, as if I was lying there asleep. Stepon
took off his boots—my old ones—and tucked them poking out at
the bottom. Then I slipped down off the cart.

I stood in the shadow between two houses while the cart drove
down the rest of the street and turned towards the gate of the
Jewish quarter. There and at the city gates, they would ask my
father for the names of all the passengers, and he would put mine
down with the others, and pay the toll for each with a few extra
coins to speed the way. If Irina grew suspicious and sent men to
look for me tomorrow, to ask if I knew where the Staryk had
gone, everyone would say in all honesty that I had left the city
before nightfall with my family; they would find the records in
their own guards' hands, and no one would admit to having been
hasty when their hands had been greased for it.

After the cart was out of sight I kept my hood pulled low and
my shoulders hunched like an old baba and went through narrow
streets all the way to the synagogue, and there asked a young man
going in to pray where Amtal's house was; he pointed me to it.
The cobblestones of the street behind it were old and worn soft,
with deep cart-wheel grooves dug into them and many loose
stones and empty pockets of mortar. The back of the house had
a little narrow place cut out of it in the middle, only just wide
enough for a single person to walk inside, and there were some
old sacks of refuse blocking it off. But after I picked my way
around them, the old sewer grating in the ground was kept clear.
I pulled it up easily, and there was a ladder there waiting for me
to climb down. Waiting for many people to climb down, here
close to the synagogue, in case one day men came through the

wall of the quarter with torches and axes, the way they had in the west where my grandmother's grandmother had been a girl.

I let myself inside and pulled the grate back down over my head before I climbed the long way down into the thin damp puddle of the sewer tunnel. There was only the dim round circle of late sunlight over my head, getting smaller and smaller as I climbed down. I didn't have a lantern or a torch, but I didn't want one. A light would let someone else see me coming from a long way off. This was a road that had to be walked in the dark.

I turned to put my back to the ladder, and I put my hands out and felt over the walls until I found the little hole chipped out in the shape of a star, with six points for my fingers to pick out. I put my hand over it and started walking slowly straight into the dark, running my fingers spread wide at that height. By the time I counted ten strides, I found another star.

They led me onward for what felt a long way, although it couldn't have been: it wasn't that far a distance from the synagogue to the city walls. But the last light from the sewer grate vanished behind me very quickly, and I felt blind and smothered and loud with my breath noisy in my own ears. But I kept counting ten, and if I still didn't find a star, I felt over the wall until I did, or I took one step back and felt around there. Once I had to take two steps back, with nothing but blank wall under my hands, and then in fear take four steps forward before I found it at last. And then the stars ended and the wall fell away from under my hand as I stumbled over a ridge of dirt in the floor and fell, putting my hands down in sticky wet. I stood back up, wiping myself off on the cloak, and groped backwards in the dark until I found the corner of the turning with my fingers, and the wall of the earthen tunnel.

"There was a tower in the wall here, before the siege," my grandfather had told me quietly, there in his small closed-in room.

"The duke's men broke it when they came in. And after, when the duke rebuilt the walls, he did not want the tower rebuilt. The foundations were solid. There was enough money for it. He chose not to. Why not?" My grandfather had spread his hands and shrugged a little, with his shoulders and his mouth. "A tower to guard the back of the city, why not? So after the walls were built again, and all the workmen had left, my brother Joshua and I went down into the sewers with rope, to search without getting lost. And we found the tunnel he had made.

"No one else knows. Only your great-uncle and me and your grandmother, and Amtal and the rabbi. Amtal keeps the grate clean. I pay him for it, I pay his rent. When he gets old, he will tell his son. We never use it: never for smuggling, never to avoid the toll. No one knows that we know. That is where they will have put him, this husband of yours, in that tower at the end of the tunnel.

"Now you must tell me, Miryem. You understand what this tunnel is. This tunnel is life. If their prisoner goes, even if you are not taken yourself, these great ones, the duke, the tsar, they will not shrug and say, ah well. They will ask how. They will look for footprints. Maybe they will block off the sewer passages. Or maybe they will follow them and find the grate. Maybe they will even come up out of it and see Amtal's house there, and put a knife to the throat of his children, and Amtal will tell them who pays him to keep it clean.

"I say this expecting you to understand, these are not certainties. If they come here, even if Amtal has told them my name, there will be things I can do. I have a great deal of money, and I am useful to the duke. He will not hurry in a rage to destroy me, that is not the kind of man he is. And there is also the chance that they will not do any of these things. They may say, he is a magical creature, he has flown! He did not go through sewers. They may leave it all as it is.

"So I do not say, put my life, your grandmother's life, on the scale. I say to you, here are the dangers. Some are more likely than others. Weigh them, put them all together, and you will know the cost. Then *you* must say, is this what you owe? Do you owe so much to this Staryk, who came and took you without your consent or ours, against the law? It is upon his head and not yours what has come of his acts. A robber who steals a knife and cuts himself cannot cry out against the woman who kept it sharp."

He hadn't waited for me to answer. He had only put his hand on my cheek, and then he had gone back out again. Now I stood there at the turning for a moment, with the dirt of the duke's tunnel under my fingers, a road to safety that I might close forever to my own people just to save the Staryk's. Or I might be caught myself, if there were guards down at the end, and do no one any good at all. I had already answered the question, but I would have to keep answering it with every step I took down that passage, and I wouldn't be done until I came to the very end.

After Miryem climbed out of the cart, I took off my boots and put them there poking out under the cloak. I did not mind taking them off because it was warm, and I was sitting in a cart anyway. I was so glad to be leaving that terrible city. It was even worse than before. The streets were all crowded with people everywhere because now there was no snow and they wanted to be outside and they all wanted to talk at the same time and make noise. I lay down in the bottom of the cart next to the sacks that were pretending to be Miryem and I tried to pretend to be a sack myself, but I wasn't a sack. I had to just lie there and cover my ears and wait until we were out. It took a long time until we came to that big city gate and Panov Mandelstam got down to pay the man at the gate some money, because that city was such a terrible place we had to pay to be let out.

But after that Sergey shook the reins and clucked to the horses just like a real driver and the horses started to walk fast, and we got away. For a little while all of us were safe. Sergey drove down the road until it turned so much that you could not see the gate when you sat up in the back of the cart and looked back. I tried when he stopped the horses and I could not see it, although I could still see smoke coming up from all the houses and all the people in there. Then Sergey gave Panov Mandelstam the reins and climbed down and looked up at me and Wanda and all of us and nodded goodbye. He was going to go around behind the wall of the city and hide and wait until Miryem came out, if she came out.

I did not like leaving Sergey behind. What if Miryem did not come out, what if the Staryk came out alone? He could kill Sergey. He could leave Sergey lying there on the ground all empty again. Or what if the tsar came out instead? That would be just as bad or maybe worse.

But Panov Mandelstam had wanted to go instead of Miryem, and then he had wanted to go with Miryem, and Miryem had said no and no to him. First she said no because the Staryk would not hurt her, and then she said no because one person alone would be more quiet if there was a guard, and then she said no because we could not trick the guards about *two* people missing, but all of those were not the real reasons. The real reason was that Panov Mandelstam was hurt. There were bruises all over him.

I knew because there were some purple marks that you could even see up his neck coming out of his shirt even though the Staryk had not hit him there. I knew how hard someone has to hit you so that you get bruises somewhere else. That is how hard the Staryk hit him, so I knew there were purple marks all under his clothing too, and even if I didn't know that then I would still know he was hurt, because he limped and sometimes he put his hand on his side and breathed carefully for a little bit as if it hurt him, and he had fallen asleep twice during the day already.

Miryem did not say that, though, she said those other reasons, and finally Panov Mandelstam said, "I will wait for you outside the city then," and Miryem also said no to that, but Panov Mandelstam was just shaking his head firmly, and he had let her say no before but he would not listen to *no* anymore, and he said that she did not even know where the house was.

That was when Sergey said to Panov Mandelstam, "I will wait for her. You cannot walk quickly. I can bring her to the house." And Panov Mandelstam was still worried, but Sergey was bigger and stronger than him already, and also not hurt, and Miryem said, "He's right, we'll make better time," so it was decided that Sergey was going to wait for Miryem and meanwhile the rest of us were going to keep going so that if anyone came to the house looking for us sooner than they came back, we would all be there keeping busy and we would say that Miryem and Sergey went away already to get the goats.

Miryem said, "But we will be back long before then," as if it was all as certain, as if all she and Sergey had to do was just walk from the city to the house, but she did not really mean that. At first I thought that she was being foolish, because she could not know if she was going to come out. But she was not being foolish; she just did not mean it. I found out because we went upstairs to our room to pack the things and Miryem came up to us and said to Sergey, "Thank you. But don't come to the city wall. When you get off the cart, just wait in the trees near the road. I'll find you if I can."

So then I knew, she did not mean it. She also didn't know if she was going to come out, and she was glad Sergey had said he would wait because she did not want her father to get hurt, and she knew Panov Mandelstam would not agree to stay in the trees. But she told Sergey to stay in the trees, and I was glad, but then Sergey looked at her and said, "I will wait for you near the wall. Maybe you will need some help."

Then Miryem lifted her hands and said, "If I need help, I'll need too much. If I don't, I won't."

But Sergey shrugged and said, "I said I would wait," so that was that, and he was going to be waiting near that wall that maybe a Staryk or a demon or even just men with swords would come out from. Those men with swords at the house who had taken the Staryk away were all big and strong like Sergey was, and they had swords and heavy coats that did not look like you could cut through them easily, so even if they were not as bad as a tsar or a Staryk they were bad enough. I did not want Sergey to be killed by any of them. I also didn't want Miryem killed by any of them, but I didn't know her so well yet and so mostly I didn't want Panova Mandelstam to be sad, which was an important reason to me but not as important as wanting it for my own self, which was how I wanted it for Sergey.

And I was so tired of being afraid all the time. It felt like I had been afraid and afraid without stopping forever. I did not even know how afraid I had been, except that morning I had stopped being afraid of anything at all for just a little while, when Wanda came up to the room with that magic letter from the tsar and I thought everything was finished, and I did not have to be afraid *ever*, I could stop being afraid of so many things, and it was so good and I was so happy, and now I was afraid again.

But it was not up to me. It was up to Sergey, and he was not going to wait in the trees. So I sat up in the cart when Panov Mandelstam drove it away and I saw Sergey walk away from the road into the trees, but into the trees the way he would walk to go all the way around the back of the city, that terrible city, and I watched him until I could not see him anymore. And then I lay down in the bottom of the cart next to the sacks. They did not have to be Miryem now, so Panova Mandelstam put the cloak over me instead and let me put my head on a sack as a pillow, and I put my hand in my pocket around the nut that Mama had given me and I told myself it would be all right. We would come to the house and Sergey would come back and I would plant the nut and Mama would grow and be with us and we would all be together.

The cart had gone so slowly when we were in the city crammed with all those people, but outside on the road it went very fast. It was strange to be on the road without snow. There was no snow anywhere at all. We saw lots of animals like squirrels and birds and deer and rabbits all running everywhere so happy about spring. They were eating grass and leaves and acorns and they were so excited they did not care about us, about people. Even the rabbits just looked at us from the side of the road and kept eating; they were so hungry they could not bother to be afraid. It made me happy to see them. I thought, we helped them, too. It was like Wanda had said about making our house a place where we would feed other people. We had even fed the animals.

We knew when we came close to the house because there was another house on the road that we remembered, with a big wagon wheel stuck on the front of their barn and flowers painted on the side. We had only seen the very top of the flowers before because of the snow but now the snow was gone and we could see the whole flowers. They were tall and beautiful and red and blue. The farmer of that house was standing next to the barn and just looking at the rye all green in his field, and he looked back at us and then I waved my hand and he waved back and he was smiling also.

"We will not be able to drive all the way to the house," Panov Mandelstam said, because there was not a road, and the trees had been so close together when we were walking, but then it turned out he was wrong, or we had not remembered it right. We saw the place we had come out and it was between two big trees and there was room for the horses to go between. And then we kept going and there was still room, even if not very much room. The cart was not a very big cart and we squeezed through. It was starting to get dark, and Panova Mandelstam said, "Maybe we should stop for the night. We don't want to miss it," but just then Wanda said, "I see the house," and I saw it too, and I jumped out of the back of the cart even though Panov Mandelstam could keep driving it all the way, and I ran around it and got ahead of the horses and ran all the way to the yard and the house was there waiting for us.

If only Sergey had been there it would already have been the best thing, but it was still very good. I helped Panov Mandelstam take the harness off the horses and we cleaned them and fed them food. I could almost reach the back of the horses but not quite, but they stayed still even when I was stretching high up to brush them. I pulled two carrots out of the garden and gave them to the horses and they liked them, and I helped unpack the cart with all the good things inside it and we put everything away and Wanda let the chickens out to run and scratch. Tomorrow we would make them a coop. Meanwhile Panova Mandelstam was inside cooking, and a good warm smell came out of the house and light came out of the windows and the door that she had left open.

"Go and wash your hands before dinner, Stepon," Panov Mandelstam said to me, and I went to the back of the house where there was a big washtub, full of water. I dipped a bowl out of it, and I was about to wash my hands, but then I thought, if I washed my hands, I would not want to get them dirty again, and then we would eat, and then it would be time to go to sleep. It was already late. And I did not want to wait anymore.

So instead I took the bowl and I went back out to the front of the house and right by the door of the house I dug a hole in the ground and I took the nut out of my pocket and I put it down there in the hole. I patted it into the dirt and said, "We are safe, Mama. Now you can grow, and be with us," and I was about to put the dirt back on top of it and pour the water on it, but I knew that something was wrong. I looked down at the white nut. It sat there in the warm brown dirt and it didn't look right at all. It looked as if I were trying to plant a coin and make a tree grow that would have money on it like fruit. But no tree would grow out of a coin.

I picked it up and I brushed off the dirt and I held it in my hands. "Mama?" I said to the nut, and then after a little moment I felt like somebody was putting their hand on my head, but very lightly, like they could not really reach me. I heard nothing back at all.

Chapter 22

Vassilia arrived for her wedding angry, of course; almost as angry as her father. She had expected to be tsarina, with the justice of all the excellent sense behind the match. Instead here I was triumphant in her place, and the next candidate in line for her hand was an unlovely archduke thirty-seven years old who had buried two wives before her, instead of a beautiful young tsar who would put a crown on her head.

That was bad enough, and now I had dragged her all the way through snow and ice to Vysnia, a small backward city next to her father's main seat in the west with its great thick-walled citadel of red brick, and she knew exactly why, because she knew exactly how she would have behaved in my place. She would have proudly walked before all the princesses and dukes' daughters of the realm with her crowned head high; when we arrived for the feasting, she would have inclined her head and deigned with cool, muted politeness to speak to one or another of us who had been particularly good at flattering and currying favor with her. I would not have been among them. So she knew I had dragged her here so she would have to bow to me and call me Majesty, so I could pay off all my own debts of tittering and smirks around us.

She had imagined it so well that as she stared up at me in my silver crown and climbed the stairs to meet me, she had her hands closed into fists, waiting to be humiliated, and she did not know what to do with them when I stepped down out of my place to meet her, too soon, and took her by the shoulders and kissed her cheeks. "My dearest Vassilia," I said. "It's been too long since we saw each other, I'm so glad you've come. Dear Uncle Ulrich," I added, turning to him, startled on the step above me, where he was facing Mirnatius and my father, and he looked at my face as I held my hand out to him and forgot for just one moment to be angry. "Forgive me: it's hard for a girl to live so far from her friends. Please will you let us not stand on ceremony? Let's all go inside, and drink a cup of welcome, and let me steal your daughter from you."

I took her upstairs to the great bedchamber with the balcony open, and sent all the servants away, and told her softly that there must be an heir for Lithvas sooner rather than late, and it might not be enough for Mirnatius to marry; I let her draw her own conclusions. And then he and my father came in together, with Ilias trailing sullenly behind, and I held Vassilia's hand while Mirnatius said, as cold as ashen coals, "The joys of the nuptial state are so many, we have decided to bestow them more widely; Ilias, dear cousin, allow me to present to you your bride."

He stood beside me in the church with his mouth twisted in cynical amusement all the time. Vassilia was happy, with cause—I had given her Miryem's golden dress, so splendid she looked more like a tsarina than I did, and she was marrying a handsome young man who would bed her that night with at least some modicum of care. My father had seen Ilias's sullen looks, and while my servants had been helping Vassilia dress, he'd taken him out onto the balcony and told him that if he meant to be a fool about the matter, we'd find another man. And if instead he behaved like a man of sense and made himself satisfactory to the great heiress he was about to marry, he could stop being his mother's lapdog and be a prince and a ruler of men in his own right when Ulrich died. When they'd come back into the room, Ilias had kissed Vassilia's hand and made a reasonably successful effort at compliments. It turned out that even great passions could be satisfied by other means.

Ulrich took over her anger and was livid enough for them both, of course, but he couldn't do anything about it: we took them from the bedroom straight to the church without a pause, and Mirnatius claimed the privilege of handing off the bride for himself. And meanwhile I took Ulrich's arm and spoke to him. Even if he had wanted to make a dash for it with her out through the ranks of his soldiers, silver gleamed on my brow; for as long as he looked at me, he forgot that he was angry, and there were already whispers traveling through the city by then, that his own men would have heard: whispers of winter overthrown by magic.

The feasting was reasonably splendid. Even if there had been nothing else, the greens heaped on the tables would have satisfied us all: not even archdukes had tasted fresh lettuce these last months. There were towers of strawberries gathered in a hurry from the woods by every hand my father could reach pressed into service, and though still small, they burst red and sweet and juicy on the tongue. Mirnatius ordered a servant to give him an entire bowl of them and ate them delicately one by one, all the while surveying the room with his hard mouth turned down. He didn't speak to me, and I said nothing to him. All I could think of when I looked at him was the high sharp note in his voice, down in the cellars.

My mother wasn't real to me. I didn't remember the touch of her hand or the sound of her voice. All of that in me was Magreta. But my mother had brought me through to safety, twice; she'd carried me under her heart until I could breathe, and she'd given me a last drop of magic almost thinned out to nothing in our blood, enough for me to find my way to winter in a mirror's glass. I had those gifts of her, and I had taken them so much for granted that it had never occurred to me before to be grateful for them. And even less for my sharp, ambitious father, who would have delivered me to a brutish husband or even to a sorcerer without hesitation. I hadn't believed there was a limit on the use he would have made of me. But with the memory of Chernobog crackling in the fire's grate, smoke and red flame, I found a clear sharp certainty in me that my father, who had told me he was proud of me, would not have sold my soul to a demon for a crown.

There wasn't much of a kindness to be found in that narrow limit. It had left me cold, all my life. But even that was more than Mirnatius had been given. I could hardly blame him any more for not caring. Where was there anything in him to care with? *No one else had a minute for the witch's get,* he'd said, the only kind words he'd ever said of anyone; of the only one of whom he'd ever had any kindness.

In the ordinary course of things, the son of an executed wife would have been tucked away in a lavish monastery somewhere to keep from getting awkward children, once his brother had been safely crowned and he was no longer needed as a spare. I had imagined that as a fate he'd wanted to avoid, one of the reasons he'd made his bargain; it would have been a punishment to an ambitious man. But of course that wasn't true. The man who spent demon-hot magic to build his own gilded cage and gave more time to his sketchbooks than his tax rolls could have gone into that retreat without regret. Mirnatius would have spent his days with pen and ink and gilt, shaping beauty, and been content. Instead his demon had murdered the brother he loved, to put a crown he'd never wanted on his head.

And now here I was dragging him along like a careless child bumping a broken doll along behind her, bargaining with the demon that sat in his belly for the sake of the kingdom he didn't care about, as if he weren't even there. As if he didn't matter, as he'd never mattered to anyone. No wonder he hated me for it.

It couldn't make me sorry for what I'd done. I was sorry for it already. Miryem had cried out to me over the horror in that tower room below, chaining up a sacrificial victim to be devoured over and over by a demon of flame, and I hadn't needed her to tell me it was evil. But I could be sorry only with my father's kind of regret. I had pity for Staryk children, and I would have stopped their winter king some other way, if I could. I would have set Mirnatius free, if I had the chance, instead of adding to his chained-slave misery. But the world I wanted wasn't the world I lived in, and if I would do nothing until I could repair every terrible thing at once, I would do nothing forever.

I couldn't even apologize to him. He wouldn't have believed me, and he shouldn't have. There was still a fault line in Lithvas to be healed, and a demon sitting on our throne. I was glad to have the winter broken no matter how it had been done, but I wasn't a fool to think we could make an ally of a thing like Chernobog. Last night it had become a choice between helping him, or letting the Staryk king bury us in ice, so I'd chosen—not the lesser evil, but the less immediate one. But I knew that when Chernobog finished drinking up Staryk lives, he'd turn and come right back for us, and I wasn't going to leave Lithvas bare before him.

So tomorrow, when Casimir arrived, still more enraged than Ulrich, my father would whisper a promise of treachery into his ear. And when finally the Staryk king had been devoured to nothing, down below, they and Ulrich would go all three together and speak to the old priests who twenty years ago had brought the saint-blessed chains out of the cathedral to bind a witch-tsarina for the flame. And that day at dawn, when the demon went into hiding from the sun, they would take my husband to the stake and burn him like his mother, to set us all free of its grasp.

I knew all of it would happen, and I wouldn't put out my hand to stop it, even now that I knew Mirnatius himself was innocent. I still wouldn't save him, in his half-life, and condemn Lithvas to the flame in his place, any more than I would try to save Staryk children with a bargain that used the lives of my own people as surety. I was cold enough to do what I had to do, so I could save Lithvas.

But it would leave me cold inside again, too. I looked at Vassilia and at Ilias, who was leaning over to her and whispering and making her blush, and I envied her as much as ever she might have wanted, now when I couldn't let myself dream anymore, even half unwilling, of warmth in my own marriage bed. That was the only thing I could do for Mirnatius. I wouldn't pretend to offer him kindness. I wouldn't ask him again for gratitude or forgiveness or civility. And I wouldn't look at him and want something for myself, like another hungry wolf licking my chops over an already-exposed red bone.

So I sat in silence during the meal, except to speak to Ulrich on my other side and offer him the best of everything, flattering and soothing him as much as I could. When the hour grew late and the sun began to sink beneath the windows, Mirnatius rose, and we all delivered the happy couple in a procession to their bedchamber down the hall from our own. Ulrich saw the other men of Mirnatius's family settling themselves in the room on the other side, and Vassilia smiling at Ilias, who had drawn her arm through his and was kissing the tips of each of her fingers in turn, both of them flushed pink with wine and triumph. And Ulrich ground his jaw, but then he accepted my father's invitation to come to his study and drink a toast of the good brandy to both their future grandchildren, so at least he had given up, even if he was not yet reconciled.

"But you, I'm afraid, my own darling bride, must resign yourself to a cold bed," Mirnatius said in savage mockery of us both, when we were alone in our room, as he tossed aside his circlet and scattered the rings from his fingers over the dressing table. The sun's rays were going down through the balcony. "Unless you'd like to send for that *enthusiastic* guard of mine; if so, you'll have a good couple of hours to enjoy yourselves. It's rather a tiresome walk there and back, and I imagine my *friend* will want to linger over his meal."

I let him spit the words at me, and said nothing. He scowled at me and then suddenly he smiled, red, and oh, I would rather have had him scowling. *"Irina, Irina,"* Chernobog sang at me, smoky. *"Once again I ask. Will you not take some high gift of me, in exchange for the winter king? Give him to me, name your price, I will give you anything!"*

There was no temptation in it. Mirnatius had saved me from that forever. I don't think I could ever have wanted anything enough to take it from his hands, with a demon smiling out of his hollowed-out face at me. I tried to imagine something that would make me do it: a child whose face I had not yet seen dying in my arms; war about to devour Lithvas whole, the hordes on the horizon and my own terrible death coming. Not even then, perhaps. Those things had an end. I shook my head. "No. Only leave us all alone, me and mine. I want nothing else of you. Go."

He hissed and muttered and glared at me redly, but he went seething out the door. Magreta crept in as soon as he had left, as if she'd hidden somewhere just outside waiting. She helped me undress, and put aside the crown, and ordered tea, and after it came I sat down on the floor beside her chair and rested my head in her lap, the way I never had when I was a little girl, because there had always been work there. But tonight she had nothing, no sewing or knitting for once, and she stroked my head and said softly, "Irinushka, my brave one. Don't sorrow so. The winter is gone."

"Yes," I said, and my throat ached. "But it is gone because I have fed the fire, Magra, and it wants more wood."

She bent and kissed my head. "Have some tea, dushenka," she said, and made my cup very sweet.

There were no more stars carved in the walls for me to follow, only a straight line, but I still went slowly. I tried to stay in the very middle of the earthen tunnel, and stepped as lightly as I could, and I let my cloak drag behind me to smooth my footprints: it was long, and its hem had trailed in the wet of the sewer. I hadn't gone far when the dark began to break, a faint light in the distance coming around a curve, making the dirt walls take a comforting real shape, full of pebbles and tree roots: I wasn't walking blind anymore, and there was a strong smell of smoke building in my nostrils. A hundred steps more, and I was looking at a star of yellow candlelight far in the distance.

It was so bright against the dark of the tunnel, I couldn't see anything else anymore. I started walking towards it. The light grew bigger, and my steps slowed; the question was getting louder in my ears with every one. It had been easier to tell my father and mother that I had to be brave when I was safe in a room with them, with my mother's hand holding mine. It had even been easier to stand in front of the Staryk and refuse to bend before him. At least I'd been *angry*, then; I'd had vengeance and desperation on my side, and nothing to lose that I valued. Now the scales had a heavy weight on them: my people, my grandfather, my family; Wanda and her brothers, who had saved me. My own life, my life that I'd fought to win back. I didn't have to do this. I could go back and walk out of this tunnel and still be myself, as clever and brave as I wanted to be.

But as I came slowly closer, so close that I began to see the stone walls of the room at the end of the tunnel and the candle-light shining steady on them, suddenly at my back there came a strong breath of hot wind flowing, and the light inside the room flickered with it. My skin crawled under it, and I knew what was there behind me. What had opened a door behind me, and now was coming down this tunnel, coming to this room.

There was a moment still to ask the question one more time. By now I was standing all the way at the far side of the city. It wasn't far back to the sewer, and it was a long way from here to the ducal palace. I had time still to turn around and run back. No one would ever know that I had been here. But I hurried forward instead, to the archway, as silently as I could. I peered quick around the edge and I didn't see a guard, only the curve of a ring of candles, dripping low to stubs, and beyond it a glowing line of burning coals in the ground. There was smoke in the air, though not as much as I would have expected: there was a draft going up.

Then I drew a breath and I stepped into the room, and the Staryk turned and saw me. He went very still a moment, and then he bowed his head slightly to me. "Lady," he said. "Why have you come?"

He was standing alone inside the ring of coals, flames licking around him. The silver chain was wrapped around him tight enough to press imprints into his silver clothing. I still wanted to hate him, but it was hard to hate anyone chained, waiting for that thing down the tunnel. "You still owe me three answers," I said.

He paused and said, "So I do, it seems."

"If I let you go," I said, "will you promise not to bring back the winter? To leave my people alone, and not try to starve them all to death?"

He flinched back from me, and straightened glittering and said coldly, "No, lady. I will not give you that promise."

I stared at him. I'd thought out my questions carefully, all that way in the dark. One to make him end the winter, one to make him leave me be, one to make him promise to stop the raiding forevermore. I had as good a bargaining position as I could have. It hadn't even occurred to me as a chance to consider that even now—he was bound, bound to his death, to *all* their deaths, and he still wouldn't—"So you want us all dead so badly," I choked out, in horror, "even more than you want to save your own people—you hate us so that you would rather die here, feasted on—"

"To save my people?" he said, his voice rising. "Do you think I have spent my strength, spent the treasure of my kingdom to the last coin, and given my hand to as I thought an unworthy mortal," and even angry, he paused and inclined his head to me as if in fresh apology, "for any lesser cause than that?"

I stopped talking. My throat had closed on words. He glared at me and added bitterly, "And after all this that I have done, now you come and ask me a coward's question, if I will buy my life, with a promise to stand aside and let him take them all instead? *Never*," and he was snarling it, hurling the words at my head like stones. "I will hold against him as long as my strength lasts, and when it fails, when I can no longer hold the mountain against his flames, at least my people will know that I have gone before them, and held their names in my heart until the end." He shook his head savagely. "And you speak to *me* of hate. It was *your* people who chose this vengeance against us! It was you who crowned the devourer, named him your king! Chernobog had not the strength to break our mountain without you behind him!"

"We didn't *know*!" I burst out, horror bringing my voice out again. "None of us knew that the tsar had bargained with a demon!"

"Are your people such fools, then, to unwitting give Chernobog power over you?" he said contemptuously. "You will be well served for it. Do you think he will be true? He clings to the forms for protection, but when he sees a chance to slake his thirst, he abandons them again without hesitation. When he has drained us to the dregs, he will turn on you, and make your summer into desert and drought, and I will rejoice to think that you have brought yourselves low with me and mine."

I put my hands on my temples, pressed my palms flat against them, my head pounding with smoke and horror. "We aren't fools!" I said. "We're mortals, who don't have magic unless you ram it down our throats. Mirnatius was crowned because his father was the tsar, and his brother died; he was next in line, that's all. We can't see a demon hiding in a tsar; there's no high magic protecting us, whether we're true or not! You didn't need my name to threaten me and drag me from my home. And you thought that made me unworthy, instead of *you*."

He flinched as if I'd struck him, and went sharp and jagged-edged in his prison. "You have thrice shown me wrong," he said after a moment, through a grinding of his teeth like floes of ice scraping against one another. "I cannot call you liar now, however I want to. But still I hold to my answer. *No*. I will not promise."

I tried to think, desperately. "If I let you go," I said finally, "will you promise to stop the winter once Chernobog is off the throne, and help us find a way to throw him down? The tsarina will help!" I added. "She wants him gone herself; you saw she wouldn't take anything from him. She'll help as long as it doesn't mean all of us frozen into ice! All the lords of Lithvas will, to have an end to winter. Will you help us fight him, instead of just killing us to starve him of his prey?"

He couldn't move, inside the silver chain; so instead he stamped his foot and burst out, "I had defeated him! I had thrown him down and bound him with his name! It is by your act that he was unleashed again!"

"Because you tried to drag me away screaming to make more winter for you the rest of my life, and threatened to murder everyone I love!" I shouted back at him. "Don't you *dare* try to say it's my fault—don't you dare say any of it is our fault! The tsar was only crowned seven years ago. But you've been sending your knights to steal gold ever since mortals came here to live in the first place, and who cared if they murdered and raped for their amusement while they were at it: we weren't strong enough to stop you, so you looked down your nose from your glass mountain and decided we didn't matter! You deserve to be bound here and eaten by a demon, and so here you are! But Flek's daughter doesn't deserve it! I'll save you for her sake, if you'll help me save the children here!"

He was about to answer, and then he hesitated, and looked towards the tunnel. I looked back in the pitch depths: there was a faint red glow down there coming nearer, a fire building, and he turned to me and said, "Very well! Free me, and this I will promise, not to hold the winter once Chernobog is thrown down and my people safe from his hunger, and to aid you to defeat him. But until that is done, I give no word!"

"Fine!" I snapped. "And if I free you, will you promise—" and then I stopped, realizing suddenly I had only one question left, not two. Hastily I changed it, and finished, "will you promise for yourself and all the Staryk to leave me and all my people—to leave Lithvas—alone? No more raiding, no more coming out to rape and murder us for gold or any other cause—"

He looked at me, and then he said, "Free me, and this I will promise: there will be no more hunting your people in winter wind; we will come, and ride the forest and the snow-driven plains, and hunt the white-furred beasts that are ours, and if any are fool enough to come in our way or trespass on the woods, they may be trampled; but we will seek no mortal blood and take no treasure, not even sun-warmed gold, save in just vengeance for equal harm given first, and we shall take no woman unwilling who has refused her hand."

"Not even *you*," I added pointedly.

"So I have said!" He looked towards the door again, and the light was getting brighter, red and leaping on the walls. It was coming quickly now. "Break the rings of fire!"

I bent down and tried to blow out one of the candles, but the flame only jumped and wouldn't go out. It was melted so thickly to the ground I couldn't even pry it off. I had to run to the tunnel mouth and scrape up dirt with my hands and pour it down, smothering it like a kitchen fire of hot oil, and it burned my hands at the last before it went out. But the coals were so hot that all the dirt I could hold in my two hands together did nothing to stop them burning, so instead I took off my cloak and folded it over so the damp part was on the bottom, and I threw it down over the ring.

"You must draw me out!" he said, and I reached over the scorching-hot ring and snatched the rope and pulled him out over the cloak, just in time; it caught fire under his foot as he stepped off, flames licking up with such fury that the long curling tip of his boot ignited. The whole thing scorched off his leg in a sudden burst of flame and smoke, and he stumbled into me gasping. I nearly fell over with his weight, and only just managed to turn him to lean against the wall. He was shivering, his eyes nearly shut, and gone translucent with pain; faint reddish lines were climbing spiderwebs over his whole foot and up to his knee, where the scorched end of his breeches hung, still smoking faintly.

I seized the silver chain and tried to pull it off over his head, and then I tried to thrust it down, but even with all my weight, it wouldn't move. I looked around in desperation; there was a shovel there, thrust into a waiting wheelbarrow full of coals. I took him by the shoulders and tipped him down lying on the ground so I could set the shovel's tip onto one of the silver links. I stepped down onto the blade with my foot like someone digging, trying to push into the ground, catching the link between hardened iron and the stone floor: it was only an inch long, not nearly as thick around as my little finger, but it wouldn't open: it wouldn't open, and behind my back I heard a sudden distant shriek of rage.

I didn't look: what was the use in looking? I lifted up the shovel and jammed it down again in desperation, and then I dropped it and knelt and seized the silver chain in my hands. I tried to change it; I shut my eyes and remembered the chests in the storerooms, remembered the feeling of silver sliding into gold under my hands, the world gone slippery in my fingers because I willed it so. But the chain only grew hot in my hands, almost burning. There were footsteps running towards us down the tunnel, and the coals all suddenly burst into roaring flame, even the ones in the wheelbarrow, thick black smoke billowing around us.

And then he stirred in my hands and whispered, "The shovel. Quickly. Put the blade on my throat. Kill me, and he cannot devour my people through me."

I stared at him in horror. I'd wanted him dead, but not bloody under my own hands; I hadn't wanted to be *that* much like Judith, hacking off a man's head. "I can't!" I croaked out. "I can't—look down at you and push a shovel through your neck!"

"You said you would save the child!" he said to me *accusingly.* "You said you would! The fire *comes for us,* will you go a liar to your death?"

I gasped in a breath of smoke, black charring smoke that burned my mouth and nose and throat, and tears burst from my eyes. I didn't want to die, and I didn't want to kill; I didn't want to go to death a murderer with bloody hands. I wanted that more than I didn't want to be a liar. But he was going to die anyway, die *worse,* and they would all die with him. There were a thousand ways to die, and not all of them were equally as bad. I whispered, "Turn over on your face," and I reached for the shovel again and stood up with it, my eyes running with tears, smoke shrouding him as he turned over—

—and through the smoke a single bright gleam shone from

the middle of his imprisoned back: a cold gleam like moonlight, blue on snow, where Irina had used her necklace of Staryk silver to bind the two ends of a broken silver chain together. I dropped the shovel and reached for it. A fist suddenly seized my hair from behind and yanked my head back, and I felt flame catch in my hair, a terrible stink of it burning, but I, straining, caught the necklace with a fingertip, and it went to gold at my touch.

The grip let go my hair. I fell to the ground coughing and sick and with my hair still smoldering as another roar of rage went up. But it went suddenly thin and high-pitched as a shrieking blast of winter wind burst through the room, a cold as bitter as the flames had been, and all around me every fire in the room went out: the coals went dead and black and the candles blew into pitch dark, and the only light left was the dull red shining of two savage eyes above me.

The next breath I dragged in was clean and cold as the frozen air after a blizzard, and it cooled my singed skin and my burning throat. From out of the dark, the Staryk said, "Your bindings are broken, Chernobog; by high magic and fair bargain I am freed!" His voice was echoing against the stones. "You cannot hold me here and now. Will you flee, or will I put out your flame forever, and leave you buried in the dirt?" And with another choking howl of rage, the red eyes vanished. Heavy footsteps went running away, back down the tunnel, and I closed my eyes and curled against cold stones, gulping fresh winter air.

I slept for a while after Magreta coaxed me to lie down again; I felt tired and painfully sore. But I stirred when a sudden rattle of wind came shivering through the open doors of the balcony, and I stood up and went to look out. I couldn't see anything in the dark past the torches lit on the castle walls, but the wind in my face was cold again, and I was sure suddenly that the Staryk had gotten free. And at once I was also sure that Miryem had done it. I didn't know how or what she'd done, but I was sure.

I couldn't find anger in me, only fear. I understood her choice, though it wasn't mine: she didn't want to feed the flame. I didn't, either, but she had unbound winter to keep her hands clean. The snow would come again: if not tonight then in the morning, and everything green that had grown would die.

The other corpses would mount swiftly after. I'd seen the hollowed sides of the animals that had come to me for bread this morning; they hadn't had much longer to live. Only the sudden bounty of leaves and berries had really made my father's feast tables tonight worthy of his rank, with all he had been able to do. There had been no whole roast pig or ox brought to the table for display: game and cattle were both too thin to make a fine show. There had probably been twice as many animals butchered as usual to make the same feasting, and I'd seen the musicians dunking their crusts a long time in the thin soup they'd been given, because the bread was stale. This at a duke's table, for the wedding of a princess. I knew what that meant for the poorer tables outside the city walls.

But I didn't know what to do. We'd only caught the Staryk king with Miryem's help, and still he'd nearly defeated us. He wouldn't make such a fool's mistake again. I would have liked to believe that Miryem had made a bargain with him, the treaty she'd spoken of to stop the winter—but the snow on the wind said that she hadn't, and we had no time for negotiations. If the snow came again tomorrow and killed the rye, all the joy in the city today would go to rioting as soon as the streets cleared enough. And if they never did clear again, we'd all starve to death buried in our homes, cottages and palaces alike. Could we make a mirror wide enough for our armies to march through? But Staryk huntsmen with their flashing silver blades cut down mortal men like wheat when they came. We might leave a song of ourselves, making a war on winter, but the people we left behind couldn't eat music.

Magreta put my fur cloak around my shoulders. I looked down. Her face was sad and afraid. She also felt the cold. "Your stepmother would like it if you paid her the favor of a visit in her rooms," she said softly.

She meant, let us get out of this room; let us not be here when the tsar comes back. Chernobog would be coming back, of course, hot and savage and angry. Fire and ice both on the horizon at once, and my little kingdom of squirrels caught in between them. But he was also my only hope of finding some way to save it.

"Go to my father," I said. "Tell him I want him to send Galina and the boys away—tonight, at once, for a holiday in the west. With sleigh runners in the carriage. Tell him I want you to go with them."

She pressed my hands. "Come."

"I can't," I said. "I have a crown. If it means anything, it means this."

"Then leave it," she said. "Leave it, Irinushka. It's only sorrow on sorrow."

I bent and kissed her cheek. "Help me put it on," I said softly, and she went and took it with tears in her eyes, and put it back on my head. Afterwards, I pushed her gently towards the door. She hurried away, her shoulders bent.

The cold was mounting swiftly at my back. The fire was dead in the fireplace, but a smell of smoke began to rise anyway, at first like an echo in a room that hadn't been aired in too long, and then the smell of someone burning too much dry tinder too quickly, before I heard the first heavy footsteps in the hall, running, and the door burst open. Chernobog came into the room only as a half-quenched smoldering, his eyes dark red and faint lines of crackled heat glowing through Mirnatius's skin; but in a moment the door smashed shut behind him, and then he was roaring at me in full force, a glimpse of yellow flames igniting deep within his throat, *"He is gone! He has escaped, gone free! You have broken your promise and let him flee!"*

"I haven't broken any promises," I said. "I promised to bring him, and I did; he isn't free by my doing, but against it. I too don't want him loose to set winter back on Lithvas. How can he be imprisoned again, or stopped? Tell me what can be done."

"He has fled, run away, where I cannot go! He will lock away his kingdom behind ice and snow, and keep me from my feasting!" Chernobog only crackled at me furiously; he started to roam back and forth across the floor in a slouching, writhing motion, the pacing of a flame. *"He is free, and knows my name, and already once he bound me . . . I would have starved on cold stone, I would have fed on nothing but bone . . . I cannot get into his kingdom!"* He stopped a moment there, trembling, and then he spat like the breaking of logs in a fire, *"I have tasted him deep. He is too strong, he is grown too great. His hands are full of gold. He will smother me with winter, he will quench my flame in endless cold."*

And then he turned on me with his glowing eyes. *"Irina,"* he crooned, *"Irina, sweet and silver-cold, you have failed me. You have not brought me my winter feast."* He took a step towards me. *"So I will keep my promise, and my feast will be on you instead; on you and all your loves. If I cannot have the winter king, I will have instead your sweetness on my tongue. You will fill me up with strength!"*

"Wait!" I said sharply, as he took another step towards me; I held up my hand. "Wait! If *I* take you into the Staryk kingdom, can you defeat him there?"

He halted, his eyes brightening like a spark fed with strands of straw. *"At last will you tell me your secret, Irina?"* he breathed. *"Now will you show me your road? Open the way, and let me go in; what care I for a single king then? I will feast in his halls until his strength falls, and I will still have them all in the end."*

I drew a breath, looking at the dressing mirror where it stood near me, my last refuge. Once he knew, I'd never have a place of retreat again. But I had only two choices left: I could run through alone, and leave him to feast on everyone behind me, or take him through, and know he could come back for me, hungry. I held out my hand. "Come, then," I said. "I'll take you there."

He reached out his hand as Mirnatius's hand, the long fine fingers coming to clasp mine, skin warm, with the smoke gathered like a large cuff around the wrist. I turned to the dressing mirror, and when he turned his head he drew a sudden hiss of breath, and I knew he saw what I did: the winter kingdom shining in the glass, snowflakes falling thickly amid dark pine trees. I went to the mirror and drew him along after me, and we stepped through into the snow-heavy forest.

But he came through as a figure of ash and flame, red lines shining bright between his teeth and a blackened tongue behind them, as though Mirnatius were a skin that he could put off, and his whole body was a living coal wreathed in smoke. Cold came surging like a blast into my face, a blizzard wind, and next to me Chernobog gave a small shriek and was blown into dark wet coals and ash by that savage wind. But after a struggling instant, the red heat came glowing again from beneath his skin: he was burning too deep, too hot, to be put out that easily. The cold retreated from around him instead, and a widening place free of falling snow opened around us. We were standing at the back of the little house, the place I'd last left; even as I looked down at the washtub full of water, the ice in it cracked and broke into small pieces that melted swiftly.

Chernobog was drawing in great gulps of the air with a dreamy, gluttonous look in his face. *"Oh, the cold,"* he sighed. *"Oh, the sweet draughts I will drink. What feasts await me here . . . Irina, Irina, let me reward you dear, before I set off on my way!"*

"No," I said, cold with contempt. He seemed to think he could make treachery over and over, and no one would notice. Mirnatius's mother hadn't had much good of her bargain with him, even if she'd been buried in the crown she'd bartered her child for. "I'll still take nothing, but that you leave me and mine alone."

He made a complaining noise again, but he was too distracted to care: the wind blew a cold shriek into his face like a knife's edge, and he turned and sprang towards it almost as if he could grab hold of it with his hands. And maybe he could, because as he leapt, he reached out with both his arms stretched out as if to embrace the air, and the wind that came to me where I stood behind him was warm. He rushed away through the trees going towards the river, and his feet left wide-spaced sinking footprints going straight down to green fresh grass buried beneath the snow, the wet smell of spring bursting out of the ground with every step. Even after he had gone out of my sight, the melting footprints kept growing, devouring the snow between them.

Chapter 23

The Staryk lifted me in his arms, or maybe a winter wind cradled me; either way I was carried like a blown snowflake up and out of a square trapdoor onto a hillside, with the city wall not a hundred feet distant from us and the city lights aglow on the other side. Whatever was carrying me dropped me again with an ungraceful thump, and I lay gasping and throat-sore on the earth—the warm earth, lush with soft green grass, and though it silvered with frost in a circle around where the Staryk knelt, his skin shone wet and glistening everywhere, as if he were melting.

But he staggered up onto his feet, one still bare, and raised his arms with his eyes shining, and the circle of frost began to spread from around him, the blades of grass curling down and tightening as the crystals of ice covered them, the ground beneath me going hard and cold, as if now that he was free, he could summon back all the winter that had been stripped away. "Wait!" I shouted in protest, getting up on my knees indignantly.

He glanced down at me and said fiercely, "He has already drunk from my people! I will not let—"

He broke off and jerked around an instant too late; I screamed involuntarily as a sword came thrusting through him, the blade piercing him from in front beneath the ribs and coming out his back shining white with frost and breathing a cold fog into the air around it. It was one of the tsar's guardsmen, the brave one who'd taken the rope to lead the Staryk out of my grandfather's house. He must have been standing watch outside the tower: he was pale with horror beneath his mustache but determined, his eyes wide and his jaw clenched and both hands wrapped around the hilt of his blade.

He tried to jerk it back out of the Staryk's body, but it wouldn't come, and frost was racing white down towards his gloved hands. His fingers sprang away almost of their own accord as it reached them, and the Staryk fell heavily to the ground, his eyes gone clouded and white. The soldier stood staring down at him, shaking, wringing his hands; the fingers of his gauntlets were tipped with white. I was staring too, both of my hands over my mouth, holding in another cry. The sword was all the way through the Staryk's body. I didn't see how he could live; it almost didn't look real, that wound, and a strange blankness filled me; I couldn't think at all.

But the Staryk, blindly groping, reached for the hilt of the sword where it stood out of his body, and it began to go entirely white beneath his touch, layer on layer of frost building. The whole sword was being frozen. The soldier and I both lurched back into motion; he pulled out a long dagger from his belt, and I shouted, "Wait," again, in a gasp, and struggled to my feet and grabbed his arm. "Listen to me! We have to stop the *demon*, not him!"

"Be silent, witch!" the soldier spat at me. "*You* have done this, *you* have let him free, to undo the work of our blessed tsarina," and then he struck my face with his other clenched fist, a perfectly ordinary blow that rattled my teeth and shocked straight through my body. I fell down dazed and sick to my stomach, and he turned to stab the Staryk.

And then Sergey, coming out of the dark upon us, grabbed his arm and stopped him. The two of them stood over the Staryk wrestling a moment: Sergey was a tall, strong boy, and oh, I was grateful now for every glass of milk and every egg and every slice of roast chicken my mother had given him. I had grumbled over them in my head, counting pennies, and now too late I wanted to wish myself more generous: if only I hadn't, if I'd put still more of them on his plate, urged him to eat up, maybe he'd have been strong enough now. But he wasn't; he was still only a boy, and the soldier was a grown man, in mail, trained to kill for the tsar. He stamped on Sergey's poor feet in their straw pattens with his heavy boot, and twisting threw him flat onto the ground, freeing the hand with the dagger.

But then the soldier stopped where he stood. A strange serene pallor came climbing out of his armor and up over his neck and his face. The sword through the Staryk's chest had broken into rough chunks of frozen steel, scattered blue-white over the grass around him. He lay flat on his back with his eyes closed, his ice-frosted lashes against a kind of pale violet color in his cheeks, but he had reached out and caught the soldier's leg where it was next to him. Ice was spreading from that touch; it had traveled up over the boot and the soldier's leg and onward up his entire body, freezing him in place.

The color deepened in the soldier's face, the skin over his cheekbones splitting and curling away black with frostbite. I hid my face in my hands and didn't look until it was over and there was nothing left of him but shards of ice everywhere, and the short dagger dropped shining and deadly on the ground.

I crawled back onto my knees, my face aching and tender to the touch. Sergey had sat up wincing also, touching his feet with his hands. The Staryk lay on the ground still glistening. Frost ringed him in a widening circle, delicate feathery patterns climbing over the blades of grass, and he was breathing; the place where the sword had pierced him was covered over thickly with a lump of white-frosted ice, as though he'd packed it hard with snow. But he didn't sit up. Sergey stared at him and looked at me. "What do we do?" he asked me, in little more than a whisper, and I stared back at him. I had no idea; what *was* I to do with him lying on the ground, spreading winter around him like ink through water?

I bent over him, and he opened his eyes and looked at me as vague as fog. "Can you call your road?" I asked him. "Your sleigh? Have them come to take you back?"

"Too far," he whispered. "Too far. My road cannot run beneath green trees." And then he shut his eyes again and lay there still, helpless and wounded and maybe even dying, now just when I'd stopped *wanting* him to die. So he was determined to remain exactly the same amount of use he'd been to me all along. I wanted to *shake* him, to make him get up, only I was afraid he'd shatter into pieces along the fracture line where the sword had gone through him. Sergey was still looking at me, and I said grimly, "We'll have to carry him."

Sergey wouldn't touch him directly, and I couldn't really blame him. I took off my wet and ash-stained cloak and laid it on the ground, and carefully one after another lifted the Staryk's legs onto it, and then his shoulders, and then heaved him the rest of the way onto it from underneath his middle. He didn't even twitch. "All right," I said. "Take the top, and I'll take the bottom," and *then* the Staryk stirred, when Sergey went to take the top of the cloak, and tried weakly to lash out at him.

Sergey scrambled back in terror, and I dropped my end of the cloak with a thump. "What are you doing?" I demanded.

He turned his head towards me and whispered, "He comes to

my aid unasked, unwanted! Am I to permit this cowering wight, this slinking thief, to put me under an obligation without end, so he may ask whatever he likes of me?"

I could have picked up the dagger and stabbed him myself. "Chernobog still sits in that castle ready to devour all of us, you're half dead on the ground, and you'd still lie here thinking first of your pride. Be proud after he's gone!"

But he only looked at me *reproachfully*. "Lady, I will be proud then," he said, "and before also; I set no limits on my pride."

I ground my teeth, and then I told Sergey, "Ask him for something!" Sergey stared at me as if he thought I'd gone mad. "What would you have him give you for your help? And don't bargain short," I added vengefully, "since he's so eager to be proud."

Sergey said after a moment, very slowly, as if he didn't entirely trust me, "For—for my crops never to be blighted by frost?" I nodded, and the Staryk didn't immediately start trying to kill him again, so he took courage and added, "And none of my herds ever lost in a blizzard? And—" I was still beckoning him on, "to hunt even the white animals in the forest?"

The Staryk scowled a little bit there, so Sergey stopped hurriedly, but I felt that was about right anyway. "There!" I said to him. "Will that do? Will you make that bargain, for the help to get you to safety? Or will you lie here until spring rains melt you entirely?"

"He bargains high, for a low thief," the Staryk muttered. "But fortune smiles on him; very well, I agree," and then he let his head sink back against the cloak, and was gone limp. Sergey very slowly edged towards the ends of the cloak and even more slowly reached for them again, his eyes on the Staryk all the while. "It's all right," I told him. "He's said yes," but Sergey only darted one quick look at me as though to say he'd take his time anyway, thank you.

We finally heaved him up and staggered away with his weight

swinging between us in the hammock of the cloak. He made an awkward bundle to carry, and after we walked ten minutes without him summoning a blizzard or trying another murder, or even sitting up to say a word, Sergey said to me low, "Wait. I'll take him on my shoulders." We propped him on his feet, and I helped Sergey tip him across his shoulders, still keeping the cloak wrapped around him. Sergey staggered a bit under the weight, and shivered, but after that we went more quickly.

The air around us was cold and biting, not quite frozen but not warm spring, either, and when I looked behind us, we were trailing white frost over the road, and trees overhead were curling back new leaves wilted with cold. Anyone could have followed us. I feared the demon, I feared more guards, I feared even just a riot of ordinary men, desperate to slay winter. But no one came on behind us, and then instead we heard a rattling of cart wheels coming towards us from the other way; then we stopped and hurried into the trees on the side of the road to hide: not a very effective hiding, when glittering needles of frost bloomed around us like a flower, but at least it was still dark. The cart came on, and passed us, a gleam of firelight going between the trees, and then it stopped and my father called, "Miryem?" softly, into the dark.

We came out and put the Staryk into the cart. I sat beside him while Sergey and my father turned around and drove us on, the cart wheels squeaking with frost turning them white and crawling over the wooden planks. The horses twitched uneasy ears around to listen behind them and hurried their stride, but they couldn't get away; we carried winter with us. At least the drive was very short: from what my father had said, I'd expected it to be a longer way off from Vysnia. But it felt like less than an hour before we came out of the trees to a little house inside a garden, surrounded by a low stone wall, and they pulled the horses to a halt.

Wanda came out to open the gate for us, and Sergey climbed

down and went to put the horses in the small shed. I shook the Staryk awake enough to say, "The same bargain, for everyone who lives here, to help you."

He looked at me with slitted white eyes and muttered, "Yes," before he faded back away.

"We'll put him in the bed?" my father asked, looking up at me from behind the cart, but I shook my head.

"No," I said. "In the coldest place we can find: is there a cellar?"

Sergey coming back heard me asking, and shrugged and said, "We can look for one," as if he thought one might suddenly appear unexpectedly; and then he took a lantern and went looking behind the house, and then around behind the shed, and then his voice called softly, "There's a door here."

My father held the lantern for him while Sergey pulled up the flat wooden door and propped it open: a cold waft of air came up to meet us, with a smell of frozen earth. We carried the Staryk down the ladder into it. It was a large open space, with walls of earth and a floor of stone still bitter cold to the touch. When we lay him down on it and took the cloak off him, the frost spread around him quickly, and now that we'd stopped moving him, it began to build up more thickly white; my father gave a small exclamation when his fingers were caught pulling back the cloak.

We stood back and stared down at the Staryk: his face was drawn and narrow with pain, and the sharp lines of his cheekbones still glistened wet for a moment, but the sheen of water hardened into ice even as we watched, and I thought he breathed a little more easily.

"Maybe some water," I said after a moment. From outside, Wanda lowered a bucket to us with a wooden cup. I dipped it, and lifted the Staryk's head to put it to his mouth, and he stirred and sipped a very little. The cup frosted at the touch of his lips, and a skim of ice was already forming over the surface of the water when I took it away again. I looked at his bare, burned foot: in parts misshapen like a half-melted snowman only vaguely recognizable anymore. I picked out the skim of ice from the water and put it onto the worst patch, and it sank into his flesh and lifted it out a little. I looked up at Wanda, who was still looking down at us from above. "Is there any ice anywhere? Or any part of the river still frozen?"

But she had gone to get water, earlier, and she shook her head. "It's all melted," she said. "The whole river is open, bank-to-bank."

"We could pack him in straw," my father suggested doubtfully. "Like keeping ice for summer."

"What we need is to get him back to his kingdom," I said. If Chernobog found us here, it wouldn't need any help to put silver chains and a ring of fire back around the Staryk. It would do it all by itself, this time, and then perhaps it *would* be able to force him to give up his name and all his people. But I didn't know what to do. His road wouldn't run under green trees, and the only winter left in Lithvas was in our cellar. When we climbed back out, Wanda giving me her hand to help me up, the nails of the ladder and the iron rim around the door all were frosted white and painfully cold to the touch, and the grass above had all died to crisp cracklings; the earth was cold and frozen solid under our feet.

But even as I stood there in the dark staring down into the cellar at him, a pale coffin-statue lying in a ring of frost, a sudden strong gusting of warm wind came through the trees, stirring my hair, and when I looked back at the road, the trail of frost we'd left behind us on the road had already vanished like dew. And in the morning, a summer sun would rise.

I'd wanted him dead, and I wanted to still be angry at him: everything he'd done to me, and he wasn't even really sorry that he'd done it; he was only sorry he hadn't believed that I could make him *pay*. But I'd walked down that tunnel to save Rebekah, and Flek, and Tsop, and Shofer, and he'd gone into the dark to do that, too. He'd laid himself out as a sacrifice for their sake; and he'd bent that iron pride of his and married a mortal, not to store up treasure for himself or to conquer, but to save his people from a terrible enemy. And now he was lying down there half dead, and the thought twisted my stomach, of watching him melt away to nothing, him and all of them gone as though they'd never won their winter kingdom from the dark.

The silver crown felt strangely warm upon my head. I held my white furs around me and watched the faint red glow of Chernobog traveling away in the distance: the fire I had unleashed upon this icy kingdom that had sheltered me. The wind blowing in my face was full of ash instead of snow, and the smell of burning wood, and I was as sorry as Miryem. But I knew I'd had to do it, and I knew what I still had to do now. I had to go back to my own kingdom, and call my father and send for the priests and blessed chains. I didn't know how long the lives of all the Staryk would satisfy Chernobog, but whenever he was done, he would come back. And during the hours of the day, while he slept curled and replete in Mirnatius's belly, we would put the chains on him and burn him out, breaking one fire with another.

The sooner I went, the better; we needed to be ready when he came back. But I still stood there watching the fire rise, and I said, "I'm sorry," though no one to whom I might have apologized was there. I was alone in a garden half snow and half green grass. There was no Staryk child standing before me accusingly, and not even my own imprisoned husband; the only living creature anywhere in view was a single squirrel that had come out to paw over the crumbs I'd scattered, a few days before. And if anyone else had been there, I would have been silent. It didn't matter that I cared, that I was sorry; what mattered was what I had done, what I would do.

"I would save your kingdom, too, if I could," I told the squirrel, which paid me no attention: it was only interested in the crumbs, which were at least of some use to one creature, as my apologies weren't. I went back to the tub full of water. I looked down into it and saw my bedchamber, with the dressing table before the mirror covered with the rings Mirnatius had scattered, and the fine coat he'd flung carelessly down. One deadly fire I'd stoked behind me, and another one still ahead, and I shut my eyes a moment as useless tears slid off my cheeks and dripped into the water.

I blindly reached my hand into the water to go through, but instead of the warm air of the bedchamber, my hand went into biting-cold water, and below the surface, another hand met mine, and put something into it. I jumped back startled from the touch, and stared into my hand. It was the nut of some strange tree, oval and smooth and pale white as milk, fresh. A little dirt was clinging to its sides. I looked at the water again; the bedchamber was still there, waiting. Tentatively I put my other hand in, and this time I didn't feel the water, and I saw it coming through on the other side.

But I pulled my hand back instead of going all the way through. I looked at the nut in my hand again. Slowly I turned and went back out to the front of the house. There was a patch of open ground near the door, just over the line between twilight and night, where the snow had melted: the ground even looked as though someone had been digging there, turning up the soil. I thought maybe it would be worth trying to plant it. I didn't know anything better to do with it, and it had been sent here, to the Staryk kingdom; I didn't think I was meant to take it straight back with me.

I put down the nut and began to open a little hole in the dirt, but before I could finish, abruptly the squirrel came in two bounds towards me and snatched it. "No!" I said. I didn't really know whether I was doing the right thing to plant the nut, but I *was* sure it wasn't meant to feed to a squirrel. I tried to catch the squirrel by the tail as it jumped away again, foolish, and of course I missed. But the squirrel only ran away to the half-buried garden gate, and stopped there and began to dig in the snowdrift.

I got up and tried to get close without startling it, although I was struggling to get through the drifts; where it hadn't melted, the snow was wet and heavy and clung to my skirts and my furs. By the gate, it was still higher than my knees. But when I came close, the squirrel dropped the nut into the hole it had made and ran away into the woods. The squirrel hadn't made much head-way digging through the deep snow, but in that little snowy hollow, the nut glistened with a moonlit shine almost like Staryk silver, something vital there beneath the surface.

I put the nut safely into my pocket this time, and started to push aside the snow, digging down through the drift. My fingers stung and burned with ice, and my feet and knees were soaked and wet, drawing the cold into my skin as I dug and dug. I tried to wrap my hands in my fur cloak, but it made me slow; I gave up and just kept digging while my hands went numb and my fingers felt thick even though I could see they were still the same size, only frozen pale white.

At last I reached the ground: frozen and packed hard, full of pebbles. I had to get a stick from the woodbox in the house to pry out the big stones and break it up, and my fingernails broke and bled into the dirt while I dug. But I kept working until I made a hole in the frozen ground, not very deep, and then I took out the white nut with my bloody hands and put it down into the hole and covered it over again, with the frozen earth and snow.

I stood up and waited for something more to happen. But

nothing happened. The woods were silent again, and I saw no more squirrels or birds moving. Even the red glow of Chernobog's flame had disappeared into the distance. I didn't know what it meant. I wanted it to have meant something; I wanted someone or something to have heard my apology, and given me some means to make amends. I wanted at least to have satisfied my one squirrel. But perhaps it only hoped that a nut-tree would grow, for it to feast on someday; or perhaps it wasn't for me to know what I'd done. I didn't have a right to demand answers and explanations: I'd come here with an invading army.

My hands and feet were aching and frozen, and I couldn't stay anymore. I turned and dragged myself with my wet cloak back to the back of the house, and stepped back into the washtub, and when I came out of the mirror on the other side Magreta came running to me exclaiming in horror over my filthy, bloody, frostbitten hands and took me to the basin to pour water over them, over and over, washing them clean.

While I stood looking down into the cellar at my sleeping Staryk king, Wanda took hold of my shoulders gently and said, "Come inside and eat. We'll put something cold on your face. It will help."

We went towards the house together. I was trying to think what to do, and then I slowed and stopped in the yard, staring at it. I turned and looked back at the shed—the small familiar shed—and back at the house. The sloping thatched roof wasn't heavy with snow anymore, but the shape was the same, and the firelight shining out of it for welcome.

The others had gone on beyond me a few steps before they saw I wasn't with them; they looked at me puzzled. But I turned and hurried suddenly around to the back, and found the deep washtub standing there full of water, that Irina had tried to take me through, and stared down into the reflection of my face. "It's the same house," I said aloud. Wanda came and looked into the water and then at me. I told her, "This house stands in the Staryk kingdom also. It's in both worlds."

She was silent. Then she said, "We found things here each day. Things we needed, that weren't there the night before. And someone spun the yarn for me, and ate our food."

I thought of Irina's chaperone, Magreta, whom we'd tucked away inside to hide her from a demon. "Did *you* make the porridge?" I asked her, and Wanda nodded.

I didn't know what good it would do. There would be snow there on the other side; there would be icicles hanging on the eaves. But I couldn't reach my own hands through to grab hold of them. I went back down to the cellar. The Staryk looked a little better; the faint signs of color were disappearing out of his cheeks. "This is the house," I told him, when his eyes fluttered open on me. "The witch's house that you told me of. The one that stands in both kingdoms. Is there some way to cross from here?"

He stared at me for a little while before he comprehended, and then he whispered, "I sealed the way between; only cracks are left. I did not want any more mortals wandering through. It must be opened again . . ."

"How?" I said. "With what?"

He shut his eyes. Then he drew a breath and opened them again and said, "Help me to stand."

Together we got him to the ladder. He looked up at the rectangle of open air standing over our heads, the stars glittering against a dark night sky, and shuddered a little. "Won't you get worse if you climb out?" I said. "It's warm."

"And will be warmer soon," he said. "From now on my strength will ebb, not grow. I must make use of what little of it I have left, while it lasts."

He climbed out in slow stages and limped slowly to the house, a hand pressed over his side, but he halted outside the door, staring at the orange coal-flickering light of the fire, his face gone flat and expressionless, and I remembered how Shofer had looked at it with fear. "Wait," I said, and went in and hurriedly shoveled a heap of ashes over the flames to put them out, and closed the oven door. Then I turned and paused, looking around the room: my mother and father were standing holding each other's hands staring out the door, Wanda next to them, and Sergey had picked up a poker. Stepon was already huddled on top of the oven under the cloak as a blanket, but even he had lifted his head. All of them watched the Staryk as he bent his head to fit under the lintel and came inside the house.

But he didn't look back at any of them. He looked around the room instead, and raised his hands and let them drop a little limply, as if in desperation, and then he went to a cupboard standing in the corner on his left, and opened it. My mother stared. "Was there a cupboard—" she said to my father, but the Staryk had already pulled both doors open and was digging through it, throwing things impatiently on the ground as he dug them out of drawers: a necklace of green beads, a cloak dark red and torn and stained with blood, a faded bunch of roses, a small sack of dried peas that burst and went rolling out over the floor everywhere—

He turned around and saw us all staring and snapped, "Help me! Or you've not given me the aid you bargained with!"

"What are we looking for?" I demanded.

"Something of my kingdom!" he said. "Something of winter, to help me open the way."

Wanda paused and then went to look around the side of the fireplace, where there were shelves, but there wasn't much on them. "There's nowhere else to look," she said.

He made an impatient noise. "There!" he said, "and there," and pointed to two doors in the walls left and right of the oven.

We all stared: we couldn't have overlooked them. But the Staryk only turned back to the cupboard and went on throwing cups and handkerchiefs and spoons out of it in frantic haste, and after a moment, Wanda went and pulled open the door to the left. There was another bedroom standing on the other side that couldn't have fit inside the outside of the house. A big wooden bed hung with curtains stood there with two heavy wardrobes on either side. Behind the other door, there was a faint thumping noise: when my father carefully opened it, on the other side was a storeroom, with ropes of dried-up ancient garlic hanging from the ceiling between bunches of crumbling lavender, and a heavy wooden table standing in the middle with a mortar and a pestle, and the mortar was rolling faintly in the bowl as if it had just been in use, with a faint smell of crushed herbs in the air.

"One person should hold the door," my mother said, warily, as we went into each one searching. Wanda stayed by the bedroom door to keep it open while we hunted through the wardrobes, and in the wooden chest at the foot of the bed: all of them heaped with the useless ordinary moth-eaten linens and dresses with pockets full of crumbling dust; rotted old boots and cloaks and blankets. But in the pocket of one dress that seemed heavy, I found a handful of smooth black pebbles that shone strangely; I ran out with them, but the Staryk said impatiently, "No! What use is that? I might wander ten thousand years in the goblin depths and never find a way out again; put them away!"

Under the pillow, my mother found an old dull-copper coin, which he rejected by saying, "I cannot dream my way home, either!" In the storeroom we found on a shelf a beautiful little glass jar of perfume, stoppered, that still had a few drops in the bottom; that only made him shrug. "Poison or elixir; what does it matter now?" he said, pulling open another drawer; three grey mice sprang out of it and ran away over the floor and out the door. The sky was growing a little light in the distance, and his bare wounded leg was leaving a wet mark on the wooden boards of the floor where he stood.

"Maybe there isn't anything!" I said.

His head was drooping, and he stopped and leaned against the door. "There is something!" he said. "There is. I feel the wind of my kingdom on my face, it murmurs in my ears and the corners, though I cannot tell where it has come in. We must find it."

"I don't feel anything but hot," I said, "even though the fire's almost out."

He was silent, and then he raised his head again and there was a terrible, stricken look in his face. "Yes," he said hollowly. "The wind is warm."

I stared at him. "What does that mean?" I said warily.

"Chernobog is there," the Staryk said. "He has gotten into my kingdom. He is *there!*" He turned away abruptly and with a fresh surge of desperation began to tear out the little drawers along the top of the cupboard one by one, flinging them on the ground, half of them breaking, scattering everywhere: marbles, pen-nibs, handkerchiefs, a doll made out of rags, unraveling strings, a handful of pennies, old candy in a bag, lumps of carded wool, a thousand and one untidy things stuffed carelessly in one knothole after another, and none of it from the winter kingdom.

"We can't find anything else," my mother said to me softly, coming dusty and tired out of the bedroom again. "We've looked three times in every corner, unless he can show us another place to look."

"It *is* here!" he said, wheeling on her ferociously. "It is somewhere!"

I threw up my hands, helplessly, as she backed away startled, and then from where he was huddled on top of the oven, Stepon said, very low, "I have this, but I cannot make it grow."

We turned. Wanda and Sergey had gone very still, looking at him: in his hand, Stepon held a pale-white fruit, the shape of a fresh green walnut. The Staryk saw it and gave a cry, springing forward. "Where came you by this?" he said, accusatory. "Who gave it to you?"

He was reaching out as if to snatch it from his hand. Stepon curled his fingers around it, pulling it back, and Wanda stepped between them and said fiercely, "Mama gave it to him! It came from her, from her in the tree, and it is his, not yours!"

The Staryk stopped, looking at her. "There is not enough breath in a mortal life to bring a snow-tree to fruit!" he said. "Though you fed it with one, with two, with three, you would have barely brought it to leaf. By what blood did you raise this, that you can claim it true?"

"Da buried all five of the babies there," Wanda said. Her face was white and hard and angry as I had ever seen it. "All five of my brothers who died. And Mama at the end. She gave it to Stepon! It is his!"

The Staryk looked at her, and then at Sergey and Stepon, as if he used them to measure the six lives missing: five brothers never grown and a mother gone besides. Then he dropped his hand to his side. His face gone faded and terrible, he stared at the white nut curled half hidden behind Stepon's fingers, and whispered, "It is his," agreeing, only he sounded as if he was agreeing to his own death.

He gave way so completely that Wanda even stopped looking angry. Then we were all standing there together with the white fruit shining in the house with the same pale gleam as his silver, and the Staryk only kept looking at it desperate and yet without saying a word, as if he couldn't even imagine how to offer a bargain for it. How could you: what could you give someone that would be a fair price for all their pain, for all those buried years of sorrow? I wouldn't have taken a thousand kingdoms for my mother.

Stepon looked down at it in his hand again, and then silently he held it out. But the Staryk stared at it, at him, stricken; he didn't reach for it, as if he couldn't take it even when offered.

And then my mother leaned forward and kissed Stepon on his forehead. "She would be proud of you," she said to him, and taking it from his hand she turned and held it out to the Staryk. "Take it and save the Staryk children. What better can you do with it?"

He only kept staring at her without moving, until I reached forward and took it, and he turned blank and helpless to me instead. "What do we do?" I asked him. "How do we use it?"

"Lady," he said, "you must do with it as you will. It is not mine."

I glared at him in some indignation. "What *would* you have done, then, if it *were* yours?"

"I would lay it in the earth and call it forth," he said, "and open my road beneath its boughs. But that I cannot do. I have no claim upon this seed; it will not answer to my voice. And I know not how you can do it, either. A snow-tree will not take root in spring, and you hold sun-warm gold and not winter in your hands."

And then he went on gazing at me—*expectantly*, as if I'd surprised him so often that now he was simply waiting for me to do it again, when I hadn't the slightest idea of anything to do. "We'll try to plant it again," I said, for lack of anything better to do. "Can you come and freeze the ground?"

He inclined his head. But when we opened the door, he shuddered back, almost falling before the wave of warm air that blew in, warmer even than the inside of the house; it smelled of soft wet earth and spring. He struggled out of the house anyway into the face of it, bent like a man turned to force his way with his shoulder into a howling blizzard.

By the side of the door we found the mound of earth where Stepon had tried to plant the nut already, a good place for a tree to grow and shade the house. But when the Staryk touched the earth, only a ghost of frost left his fingers, and vanished quickly as a breath blown over cold glass. I put the nut back in the ground quickly and tried to press it down with his hand; only a brief silvering outline spread around his fingers, and faded away again.

He took his hand away, and we watched the earth a little while, and he shook his head. I dug the nut up again, and held it in my hand, trying to think: it wouldn't grow in spring. And then I thought suddenly—how had Chernobog come into the Staryk kingdom, now, when he'd only ever been able to breach it from a distance before?

I got up and ran around to the back of the house, to the deep washtub there. I looked down into it. It was only water in a wooden tub, but it might be something more on the other side—if Irina was standing on that other side, with her crown of silver, after she'd taken Chernobog slithering through into the winter kingdom, trying again to save Lithvas from the Staryk king I'd freed.

I didn't know if she was there, or if she'd even try to help me if she was. And if she was, and would, I couldn't even explain what I wanted her to do. But I knew I couldn't do anything more on this side, alone. I thought of doors that opened where they hadn't been, and rooms and cupboards appearing out of nowhere, and then I shut my eyes and plunged my hand into the water, reaching out for hope, for help.

My knuckles didn't hit the bottom. I kept reaching down, deep, and for a moment I felt a hand on the other side, reaching back. I caught it and pressed the white nut into it, and then I pulled my arm out of the water and stared at my empty palm. I looked into the tub as well, and the nut was gone. I could see the bottom of the washtub clearly through the water: there was nothing there.

I stared down into the tub another moment, half disbelieving that it had worked, and then I ran back to the front of the house: everyone was in a circle staring at the Staryk, and he was leaning against the wall of the house, gone thin and shining almost as if with sweat, blind agony in his face. I caught him by the arms. "It went through! It went over! What else do I do?"

He opened his eyes, but I didn't think he saw me; they were filmy and smeared white and blue. He whispered, "Call it forth. Call it forth if you can."

"How?" I said, but he closed his eyes and said nothing, and I sat blankly.

Then my father said, "Miryem," slowly. I looked around to him in desperation. "It is the wrong month, but the trees have not been in bloom before, and the fruit is not grown. We can say the blessing." He looked at Stepon, and at Wanda and Sergey, and added gently, "Some even say it helps those whose souls have returned to the world in fruit or trees, to move onward."

He held his hand out to me, and his other hand to my mother. We stood up the way we always did in spring in front of the one little apple tree in our yard, and we said it together, *"Baruch ata adonai, eloheinu melech haolam, shelo hasair b'olamo kloom, ubara bo briyot tovot v'ilanot tovot, leihanot bahem b'nai adam,"* the blessing for fruit trees in bloom. I had always loved saying it: it meant hope, a deep breath of relief; it meant that winter was over, that soon there would be fruit to eat and the world full of plenty. As a little girl, in the early days of spring I'd go into the yard every morning and look over the branches for the first sign of flowering, to run and tell my father when we could say it. But this time I said it more fiercely than ever, trying to hold every word of it tight in my head, imagining them written in letters of silver that turned to gold as I spoke them aloud.

When we finished, we all stood in silence. Nothing happened at first, as far as we saw. But then Stepon suddenly gave a cry and ran away from us towards the gate of the house, waving his hands to chase away a small bird that had just landed on the ground there to peck. He stood staring down with his hands clenched until Wanda and Sergey and then all of us went and joined him. A small white seedling was coming out of the earth, a little soft squirming worm just poking up.

We stared at it. I'd seen seeds pop before, beans come out of the dirt, but this one came quicker, an entire spring going before our eyes in moments: it straightened into a thin white seedling tree and began to lurch up like someone trying to climb a rope, stopping every so often to catch their breath before pulling themselves up a little farther. A crown of tiny white leaves unfurled like flags at the top, ghostly pale, and they began to flap and stretch themselves urgently, pushing upwards. When it was as tall as my knee, it began to put out thin branches that sprang open from its sides like tiny whips, and more of the white leaves opened. We had to back away to give it room, and it was still growing; smoothly now, steadily and rising.

I turned and ran back to the Staryk. He didn't wake or move; he lay against the house gone very thin and deep blue, as if some core of him were emerging from a shell of ice, and when I touched him my hands were wet, but Wanda came and helped me. Together we pulled him over to the tree, and lay him down beneath it, and suddenly crackling frost was climbing all over the ground beneath him and up the white bark and over his own skin, the deep blue vanishing again under that frozen layer. He breathed out winter air and opened his eyes and looked up at the spreading boughs of the tree, and he wept, although I almost couldn't tell, because his tears froze into his face at once and there was only a shining coming out of him.

He stood up, and as he stood the tree was tall enough for him to stand beneath it, although it hadn't seemed quite that large yet a moment before, and when he put both his hands on its trunk, it burst into flowers of silver shot through with gold. He reached up and touched a blossom with his fingertips, looking at it bemused.

"It grew, it grew," Stepon was saying; he was gulping with sobs himself, crying as if he didn't know whether he was happy or sad, with my mother kneeling with her arms wrapped around his thin shoulders, stroking his head.

And then the Staryk turned away from it and put his hand on the gate, and when he swung it open, on the other side of it a white road was standing, a white road lined with other white trees, but it didn't run on forever into winter anymore: there was a darkness at the other end, a cloud of smoke and burning. He looked at it with his face set, and then he stepped through and walked a little way down the road, and a white stag came bounding out of the trees. We had followed him to the gate, but my family all drew back away into the yard when it leapt out. For a moment I saw it with their eyes, the sharp claws and monstrous fangs hanging over its top lip and the red tongue, but it was only one of the deer for me, now. He went towards it, and as he mounted, his foot was no longer bare; a silver boot closed round it, and then he was all in silver, in armor and white fur, looking down.

Then he held his hand out to me, and said, "Chernobog is in my kingdom. As I have promised, so will I do: if he is cast out, and my people made safe, I will not bring back the winter. You asked for alliance to see it done: will you still come and lend your aid, though he is no more in your own world?"

I stared up at him, and wanted to demand, half indignant, what good he thought I would do against a demon of flame in outright battle. There was dirt under my fingernails; my face ached and my cheek was still swollen and red where the soldier had struck me, and I was tired and only a mortal girl who'd bragged too much in his hearing. But I looked at the white tree standing next to me, with its branches high and covered with flowers, and I knew there was no use asking him. He would only shrug and look at me expectantly again, waiting for high magic: magic that came only when you made some larger version of yourself with words and promises, and then stepped inside and somehow grew to fill it.

"Yes," I said. "I'll come, and do what I can—*if* you'll bring me back after!"

"My road still does not run under green trees, lady," he said, "and you have already made me promise to lift the winter, if we are victorious. But summer will not last forever, even if I lift my hand, and this I much can offer you: on the first day the next snow falls, I will open my road hence, and return you to your family's home."

I turned back: my mother and father were standing in the yard, and they weren't alone. Wanda and Sergey and Stepon were with them, and the house behind them with plenty of room, now. They would be safe, they would all be safe, even if I never came back after a wild leap down a winter road; they had each other to love and live for, and to grieve with, and to help each other on their way.

They seemed somehow far away from me already, a few steps removed, and their faces looked almost dreamlike when they gazed at me. But I ran to them quickly, and kissed them all, and I whispered to my mother, "Look for me on the first day of winter," and her fingers trailed out of mine as I turned back and went through the gate, and took the Staryk king's hand, for him to pull me up onto the back of his stag behind him.

Chapter 24

We rode down the white road with snow and ash blowing together in our faces. The hot flecks stung on my arms, but we were going quickly; the road was blurring silver beneath us with every leap of the stag, going as fast as the Staryk wanted to go, as fast as it could, and with one more leap we were under pine trees burning, a terrible red roaring flame all above our heads, and with another leap after that the road burst out from beneath them and was running next to the river.

But a river in spring, roaring, full of cracked chunks of ice bobbing and smashing against one another as they swept past us downstream. Scattered silver coins were gleaming among them, and the Staryk gave a cry of horror as he saw ahead the waterfall alive again: a roaring torrent, bursting from the side of the mountain and crashing down in clouds of steam. At the base of it, Chernobog danced and twirled with his arms in the air shrieking in delight. He wasn't burning all over anymore. He'd swelled out of human size and become monstrously large, a towering figure of charcoal covered thickly with ash, laced with deep cracks where glowing red veins of heat showed through, open flames only flaring here and there from his body. He put his face into the falling water and drank in enormous thirsty gulps and grew a little more, as if he were somehow making more of himself to burn. Coins of Staryk silver were shining like a carapace over his face and shoulders, scattered on him by the falls.

He wasn't standing there alone: a knot of Staryk knights were trying to fight him, flinging silver spears at him from the shore of the spreading waterfall pool, but they couldn't get close. There was a forest of spears floating on the water, scattered and scorched, and he wasn't bothering to turn away from his gluttonous drinking. The Staryk king leapt off the stag and cried to me, "The mountain must be held against him, do whatever you can!" and then he drew a silver sword and ran to the pool and put his foot out onto the surface. Where he stepped, ice grew solid underneath him, and he ran straight at the demon on a shining white road. In his ecstatic hunger, Chernobog didn't see him coming; the Staryk swung the sword into his monstrous leg, carving deep, and Chernobog roared in fury as ice spread in a crackling wave over the surface.

I ran up the road to the tall silver doors in the mountainside and pounded on them. They had been shut and barred. "Let me in!" I shouted, and abruptly there was a grinding on the other side, and Shofer was there, heaving up a great crossbeam of silver that had blocked the door, and pushing it open just enough for me to squeeze inside. A gust of cold air blew out, escaping, cold enough to make me realize how warm it already was outside, and even only standing in the cracked opening, Shofer's face instantly began to shine with ice-melt. He dragged the door shut again behind me, and lowered the bar back into place, and sagged away, pale.

"Shofer!" I said, trying to hold him up. He wasn't there alone; behind him, guarding the door, was a whole company of Staryk knights or lords, all of them holding tall shields of clear blue ice bounded in silver, overlapping one another like a wall. They'd retreated well back from the opened door, but once it was shut, they rushed forward again, and there were hands reaching to help us back behind the ice wall of shields. Behind that shelter, Shofer wiped the wet from his face and struggled back onto his feet.

I caught his arm urgently. "Shofer, the mountain—where the mountain is broken, where the waterfall comes out. Do you know where it is? Can you take me there?"

He stared at me wet and cloudy, but he nodded. Together we ran up the road into the heart of the mountain, slipping a little with almost every step; the surface had gone slick, and there were tiny trickles of water running along the surface in places. When we came out finally into the great vaulted space, it already felt somehow smaller overhead, as if the ceiling had drawn in closer on us, and the grove was full of Staryk women huddling close together beneath the white trees, making a smaller citadel of themselves. I saw between their bodies the deep blue cores of children being sheltered from the growing warmth. They looked up as I ran past with Shofer, with desperation on their faces; the ground was softening underfoot, and the limbs of the white trees were drooping. The narrow stream was gurgling up out of its wellspring and running away through the grove, into the mountain walls.

He led me into a tunnel running parallel beside it, the deep crystalline walls breathing faint fog around us, full of the low groaning creaks of a frozen lake beginning to break up in spring. And then the path ended suddenly in another tunnel, its sides very smooth, and the river became wide running down it. He halted at the edge, staring down at the running water in misery and fear, and I said, "I can follow it from here! Go!"

I kicked off my shoes and plunged into the water and ran along the dark tunnel with the current, splashing along until it came out again inside the vast empty storeroom. I ran through it and into the other side and kept going in a scramble over the narrow, choked space left by the water and the crammed heap of silver coins, mounds of it dragged along by the water. The waterfall was roaring up ahead. Chernobog was a blurred capering shape on the other side of the mountain as I drew near, a shadow glowing red with coal. I managed to climb a final massive slope of coins that had built up in the tunnel to the crack in the mountain: a wide and terrible maw of broken glass that looked like it was lined with teeth that had been softened around the edges: seven years since Mirnatius was crowned, and the mountain had first broken.

I imagined an earthquake or reverberation shuddering through the Staryk kingdom, and the crack spreading to let summer's heat come in. I could even see where they'd tried to patch it or block it, and the water had broken through again and again, widening the crack, each year draining away a little more strength that Chernobog could lap up from his seat upon the throne. So their king had fought off summer every year instead, as long as he could; he'd stolen more and more sunlight from us, trapped in gold, so he could summon blizzards and winter storms in fall and spring, and keep the river frozen, if he couldn't close the mountain. And at last he'd come for me, a mortal girl who'd bragged that she could turn the silver that filled his treasure-rooms into an invincible hoard.

Silver coins were going out with the water like leaping fish, tumbling away between the shards, a treasure that was nothing next to the water itself: that clear cold water that was life, all their lives, draining out of the mountain to slake a thirst that had no end. Chernobog would drink up the whole mountain and all the Staryk in it, and then he'd go back to Lithvas and suck everyone there dry as well. Even if the Staryk king hadn't told me, I would have known. I recognized that hunger: a devouring thing that would gulp down lives with pleasure and would only pretend to care about law or justice, unless you had some greater power behind you that it couldn't find a way to cheat or break, and that would never, never be satisfied.

The Staryk king was below and all his knights with him, on a ring of ice that the king was keeping frozen around Chernobog. They were fighting together, determined, and where their silver swords struck him, frost crawled away over his body. But they couldn't put his fire out. He shrieked with rage, and the frost evaporated away into steam again as gouts of open flame erupted from the wounds. Yet they couldn't get to the core of him. He'd grown too big, and he was still growing; he was still draining them even as they were trying to fight him. He cupped his hands beneath the falling water and brought gulps of it to his mouth, throwing his head back and laughing with horrible gurgles, and with every swallow he was growing a little more.

I gripped the edges of the crack carefully and leaned out and shouted, "Chernobog! Chernobog!" He looked up at me with eyes that glowed like molten metal in a forge, and I called down, "Chernobog, I give you my word! By high magic I'm going to close this mountain crack now, and shut you out for good!"

His eyes widened. *"Never, never!"* he shrieked up at me. *"It is mine, mine, a well for me!"* and he flung himself at the mountainside and began to claw his way up towards me.

I darted away from the opening and back into the tunnel, scrambling over the hills and valleys of silver, and I waited until he came peering into the dark at me. He laughed at me through the crack and struck the edges with his fist, shattering more of the mountain's crystal wall to open it wide. *"I will come in, I will drink my fill!"*

He dragged himself through and came after me, gouts of steam rising around his hands and his belly as he squeezed down the tunnel. He put his face down into the stream and took in a great swallow, throwing his head back in pleasure to gulp it down, grinning at me as he let some of it run out the sides of his mouth and crawled onward. I kept backing away down the tunnel, until I'd climbed over the last hillock of silver and the mouth of the storeroom stood behind me. He was still coming, a red glow rising in the tunnel. The water was boiling and seething away around him, climbing the walls; only a river of silver coins left beneath him, sticking to his crawling body, his chest and belly and the front of his legs; silver coins that tarnished around the edges but didn't melt, and he laughed again, the sound echoing, and raised a hand covered like armor in silver coins out of the water and wagged it at me jeering. *"Staryk queen, mortal girl, did you think a chain of silver could stop me?"*

"Not silver," I said. "But a friend tells me you're not very fond of the sun." I put my hand down to touch the last heap of silver standing before me, the coins that were just barely cool enough to touch, the coins that were a part of that whole enormous hoard; and all of it together, every last one, I turned at once to shining gold.

He shrieked in horror as the silver changed around him. The coins beneath him began to melt at once, blurring into a single stream like drops of water running together, and as they melted, the tunnel filled with a blaze of sunlight escaping, so bright that my eyes watered. It shone through the crystal walls of the mountain, the whole of it illuminating, and he shrieked again and cringed behind his arms and started desperately trying to wriggle back down the tunnel to get away.

But everywhere the light touched him, the ash and coal of him began to break off, exposing molten flame beneath. The coins heaped on his head and shoulders began to melt in thick cobweb streams running all over him, letting still more sunlight out, and pools of gold were coating his belly. Whole great chunks of him came shearing off in the light, his limbs cracking. He was shrinking even as he struggled and wailed and dragged himself back down the tunnel. The water was still coming, running past my legs, but it wasn't feeding him anymore: it was cooling the wide trail of dull molten metal he was leaving behind, erupting into clouds of steam that dewed the walls without ever reaching him.

I almost couldn't see him through the mist anymore. He had already shriveled small enough to turn around, his arms and legs growing spindly and long as his body thinned, and breaking off in chunks, the ends splitting into new fingers and toes that almost at once also began to splinter and break off, going up into small bursts of flame that consumed them. He'd almost reached the crack up ahead: I heard his weeping and moaning as he saw the monstrous slope of golden coins piled up, but the tunnel around him was brighter than full noon—a hundred years of summer sun paid back all at once, coruscating through the depths of the mountain and coming back again, and he was shrinking with every moment.

He flung himself with desperation at the slope and went crawling frantically up towards the crack as the gold melted into an ocean of light around him. As he squirmed back out through the jagged hole, he plugged it up himself: the teeth of glass scraped enormous thick lumps of melted metal off his sides, more massive chunks of his body breaking away with them and bursting into open flames. The glass wall itself melted into incandescent glowing liquid, ropey strands dripping down over the crack, closing off the opening. Another great chunk broke away, and he fell out of the mountain shrieking, a small wriggling remnant of himself.

I was gulping for breath on a riverbed of dull metal, a few scattered lumps of gold that hadn't quite melted stuck into it here and there, and water running like rain down all the tunnel walls. As the golden sunlight faded out of the mountain walls—escaping back to where it had come from, I hoped—the water running past me climbed up the slope and reached the crack in a great cloud of steam, and cooled the glass and metal solid again, sealing the mountain face in crystal entwined with lines of metal flecked with gold.

The air in the tunnel started growing colder rapidly, enough to chill the sweat that had for once broken out on my skin. The lines of water trickling down the tunnel walls were already freezing into solid white, and gleaming thin icicles stretched narrow points down from the ceiling as ice began to crust the river. I turned and had to struggle against the quickly freezing current back to the empty storeroom: by the time I reached it, all the river was a mass of jagged shards of ice sloshing around me, like broken pieces of glass themselves rising and falling in waves, and the doors of the great storeroom flung open suddenly and the Staryk king rushed in.

He reached down and caught me by the waist and lifted me out onto the bank. He was breathing hard; he'd lost some of his own sharp edges in the fighting, melted away to smooth curves with blue showing through beneath the surface, but new layers of thick ice were already building over his skin as quickly as over the surface of the river, and fresh gleaming icicle points were sprouting in clusters from his shoulders, frosted with white at first but already hardening to clear.

He stood there holding me by the waist a moment longer, his face almost stricken as he looked down the tunnel, at the lacework vein of metal binding the mountainside shut. Then he turned back and seized both my hands in his, gripping them tight as he stared down at me, a glitter of light caught in his eyes almost like the sunlight shining through the mountain walls. I stared back up at him, and for an instant I thought he would— Then he let go both my hands and stepped back and in a deep graceful courtesy went down on one knee before me and bowed his head, and said, "Lady, though you choose a home in the sunlit world, you are a Staryk queen indeed."

My poor Irina's hair had fallen half loose, a great tangled mess, cold and wet and snarled black with the same dirt as under her broken fingernails, her bruised and frozen hands. I took the crown off her head and put it aside, and I washed her hands until the dirt and blood came free and they did not look bloodless anymore. She was drooping, her shoulders bent, and I was putting the bandages around her hands when she jerked her head suddenly up and looked at the mirror, her face pale.

"Irina, what is it?" I whispered.

"Fire," she said. "The fire is coming back. Magreta, go quickly—"

But it was too late. A hand came out of the glass, terribly, like a fish surfacing out of still water, and it caught the edge of the mirror's frame with its fingertips. It looked like a low-burning log, grey with ash and scorched soot-black beneath, with a core of glowing flame. A second came out also and together they pulled the demon's head and shoulders out all at once. I could not move. I was a rabbit, a deer, halted in the trees, trying to be small and still and unseen; I was hiding in a dark cellar behind a secret door, hoping not to be heard. My voice was locked in my throat.

The demon came out so quickly, uncovered by any illusion of being a man. It crawled with dreadful speed out of the mirror and onto the floor, smoke rising in curls from its back, its legs dragging and dark behind it, and caught with a thrashing hand at the table nearby to pull itself up, the table where the magical crown stood. *"Irina, Irina sweet, what betrayal you have wrought against me!"* it hissed at her, even as it came. *"Never again can I feast in the winter halls! He came, he came, the winter king; the queen closed the mountain against me!*

They banished me forth, they carved my strength, she stole my flame to mend their wall!"

It turned and with a great sweep of its smoking arm it struck away the mirror and the table over; the glass shattered everywhere, and the crown rolled over the floor beneath the bed. Irina moved for me; she pushed me away towards the door, but the demon went darting quicker than we could, in a sudden violent rush over the floor despite its dragging feet, and blocked our way. It stamped on the floor heavily, and a little of the flame glowed red again in its thighs and down to a few spark-flickers deep in its feet, hot coals being stirred to wake a fire. *"I am so thirsty, I am so parched!"* the demon said, a complaining crackle. *"I must drink deep again! I wanted to linger, Irina, on you! How long I would have savored your taste! But at least weep for me once, Irina sweet, and give me a measure of pain."*

I was weeping, I was afraid; but Irina stood in front of me straight and said, cold as ice, even in the face of the demon, "I brought the Staryk to you, Chernobog, as I promised, and I let you into the Staryk realm. And I have wept already once, for what you would have done. I have given you all you have asked for. I will give you nothing more."

He snarled at her and came upon us. I sank in terror as my legs gave way beneath me, falling back upon the couch; I could not even look away as he thrust himself across the room and seized Irina by her arms, his hot breath a wind in our faces, horror—and then he recoiled with a howling as if he was the one burned, and jumped back cradling both his hands.

They looked like cold coals fresh from the scuttle that had never seen a fire. He moaned and hissed and wailed over his hands, opening and closing them as though they pained him after a day of long work. Gouts of steam came rising as he stretched them until a crackle of flame burst out through the surface and they were glowing furnace-red again. Then he looked up from them at Irina in wide burning fury and shrieked in rage, *"No! No! You are mine! My feast!"* and stamped, and then he turned—turned upon me, and I screamed at last, my throat opened, as he lunged to seize me instead.

For a moment only I felt the touch of his dreadful fingers on my face: heat like a fever beneath them, sweating and sick. But it was a fever in someone else's body, and it did not come into mine; instead the demon sprang back from me with another crackling wail, those fingertips gone dull-cold once more. He stared down at me with an open mouth of rage, flames of hell leaping within like a deep furnace. Irina put her hand on my shoulder. "Me and mine," she said slowly. "You must leave me and mine alone, Chernobog; you gave your word, and I have had nothing else of you."

He was staring at her when the door of the room opened. A scullery-maid looked in timidly, as if she'd heard my scream and come to see what was wrong. She stared at the demon and her mouth opened, but it was too much wrong; she too went animal-still in horror. The demon turned and saw her; it went lunging at her, though it paused for a moment, gone wary, and reached down with one finger only to touch her soft young cheek as she turned her face cringing away in terror, her hands held up to ward.

I covered my mouth with my hands; I almost screamed again, but next to me Irina did not even move. She stood still, tall and proud, looking across the room at the demon with her cold, clear eyes, and there was no surprise in her face when the demon pulled its finger away with a snarling noise and twisted back and came towards us again, enraged. But he was not so wild as to try to put his hands on us again, though he wanted to: he stopped short and stamped furiously. *"No!"* he shrieked. *"No! I promised safety only to you and yours!"*

"Yes," Irina said. "And she also is mine. All of them are mine, my people; every last soul in Lithvas. And you will touch none of them again."

The demon stood there staring at her, his shoulders heaving, the flame burning low in the sockets of his skull and his teeth dull coals. He ground them together and spat, *"Liar! Cheat! You have denied me my feasting! You have stolen my throne! But this will not be my end. I will find a new kingdom, I will find a new hearth, I will find a way to feed again!"*

He shuddered his whole body over. The flame sank down low within him, and skin closed over his flesh again, the tsar's face unrolling like a shroud over the horror beneath, even his beautiful clothes taking shape, of silk and velvet and lace. I covered my face so as not to look and huddled back against the couch as he turned away towards the door, until Irina let go of my shoulder. She said, sharply, *"He is mine, too, Chernobog. You must leave him alone as well."*

I looked up in horror: she had put herself in his way. The demon stopped, glaring at her with red light still shining in the tsar's jewel eyes. *"No!"* he spat. *"No, I will not! He was given me by promise, by fair bargain made, and I need not give him to you!"*

"But you already have," Irina said, "when you made him marry me. A wife's right comes before a mother's," and she pulled the silver ring from her hand, and reaching out caught the demon's. He tried to jerk back, but she held him fast, and pushed the ring swiftly onto his finger down to the knuckle.

He stared down with red fury twisting his face, his mouth opening on another shriek, but it didn't come out, and the demon's whole body bent away like a curving bow. There was a glowing light deep in his belly, which began to move upwards: red light came shining before it like a candle coming from around a corner in the dark, growing brighter and brighter, and then the tsar suddenly convulsed forward and a single enormous glowing coal of fire came up out of his throat and was flung down onto the carpet before the fireplace. It burst up into a lump of curling orange flames, smoking and seething, that hissed and spat and crackled at us all with rage, a mouth of red opening to roar.

But even half crouching against the wall and her face still wide with alarm, the scullery-maid lurched at once instinctively for the iron bucket of sand and ashes and cinders beside the hearth. She poured it straight down onto the flames, smothering them, and clanged the bucket down on top of it all.

She left it there, stepping back hurriedly. Thin wisps of smoke leaked out from underneath it, a black smoldering ring darkening in the carpet around the base of the pail, but it did not go far. After a moment, even the smoke went out. She was staring at it, breathing hard, and then she looked over at me with her eyes wide, startled, and reached up to her cheek, where there was still the one small black smudge. But her hands were sooty, and once she touched her skin, you could not have told the one from the others.

I was trembling in all my body. I couldn't look away from the pail, for terror, for a long time. Only after the last wisp of smoke was gone, then at last with a jerk I turned to look at my girl, my tsarina. The tsar was holding her hands against his chest, the ring on his finger gleaming pale silver like the tears running in silver lines down his cheeks; he was gazing down at her with eyes shining jewel-green, as though she were the most beautiful thing in the world.

Chapter 25

Sergey and I went back to Pavys three weeks later, once Papa Mandelstam was all the way better, and he and Stepon could look after the fruit trees while we were gone. All of them were growing very well anyway. Sergey had gone back out to the road and got the farmer who had the barn with the flowers to come and help him cut down some trees, for a share of the wood, and clear some land. We took that wood to Vysnia and sold it in the market there and bought the seedling trees: apples and plums and sour cherries. All of them were in flower.

While Papa Mandelstam was getting better, he wrote us many letters to take: one letter for everyone who still owed him a debt. "We have been lucky," he said, "so now let us be generous. It was a hard winter for everyone." I think he also thought that if we came with those letters, then everyone in town would be happy more than they would want to hang us. We took the tsar's letter with us, too, but after all, the tsar was far away. We did not have to worry that they would come and get us, because nobody was spending time on hunting for us: all the work that everyone would have done in spring, they had to do now, in a big hurry, because it was already beginning to be summer.

But we were still surprised when we drove into town. Panova Lyudmila was standing in her yard sweeping it and she called to us, "Hello, travelers! Do you need a meal on the road?" and we looked at her and then she saw who we were and shrieked and threw up her hands and some men came running, and they all stopped and stared at us and one of them said, "You aren't dead!" as if he thought we should have been.

"No," I said, "we are not dead, and we have been pardoned by the tsar," and I took out the letter and opened it and showed it to them.

There was a big noise for a while. I was glad Stepon was not with us. The priest came and the tax collector, who took the letter and read it out loud in a big voice, and everyone in town listened to it. The tax collector handed the letter back to me and bowed and said, "Well, we must all have a toast to your good fortune!" and they brought tables and chairs out of the inn and out of Panova Lyudmila's house and jugs of krupnik and cider, and everyone had a drink to our health. Kajus did not come, and neither did his son.

I was very puzzled the whole time why they thought we were dead, but I did not want to ask. Instead I brought out the letters from Panov Mandelstam and gave them to all the people who were there, and the ones who were not, I gave to the priest, to give to them. Then everyone was really happy, and they even drank a toast to Panov Mandelstam's health.

After that we went to the Mandelstams' house and packed everything into the cart. Panova Gavelyte was the only one who was not happy to see us. I think she had planned to tell Panova Mandelstam that the goats and the chickens were hers now and Panova Mandelstam could not have them back. But she knew about the tsar's letter like everyone by then so when me and Sergey came she only said, "Well, those are theirs," and pointed to some thin sickly goats.

But I looked in her face and said, "You should be ashamed." Then I went and took all of the right goats, ours and theirs, and we tied them to the end of the cart. I went and got all the chickens too, and packed them into a box. We took the furniture and the things off the shelves and packed it all carefully, and the ledger we put under the cart seat carefully covered with a blanket.

Then we were done and we could go back, but Sergey sat on the wagon seat silently and did not start driving, and I looked at him, and he said, "Do you think anyone buried him?"

I did not say anything. I did not want to think about Da. But Sergey was already thinking about him, and then I was thinking about him also. And I would keep thinking about him there, on the floor of the house, not buried. And Stepon might start thinking about it too. So Da would always be there on the floor, even once he was not anymore. "We'll go," I said finally.

We drove the cart out to our old house. The rye was growing. It was full of weeds because nobody was taking care of it, but it was still tall and green. We stopped the cart in the field so the goats and the horses could eat some of it, and then we went to the white tree. We put our hands on it together. It was quiet. Mama was not there anymore, and the tree outside our house did not speak to us. But Mama did not need to talk to us out of a tree anymore, because we had Mama Mandelstam now, and she would talk for her.

There were silver flowers on the tree's branches. We picked six of them and we put one on Mama's grave, and one for each of the babies. Then we went to the house. Nobody had buried Da, but it was not that bad. Some animals had come, and it was only some bones and ripped clothes left, and not a bad smell, because the door had been left open. We got a sack and we put all the bones into it. Sergey got the shovel. We carried the sack back to the white tree and we dug a grave and we buried Da there next to all the other graves, the ones he had dug, and I put a stone on top.

We didn't take anything else from our house. We went back to the cart and we drove all the way back to town. It was getting late then, but we decided we would keep going. We would stop for the night at the next town instead. It was ten miles to go, but the road was clear, and it was a very pleasant night. The sun was not all the way down yet. As we drove out of town, there was another cart coming, with one horse. It was empty so the driver pulled off to the side to let us go past because we had a big load, and as we came close and passed him, I saw it was that boy Algis, Oleg's son, sitting there on the seat. We stopped a moment and looked at him, and he looked back at us. We did not say anything, but then we knew that he had not told anyone where we were. He had just gone home and he had not told anyone he had seen us at all. We nodded to him, and Sergey shook the reins, and we went on. We went home.

The walls of the glass mountain were secure now, but even so, inside them it had been a lean summer and fall: many of the pools down below had gone dry in Chernobog's attack, and more of the vineyards and orchards had died. But we'd fed the children first, and then shared what there was left, and the Staryk king had told me, "They will fill again when the winter comes," when we'd walked through the lower passageways together, to see what harm had been done.

We'd buried the dead and treated the wounded, laying them in quiet rows beneath the white trees: the king carefully took shavings of ice from the very wellspring of the stream, and laid them on their wounds, and put his hands on either side and coaxed it to grow and merge with their bodies. Some of the great caverns had closed themselves up like turtles pulling into their shells, and had to be opened again, and in the fields below we cut back the dead vines and trees, and started cuttings from what had lived, to make ready for a new planting.

At least now I was able to find my own way around. Either I'd learned the trick of it without realizing, or the mountain itself was grateful to me, because when I went looking for some room or cavern, the right doors and passages softly opened for me. And amid all the work, I found more than enough to make a place for me. The Staryk didn't know anything of keeping records: I suppose it was only to be expected from people who didn't take on debts and were used to entire chambers wandering off and having to be called back like cats.

But with everything in disarray, we needed something better. I had to commandeer pen and paper from their poets just to have something to keep track of all the fields and pools and what state they were in, and how much we expected to have, to last us until the winter. I divided up the supplies and measured out days, so none of us would go hungry before the end.

The tally of those days seemed a long one at the beginning, but every hour was filled. By the end, they were sliding away so quickly that it took me by blank surprise the day I woke up and found the trees outside the mountain frosted with the first new snow, and I knew the king's road stood open once again. And I missed my mother and my father, I ached for them to know I was well, but still I stood there looking out for a long time before I rang the bell to call the servants to help me get ready.

It didn't take me long. I'd taught Flek and Tsop how I kept my papers sorted, and my books were clean; my grandfather wouldn't have found any fault. I packed one small bundle, only a few things in it but dear to me: a few pressed silver flowers, a pair of gloves sewn very badly that Rebekah had made for me, and the dress I'd worn for the midsummer dancing. It wasn't a grand gown; the celebration had been a rejoicing for survival, a few weeks after we'd buried our dead, and there hadn't been time or strength for anything grand. It wasn't much more than a simple shift, but of cool silvery silk that ran through the fingers like water, and caught the light coming in through the mountain. I'd worn it with my hair braided up in flowers, and danced in a circle holding hands with my friends, the new ones and the old, who'd worked beside me, and at the end the king had come to me and bowed, and together we'd led two lines through the grove, dancing beneath the white branches as they shed their last flowers to rest until the snow.

He'd kept his own promises, of course; he'd made no more claims upon me, and down in the grove the sleigh was waiting. I drew one final breath and turned and left my chamber, and went down the narrow stair. The white trees had bloomed again this morning, full of leaves and flowers. There were still a few gaps left in the circles, where some of them had died in Chernobog's attack. But in each of those spaces, one of the fallen knights had been buried with a silver fruit upon his breast, and thin white saplings had come out of the ground when I called them with the blessing. They'd keep growing here, even after I had gone. It made me glad to think of it, that I'd leave them living behind me.

But as I came low enough to see beneath the leaves, I paused, my eyes stinging: behind the sleigh, a full and dazzling company of the Staryk had assembled, mounted on the backs of sharp-antlered deer. The knights and nobles carried white hawks on jeweled gauntlets, and white hounds clustered around the hooves of their mounts, and silver and jewels gleamed on their pale leather: many of them I'd seen at the gates, or helped to tend beneath the trees. But it wasn't only them; even some of the farmers were there, looking at once excited and afraid, plainly uneasy about going to the sunlit world but coming to see me off in their best finery, their hair strung with silver. And in the very front rank, just behind the sleigh, were Flek and Tsop and Shofer, with Rebekah there sitting nervous and wide-eyed in front of her mother, her long fingers wound into the braided reins.

All the beauty and danger of a winter's night caught out in living shape, and when I came down and the Staryk king held his hand out to me and helped me into the sleigh, I stood in it a moment longer, holding on to his hand for balance, looking at all of them, and last at him, to have a picture to hold in my heart when the winter kingdom's door had closed behind me.

I sat down blinking away tears, and he sat beside me, and the sleigh leapt off over the snow. Almost at once when we came out of the mountain, the white trees unfurled to either side of the shining road before us, icicle drops of silver hanging overhead. We flew down it with cold wind rushing into our faces and the great assembled hunt coming on behind us, blowing the faint high horns that sang clear as a winter bird's song. The people of Lithvas wouldn't have to fear that music anymore. The Staryk wouldn't come among them again as anything other than a whisper beneath the snowy trees that they'd only half remember. Perhaps I'd have a daughter of my own one day, and when I heard that wistful sound through the window on a winter's night, I'd tell her stories of a mountain of shining glass, and the people who lived within it, and how I'd stood against a demon with their king.

I looked at him sitting beside me. These last months he'd more often worn clothes as rough as any laborer's, even if they were still of purest white, while he'd worked to reopen deepest chambers and tunnels that had collapsed, healing the mountain's wounds as he'd healed his people. But he was as splendid today as all the rest of them, and he sat proud and glittering with his hand tight on the railing of the sleigh. He didn't hold back at all; the journey was over too quickly. It felt as though we'd barely left when a wind bright and fresh with pine came into my face, and the white trees opened wider into a grove where one single tree stood, still only a young tree but beautiful and full of pale white leaves, behind a wooden gate, with a house gently blanketed in snow behind it.

I couldn't help smiling as soon as I saw it: they'd done so much with it already. My eyes were wet, blurring the thin slivers of golden light shining out around the cracks of the windows and the door. Friendly plumes of smoke wound from three chimneys, fireplaces in the rooms on either side, and the shed was attached to the side of a proper barn now. I saw a large coop of chickens, boxes for grain; a few goats were wandering the yard. Just behind the house, orchard ranks of small fruit trees were standing, and a lantern hung from a post by the door, spilling light onto a welcoming walkway of swept-clean stones coming all the way up to the gate.

The sleigh stopped before the gate, just by the tree. The Staryk stepped out of it, and gave me his hand to help me. The hunt was still gathered behind us, but Flek and Tsop and Shofer had climbed down; one of the others was holding the reins of their mounts. They all bowed to me. I drew a deep breath and went to each of them and kissed them on their cheeks, and I reached up and took off the necklace of gold I was wearing, and I put it around Rebekah's neck. She looked up from it on her palm and said, "Thank you, Open-Handed," a little softly and tentatively, and Flek twitched a little as if in uncertain alarm; but I bent and kissed her forehead and said, "You're welcome, little snowflake," and then I turned and walked to the gate, and put my hand on it.

It swung open at my touch, and one of the goats, who had been browsing under the light snow at the posts, startled and made a loud complaining *baa*-ing and fled away towards the barn, probably unhappy to have a mysterious stranger erupt out of nowhere into his comfortable yard. The door of the house opened at once, and my mother was standing there, a shawl clutched around her shoulders and hope in her face, as if she'd been waiting by it; she gave a cry and ran towards me down the path with the shawl flying off behind her red onto the snow, and I ran to her and fell into her arms laughing and crying, so glad it drove out regrets. My father was right behind her, and Wanda and Sergey and Stepon piling out after them; they all came around me: my parents, my sister, and my brothers, and there was even a thick-coated sheepdog jumping around us in excitement that I'd never seen, trying to lick all of us at once, and then it planted its feet and barked loudly twice and then yelped and ran back to Sergey's feet and peered from around him instead.

I turned round: they hadn't vanished yet, that glittering hunt, and the Staryk king had come into the yard behind me, a winter's fairy-tale standing there half unreal in the warm lamplight, only made possible by the cool blue gleam of the snow behind him. My mother and father tightened their grip on me a little, looking at him warily, but I had his word and I wasn't afraid. I swallowed and made myself raise my head and smile at him. "Will you let me thank you, this once, for bringing me home?"

He shook his head and said, "Lady, I would scorn to bind you with such a trick," and then turning, beckoned, and Flek and Tsop and Shofer each of them came into the yard, carrying a chest, and Rebekah followed them, holding a small box. They put them down on the ground and opened them: two full of silver, one of gold, and the little box full of clear jewels, and the Staryk turned to my parents, and said as they stared at him, "You have a daughter of your house unwed, whose hand I would seek; I am the lord of the white forest and the mountain of glass, and hither I have come with my people assembled for witness to declare to you my intent, with these gifts for your house to make proof of my worth, to ask your consent that I may court her."

My parents both looked at me in alarm. I couldn't say a word. I was too busy glaring at him: *six months,* and he hadn't so much as said a word to *me;* because now he was determined to do it all exactly by whatever mad rules undoubtedly governed the formal courting of a lady by a Staryk king. I imagined dragon-slaying and immortal quests were meant to be involved, and possibly a war or two. No, *thank you.*

"If you really wanted to court me," I said, "you'd have to do it by *my* family's laws, and you'd have to marry me the same way. Save your time!"

He paused and looked at me, and his eyes kindled with light suddenly; he took a step towards me, and held out his hand, and said urgently, "And if so? Whatever they are, I will venture them, if you will give me hope."

"Oh, will you," I said, and folded my arms, knowing that would be the end of it, of course. And I wasn't sorry; I wouldn't be. I wouldn't regret any man who wouldn't do that, no matter what else he was or offered me; that much had lived in my heart all my life, a promise between me and my people, that my children would still be Israel no matter where they lived. Even if in some sneaking corner of my mind I might have thought, once or twice, for only a moment, that it *would* be worth something to have a husband who'd sooner slit his own throat than ever lie to you or cheat you. But not if he didn't value you at least as high as his pride. I wouldn't hold myself that cheap, to marry a man who'd love me less than everything else he had, even if what he had was a winter kingdom.

So I told him, without sorrow, and when I finished, he was silent a moment looking at me, and then my mother said, "And a way for her to come home, whenever she wants to visit her family!" I stared at her: she was holding my hand tight and glaring at him fiercely.

He turned to her and said, "My road opens only in winter, but while it does, I will bring her at her will: does that content you?"

"So long as winter doesn't up and vanish whenever you don't want her to go!" my mother said tartly. I wanted all of a sudden to burst into tears, and cling to her, and at the same time I was so happy I could have started to sing aloud, and when he looked back at me again, I reached out to him and took his hand with mine.

We were married two weeks later: a small wedding only in that little house, but my grandfather and grandmother came from Vysnia with the rabbi in the duke's own carriage, and they brought with them a gift, a tall silver mirror in a golden frame, that had been sent from Koron. And my husband held my hands under the canopy, and drank the wine with me, and broke the glass.

And on the wedding contract, before me and my parents and the rabbi, and Wanda and Sergey for our witnesses, in silver ink he signed his name.

But I won't ever tell you what it is.

About the Author

NAOMI NOVIK is the acclaimed author of the Temeraire series and the Nebula-winning novel *Uprooted,* a fantasy influenced by the Polish fairy tales of her childhood. She is a founder of the Organization for Transformative Works and the Archive of Our Own. She lives in New York City with her family and six computers.

naominovik.com
Facebook.com/naominovik
Twitter: @naominovik

About the Type

This book was set in Baskerville, a typeface designed by John Baskerville (1706–75), an amateur printer and typefounder, and cut for him by John Handy in 1750. The type became popular again when the Lanston Monotype Corporation of London revived the classic roman face in 1923. The Mergenthaler Linotype Company in England and the United States cut a version of Baskerville in 1931, making it one of the most widely used typefaces today.